Also by
Brandon Rolfe

Countdown To Doomsday
The Analyst
The Dromyrk File
Checkpoint

BETRAYAL

предательство

Brandon Rolfe

Published by Dolman Scott Ltd in 2021

ISBN:

POD: 978-1-8381944-6-8

iBooks: 978-1-8381944-7-5

Kindle: 978-1-8381944-8-2

Dolman Scott Ltd
www.dolmanscott.co.uk

Dedication

To Annita

1

Down in the darkness of deep waters, a great black hulk stirred, with a low belly-groan, from its slumber. Suddenly the bright Arctic moon blinked repeatedly as a clamorous swarm of gulls gathered beneath it, criss-crossing and swooping down round the 'thing' rising out of the water, coming up out of the fathoms of Norway's Hardanger Fjord. Rising up as a sharp 'fin' at first, it suddenly swelled out into a long body glistening in the moonlight, the water running off its massive round back and cascading down its sides with a mighty roar boasting its colossal weight.

Were it from a biblical text, the small dark figure emerging from the gigantic dark body would have been seen as Jonah making his hectic exit from the Whale. But apart from being a few millennia and a day or two late, this whale's skin stretched a whole three hundred and eighty-one feet from head to tail in 2.5 inch thick high-strength alloy titanium steel. A great 'dorsal fin' was the twenty foot conning tower jutting up from the curved back, bristling with classified electronic gizmos that virtually looked round corners by scanning beyond the horizons, thanks to those satellites looping the globe faster than Santa's reindeers --- as well as with white-capped heads that were beginning to pop up, to dot the darkness, one after the other.

Major Frank Falzoni was the one not wearing a naval cap. As US Army Intelligence liaison officer with US Navy-NATO operations, he wasn't required to. Instead, his head hugged the shelter of his fur-lined

Called out of his shallow sleep at 01.46hrs, the young officer's message had been short and precise: 'We're here, sir.' The coded instructions he handed to Frank fought a short battle with the Muscae volitanti spots dancing in his inner ocular fluid and the yawning brain struggling to form some intelligence out of what it was seeing. The words, stippled across the paper in primary code, then secondary code, held an inner message in tertiary cypher; the last, solely for Frank to recognise and decipher. Nothing more was needed to set up the alert signals in his mind. All aspects of the 'hit and miss', 'dodge and dive' game spiked up in his mind, like those pin-pricks of light you try to comprehend on the radar screen. These always tended to create pressure points of frustration, where impatience with monotonous waiting left you no more to do than restless tapping of the feet.

Your stomach habits changed no more than work did. HQ expected you to take all this in your stride with no more fuss beyond that first shiver and cigarette of the morning. Frank tapped his pocket by reflex. And guess what loon had forgotten to pick up his cigarettes. Damn!

Frank's companion, seated across the dark space of the tiny cabin, Lieutenant Ferten, was deep in his own thoughts. He alone had accompanied the Major in the dinghy. Neither of them had exchanged much conversation. What few words they had uttered had barely managed to leave the strained jokes stage. Ferten seemed to have no inclination to see the serious side of things. A jolly young blond product of the US Naval Academy in Maryland. That was a difficult institute to be enrolled into, unless your old man had lots of influence and dollars to put in the way of that lot in Washington with 'scrambled egg' on their service caps and a mini Fort Knox of gold braid on their dark coat sleeves. With a tall frame that took in all sports, from A to Z, he saw all problems remedied with a tap on the knee from the MO's rubber hammer, followed by a brisk jog around Annapolis in the fresh morning air before reveille.

Not quite like Frank's straddled situation, with one foot planted in Military Intelligence, while the other was an insecure footing on the shifting ground that was the Central Intelligence Agency. A mind-jangling job where

1

Down in the darkness of deep waters, a great black hulk stirred, with a low belly-groan, from its slumber. Suddenly the bright Arctic moon blinked repeatedly as a clamorous swarm of gulls gathered beneath it, criss-crossing and swooping down round the 'thing' rising out of the water, coming up out of the fathoms of Norway's Hardanger Fjord. Rising up as a sharp 'fin' at first, it suddenly swelled out into a long body glistening in the moonlight, the water running off its massive round back and cascading down its sides with a mighty roar boasting its colossal weight.

Were it from a biblical text, the small dark figure emerging from the gigantic dark body would have been seen as Jonah making his hectic exit from the Whale. But apart from being a few millennia and a day or two late, this whale's skin stretched a whole three hundred and eighty-one feet from head to tail in 2.5 inch thick high-strength alloy titanium steel. A great 'dorsal fin' was the twenty foot conning tower jutting up from the curved back, bristling with classified electronic gizmos that virtually looked round corners by scanning beyond the horizons, thanks to those satellites looping the globe faster than Santa's reindeers --- as well as with white-capped heads that were beginning to pop up, to dot the darkness, one after the other.

Major Frank Falzoni was the one not wearing a naval cap. As US Army Intelligence liaison officer with US Navy-NATO operations, he wasn't required to. Instead, his head hugged the shelter of his fur-lined blue anorak hood, away from the biting Arctic night air. And that air sure stung his lungs, sharp in its freshness, in contrast to that 'cosmetically treated' soft warm atmosphere of the sub's interior that he had breathed in for several days, when they had needed to remain submerged in strict compliance with operational tactics. USS *Arkansas*, this new age's breed of sea-monster, was a Python class SSN-594B nuclear-powered fast attack hunter submarine armed with UUM-44 SUBROC anti-submarine torpedoes and UGM-84 HARPOON anti-ship torpedoes.

Nothing moved. Everything in the vacuous expanse stood still. Movement was measured in geological eons that reduced Homo sapiens to a nonentity. Man did not feature in the titanic combination of time and strength that had brought forth this landscape. Nothing short of millions of years of seismic upheaval had been sufficient to contort and weld the strata together with colossal pressure and heat, to form this indelible sculpture of a landscape. Enormous rock masses reposed with a lethargy that was reminiscent of a slothful Mezozoic Period, where brontosauri had probably weltered in the sun on these very banks. Now, supposedly, it was Troll territory if local folklore was anything to go by.

Well, none of those crazy mythical ogres were about, swinging their tree-trunk clubs, it seemed. But maybe it wasn't just quite the right night for the old moonlight wassail flowing with ale, grilled human steaks and french fries. No-one else was about, either. But then things always weren't what they seemed, especially in this game. Noting the large binoculars dangling on the chest of the young lieutenant beside him, Frank gave him a nod, pointing to them. 'Sure, Major.' The lieutenant handed them over.

Falzoni made a long slow sweep all round with the infra-red lenses to snatch in out of what had been a dark landscape, sharper 'daylight' images than what the naked eye had managed. Only to be greeted with the same inert stillness.

'Anything?'

The Major shook his head. 'Clear.' He handed the binoculars back to the lieutenant.

Falzoni returned his attention to the crewman who had emerged earlier from the deck hatch. The guy was now being joined by another two figures climbing out of the black void, hauling out behind them a long rubber dinghy. That would get him to the small wooden jetty, dispelling his crazy thoughts of a moment's inaccurate manoeuvring of the sub's two and a half thousand ton bulk crushing the timber structure to matchwood. Easy to see he wasn't a Navy man.

Falzoni watched the quiet activity going on outside from his chair by the cabin window. Specifically, at that around the small white Bombardier CL-415 amphibian flying boat, its twin Pratt & Whitney PW123AF turboprop engines providing the right balance of decreasing thrust to neatly skim in to land on the fjord's generous expanse of water, now being serviced by the *Arkansas* maintenance crew. The eyes looked on, while the mind worked elsewhere, running facts over and over again through its treadmill. Not fully satisfied that there was nothing to worry about, he tried to ignore the burning unease in his mind, relaxing until his grey concentration began to ebb away.

Amusement poked through his dark mood for a few seconds, as did the awakening pang of hunger in his stomach, as he watched the antics of the old man in the corner of the wooden cabin. Part woodsman, part poacher, part fisherman, he was now imitating the long-necked cormorant, holding on high, head tilted back, a whole pickled herring, bones and all, to be dropped into the gaping mouth and swallowed, without chewing, down the throat, in the manner of that great voracious seabird. Frank wished he hadn't turned down the galley chef's offer of that mouthful of venison steak before leaving the sub's warmth for this cold air. But it was always the same when you were called out. Just as he had been *shaken* out by the young Duty Officer; right out of that tiny haven of sleep that he'd just managed to fall into, having finally escaped the background droning of the sub's powerful nuclear-driven motors. Out of his bunk and into a new round of 'Battleships (and Subs)', rolling the dice, not on a kid's play-board, but on green-glowing electronic screens.

Called out of his shallow sleep at 01.46hrs, the young officer's message had been short and precise: 'We're here, sir.' The coded instructions he handed to Frank fought a short battle with the Muscae volitanti spots dancing in his inner ocular fluid and the yawning brain struggling to form some intelligence out of what it was seeing. The words, stippled across the paper in primary code, then secondary code, held an inner message in tertiary cypher; the last, solely for Frank to recognise and decipher. Nothing more was needed to set up the alert signals in his mind. All aspects of the 'hit and miss', 'dodge and dive' game spiked up in his mind, like those pin-pricks of light you try to comprehend on the radar screen. These always tended to create pressure points of frustration, where impatience with monotonous waiting left you no more to do than restless tapping of the feet.

Your stomach habits changed no more than work did. HQ expected you to take all this in your stride with no more fuss beyond that first shiver and cigarette of the morning. Frank tapped his pocket by reflex. And guess what loon had forgotten to pick up his cigarettes. Damn!

Frank's companion, seated across the dark space of the tiny cabin, Lieutenant Ferten, was deep in his own thoughts. He alone had accompanied the Major in the dinghy. Neither of them had exchanged much conversation. What few words they had uttered had barely managed to leave the strained jokes stage. Ferten seemed to have no inclination to see the serious side of things. A jolly young blond product of the US Naval Academy in Maryland. That was a difficult institute to be enrolled into, unless your old man had lots of influence and dollars to put in the way of that lot in Washington with 'scrambled egg' on their service caps and a mini Fort Knox of gold braid on their dark coat sleeves. With a tall frame that took in all sports, from A to Z, he saw all problems remedied with a tap on the knee from the MO's rubber hammer, followed by a brisk jog around Annapolis in the fresh morning air before reveille.

Not quite like Frank's straddled situation, with one foot planted in Military Intelligence, while the other was an insecure footing on the shifting ground that was the Central Intelligence Agency. A mind-jangling job where he had to correlate all the information gathered between the services. That wearisome chore having Frank's cigarette butts fighting for space in the overflowing ashtray, when petty bickering among rival intelligence officers caused snippets of information to be snipped even further. That caused no end of bother with needless delays and certainly didn't go easily on the dollars. That was why he had to investigate individual points on the spot, and gather all the data into a form that kept departmental heads happy --- and let the country sleep peacefully at night – theoretically.

They had come ashore at 03.11hrs, to wait for the Bombardier supplies/transport plane to fly in. And it did, a little over forty minutes later. That was just an hour ago. Since then, two reports had come through from the sub's communications room, at progressive stages, assuring only '*CIRRUS*' at that stage. With the technical crew working to and fro between the tiny Bombardier and the mighty *Arkansas*, they were now waiting for clearance at this end.

Frank fingered the crisp notepaper with the coded message which the radio operator had passed on. The next two reports should have set his mind at rest. But they didn't. He was still uneasy about something, somewhere, at the back of his mind. Nothing specific, nothing more tangible than that faint thread of tension that you can't dismiss until you've finally put the lid on the job. Totally irrational, of course. You always knew this, and accepted it as the habitual uneasiness that you called alertness, that waylaid you at this early stage of your assignment. You just couldn't do this job without being suspicious. That was what those pen-pushing grand wazirs back in Washington paid you for --- to be suspicious and safe, rather than satisfied and sorry. Frank went over the Grade 5 security cypher's points in his mind again, seeing Marley Goodblood's hand in the coded message as clearly as the Boston Chimps' score-board.

The rough rasp of radio static, from the Lieutenant's walkie-talkie lying on the stool in the corner, pierced the silence, cutting into their thoughts.

Lt Ferten jumped up and went over to the squawking box that was threatening to fall off its perch, in its eagerness to spill out its urgent tidings. Picking it up, he the grunted into it, while making the toothpick flit nimbly across his row of upper teeth, like a miniscule acrobat. 'Yeah?' He waited, searching with his tongue for the gum that shared the mouth space with its companion wooden performer, while the scratching voice burrowed into his ear. 'Yeah?' he said again, finding time to transfer the midget artiste for a performance on the lower row of shining white teeth.

All the while Frank sat waiting, watching the Lieutenant standing waiting, listening.

'That's it, huh?' A pause. 'Right.' Putting the walkie-talkie back down on the stool, the Lieutenant went back to his seat, seeming oblivious to all but the timings of the next 'buccal cavity performance'. Officers' etiquette said it would be rude to speak to the Major with the toothpick in his mouth. He promptly took it out before sharing his new knowledge with Major Falzoni. 'It's all clear. That was them on just now. They've fallen for it. Seems to have got through and accepted by 'them' that it was just a freak malfunction in the turbine thrust units that caused the *Arkansas* to divert from its scheduled route, and take berth here, to await appropriate 'technical replacement'. But anyway, things seem to be flowing smoothly, as planned. No sign, so far, of Red Whales and Minnows adjusting positions in redirected manoeuvres. No trace of their 'cats' whiskers' twitching unduly in tracing our action. A nervous Board of Inquiry lot will have to be placated, hopefully, with falsified reports, of course. Otherwise, okay. Does that sound okay to you, Major?'

Ferten's nonchalant manner, with its matter-of-fact sum up, sounded as if he was taking full credit for everything being 'okay'. Falzoni could have bet that he harboured a secret yearning for the simplicity of a bygone era officers' chivalry in clear air, clear water, free of blemishing 'dirty water' tactics below surface. Well, perhaps a lot of us did. But he could have done without the intonation of the Lieutenant's final remark. It had carried, not too openly, but still its hint of disapproval, if not chiding, for this charade of a holdup.

Frank resisted the urge to show annoyance. 'Yeah, I suppose so, Lieutenant. It *sounds* all right. But what do *you* think? You're the gunwale and oars man. I've just a liking for *terra firma* beneath my feet. *You* tell *me.*' What juice are we *really* picking up on the other side? Can you say for certain?'

'Do you mean will it fail to sell, and collapse with the weak dying squeak of a burst balloon?'

Hell, this guy was sure slow on the helm-wheel for turning corners. 'That's as good a way as any of putting it, I suppose. Yeah, I mean something like that, Lieutenant; *something* like that.'

'Not that we can afford to ignore that mal chance, from what we have so far. But, no, at least I shouldn't think so. Not even with this latest integrated link-on set-up for detection they have now. I gather that it works something like the idea of Nobel's dynamite. Kick it, beat it, but it still won't release from its programed quarry without reciprocally programmed stand-down instructions. That's perhaps an odd way of putting it, maybe, but I think you follow my meaning, Major.'

The Major's faint personal stab had got through. Ferten, for all his apparent preoccupation, took the message quietly, casting a wary eye at him. 'But I'm gathering that you haven't seen any *real* action since your wartime days, have you, Major? Just like we did in Viet. With flak and anti-aircraft tracer bullets strafing your ass, you had to count your balls regularly, I tell you.'

'You were a *flier* before this?'

'Reconnaissance, but only for a very short time. Having almost lost my plane on only my second mission, I reckon 'Uncle Sam' considered I'd constitute a strain on the Defence Budget, so being a safer bet grounded to the steel deck of a ship.'

The challenging hold that had sparked up moments before in the young eyes dimmed, striking the Major as a boyish step-down after losing his swipe at the ball. A follow-through to old college fraternity house rules, perhaps? 'Strictly speaking, Lieutenant, Captain America books are more in my line of fire.'

The casual small talk lost its edge as suddenly as it had begun and immediately dried up. Both minds came back to the more important matter in hand. Ferten leaned forward on his seat with a philosophical look, over a pensive few seconds, ready to speak. 'You'll no doubt want to see some analysis figures for yourself, after our Intelligence Section has integrated them thoroughly, Major?'

'Faster than fast. As soon as your people are finished, we want in, without a second to spare. As it happens, we know a lot about them already. But I could do with a fresh inflow.'

Ferten knew his lot, reading the details off from memory, while his fingers kept pace tapping out the points, holding the Major's attention. 'That 'shadow' we've shaken off at last, after its tailing us for days, is – *was-* the Kila class sub, *Meerni*, nuclear powered, liquid-metal engines. Captained by one Grigori Zartenov; one child, a daughter; graduated in Chemistry from Leningrad University, the *daughter*, that is, not the Captain. The submarine left Murmansk, on Kola peninsula on Tuesday the fourteenth, to take up watch on our NATO Summer-time Operation off Norway's Spitsbergen Island – or *Svalbard* – if you want to twist your tongue.' Ferten paused for an apparent mental breather, looking at the floor with his inner puzzle, before looking back at the Major. 'At least that's what it's supposed to have been doing after leaving Murmansk. That's our *official* statement for keeping face, so to speak. Where the thing went after we lost it on the seventeenth is pretty much unclear. Damned well anyone's guess, really.' Although Ferten's words came out in a constantly calm pace, Falzoni could virtually hear the situation gnawing away like a true rodent across the room in the other man's mind.

'Kila class? They're quite fast, aren't they?' remarked Falzoni with what sounded like a faint touch of envy.

'*Very* fast, Major. From what we've managed find out so far – they're capable of reaching about forty-two knots underwater. Their deep-diving capacity is giving us in the West a sore head. Apart from conventional torpedoes, they can also launch nuclear ones, as well. These nuclear babes could devastate a whole carrier group of ours without even having to score a direct hit on a target. Their potential nautical range, we're not sure of. Not quite the length of the *Arkansas*. Pretty impressive, I've got to admit – as well as worrying.'

'Yeah, pretty impressive.' Falzoni's reply was a low brooding, almost inwardly-directed one, pulled down by the gravity of the situation that the statistics denoted. The very prospect of nuclear torpedoes would have those Hawks and Doves on Capitol Hill baring their talons at each other. But he managed to find amusement in the Lieutenant's psychological trick of lessening the gravity by finishing up with a 'lighter' statistic.

Falzoni saw the change in mood and took the opportunity to stress his question urgently, without having to pull rank with priority orders. 'Can we go over again what exactly it is that we have got, so I can check with anything I've missed. No room for errors, right?'

'Yeah, let's do that. Well, in actual fact we have, as you yourself know, all their Strategic Nuclear Strike Command codes – codes for patrolling Western air space and waters; targets, codenames, the lot.'

Falzoni scribbled down what codes he could remember in his notebook, putting a stroke through each of them. 'A tiny bit of a problem there, Lieutenant. Only double shift work for the poor 'technics' having to relocate routes and targets and reshuffle codes, when Moscow finds out, as indeed, it will eventually.' You couldn't last in this game if you didn't realise that bad points inevitably had their turn of popping up to put a spike in things. Falzoni's calm words did little to reassure either of them in their minds, as they both visualised the mountains of paperwork and headaches that would come their way in the progress of putting things right. Not to mention having to stare down, if not satisfy, angry Naval Board Enquiry Committees.

Ferten pondered the implication, with its uneasiness, in the Major's words. 'Not for a long time, let's hope.'

Clearly not fully cheered with his own remark, Falzoni drummed his pen down sharply on his knee. Ferten caught the unsettled motion. He wasn't feeling too happy himself. Looking up from his notepad, Falzoni stared out the small dirty window. The darkness had thinned slightly, where a waking sun was trying to scrape a way through from behind the black blanket. Maybe it was waiting for a conductor's baton to summon Grieg's soft musical raising up of the curtain on a new morning.

Just visible was the mobile compressor, servicing the plane, chugging and shuddering away on the end of the cable snaking out to the *Arkansas*. The working crew from the *Arkansas* had all dispersed, their lot done. That had all been a dummy run, of course. An open secret operation, on hush hush orders from above, to pull the wool over the eyes of the Red Fleet monitoring the US/NATO wargame manoeuvres. But even this had a double lining. A ploy within a ploy. Marley Goodblood's brainchild, of course.

05.11hrs. Falzoni watched the ginger-haired ensign striding smartly towards their cabin, to tell him that the helicopter would be landing shortly, to take him inland. Zipping up his anorak, he stood up to go. Ferten looked up at the Major. 'Time for you to shift, Major? Right.' Ferten looked at his watch, and then reached over, to pick up the walkie-talkie.

Frank followed the other's longing look at the empty hotdog foil tray. That faint pang of hunger he had felt earlier, when offered breakfast by the galley chef, was now gone. He had to 'stomach' other things first. 'You go get yourself another one of those, Lieutenant. I'll push on with my lot. I've still a couple of things I need to see to first, before the chopper flies me out.'

<h1 style="text-align:center">2</h1>

The bright spot in the distance gradually grew into a headlamp flux as it entered the forest, reappearing as flashes between trees as it travelled along the winding road. Flashes sharpened every so often into silver rapiers of light thrusting expertly between the slender trunks, and then withdrawing again with equal adroitness. Falzoni's black Porsche swept round bend after bend, flanked on both sides by legion after legion of tall stalwart pines honouring the passing regal chariot. With the way ahead continually twisting sharply from left to right, Frank could only hold his patience and drive on and on – perhaps '*tunnel on*' would have been more appropriate -- where the dark dense foliage of this great Norwegian forest never seemed to be ending. When at last a torch-light suddenly popped up, moving from side to side some fifty yards down the road, Frank pressed his foot down to have the car slowing down and gradually halting.

With the engine purring quietly, in readiness to race off again in an instant, and his throbbing suspicion and alertness equally tensed for action, Frank waited, watching. The dark figure started to walk forward slowly. Closer and closer it came. Eyes trained all the time on the man looming up closer, Frank felt for the .38 Ruger automatic lying beside him on the passenger seat. Still no sign of hostility. He let the widow slide down slowly. The cold air space filled up with a large face, searching eyes trapped between massive spiky beard and fur hat pulled down to the eyebrows. Seconds stretched out until inspection, both ways, was satisfied.

'SAILOR BOY?' The code-words came out in a surprisingly light tone, instead of a heavy bear growl to match the heavy bear face that Frank had expected.

'SAILOR *MAN*,' replied Frank in required corrective code.

Nodding in approval of the response, the man stepped back, beckoning Frank to follow him. Pocketing the automatic, Frank got out of the car to follow on, still taking the precaution, code-words or not, of not walking too close behind for the man to suddenly turn round in surprise attack on him. Stepping down off the road, they passed through the great wall of trunks and into the heavy undergrowth of the forest. With only the torch-light and snapping twigs in front to steer him, Falzoni had a hard job stumbling, tripping, and fighting off branches springing back at his face, in his effort to follow his guide. All at once, after what had seemed to be a never-ending trek, obstruction from menacing branches fell away and they were suddenly in a small clearing. Correction – *he* was in a small clearing alone by himself. The guy had skedaddled, leaving the torch behind, God bless his kind consideration! Still lit, and perched on a branch-end, the torch seemed to signal this to be a tryst of a stopping point.

Frank looked around, inspecting the tiny circular space. If this was where the local coven held its nocturnal pagan rituals, there wasn't much standing room for the chorus with its vibrant *Carmina Burana* or without the central sacrificial bonfire scorching a few of those bare feet dancing around it. But this wasn't the States, so you had to respect a foreign culture's oddball way of doing things. Then he noticed the stone jutting out of the ground on the far side. It seemed too regularly shaped to be natural. It had been placed there deliberately. Now that he looked, there appeared to be markings of sorts on it. Something was written on it. Stepping in closer, he leaned down to try reading the crudely scratched words.

'He was awarded the Nobel Prize for Literature, no less,' The words, suddenly cutting the silence from behind Falzoni, broke his attention in trying to read out and pronounce the strange foreign name.

'You don't say. How about that!' Frank didn't need to turn round to identify the speaker, long-time familiar as he was with the New England rounded accent.

'And he was executed by firing squad the next day.'

'His spelling was *that* bad? They reckoned money was better spent on bullets than on casting a gold medal?' Frank turned round abruptly to face his associate 'advisor' and handler in the field, in things that were much better left unmentioned --- forever dubious as he was trustworthy --- Marley Goodblood. As he did, he gave a slow shake of the head of mild rebuke that hardly needed his cynical smile to reinforce his open show of annoyance. He half turned to have another look at the stone. The dirty surface made it difficult to decipher the words. 'This – Hi-? -- or Ho-? Stohl, guy?'

'Hirtven Stohl.'

'Yeah, sure, whatever you say; who the fucking hell is this guy that you had to have me come all the way out here to see his final dice-roll stepping-off block? Couldn't you have just as easily wired me the dossier 'ink blots' straight through to the sub? Drowned in that flow of Navy Operational info coming through all the time, nobody's going to notice that it was in a separate cypher that only I could read; well, not straight away, anyway. I would have deleted it immediately after reading. So what's so important about him? What's his security label? How the hell does he figure in the game?'

'Frank, Frank, take it easy.'

' "Take it easy"!'

'Yeah, cool down and hear me out.'

'This will turn out to be a good one, I bet, just like all the endless good ones you load onto me under the murky heading of 'for national security. So let's have it.'

'I just figured that you could do with a break from playing Navy games, with you being holed up ten days in that fancy electronic wonder of a titanium can, playing hunt the Pirates; I thought you could do with some fresh air from a walk in the country, Frank --- *this* country.'

Frank recognised Goodblood's devious smile after getting his way in dowsing the child's anxiety tantrum, with only the stereotyped rubbing of hands missing to complete the scene. 'Jeez, Marley! That might wash down well with coke-headed college kids with asses still dripping oil from their Alpha House initiation rituals, but not with me. Fairy tales went out the window with me when I realised that Rudolf got his red nose from swiping the seasonal brandy. Save the schmaltz for unblemished virgin ears in your next Langley recruitment class lecture.' It was another feather in Marley's cap, joining the already thickening plumage, for him to lay down the sacred tablets of CIA's official rules of protocol before fresh college kids stepping forward to take up sword and shield for their country. Yeah, well, we can all fantasize at some time in our lives. Pausing for a cigarette, after his heated verbal fusillade, Frank was bluntly reminded for the second time that he had forgotten to pick them up. He had to satisfy himself with a piece, his last piece, of gum. 'So answer the question. Where does this guy, or what he was, figure in our own little private board-game?'

Then the thought, vague at first, started to come clearer to Frank. 'Hold on a sec --- you said: "*this country*"; Norway! Right, I'm beginning to see now, or perhaps at this stage, only what I'm *allowed* to see.' His jaws worked more slowly on the gum as he pulled the connecting parts into shape in his mind. 'So our little trick of using the Navy's latest hush-hush submarine detection sonar deflection equipment to evade the *Meerni's* searching sonar beams and disappear from its screens, was not entirely dreamed up and pencilled in solely by gold-braided Navy Chiefs alone, was it? It was you who initially handed them the pencil. Stopping off here for so-called 'minor technical modifications' in this backwater pond, was all part of the plan from the very beginning of Operations. Have I got it right?' Of course I'm right, if I know you, Goodblood' If ever any family name was synonymous with power in Washington, be it in politics, industry or military dealings by the side, it was Goodblood. You could be sure that Marley got more than just a word in edgeways where specific strategic lines were to be drawn in across giant screens in the Operations Room.

'You're not quite the parrot brain I sometimes take you for, Frank. You can hatch a good egg from time to time.'

Frank shuffled to show his restlessness, looking round the small clearing. 'So why am I here, in what's not exactly Central Park, if it's not looking for Red Riding Hood. Spit it out.'

'The significant point is that *you* are not here, Frank. The US Navy's submarine *Arkansas* is here in a Norwegian fjord for all to see with the naked eye or electronic screen. But you are *not*. Repeat: you are *not*. *Capisce?* Knowledge of a civilian stepping ashore from that naval vessel and onto Scandinavian soil is shared by a very select few.'

Still only half clear on what was happening from that sparse briefing, Frank pointed to the small stump of stone. 'And where does our pal, here, come into the picture?'

'He doesn't. Forget him. I came across him when I was checking the area for a suitable out of the way place for us to have our briefing in private, and I found this place. It seems that who he was, or what he was at that time, nineteen forty-two, was somewhat unclear to those concerned. He was either a collaborator informing the Abwehr (German Military Intelligence) of local Resistance movements, or a double agent supposedly working with German Occupation Forces, while all the time passing valuable information back to the Resistance. With unresolved suspicion outweighing absolute certainty on both sides, an Iron Cross or a hero's bronze memorial plaque was not to be the order of the day. Possible embarrassment from tarnishing of reputations on both sides, made swift, remote disposal of the 'problem' the mutually best plan of the day.'

'And that's it? That wraps it up? All this.' Frank swung a hand, indicating all around them and not hiding his irritation of the time wasted on a pointless guided tour.

'Just thought I'd let you know and quell your anxiety in putting you off on the wrong track.'

'You managed to do that well enough, for sure. Right, so putting that behind us and moving on, the next question is: what pawn's square are you playing me from in this new game you've arranged, as if I hadn't guessed.'

'All in good time, kid, all in good time. I don't have to remind you of our thumb-rule: you need know only what you need to know.' Goodblood paused as he felt something touch the tip of his nose. Taking it off with his finger, he looked at it. A tiny white snowflake. He looked up to see that the little thing hadn't descended on them without bringing pals along. In spite of the dark umbrella of the forest's thick foliage sheltering them overhead, snowflakes were managing to filter though. 'We'll get back to that later, Frank. In the meantime, I think it's time to get out of here. One buried here is enough; we don't want it to be three.'

Turning to move off, Goodblood stopped again to take something out of his pocket. He handed it to Falzoni. 'It should help you, carrying this on your person.'

Frank opened the small plastic wallet. The photograph was of him, but the name wasn't. 'Lewis. Frank Lewis. Food critic, writing for Boston gourmet magazine, *Bon Appetit*. Is this who I am for this assignment?'

'Enjoy the Scandinavian cuisine, Mr Lewis. Now let's get going. We'll go in my car. Some things we need to go over on the way. Give me your keys, and someone will see to the Porsche.'

'Hold on; wait a sec and satisfy my curiosity. What's *your* opinion on him?'

You can make up your mind on that for yourself, when you meet him, Frank.'

'No! No! *Him!*' Frank jerked his head, indicating behind him at the grave.

Goodblood's patience won over his anxious haste to leave, to let him ponder the question. 'That damn fiasco a few years ago where we all became heroic victors wasn't a ball game with only Allied Forces and Nazis on the field. The referee wanted to join in with his stringent rules to overrun us all, waving his glorious red flag.'

'*Red flag?* You mean ---. Right, got it.'

'Bravo! Somebody give Wonder Boy Frank, a gold star. Now, for God's sake, let get moving. We've wasted enough time, without having to go into history lessons about Johnny Red Bolshevik coming into the game and pushing everyone else off the field.'

3

The parks were first to sense the coming weather change. A darkening of grey skies came first, followed by leaves twitching to a low sough sifting through them, the green fingers swaying in the breezes. Upsurge currents whispered the cry for change across the city, so that plant growth everywhere was shifting feverishly, in readiness for the coming. Just as suddenly, a stalling stillness returned. Then down came millions of them. Each with a separate identity, in a swirling motion to answer the clarion call for this new purity. The snowflakes landed where they were welcome, abandoned by the wind, as it tended to millions more earth-bound passengers. Parks and streets slowly changed colour, like a giant kaleidoscope. The white particles floating down onto soft turf and hard stone, covering greys and greens of the rough and the smooth. Only the lamp standards stood out aloof over their territories. Buildings, whether grand imposing edifices, or lowly homesteads, all gradually lost their huffy divisions, united at last under the thin blanket covering the city, except where the river and lakes swallowed up the white invaders without mercy.

That was how Frank saw it as he drove across the city in his hired Volvo, to his rented apartment in the quiet district where, on Marley's assurance, his presence would not arouse undue attention. Worn and tired, like the rest of the ancient vehicle, the windscreen wipers struggled and groaned, almost losing the battle, to cope with the snow piling up on the glass.   With everything getting wetter under the falling snow,

19

his patience grew thinner with his crossing off street after street in never ending succession. What he was impatiently wanting see springing up just short of magic before him out there didn't appear to be willing to grant his wish.

Continually craning his neck and straining his eyes, peering out to read partly obscured street names distracted Falzoni from what he should have seen. Until he saw it in the rear-view mirror. And yes, the car was following him. Time for crazy maze games. Ramming the pedal down fiercely, he had the car lurching forward, its wheels spinning in sudden wild acceleration, spurting out great arcs of snow to shower grim-faced passers-bye who were none too pleased to have the slush, in addition to the bitter wind, bite into their faces. Turning rapidly down side-streets, one after the other, without knowing where he was going – without *caring* where he was going --- didn't seem to be doing any good. That damn blob of a stalker was still stuck there, square in the centre of the mirror.

Perhaps sensing Falzoni's annoyance, the 'blob' started flashing its headlights. No, it wasn't a trick of the light. There, in the mirror, the double spots of blue fog-lights were blinking in positive pattern. On and Off twice; pause, On and Off once; pause, On and Off twice. Repeated over and over. A finger was either jammed on a switch, or someone wanted a parley.

The 'Indianapolis-500' car rally ended slower than it had started, both of the vehicles pulling in, at a 'safe' distance apart, at the kerb. Two car door clicks, distinctively clear in the quiet night air. Blowing on his cold fingers, Falzoni looked down the street, taking in the dark figure cringing in the night, the face half covered by collar, the other half by snow. From the way the guy was holding that thick package, fingers splayed out, to his chest, you could have taken him to be a Dickens-style Bible-thumping evangelist in timely keeping with the 'no room at the inn', stable at Bethlehem theme.

Which, of course, he *wasn't*. Blowing on his cold hands as he walked towards the guy, Falzoni recognised, with a knowing eye, the polite just discernible servile manner of the raw diplomat recruit. The courier from the Embassy.

'Mr *Lewis*?'

'The one and only, in person. Yeah, *c'est moi*.' The playful words to put the nervous young rookie at ease. Frank looked up pointedly at the guy's car roof. 'Couldn't Expenses afford to squeeze a neon sign in on its budget?' Frank couldn't help thinking that one of those contraptions glaring out its message could hardly have attracted more attention than the wild flashing of headlights had done.

'*Sorry?*'

'Skip it.' Frank reached out to take the package. He saw through the open end of the small diplomatic bag what he reckoned to be a long night's reading in the form of two fat folders. 'My homework, *right*? That'll take more than a packet of Camel and a long stream of coffees to get through. What do you reckon?'

Not knowing what to answer on that, the man blurted out: 'I gather that it's important --- *useful*, anyway, for you. According to Mr Hawkesly, that is.'

' "*Useful*," huh?'

'To be delivered to you immediately, he said --- Mr Hawkesly, that is.'

'Ah, of course, Mr Hawkesly,'

'You know how he likes things done quicker than lightning. But you'll already be acquainted with his ways.'

Frank gave a soft avuncular smile, shaking his head slowly. 'Ah, no, sorry to disappoint you, but no, I don't know your Mr Hawkesly.' He held up the bag, with its 'precious' lot in a gesture of gratitude. 'But you can tell him that I said thanks for this, and that I'll get on with the good work at "*lightning*" speed, have no fear. We don't want him developing ulcers from undue worry, do we?'

The young man gave a short laugh, realising now, that it was his own behaviour that was the butt of the humour. 'I guess not, Mr Lewis.'

Looking down at his watch, Frank began turning away slowly as a signal before looking again at the courier. 'Well if that's all there is, I think we can call it a night and disperse, before the local Keystone Cops arrive to haul us in for ungodly soliciting in the street.' He walked away with a quickening pace. Enough time wasted.

The courier called out. 'Incidentally, Mr Lewis, we're holding an informal cheese and wine sort of do on this coming Wednesday. Perhaps, in your capacity of professional gourmet, you'd care to come along and enlighten us with your valued opinion on the refreshments; the wines especially?'

Frank stopped, to turn round. He pulled on a frown, not that it could be seen at that distance in the poor light of the street lamps. 'Now I do like the sound of wines, like music to my ears; but cheese? Cheese makes me think of mice. And mice scare the pants off me, but don't tell anyone. So I think we'll leave it there.' He turned to walk away again, then stopped, looking back at the guy. 'Say, kid, what the heck is your name, anyway?'

'Hawkesly, sir.'

'*Hawkesly?*'

'Yes, Hawkesly. Hawkesly *Junior*, that is, sir.'

4

That his father was now gone, alas, having lain a mere fifty-one hours in the grave, gave Frank only the compensation of partly pulling his mind from that other painful connection with the past – Charlie's death. It moved him in reminding him of the only other time that he had paid a visit, to that antiquated suburban corner of San Francisco that had spawned and spewed him forth, to die-cast him in his ever-lasting like-or-lump-it personal mould. Coming down from the university, back to the quaint little apple-blossomed hometown had given him a feeling of personal conquest. But where sadness of farewell filled the day, a drabness flowered over former familiarity, like weeds springing up and cluttering what had once been welcoming doorways. Thus he had been able to look down in a quiet satisfaction of completion. He did not recognise the town, any more than it recognised him, or failed to grant him recognition after it had once sent him away, a long time ago, to offer his life in service for his country. He had not felt alone or alienated in that strange town that day. Rather, he had felt an elating sense of freedom – of his having broken the chains of familial bonding – of having wiped away blemishing faults of the past. Or so he had thought then, watching the coffin's slow descent. But that very lowering into the earth had mirrored that earlier coffin drawing out of reach forever, making him realise that the past was continually stalking him, a skulking predator snarling on his heels, its hunger increasing of late.

Laden with this morbid mood, it was thus through a whirling snow blizzard that Falzoni, after parking the car, tramped his way uphill, his form bent forward, to the town's Sorjen Institute of Natural Studies. As far as he could judge, a place rarely visited by the common crowd but most avidly by that peculiar 'absent-minded' lot forever in search of something more extraordinary, like a mutant strain of banana with two left feet. A high spiked wall hid the select institute, except at the gateway, where the building leapt out in bright patches of red sandstone, to penetrate the grove of snow-sprinkled larches. The trees moved aside so that a forest of twisted chimney turrets took over, smoking heavily to recover the heat lost through the tall French windows. Where Falzoni churned the snow underfoot, he was able to deduce that the large building had reproduced itself in countless little red pieces covering the driveway and scattered up the stairs under the stone portico.

Scraping his soles on the iron frame to remove the snow, Falzoni pulled down on the heavy iron door handle and pushed open the heavier iron-studded oaken door. He entered the main hall, brushing under the tropical palms held in the grip of two grimacing Burmese jungle warriors standing beside two fiercer grimacing jade dragons. Teak parquets and raw sienna carpeting stretched out before him, with finely veneered wood panelling rising to the Renaissance ceiling's frescoed pale-flesh frolics of naked nymphs. And shelves and shelves holding up a sea of dust-covered, time-forgotten, volumes visited mostly by the odd adventurous spider. Frank took in the room's dull atmosphere, along with that unique smell of books quietly decaying all around him. It gave off a cool feeling, but not as cold as he'd been out there in the snow. Looking cooler in their redundancy, just like the books, the two suits of armour standing on both sides of the large crest emblazoning the balcony balustrade caught Frank's attention. '*Semper paratus* – always ready,' he said quietly, reading from the large shield. 'Yeah, pal, I get it, no need to remind me,' he muttered again quietly to himself. He stole a glance all round about, without looking suspiciously on guard. In this game, you could never be sure who was who, tailing you or not tailing you. Not unless any KGB (*Komitet*

Gosudarstvennoi Bezopasnosti) agent would be crazy enough to be sporting a Ku Klux Klan- style of tall conical mask headgear.

His inside started for a brief instant at the sight the woman's face framed in profile against the light of the window. It reminded him of *her* for a moment, the surprise catching him inside. But the woman straightened up from her leaning position over the glass case, turning her head to reveal an entirely different person. His inner glow subsided. It wasn't Charlie. She was dead. Killed by a bastard traitor double agent just doing his duty to protect what he supposedly believed in before fleeing to the safety of the Soviet Motherland. Now in game rebound, it was apparently Moscow's turn to be betrayed by one of its traitors scheming to help the West.

The woman stepped away from the display cabinet with a slow unsure motion that quickened into the brisk official walk of a curator. 'Kan jeg hjelpe deg' The woman's voice tried to convey a friendly tone, but didn't manage to lose its official note completely.

Snapping out of his dark thoughts, Frank broke out in a wide smile, shaking his head politely. 'Sorry, ma'am, I don't speak your lovely lingo. In any case, I don't think my tongue would curl round those cute vowels with quite as chic a click as yours does.' And she was a chic chick in Frank's eyes, in spite of the officious message that came across from her impatient fidgeting with those keys on the long gold-linked neck chain draped over and dangling from her generous bosom balcony.

'Ah, American,' she exclaimed. Did he detect a note of disdain in her remark?

Switching to English, she tried again. 'Can I help you?' Turning slowly, she swung an arm around, indicating the glass cases with their display of precious specimens.

Taking a quick step back, Frank gave a short laugh, declining the kind offer with a shake of the hand. 'No, no, it's okay; I'm just browsing – looking around at your super collection here. That's awful kind of you. Thanks all the same.' Turning away, whilst trying not to appear rude, he made his escape. She followed the American's retreat with dagger eyes, her face creasing into a frown of disapproval. Another foreign tourist insulting the museum's precious specimens by coming into the building simply to shelter from the inclement weather outside.

All the way from Lavik to Bergen in the back of Marley's car, Frank had made a rough perusal through the CIA classified notes that Marley had loaded on him. Dropped off at a convenient suburban coach stance, a local bus had him arriving discreetly in the city with its picturesque image of yester-year multi-coloured wooden buildings. In his rented room in the town's quiet district, he had spent the night running over dossier after dossier, field reports, recorded phone-calls and letters, until he felt that he knew him, in spite of the fact that he had not yet set eyes on the damn guy; none of our lot had seen the guy --- if it *was* a guy, or a dame. Nobody knew. Even with all the scant snippets of information collated by our agents spread over Europe and everywhere else outside of Russia, anything beyond what we now had was a total obscurity. It sufficed for the moment, to allot him the codename: COMPASS.

Tomorrow's low-profile entrance, this time in Oslo, would let him see the guy face to face.

Now he was here in this gloomy mausoleum to meet this crazy phantom 'Red' Pimpernel, who was offering to tear a hole in the Iron Curtain, if you could excuse the pun. Taking a final checking sweeping glance around the room, Frank turned his attention on the broad staircase, walking with a determined step towards it, muttering: 'Okay, pal, so let's be meeting you, whoever you are; let's put your invisible mug-shot in the frame.'

5

Clearly, what had been of compelling interest to scholars for centuries had now waned in drawing power with the two men in the ancient manuscripts room of the Institute. Neither Falzoni nor the blond-haired man in russet Norfolk jacket was giving any real attention to the manuscripts in the glass cases over which they stooped, shifting and turning like restless bloodhounds. And what scent was that they were each picking up? Both of them were acutely vigilant of all that was happening around them. Their senses were tuned to every creak of the worn-weary floorboards, to every voice or whisper that filtered in from the surrounding rooms of the building. Both of them were acutely aware of each other.

Falzoni bent in closer to the glass case, his nose almost touching it, all the while watching the man's angled reflection on its surface. When the reflection turned its back on him, Falzoni stole a quick glance at the man across the room. The man's height and broad, robustly filled, frame were two factors tying in with the image of him Falzoni had conjured up in his mind the previous night when going over the will-o-the wisp guy's details. Military boots, gleaming bright from devoted polishing, stood proudly out of the cavalry-twill trousers, and could well have strode with resolute pounding across a hard concrete barracks parade ground at one time in the past, although the footsteps were sounding differently on relatively soft wooden floorboards today. Cautiously light, *furtive*, steps. Not wishing to draw undue attention. Yeah, that was making sense, joining up the dots in the vague sketch they had of him so far, built up from equally vague field reports that had been gathered on him from far and wide. Collectively it all added up – from military to civilian – from soldier to engineer – from dedicated comrade to disillusioned traitor.

But this dawning clarity was suddenly giving rise to an uneasy feeling in Frank's mind. Was he mistaken? Was he being over-alert comparing the sound those military boots would have made, to the sound he remembered hearing – *thought* he had heard -- striding resolutely after him in the shrouded depth of the evening mist last night? Trailing him? Hell! Or was it just the light of day blowing away the night's gossamer phantoms of the mind, like a child's nightmare dissolved with the coming of morn?

All in all, who was this fucking guy who appeared to be one step ahead of us, keeping a tab on *us*, in the game we thought *we* were running? If Moscow was unaware of agent Falzoni's presence in Norway, as Marley had so resolutely assured him, and this guy was dogging the steps of our operation so closely, you had to see a new mantle of professionalism flapping round those broad shoulders. And it somehow didn't seem to tie in with the image of the quiet docile laboratory worker interested in nothing else but what he read through a spectrometer, measuring the laser-beam power of possibly what could be another asset to be added to the Red Army's already massive armoury. No, it didn't.

What the reports he'd read on the guy didn't give was the dark, faintly Slavonic, bearded face, pock-marked high on the cheek he could see, by what looked like those cruel 'love-bites' that ripping shrapnel left you with as a reminder of how lucky you were to have been spared death. How many cases would have considered it *unlucky* to have been spared, you were often led to wonder? Frank certainly wondered, mindful of his own near scrape with those furious flying fragments of demon steel when his unit, the 2nd Armoured Division, confronted Goering's elite Panzer Division and the 15th Panzergrenadier Division in Palermo, '42. Dark and weathered just like the face, two large toughened hands spread open-fingered around the corners of the display case with a firmness that threatened to shatter the seemingly fragile structure. Frank reckoned the guy to be about his own age --- but not the sort of person to be wasting his time peering down at an exhibit of *Drosophila melanogaster*. And that giant fruit fly, invaluable as a base source for genetic research, certainly knew the feeling of cruel steel, trapped in flight and skewered down in its final frozen pose.

The man moved to another case so that he was now facing Falzoni. Straightening up, Frank went over to the same case. Standing over the glass panel, he looked down at the faded yellow decomposition that was the brittle remains of the fifteenth century Zhutenberg Treaty. One touch of a finger, and the entire scroll would disintegrate. 'Truly a remarkable specimen of preservation,' said Frank, his eyes remaining fixed on the scroll.

'Indeed, sir; indeed.' The tone was that of one who didn't give a damn about decaying paper scrolls, but only about someone else stooping over them *pretending* to care.

'I guess,' continued Frank, 'that it wouldn't take too many poking fingers. Like a party mask, finger it too fretfully, and it falls away, so revealing the face and the game is ended.' Frank stood up straight to stare the other in the eye. The message was clear that he was more than a little peeved at being kept waiting. 'Is the game ended?'

'Sir?' A lesser person challenged so would have shuffled uneasily, or fidgeted a nervous finger, under Frank's steely stare. But this guy didn't twitch as much as a single hair of his heavy brush eyebrows. His dark brown eyes twinkled with open amusement, whilst awaiting Frank's next move; like a child dangling a frog or spider by its leg, watching its frantic wriggling, before deciding on letting it run free or dashing it underfoot.

Falzoni handed the man the note passed on to him from the CIA station the previous evening. 'Yours, I think?' The man barely glanced at the paper before crushing it in a mass of dark-haired fingers and putting it away promptly in his pocket. With equal brevity, Falzoni looked at his watch, tapping it with obvious message. 'Maybe we can get the ball rolling soon, huh? Preferably before we become parched and crack up, like that thing.' He nodded pointedly at the ancient scroll.

The man glanced round the large room and back at the American 'You came alone?' he said at last.

'Your eyesight is working just fine, pal. Relax, there's just me and my shadow, or at least there would be if there was more light in this gloomy mausoleum. No one else.' Falzoni smiled whilst reading the other's eyes. A brief return smile was allowed to touch the man's hard face. A black eyebrow arched momentarily, acknowledging the American's strangely humorous words. Spare in his own words, the man moved off, pausing only to turn and beckon Falzoni with a casual flick of the finger to follow him.

Stooping to put his eye to the snub-faced, double-fanged head, of an Inca ceremonial marble reptile, and looking along its long slender body, like the hunter assessing his target, the Russian sized up Falzoni for his opening shot. He waited for a sign from the man. Frank obliged with a questioning slight tilt of the head. COMPASS straitened his posture, coming round to Frank's tail-end of the artefact, patting the cold stone surface as he did so. 'To the layman, Mr Lewis, this is a mere six feet stone replica of the Crotalus Durissus highly venomous pit viper, indolent in its silent repose; but to the archaeologist, it opened a truly colossal gateway to the hitherto forbidden territory of that long-lost civilisation. Owing to that ancient tongue's unique form of hieroglyphics, akin to no others, it had proven impossible, for far too long, to decipher the basic semantic key. But, because of these inscriptions in the three tongues of hieroglyphics, demotic characters and Greek characters, had now considerable progress has been achieved in converting former skull-cracking symbols into modern language. And all because, for the first time, we know what the other side is thinking, so to speak. A fundamental lesson in the strategy of communication.'

'Bravo! Encore! Encore!,' Falzoni let out a wide smile that didn't hid his vexation, giving a slow mocking hand-clap for back-up. 'This is your hobby, then, is it? What you do, in place of exploring the well-rounded body 'hieroglyphics' of hookers, on your night off, away from spectrometers and lasers?'

'Sorry? *Hookers?*'

'We'll dump that one. I'm sure neither of us agreed and arranged for this meeting here, at the expense of valuable time and risk of danger, for the sole purpose of a remedial recourse to a belated lesson in linguistics. As it is, I can't remember where I put my early schooling ABC spelling book, anyway.' If Frank sound vexed, it was because he was, at the Russian's detracting reference of him as the 'layman', with his presumptuous need to give this time-wasting lecture. Taking a slow deep breath to let his simmering irritation settle down, Frank rubbed his palms together as a sign for shifting. 'So let's move on.'

COMPASS smiled in open amusement at the American's deliberately stilted delivery of words. 'I incur your pique, I see, Mr Lewis, with my circuitous choice of words. How remiss of me. Permit me to apologise most profoundly.' The silken eloquent speech of the educated man. Yes, they had a few of those, even in that glorious motherland of all-equal plebeian hammer and sickle wielders. 'Yes, you are correct; I waste valuable time with my unnecessary detour into linguistic enlightenment. However, one must agree that a tactical approach to gaining access to new ground calls for a need to tread warily. The matter that I am presently concerned with is a most delicate one, the details of which are somewhat ---' The Russian's hard-faced expression, retentive of many secrets, still let out a betrayal of embarrassment, in his searching for the appropriate word.

'Money, perhaps?' suggested Falzoni. 'Or perhaps I should say Swiss francs? How does that sound? Touches your ears with a swell ring, I bet. Fits in with your fancy vocabulary as easily as it would a begger's.'

The man's apologetic look was replaced with quiet relief, and this in turn by his usual calm-eyed control once more. Shaking his head, he looked at Frank, grateful that the American had been the one to broach the delicate subject of money for secrets without stipulating hard conditions or showing any sign of deferment. Not yet, anyway. Those thirty pieces of silver had their way of weighing heavily on the conscience, if not fatefully.

'You would appear to be a bird who knows his wing, discerning his nest from afar, Mr Lewis. Please do not let me hinder your flight.'

Falzoni guessed that there was still a play of nerves behind the other's calm expression. With the gross pilfering of highly classified, highly guarded, government intelligence being on an easy agenda for this character, so also could double-dealing come easy for him. There was no way of 'measuring' the man yet, not knowing who, or what, he really was, but they would find out soon, one way or the 'other'. The Department's IBM Fortran computers were already spinning their wheels just short of burn-out, thanks to Goodblood's Level 2 memorandum to Administrative Executive at Langley.

Falzoni attempted no words at the Russian's genial invitation to continue. That matter was completely out of his power, and was entirely Marley Goodblood's worry. Presumably Marley would have procured such sensitive material for him without needing to cope personally with the consequences. A favour for services rendered. Frank, of course, could have held back on these last points, but this was the method of convincing COMPASS of the folly of holding back further. To goad him into revealing his hand, so to speak. Like the skilful poker player's prompting wrong moves from that guy across the table. Not that he'd spared much time for that game since leaving college.

COMPASS was about to speak, when he stopped. They both stood still, silent. They'd both caught the fleeting flash of a movement reflected on one of the glass cases. It was the female curator that had come up to look around the room, seen them in close conversation, and retreated back down the stairs.

When COMPASS did speak, it was to delve into what he sensed to be the stirring undercurrent of shifting politics rippling below the surface of Moscow's otherwise settled aplomb. Separatist groupings of hitherto forbidden alien theories were building up in the labyrinthine maze of minds that constituted the Politburo's far-reaching fingers of power. But so far this did not appear to be calling for increased policing and subsequent purging. Far less disturbed was the KGB, since it could gain valuable intelligence by measured observation and treatment of the festering open wound with more finality than that of the insidious build-up of rogue cells in the malignant tumour growing beneath the skin. Proper surveillance mounted on this rising wave of subversive thinking was the required means of stemming a crisis of political chaos through multiple stalemates. In contrast, there was relative solidarity in the military. Like Germany's resolve to rebuild its strength, following the humiliation of defeat in World War One, the Red Army was united in its need to regain face, after Khrushchev's knuckling-down to Kennedy's naval blockade of Cuba's nuclear threat in '61.

With security minds thus looking to forestall a looming case of political impasse, the close attention given to this serious issue gave distraction away from any security violations possibly occurring in the military sector. A limited window of opportunity for purloining highly classified military intelligence, in fact.

'And this incited you to make your move now and throw your bag of loot to us in the West through what you consider to be a safe tear in the 'Curtain'?'

The Russian felt a tiny inner tremor of uneasiness at what he hoped wasn't a change of mind in the American, going by his tone. 'Or perhaps you would consider this to be *not* the opportune moment for such an arrangement between us?'

Frank laughed quietly, looking away and then back, at what he saw as simple naivety in the man. 'Oh, sure, it's the right moment, all right.' He laughed again. '*Any* moment is the right moment in this game, pal. It's only when your Case Officer in the field disowns you, claiming to have no knowledge of your mission, and leaves you on your own, isolated in cold indifference, that you know that it was not the *right moment*. The steel cuffs, cold against the wrists, in the interrogation cell help to confirm this. That and Pentothal mind games between cold showers from high-powered pressure hoses at brain-screaming irregular intervals.'

'I am understanding you, Mr Lewis.' The slow solemn tone said that he did, indeed, appreciate the depth of danger involved.

'Fine. So long as we've got that. Good.'

As they passed through the rooms towards the institute's entrance, it seemed that the discussion's pendulum had swung as far as it could in a positive direction. 'So, am I being officially recruited by your intelligence department for ancillary duties of a clandestine nature, Mr Lewis?'

Frank halted abruptly, so that COMPASS only just avoided colliding on his heels. He gripped the Russian's forearm and looked into the dark eyes shrouded under those bush eyebrows to register the guy's understanding. 'I never heard you say those words, pal; nor will I ever. However, forthright you may want to stride for your cause, no banners can ever be hoisted high on this battlefield, except at half mast, at the end of a bitter life-long campaign. But you already know that, don't you; no need for reminders, right?'

'I am very much actively acquainted with such a strict code of secrecy, as decreed by my own department – as presumably *you* in turn, must know.'

'And you figure you're ready and have the balls to handle it?'

COMPASS stared back his strength of affirmative, at the same time removing Frank's steely grip his arm. He narrowed his eyes to search into the depth of the mind that was already searching his own, seeking out the littlest tremor or crack of American grand-plan deception. Satisfied as much as he could be for now, he nodded slowly in positive assurance, voicing a low guttural murmur: 'Y-e-s. A leopard among leopards. Distinguishable from those around it only by its spots.'

'Yeah, we understand each other, pal. We got that right.' Smiling and taking out a cigarette, Frank took his time lighting it so giving him the time to look the Russian over rudely from head to foot in open assessment of how the man would react to this inspection. He wanted something more than what the scant details on the dossier notes were giving as a personal profile. With Marley Goodblood directly answerable to the State Defense Secretary for any '*misdemeanours*' that should occur, and not himself. This made things smoother for Frank, considering the already dodgy tightrope-strolling nature of his work. His motive for recruiting COMPASS was on the strength of department reports that the man could prove to be very useful to them, not solely on account of his scientific role, but on his high-grade position giving him access to other invaluable interrelated material. A reasonably good horse to put your money on, so they hoped. And that was just what they needed --- a guy who could blend in easy with generals and other 'high brass' without being a dumb 'yes' and 'no' man. A teeny risk, perhaps, on account of his breeding, the ethnic strain that had not served well for the parents. But they could carry that. He could also be made to 'fall' for that matter, when they no longer needed him.

That, at least, was the *ghost* plan, thought up, but *not written down*, by Marley, of course. Now was the time for inspecting the 'goods' prior to testing. Another look at the hard blank face that gave out little from behind it, so not arousing undue attention or suspicion, or staying in memory for long. Good. The heavy build spoke of great reserves of strength simmering quietly for outlet. Frank had to look closely to see a degree of nervousness playing behind those deep brooding eyes. But there was something else turning over at the back of dark pits. Whatever it was, it burned with the strength of – of – what? Frank wondered. He reserved a place for the answer to the question later at the back of his mind. An unexpected reserve of strength behind a disciplined calm was tantamount to the tethered goat luring the unexpected tiger. It would serve their purposes well to have someone with a sinister side who was not afraid to step out and wander off the secure path of the straight and narrow.

Frank blew out a long stream of smoke as a signal to closing the 'meeting' 'That seems to be it, pal; my boss will be looping the hoop on reading my report. I hope you're satisfied too.'

Before anything else could be said on the issue, they both jumped inwardly at the sudden metallic clank immediately behind them. They looked round to see cleaner, bucket and mop approaching, the mop snaking closer and closer, menacingly encroaching on their mini cabal. Was he a cleaner? Silent from a scary moment of being so caught off guard, Frank stepped out the way. In contrast, COMPASS laughed aloud heartily at the interruption. Frank felt a twinge of annoyance at COMPASS so easily taking amusement at what could have been a thunderclap disaster with their cover being blown along with their being arrested, to disappear forever in Lubyanka; the only way out of there was via a window seven floors up, with only the one direction to take thereafter, courtesy of Isaac Newton.

A moment's truer thought gave way to that earlier trickle of initial preparatory suspicion. The very ease of reaction with every contingency that he encountered, turning it to his advantage with the smooth aplomb that had the smell of special craft-training for spooks. But the man was purportedly an engineer, or so they so far had been led to believe. Like before, Frank wondered – who the hell *was* this guy? He was brave enough to approach CIA, offering information valuable to Western defence, but would not reveal his identity at this stage, for fear of being snared by KGB surveillance.

Collecting their thoughts from the brief distraction, they both returned their minds to the grimmer facets of the situation facing them ahead. As they looked each other over without words, the silence was enough to say that the meeting was ended. Pulling on his leather gloves as he moved away, COMPASS looked up into the air in display of pulling a distant point to mind. 'Lewis? Lewis? Unless I am mistaken, I am recalling that it was on the sixteenth of April, 'forty five, that our First Belorussian Front battalion, commanded by Comrade General Georgy Zhukov, launched its night-time attack, aided by floodlighting, on the heavily-fortified German position in Seelow Heights on the outskirts of Berlin. With our unit to the forefront of the assault, followed by tanks and infantry, we achieved a glorious capture of Berlin. There was much celebrating the historical victory and fraternising with allied martial forces – British – American. If I remember correctly, there was a young Sergeant Lewis. Yes – I am sure the name was Lewis. A much younger person than we are now, of course. We were all younger and fresh in experience all those many years ago. They were much needed for our learning of life.' COMPASS glanced at Frank's gloved prosthetic hand. 'As, indeed, you, yourself, have had much experience. He was perhaps of your family or relation, this younger Lewis?'

With barely twenty four hours to have taken on his false name for the assignment, Frank felt it come to ear as if it was someone else's. As it always did when on a mission, you were apt to assume every query as possibly being fired at you by the enemy, to shatter you out of your cover. The memory of an operational pseudonym never losing its alien scrape in the mind never lost its effect on you however many missions you had clocked up. His negative headshake had the Russian's face snap shut with nothing more ado about that subject. Almost as if a secondary motive behind the question had failed. A cautioning reminder of who was who, or *wasn't* who, with the possible dividing line still hanging around, waiting to claim its specific position. And you had to make sure that you were on the right side of that line.

Giving his gloves a more tightening tug, COMPASS made to move away. 'I shall make myself scarce, as you Americans would say in your idiomatic tongue, and go first.' He hesitated for a moment's thought that was amusing him from what he had just said. 'It is perhaps not the weight of wisdom, but rather, the lightness of folly, that tips the scales.'

'Yeah, well, I took in all the philosophy I needed in the first half of an hour's lecture in my Freshman's Year at Yale. That was enough for me.'

As Falzoni watched COMPASS go down the broad steps and crossing the foyer, he noted how the man's dark-bearded face matched with another large figure's dark hairy countenance. That of a large gorilla of massive physique. ' --- distinguishable from those around it only by its dark demeanour and foreboding powerful form,' Frank murmured in quiet thought to himself. Yeah, he could well imagine that man wielding powers akin to that great beast, if he turned out to be what you just hoped he would not be, with his own official labyrinth of Moscow corridors of influence making him a sore man to cross. Frank hadn't forgotten how he had ventured along that perilous route before, being only narrowly spared a 'Lubyanka Special' brain-scourging session, followed by free State-paid leisure time in Siberia. At the time, it had been difficult to measure the difference between his own wrath, and that of his captors and interrogators. Only covert CIA dealing, euphemistically named 'diplomacy', had whisked him back to the States faster than that Oz guy in the movie had delivered his lot back home. But enough of 'happy' reminiscences.

With another matter to in attend to, in preparation for tomorrow's stage in the game, Frank waited a suitable interval after COMPASS had gone, and then stepped out into the sharp brightness of daylight reflected back from snow-covered ground, blazing in comparison to the Institute's dark interior. As a further precaution, he then boarded a municipal service bus and riding for three stops, alighted and boarded a second bus. Repeating the procedure again, he alighted this time after riding for only two stops, before he could be reasonably sure that he had not been tailed. A further twenty minutes of walking, turning abruptly down dim-lit alleys and quiet empty streets that allowed you to look back to check, had him arriving at the Department's safe house. And yet, after all the zig-zag tactics to elude possible surveillance, success could still not be taken as an absolute certainty. That was the tight-rope balance of the game you played.

6

It was much to COMPASS's surprise, when, two nights later, he was set upon and bundled violently into the car that had ghosted up out of the evening mist to stop alongside him with its door open. As the door slammed shut and they moved off, a match flared up to reveal the now familiar face of the American, Mr Lewis, opposite him. The other 'assailant', seated beside Lewis, was not familiar to him. The man sat straight-backed, staring at him, watching, listening, saying nothing, missing nothing.

Frank Falzoni watched the watching game in the other two, letting it prolong for several moments before intervening. 'Don't worry about my colleague here. He only barks and bites when he needs to. Further to that, I should add that he does bite deep.' Frank smiled, looking round at Marley Goodblood sitting beside. Goodblood cocked an eyebrow at the joke, whilst still holding his stare on the Russian.

Measuring this remark, and how it was put across, COMPASS concluded the man to be in some way a superior of Lewis. But at to the reason for, or the meaning of this unscheduled mystery tour, he was as much in the dark as the vehicle's interior. Not sure if he should show anger or calm composure, at this rough abduction, he settled for snubbing the cigar Goodblood offered him. He looked to Lewis for immediate enlightenment. Reading the dithering perplexity in COMPASS's expression, hidden as it was in his control of impatience -- and the guy was good at it. -- Falzoni made a point of drawing out further on that control. He waited, to let Marley put extended play to work, cracking the cigar at his ear, and cutting it with deliberate slow precision, then settling back to savour the taste for a few more seconds.

COMPASS found the other's delay tantalisingly long, as they, no doubt, were intended to be. But he recognised the pattern of play. The last time it had been a display cabinet in a museum, now it was a cigar in a car going to God knows where. At least they made a point of not racing at breakneck speed through any red traffic lights in haste to wherever it was they were heading, In fact, first the horse, then the open carriage with its two tourists pointing about round them, floated into view alongside with the gentle clip-clop sound of hooves just filtering in through the loud hum of the six cylinder engine. Goodblood leaned forward to tap the driver on the shoulder, telling him to put his foot down. They could afford the gas. He brushed off the cigar ash from the man's shoulder. The horse and carriage floated back with leisurely ease out of sight.

Goodblood held his head back to blow out a final long stream of smoke to signify the end of his sampling. Now for another 'sampling' of sorts. He turned to Falzoni. He knew why the Department wanted the Russian. But why had the man so readily consented to joining them? An academically proficient man who could go on to shine brightly in his field, wanting to engage in their work, so dark and obscure, and even dangerous? He sensed entrapment in the person sitting there with them, so still, so reticent, so near but so distant. Was it a mad craving to be singed by excitement's flame, or the need to escape from doldrums, or *something deeper*? Did he see a conflict of wills in that face? As in two contesting terrible twins, with COMPASS content with neither one nor the other, being in constant variance between the two? But this was real, and not some Grimm tale for children. Or was it somehow unreal in a grim adult tale? Goodblood checked himself before he was drawn further into a spiral of hair-splitting logic. He had no time for such mind games, in spite of the problem its answer could possibly place before the Department. But not yet, anyway. He guessed it would appeal more to the Russian's intellect to pursue such a puzzle, ironic though it would be, like a cat chasing its own tail. He tapped Frank's arm, whilst looking pointedly at the Russian. 'It does good to see the new horse's form before entering it into the race, right, Frank?'

'Yeah, I've got to agree with you there. No point in betting our lot on a loser.'

'Ah, y-e-s,' muttered COMPASS slowly, taking in the subtle meaning of the words and nodding collusion between the other two. He nodded back, smiling to demonstrate his full understanding; but this was an automatic stalling reaction to cover his inner fleeting moment of dented importance. Natural importance made him resent having his competence questioned, but the scientist in him saw the good sense in preliminary testing. So he played the game their way – for the moment. 'And do you envisage this "new horse" having the stamina to run its course, outrunning all its pursuers?'

'You could say this is just the initial trotting phase. Let's wait until we progress to full gallop; then we'll decide on the betting spree. Okay?' Frank had been understandably reserved in his answer. He expected COMPASS to be just as reticent. He judged correctly. Retribution for gross family injustice, and not politics, was the *real* reason for COMPASSS joining them. Not forgetting, money, of course. That was how Lewis saw COMPASS's motivation, after he had prompted him hard enough.

But as their discussion continued, Frank noted how the Russian's words appeared to flow somewhat mechanically from the mouth, while the mind behind it seemed to follow a different train of thought entirely. Frank considered how this could be an asset in conversing with a contact, whilst having an agile mind that could plan answers in parallel. So long as the contact did not perceive this, as he was seeing it now. Even the smallest of suspicions could swell up into great mishap. And those KGB 'quiz masters' in Lubyanka knew their craft. They wouldn't need to bother chasing their horse and tripping it up to make a flat egg of their bet in the race -- yanking out COMPASS's fingernails would be effective enough. Everyone had an eventual breaking point, and Frank didn't think this guy, in spite of his hard look, would be an exception – if it came to that – which it wouldn't – if it turned out that he wasn't what he was claiming to be. Yeah, a real twister with more goddamn turns in it than that broad's ass wriggling and slithering round that dance-pole. And for sure, as was always the case on every mission, that mind-bender of uncertainty was not going to leave him all through this assignment, no matter how broadly the guy smiled. *That* was a certainty. Lighting a cigarette to hide his preoccupation with the gruelling thoughts from the others, Frank decided to let the issue go for the time being.

As they travelled in a roughly circular peripheral route round the city, Goodblood turned the conversation to the driver. The man, Sheldon Myers, would be Mr Lewis's Case Officer, and handler in the field responsible for Lewis's guidance and safety, and for conveying reports back to the Oslo American Embassy's CIA station instead of Lewis reporting in directly himself. Lewis knew his handler, but withheld the name from the Russian. These instances required a triple coded form of communication, allowing for the contingency of material falling into enemy hands. Goodblood Had already passed on the encrypted codes to Frank and Myers, along with the locations of 'dead letter boxes', for using when personal contact between them in the field should be deemed unsafe. Frank and the Russian would be using a *separate* set of locations. The car stopped several times in order that COMPASS could alight with Falzoni to be shown the exact secret locations for concealing messages to be collected later. The points had been paced to be roughly equally distanced around the city. A good strategy that made allowances for being in different parts of the city whenever urgent messages required passing on.

When at last the briefing appeared to be at an end, the car stopped and Falzoni opened the door on his side. With neither Frank nor Goodblood moving or saying anything and both of them staring expectantly at him, COMPASS was puzzled for a moment. He then realised that he was being made to get out. He got out. Looking around he saw that he was in a desolate locality that he did not recognise, except that it seemed far out from the city centre – more so from where he remembered his hotel to be. With the car engine giving a low rev of its impatience to move off, and the car door closing, COMPASS called out: 'Where are we, and how am I to get back to my hotel on foot?'

Through the few remaining inches of open door space, Falzoni laughed and called back: 'That's up to you. Call it the canter phase.' The door clicked shut and the car was away, as mysteriously as it had come, back into the mist.

Arriving back at his rooms once more, Falzoni had had ample time during his long trek back to turn things over in his mind. COMPASS's questions, cunningly burrowing for information that lay deeper than the answers they plucked out, now reverberated in Frank's mind, this time to a different sound. Whilst he had believed his answers to have satisfied COMPASS, he was not so sure now that they had. On top of that, he was feeling unsure over his wisdom of motivation for entering into this very dangerous commitment; for dangerous commitment it surely was. If anything, it promised to be a very time-consuming undertaking. So why had he offered his services? Why, when time was already so critically short? For a man of ever iron-firm conviction, this uncertainty over a serious decision was unsettling. To be sure of an issue one instant, then unsure of it so soon after was alien to his logically organised way of thinking. It implied that he was not in full control of where he was heading. This perspective of a possible momentary lapse in certainty, was not encouraging. Not encouraging at all. Was all this now sliding into jeopardy?

It occurred to Falzoni that the peril COMPASS had faced in his earlier wartime experience had been of a 'safer' kind, where only glory in either victory or death awaited him. Now here he was popping up over the horizon to enter into their game of spooks, where treacherous waters required great determination to swim contraflow. So why was COMPASS so ready to take this risky path, knowing that he could be teetering on the brink of possible danger? Why? Did his need for vengeance answer the question?

Plumping himself down heavily in an armchair, Frank tugged away thoughtfully at a loose stud whilst thinking. He hadn't forgotten how he, himself, had been fired up with the devil-seed of vengeance in his mind when 'Charlie' had been killed. Urging him to do something stupid -- to break the rules, -- to infringe on department protocol -- to contravene Marley's specific mandates; something which he had *not* gone and done.

Perhaps it was the embittered Russian's token of penance in reflection of his parents' vile removal from the land in the manner of unwanted weeds? Maybe even to meet death and so be with them? Frank shuffled the ideas to and fro, like cards in his mind, wishing it could be a better deck he had for playing with.

7

'Just as with those Doric pillars of ancient Athens' Acropolis, one need only apply that initial force of imbalance, and a whole civilisation collapses under the weight of its own decadence.' To give added weight to these words, the informer contact, codename, COMPASS, looked up from his cup of black coffee and around him at the swaying piles of fish baskets being trundled along on trolleys, from trawlers to quayside market stalls. 'What one would call, I believe, in your most strange mother tongue, a push-over.' He looked round, from the wobbling piles, in sharp scrutiny of his companion. 'Would you agree, Mr Lewis?'

'Yeah, sure thing; just as sure as my mother was Irish and came from Killarney, an' all.' Frank's words came out in a weak impression of his imagined version of old Erin brogue, firm but meaty, like the succulent griddled swordfish steak, savoured with fresh mint and marjoram sauce, he was chewing, in keeping with the fancy food geek guy he was pretending to be. It gave him a momentary degree of relief to escape from the stress of his official role and serious duties with all the rough edges it forever entailed.

About to reply, COMPASS paused as a waiter hovered near to their petit wrought-iron table, perched as it was, on the restaurant's outside terrace, giving a panoramic view of the harbour's bustling activities. Looking out to sea, you wondered which of those innocuous little spots, that were fishing boats, could be sporting high-powered lenses

45

and electronic 'ears', in place of nets, trawling for shoals of human fish, without being holy apostles. He smiled, waving the waiter away politely, before continuing. 'By which, I assume, in disagreement, you imply that she was *not*?'

'She was *not*; you got it in one.'

COMPASS studied the American, seated facing him, across the table, with unsettled feelings of curiosity mixed with caution.

Falzoni stared back in turn, studying the Russian. A silent duel of minds wrestling with vying opposite answers. Was he imagining it, or was he seeing in that hard face, that COMPASS was deriving his own fleeting sense of release from the comic 'Oirish' mimicry that was allowing him to cast aside the fetters of his society's iron-rigid rules that he had been forced all this time to comply with? Forced? Perhaps that was the wrong word. Perhaps he should have seen that behind the faulty façade of loyal Party Card bleating, the guy was something of a social Houdini contorting from communist worker to capitalist entrepreneur. What the face pretended to give, the pocket retrieved again in back payment. In uncanny semblance of confirming this image, as if reading Frank's mind, COMPASS took out a short pencil stub and battered notebook to tote up the collective cost of both their meals, while pushing Frank's Diner card back across the table and putting down his own wallet. Further to this image, you could see the Russian duly wanting to trade in that old scarred goat-skinned eyesore with the more sophisticated glossy square of plastic that would give virtually unlimited privileged access to those better, more sophisticated, eating joints. That's what good old capitalist money did for you. But taking all that in only gave way to more room for testy speculation with small problems growing into large problems. Easy to see how Marley approved the Company's (CIA) protocol of his being a Station Chief not permitting him the role of active handler to the agent in the field. That gave him space to clink glasses with his buddies at classy exclusive Washington soirees.

Giving a neat napkin dab to his lips, before taking out his packet of Camel cigarettes, Frank cast a quick searching glance at COMPASS. The man's russet hound's-tooth check jacket and bright blue tie were on a softer line than the army uniform they had replaced. Watching the figures, dark and thick like their writer, being entered down the page, Frank could see the tiny wheels, in their Cyrillic characters, turning round in his mind. So unlike the almost perfect English that he spoke. You could cross over a frontier border or two, changing tongue, writing and dress-style, but old ideas – old *ideologies* – could be slipped past undetected.

'I won't keep you waiting much longer, Mr Lewis. If you'll bear with me just another few moments.' COMPASS managed the words without looking up as he wrote on. A true engineer to the end, dedicated to entering up precise reports.

'Sure thing, pal, take your time. The race is only beginning. Not a good time to mistake the odds you're betting on.'

COMPASS laughed and Frank played along with an empty laugh of his own, playing the game, for game it was, with both of them weighing the other up for any sign of a breakthrough point. Looking up, he beamed. 'Nearly there, if you'll hold on just another second. I'm sorry to keep you waiting like this. It's an incumbent task to keep happy our masters forever awaiting our satisfactory reports. I am required to report to the Delegation's Comrade Purser Officer with an accurate account of total expenses incurred in my personal excursion through this beautiful city of Oslo.'

'Yeah, I know what you mean there, pal; I certainly know what it means when it comes to filling in expense sheets to keep the boss happy.'

After a further spasm of cursive writing, COMPASS slammed his notebook shut and put it away. He looked at Frank and then down at his own demi-tasse that could have fitted as a thimble on one of his massive fingers. He pointed at the tiny cup, but the American shook his head. Taking up the small plate of mint sweets from the table centre, the Russian proffered that in turn.

Frank waved it away. 'Save that one for the horse. You never know, it might need it, the way things could turn out.' He watched the sparkling bright wrapper being pulled off imprisoned behind the stockade of thick fingers.

COMPASS laughed at the American's sly innuendo attempt at probing him. 'Touche!'

They both laughed out their bluff once again and the glass bowl on the table joined in the fun with a light ping as the tiny ball of sweet wrapper landed in it.

But more serious issues needed settling. With talk on the money-for-information exchange deal still dodging final agreement, you could sense that they were just circling round what was really wanted. Like bears edging round a pit of spear-headed wooden stakes. And you didn't want to ruin things falling into that. With minutes passing like hours, they haggled over 'reasonable' figures, knocking them back and forth like ping pong balls. The Russian studied the American with weighted thought, his dark eyes twinkling like broken glass and seemingly with as much cutting power. Frank could feel those piercing eyes trying to read right through him. He wondered, more than he could decide, which of them was doing the better job of reading the real thoughts behind the other's words, and gaining better insight of the other's inner strategy.

COMPASS cleared his throat with apparent nervousness in clearing a point of negotiation. 'So we are agreed on my being paid that sum in monthly increments into an anonymous numbered Swiss account. We are agreed on that, yes?'

'Yeah, on that we are agreed.' Marley had done his job so far as intermediary, laying out for Frank how much of a carrot in Swiss francs they were going to dangle in front of this potentially precious Russian informer. Now, having done that, Frank had to continue dangling the carrot to lure him further. 'And you say that you can provide us with more sensitive information that would highly benefit it us – *the West*, that is – for the sake of maintaining peace?' Confirmation was a slow nod. Hello? Was that uncertainty he saw there? 'Good. We're particularly interested in your latest technical data that would enhance our own developments for low level radar detection that would enable us to duck under your MiG- 25 patrol corridors.'

'This I can provide.'

'All this, and yet you still back away from revealing your name?

'Suffice it to say that I am engineer of Priority Grade One.

Frank, having worked among some dangerously devious characters, arranging deals above and below the 'waterline', so to speak, was familiar with recognising a sudden reversal of mood in another when it blew in out of nowhere like that typhoon that nobody wanted. He knew how to keep hidden his unease at the other's apparent dive in spirit. What the heck was irking the guy? In an effort to shift things out of a rift, Frank nodded his standing agreement on what they had reached so far on the deal. But the guy needed prompting. 'And?'

The Russian came back from wherever he had been, far away in his mind. 'So little was I then, to know the reason for my father being taken away from me, my being barely – how would you say? – high as the leg of goose. For sure, I was that. Dragged, not merely taken, my mother had told me. He had been a clever man, she had said. Not academically as we would measure an individual today; but with his hands – with his natural woods and things of the land. A man of the soil. His soil. His land and what few livestock he had. All this taken from him – destroyed – the buildings burned down – the animals confiscated by a landowner more worthy of them. My mother had once told me that he had lost most of his teeth holding the plough-blade in his mouth when we were too poor to have a proper plough. It was either that, or all that great fighting in the early days of the Uprising. Of that, alas, I am not certain.' A faint semblance of a smile at that last remark was allowed to blanch the morose expression for a second.

But look out, that face was darkening again! Frank saw another Lenin-ghosted spiel looming.

COMPASS gazed around him at Oslo's glittering skyline that had since lain down alongside the water, like a dozing animal resting beside its water-hole, never again to rise from its satisfying recline. 'There is much design for shifting the slothful beast of burden, lest it should never rise to do its work.' In the devious cavern that was his mind, COMPASS seemed to be still basically at war with the West's social stagnation, so that any form of rest or order was in itself an accursed impediment to change and improvement by progress that was the essence of Soviet spirit. Total disorder from public demonstrations were the means to incite civil unrest. And this in itself was the instrument of change resulting from the reactionary thinking of an established society's resistance to challenging new philosophies that questioned the value of that society's fundamental rules. Looking at him through dead eyes from the steaming silver platters carried by hurrying waiters, were taunting examples that blatantly signposted the roaring trade that catered for established tastes of a settled society. No matter what deliciously palate-tingling dishes the local culinary waters offered, be it fjord trout, monk fish, blue mussel, salmon, or popular special cod delicacy, klippfisk, the vacant expression and very stillness of the fish seemed to irritate him with the orderliness that they represented. Squirming lobsters did little to placate him.

Turning away from this display of Capitalism gorging its gluttonous self, COMPASS looked at 'Lewis'. 'There is much serious misjudgement in your advice to let a sleeping dog lie. Such an animal lying in one's path constitutes an obstruction, so impeding one's natural impetus to go forward. The dog must be removed by force!' He was emphatic to the point of stabbing a finger hard into the warm savoury smelling-air of cooked fish and crustacean.

Frank resisted the impulse to smile, recognising the man's earnest effort to make serious political issue out of misinterpreted proverbs. But perhaps he could throw in some mischief. 'And what if that crazy dog bites?'

'One must be sure to apply the force so that the dog is made to chase and bite its own tail, so inflicting itself with more pain, more chasing, more madness, to the point that it is finally put down.' COMPASS swung an arm round in a sweeping gesture that indicated the fat Capitalist diners seated all around them, flashing their money. 'Your society sleeps the terrible sleep of the palsy. Your pathetic laissez-faire attitude barely credits your social structure with the indolent pulse of the hibernating bear. Even your so-called police preventive measures for curbing the occasional upsurge of civil unrest is laughable from your own point of view. You would surely be better to root out the trouble and so rid yourself of it forever, like a bad tooth. But, alas, you cannot even carry out this action which would be of immense self-benefit. It is truly pathetic.'

'Doesn't that mean that these troubles can occur again and again, something like the continual unrest that you want, in the first place? Seems to me you've got a bit of contra-flow current there, pal.'

'Fool! It is the same recurrent action, like a dormant sore awakening in the body from time to time. If that trouble is removed forever, then it is forever in the past, making room for new developments, as forever it must be. That is, until we reach the social strata of People's co-existence with rules generated by the People, for the People, being the only self-imposed parameters necessary.'

'And is that how those guys taking the May Day salute, from up on the balcony in Red Square, are thinking? I can't help thinking that your idea of the perfection of being imperfect will have then lost its perfection by becoming perfect. One of us has got it wrong there. Do we really need to throw the dice to decide who? A tongue-twister to put a needle in COMPASS's long-winded philosophical balloon.

COMPASS looked at Lewis in annoyance for his intrusive attempt to trip him up. He was not sure if he liked this. He regarded himself as intellectual, whilst looking upon the American as the instrumental extension of his superior's commands, like the artist's knife shaping the clay. There was that oddity of his hands and face having the irrevocable peasant's coarseness of skin that spoke of his plebeian roots, in contrast to the pensive depth of his strangely distant eyes and the surety of solid, determined, engineer's hands.

The inconsistences did not escape Frank's notice. And that was giving rise to an unsettling clash of contrasting views. Here was this Russian actively betraying his country for money, yet at the same time mouthing off all this Marxist anti-Capitalist palaver. Could we be possibly taking on a crazy moron? A dangerously unstable schizophrenic? Not knowing which flag to salute, which flag to throw on the bonfire? That would shake things up a bit, not least of all in Washington. Trying to see the issue in a more favourable vista, Frank put on his shrink's hat. Were COMPASS's criticisms of the West an inner personal penitential squeal to compensate for his guilt of selling his precious comrades down the river? Mea culpa, mea culpa, mea maxima culpa, and after that, all was well? That would need close watching.

Coming out of his inner reflections for a second, Frank looked down to see that the lengthening ash on his cigarette was about to drop off. Knocking it off promptly in the ashtray, he looked across at the source of the conundrum. 'My colleague spoke well of you yesterday, but can you act with the positive precision you assured us you would, when the moment arises, in the face of the adversary?' Slipping through the KGB's security net will not be kid's-play. It's one thing being 'Grade One Engineer', where you can clank your monkey-wrench as loud as you want, but the cards have to be dealt quietly in this spooks game.' Frank looked at his own hands and then pointedly at the Russian's hands. 'All is *not* truly revealed in the handshake, it seems, contrary to what we'd like to believe. So you tell us that your family suffered searing injustice by way of Czarist inspired pogroms of Jews. Are we to read this personally related scourging then as the invisible writing on the wall -- your *real* reason for spiking the guns of Communist ideology? Unlike all the many hair-brained philosophies that your country forever sends out across the waters to enlighten the world?' There was as much ridicule as there was indecisive query behind Frank's prying eyes.

COMPASS read in Frank's expression what he figured was the American thinking of unearthing his identity via the 'back door' method by reading up on archive files in long-forgotten storage. He gave a gruff laugh. 'No, no, Mr Lewis!' Another laugh and a cough. 'You will not find writings of such brutal ethnic-cleansing atrocities recorded in files. Governments do not concede to ever being aware of such *misdemeanours*.' He threw a piercing glare at the American, pointing a finger at him. 'Not even your own democratic government would confess to officially endorsing such criminal acts.'

With all that needed to be said having been said, a languid stalemate silence fell between them. This was pushed aside by an inrush of the hubbub of voices around them. Heeding this change, COMPASS suddenly took up his slim liqueur glass of Asbach brandy, holding it out, up high, to the American. 'Na zdarovye!'

'Yeah, sure, 'Na zdarovye! Cheers, Comrade!' But Frank saw what certainly wasn't a cheerful expression on the Russian's face.

Consumed by an upsurge of dormant anger released from deep-down subterranean memory vaults, COMPASS drew back his seat suddenly with a loud grating, to get up and walk out. Frank got up and followed him across the sun-drenched concrete quay. They both stood silently on the quay's edge, looking down at the water. In demonstration of his burning anger, COMPASS took up a wooden slat from a broken fish box to throw it into the water. Stepping up onto a gleaming iron bollard, his thumbs thrust in his pockets, he stood watching the wood fight and leap the crests of the waves, like a square-shaped salmon, thrown up in the wake of a passing trawler. The foam-freckled wash floated out from the trawler's shining brown hull to meet the lesser mass at a restless line marked by froth and bobbing debris.

Frank stood by the bollard, watching the progress of the sun-bleached-lettered wood outlined against the water where it seemed out of place. But was it the only thing out of place? He wondered. 'For a guy who's saying he's ready to embark on a pretty dodgy game loaded with its many penalty points, you would appear to be harbouring, what I can only guess to be, some opposing thoughts of indecision in your quieter self. Do you think you're able to hold these two positive and negative forces apart without the danger of conflict ruining our plans?' Frank searched for a true response in the secretive depth of those eyes. He needed it now.

'Are you saying that I can't fulfil my part of the agreement?'

'*Can* you?'

In a whirl of hurt emotion, COMPASS jumped down beside Frank, jabbing a forefinger angrily into the American's chest, at the same time whipping out a knife from nowhere with the other hand. 'Just you transfer those francs into that bank beneath the pavement in Zurich, and I'll give you a hole in the Soviet defence programme bigger than your very own Grand Canyon. And you have assurance of my permission to slit my carotid with this blade if go back on my word.' In angry ramification of his pledge, COMPASS plunged his blade into the eye of a resplendent sole, to hold the fish out at arm's length. At this, a huge fisherman came stepping over to them, wielding fists that made midgets of the bollards. Giving the man a defiant grimace, COMPASS flashed his teeth and flicked the knife so that the sole flew off to thud into the man's rubber-aproned chest with a plop that could have come from his gaping mouth. 'Do not think for a moment, fisherman, that I crave for your puny-sized fish! For surely, it is in Tartu that we have the tadpole that is bigger than this poor specimen, and that is the human one!'

Although the fisherman was built with the semblance of a walking wharf, there was something daunting in the Russian's hostile glare and the glint of steel in his hand that made him hold back any aggressive correction he could have given to people messing with his fish. But not everyone was put off by the angry Russian. Raucous taunts screeched out from above, a second before something slapped Frank on the shoulder. 'Shit!' he cried, at the sight of the white splattering of bird-dropping on his suede jacket shoulder. All heads looked up at the irate cries, but missed the gull's shadow racing along and off the quay and out over the water.

8

With no visible movement to identify it, the sporadic distant clinking of metal on metal gave an eerie atmosphere to the otherwise thick silence of the smothering darkness filling the great cavern of a warehouse spanning 25,000 square feet. The spell was broken by a side-door opening with a screech along its steel rail, to throw in a splash of daylight to slice the interior darkness with a solid golden sheet of sunlight filled with millions of dancing dust particles. A head with its welding mask raised, peered round the door, only to withdraw sharply in lightning reflex at the sight of an approaching colonel. Nervous pigeons, alerted by the change, fluttered away to safer perches among the spider-work of steel roof-beams.

A 'blob of darkness' seemingly shifting in the distant gloom, materialised into a truck coming right up from between mountains of wooden crates, causing Colonel Antonin Yuri Georgievich to step aside to let it pass, with its three ton load of nine inch diameter titanium tubes. His eyes were not fully adjusted from the blazing sunlight outside, and he had a little difficulty seeing what other components were stored in the crates around him. There were obviously many different kinds, judging by the varied sizes and shapes of the crates. The components that were made under Moscow's official Central Committee contract looked no different from the others, except that they were sectioned off behind thick wire partitions with the gates heavily padlocked. Even Colonel Georgievich didn't know what he was passing, when he passed the wire mesh with the glaring red warning notice with its grim message: **NO ENTRANCE WITHOUT OFFICIAL PASS.**

Enforcement of compliance with this was ensured by the Kalashnikov AK-2 Assault Rifle held in the hard grip of the 2nd Guards Motor Rifle Division soldier, with the equally hard expression on his freezing face, in spite of the Afghanka uniform's fur hat and collar. The fur hat turned stiffly as he saluted the Colonel.

Georgievich returned the salute, extending it, with a turn of the head, to another soldier climbing up into the large grey 5 ton 104 hp ZIL-157 Army supplies truck. He watched the vehicle trundle off on its massive wheels, to disappear down a narrow metal canyon between mountains of large corrugated steel cargo containers. However, he did have it within his official knowledge that the factory, like many others of its kind, was commissioned by the Ministry to produce specified parts of an integrated armaments programme. Each part, isolated this way, looked meaningless enough to its production team, giving no indication of how many cities of the West it could help to raze to the ground. It also reduced the risk of precisely detailed information on the plant's manufacturing programme being leaked out. This was becoming a serious concern with the West's increasing attempts to infiltrate the motherland with its agents. Whilst many of these attempts were foiled, others getting through the security net --– *even one* --- was danger enough. And this was increasing in possibility with the number of factory inspectors from satellite state republics coming in to negotiate the schedules of their allotted quotas of government contracts. Money always constituted a blindfold to problems like this. More so, when there was a scarcity of it. With a growing number of Moscow's worried influential sources stirring to the issue of late, one Comrade Politburo Member had approached Comrade Colonel Georgievich in order to 'request' his compiling a security assessment report on the gravity of the situation, in his accredited high station as Grade 1 Engineer.

But that wasn't the Colonel's purpose for being here this morning.

Georgievich ducked under the low wooden door, out into the bright daylight again. The narrow corridor connecting the warehouse to the main office block had glass walls and a glass roof. He took in the panorama with a hand shading his eyes for a few seconds, to spy out his contact. There he was, standing on the second stage of the steel staircase that zig-zagged up the gable end of the building like a giant ivy climber. The man had sounded anxious on the phone and he'd openly stated that he was anxious for someone from Security to come along to help him out. You couldn't help but conclude that the man *must* have been anxious, considering that he had come all this way from Moscow to this top secret Soviet People's Heavy Industrial Manufacturing installation on the outskirts of 'nowhere'. Georgievich felt a horrible tingle of bad premonitions starting up in his mind.

At a closer look, as he came up the last few clanging stairs, Georgievich saw the man, in his thick leather coat, broad-brimmed Fedora, heavy steel frame spectacles and leather gloves, looking the exact stereotype of what the he hoped he wasn't. With that long pale face betraying no trace of feelings, the man had no age bracket to fall into. The man's feet shifted with impatience and he consulted his watch to 'politely' demonstrate his irritation. 'You're late, Comrade Colonel. Seven minutes to be precise.'

Georgievich only just realised that he'd let out a quiet sigh of relief at only the man's watch appearing, and not a warrant for his arrest. In order to hide his inner relief, he made the effort to be not too friendly. 'Miracles do happen. I always observe my schedules, being always on time for my appointments.' A short pause. 'You are from Security, I take it?'

'Comrade Zilianov.' An extended arm held out the wallet with its three plastic windows flashing their credentials. The photograph in the middle panel was a right nightmare snap, but it was enough to confirm that the man was indeed Major Mikhail Zilianov. The third panel stated him to be an officer of the GRU (*Glavnoye Razvedyatelnoye Upravleniye*), the smaller secret military intelligence affiliate of the KGB (Komitet Gosudarstvennoi Bezopasnosti).

Georgievich smiled a hard smile of his satisfaction, nodding for the intelligence officer to put his credentials away. 'That seems to be in order. So what exactly is it that you think I can do for you, to have me running along here, when I should be seriously engaged in my work elsewhere, instead?'

'To be precise, we can get down to that better by going inside for a start.' Zilianov thumbed at the building behind him. I've already been inside, but it seems my presence was inadequate in throwing any light on the problem. They required a scientific officer to review the problem.'

Georgievich nodded with a neutral cold face. 'I'm sure that you'll understand that we can't be too careful in these matters. But then you can tell me all about it. Let's go inside first. These open stairways expose you cruelly to the cold wind. '

They went through the glass storm door, on through the semi-glass Staff door and through the first fire door, before the receptionist looked up from along the passage. Zilianov halted for a second between the two fire doors. 'It appears that there are some 'discrepancies' that require explaining,' he said warily, searching the Colonel's face for reaction.

Georgievich felt a slight tightening in his stomach. He kept a straight face, as tight as that in his stomach. *Discrepancies?* Yes, well, that's something for us to start on.' The mind scraped around wildly for suitable answers to give beyond that, but not readily knowing any. No more than he knew the questions that would be coming at him. There was that uneasy feeling coming over him, when you know – just know – that it's not going to be your day. Not by a long chalk. He wondered if he had been careless, rushing breakfast in the laboratory canteen to come out here out here, now that it was trying hard to climb back up his throat. It felt now that he had been 'summoned' rather than asked to come out here. An indigestion tablet, no better a remedy than hard horse-dung, materialised in his hands, and he popped it under the tongue to suck slowly with a rueful twisting of the mouth. Just like when you concede argument to the old dragon of a *dezhurnaya* (female corridor attendant).

Zilianov's mind buzzed at the Colonel's remark. *Started? Only started?* Heck. Didn't he just love these intellectual boffins who can't keep things simple. 'I wonder why I don't think I'm going to like what's coming after your initial "yes" ' Zilianov's frown deepened as he turned and pushed through the second fire door.

'Perhaps we should first consider ----'

'Later.' Zilianov snuffed the Colonel's words with a sharp wave of the hand, at the same time holding up his GRU pass to the girl. 'Comrade Officer Major Zilianov. I phoned earlier. I need to speak to your Comrade Works Superintendent Pentrovsky. It is imperative that I have Comrade Pentrovsky's immediate attention. Immediately!' Major Zilianov reinforced this 'request' with a hard wrap of his knuckles on the desk.

Her eyes didn't jump at the sight of the security pass, but her voice was extra hushed. 'I'll tell him you're here. If you'll just wait a moment.'

Superintendent Pentrovsky took them along to a door marked with Senior Technical Executive, and disappeared inside. They waited until he reappeared, gave them a nervous nod, and retreated back along the corridor. Angered at this surprise departure, Zilianov was about to call the Superintendent back, when he saw another man come out the office. The Senior Technical Executive. 'Comrade Petra Yanin.' A friendly arm reached out for a friendly handshake in keeping with the friendly statement.

There was a mixture of confusion vying with annoyance in Zilianov's face with his taking in the new arrival, before looking back in the direction of the now vanished Pentrovsky. He took a step towards this new surprise person. But without raising his hand to shake. 'I was given to understand that Comrade Pentrovsky was the governing authority of this establishment. Explain, please, Comrade Yenin.' As always, Major Zilianov's 'requests' were never 'requests'.

'*Yanin*. Petra *Yanin*.'

'I'm waiting.'

'Of course.' The young face didn't lose in its bright sparkle, in spite of the aggressive tone thrown at him by the GRU man. 'The Old Man likes to delegate work to others, while he relaxes, refilling his pipe in his office. He's too old to do anything else but count the days to his retirement off on his office calendar.'

'I should most seriously remind you that there are no *old men* too old to do their work in our glorious Soviet Union. Only those sent to rehabilitation sanitaria in Siberia.' A brief pause to let the words sink in. 'Are we understood?'

'Understood.'

'Are we agreed?'

'Agreed.'

Georgievich was deriving a faint inner degree of comfort from the ways things seemed to have digressed from what he had dreaded was going towards a security check. But this was short-lived. After a few more words between Yanin and Zilianov in their private eye-to-eye battle, the air cleared and Yanin took them along to yet another door marked Time Records Office. At the GRU officer's 'request', he left them on their own. The office's inner walls were glass and wood, and looked on to a warren of similar glass and wood offices. A small panel on the third wall looked on to the factory floor, where lathes turned smoothly, snivelling out long curly snots of gleaming steel.

Zilianov sat down on the cold radiator with his back to the glass panel and toyed with the cactus plant named a whole mouthful of *Blosfeldia liliputian*. He let Georgievich carefully run through seemingly miles of work schedules, attendances, as well as sick-leave dockets, the latter, to discriminate between the genuinely sick and skivers criminally soiling the glory of the Motherland's Phase Four Industrial Programme with their false sick claims. His patience thinned as he waited, the seconds ticking by into minutes on the wall clock. The secretive rustling of the thick sheets didn't help much, any more than did Georgievich's maddenly low mutterings as he diligently poured over them closely with a professional eye.

Zilianov could bare it no longer. He sat bolt upright, staring into Geogievich's bent back. 'So what is it that I am so urgently needing to hear from you after all this, if I'm to think that I have not been wasting my time waiting?' He swept an arm all around, so that his 'this' took in, not only the mass of paper records sprawled out across the large desk, but virtually almost everything else you could lay eyes on in the office.

The statement came out with just enough measured control to make the command sound like a polite question.

Georgievich looked up. 'Do you want it in plain language?'

'*Please.*' A word that rarely scraped that habitually harsh tongue.

'To be precise and simple, these machine parts, in their eventually being put together, will not be assembled in accordance with their officially planned timings. They're 'miles' behind in their schedules, in fact.' Geogievich's remark was clinically precise and unemotional, unaware that he could be annoying anyone.

Zilianov felt his control plunging rapidly down the tube like mercury, and folded his arms resolutely. 'So let's get this straight, now. Am I to understand that, contrary to it being mere rumour, it is solid truth that the State is being robbed of time and money by way of outrageously false record inputs of the workforce? Not just here, in this factory, but as we've been given to suspect, in a great multitude of industrial establishment spreading across the whole country. And all this, as we've hitherto feared, with nothing more solid to rely on for evidence, now substantiated by your professional examination, as testimony that there is a massive rebel plan of the People's Workers' Union for industrial disruption in order to force negotiates for higher wages.'

Zilianov's anger was out in the open now. 'Forgive my ignorance on the technical side, Comrade Engineer Georgievich, if I'm thinking that these serious errors can be remedied by a simple flick of the draughtsman's pen. After which the imbecile criminals responsible for the errors would avoid being severely punished? Most severely.' He sat back, pleased at having squashed the importance of what the engineer thought that only he, in his professional capacity, and not a layman, could bring to the surface.

It was Georgievich's turn to be annoyed, his hard features firing with the feeling. That he'd been dragged all this way out here, to the confounded back of nowhere, just to be told that a couple of little numbers need correcting — a couple of lines needing straightening out? That his analysis could be so misunderstood clocked up like sacrilege in the engineer's systematic mind. 'I think I've made myself clear enough for you to comprehend the situation, Comrade Zilianov. This is not a case of accidentally occurring errors by some young whelp apprentices who do not know which end of their pens to use – the sharp end or the blunt end. No, the technical specifications here are so miniscule and precisely inserted among the mass of similar technical details as to be deliberately 'invisible' to the point of being undetected. How does that sound to you?'

The GRU officer stood up abruptly from the radiator. 'If I'm hearing you correctly, you're saying deliberate sabotage. *Am* I? Is that what you're telling me? Definite enough to be entered on official report?'

'I am.'

This newly evolved situation was conjuring up contrasting vibrations in Geogievich's logical thinking. That there was other dissident motivation at work against the government out there, gave him a little comfort. So he had not been made to come here this morning owing to any suspicions pointing at him. But this relief diminished with the realisation that military technical fields were not totally devoid of security scanning, as he had originally thought, and expressed to the American, Lewis. It also meant that the blame for this technical out-of-the-blue 'mischief' could, with the worst swing of fate, wrongly fall on his shoulders. But apart from that, there was still some unexplained logical reason that didn't make it clear why he, a Grade One Engineer and Scientist, should be called upon to perform this simple task of technical checking. And it was making him uneasy. The condemned, tied to that post, would not feel any differential impact of those firing squad bullets on the body, be he guilty or not guilty.

9

The 'cats' were squalling in the pit, as the orchestra 'preened' itself in pre-performance warm up for its presentation of Dvorak's opera, *Rusalka*, in the Wiener Staatsoper (State Opera House), when Frank Falzoni took his seat. The seat beside him was empty, reserved for his contact. He scanned the auditorium, just as it scanned all. A sibilant sea of discordant conversation flowed out from it in unceasing waves, as if by two giant sea shells held to the ears. Here before him in the fleeting glances exchanged between fluttering programmes and sweeping binoculars, was all that the 'cultured club' of Viennese society never tired of. From the highest wit, to the lowest gossip and impertinence of scandal.

The seat remained vacant beside Frank even when the lights dimmed.

He would normally have been looking forward to the performance, but this was not one of those normal nights, so that his fretting anticipation was for something other than magically evocative Bohemian romantic folklore. Hopefully leaving out the tragic vein that ran through it. Whilst he should have been enjoying the forlorn water-sprite's sublime *Song to the Moon* riding the waves of orchestral sound, instead, the music was passing through his ears like water through a sieve, his mind occupied elsewhere. The only thing catching his attention without requiring much concentration was perhaps the beautiful swell of the soprano's silken bosom rising and falling in time with her emotional pleading outbursts. After an hour long performance completing Act 1, the great curtain made its slow descent to announce the thirty-one minute intermission. Frank took another worried look at his watch. Missing your appointment wasn't a good thing in this game. A contact not arriving as scheduled could mean many things. And some of those things you just didn't want to think about. He resisted going to the bar for a 'stiff strengthener' lest the contact should turn up and find *his* contact's seat empty!

With the lights dimmed again, and the curtain rising for Act 2, the box's curtain behind Falzoni shifted, to split the darkness into a bright slit and a dark figure ghosted in. It sat to the rear of Frank, shrouded in the box's inner shadows.

'You got here, then?' Frank's held his gaze to the front, possibly to hide the unease he'd felt at his handler in the field, Sheldon Myers, not turning up.

'Yeah, sorry about the late arrival.'

Falzoni turned to make a glancing inspection of Myers, returning his apparent attention to the stage, before speaking. 'And she wears a beguiling perfume.'

'Being pre-conclusive in this game can carry its own fall-backs. How can you be so sure that's not my after-shave you're catching a whiff of?'

'Unless you're batting for the other side, then the day I can't tell the difference between the two is the day I hang up my spook's stirrups.'

'So that's another international crisis solved -- great! So let's push on.' Myers, longer in the tooth and longer in the murky undercurrent of the spying game than Falzoni, had that experience etched into a long haggard face of dry skin tightly stretched over prominent bones that wanted to break through. The dark brown cotton three-piece allowed the thin frame it covered to betray an occasional nervous shifting that marked his end as an active agent in the field. Mounting stress over the years from danger on missions run by Marley Goodblood, had seen his inner self shredded to a point beyond further endurance. No longer capable of the role with all its risks, he was now a wise guru passing tradecraft advice on to those in the field who needed it. It was easy to miss the fact that he was the same age as Frank.

'This is the second time he's failed to turn up since moving on from Oslo. The second weekend in Copenhagen, and then here, last weekend, outside the bookshop, in the street adjacent to St Steven's.'

'How long a vigil did you keep at the Cathedral?'

'What we'd agreed -- every hour, on the hour, for three hours, for three days.'

Myers looked away for an instant, distracted by a long extended contralto cadence reaching out from the quiet of an orchestral pause. 'It figures, him not having been shown the how's and where's of the business, with his approaching us from nowhere. To make that initial move, it has to be reckoned that he has some grasp of surveillance surrounding his circumstance. But as for those tricks you have to pull out of the hat when you only just manage to catch that otherwise almost inaudible faint ping-ping of alarm ------?' Myers splayed out his hands in a limp gesture of leaving the question with no answer.

'We did a rough run through on 'Brush Past' contacts for passing on withdrawal signals in seconds when safety was deemed to be threatened.'

'And have you *had* one?'

'Not as such.'

'So *how*, then? Let's have it, for God's sake! You're keeping something back. What are you not telling me, Falzoni?' Myers, in the throes of impatience, rocked and twisted in his seat, forgetting for a moment that he was a gentleman member of an audience who was expected to sit quietly and not cause a disturbance that turned heads.

Falzoni, noting the undue attention they were attracting around them, murmured in a low voice: 'Maybe we should get out of here first'

'No, no, letting them note the colour of our socks as well, as we leave, is the last thing we want to do. Just sit tight and give it to me in the same soft whisper your mom used to let your old man know that you would be along in nine months or so.'

'As it was, my old man had to settle for a note, virtually illegible, scribbled in semi-illiterate hand, from the village half a mile away across muddy ploughed fields in sunny Palermo, having just gone to visit Uncle Alfonzo. Telephones were few and far between in those days in rural Sicily.'

'Yeah, well, he got the message in the end, didn't he? As you do now.'

'That his movements have become more restricted is the last thing he was able to pass on to me.'

'*Restricted?* How do you mean?'

'Ironically, he's been taken on by one of their GRU officers to look into, and help eradicate some dissident effort – probably unhappy factory workers – to upset production performance.'

'His being indirectly under the scrutiny of the GRU can only mean a lengthening of the odds. That's all we need.'

'His name is Geogievich. Antonin Yuri Geogievich.'

'The GRU guy?'

'No, COMPASS. The GRU guy is Major Zikianov.

'And he's now using our guy as a bloodhound on the end of a leash. Yeah, I can see how that restricts things. Just great.' Still noticing the odd look of attention coming their way, because of their continued whispering, Myers squared himself back in his seat. 'We'll talk more later, after the show, outside. What are we watching, anyway?'

'*Rusalka.*'

'*Yeah?* Is that the one where the guy with the bow and arrow shoots the coconut off his kid's head?' Seeing the surprised look on Falzoni's face, Myers' own face broke into a wide smile for the first time that day – and perhaps that week. 'Just kidding, Frank. I know it was an apple, not a coconut.'

With the performance ended, a solid mosaic river of people poured out of the auditorium dutifully following the course between the broad river banks of brown staircase marble, to ooze out through the open doorway like pus festering from the open wound. Falzoni and Myers fought their way to the side, and clear, of the swelling mass of bobbing, babbling, 'culture', as its volume increased with the mounting pressure within, before it spilled off the pavement and out onto the road.

Making a slow shuffling move in the Vermont direction, Myers nodded to Frank for them to go that way. 'There's a cute little joint along this way, towards Stephansplatz. Just along from the Kammerspiele cabaret joint. Nice ancient Bavarian atmosphere as well. It's only two minutes away from here. They do a decent bar lunch, twenty four hours.' He pointed back with a thumb at the Opera House. 'What they're charging in the bar back there is plain robbery. Makes Bonnie and Clyde take on an honest role. At least they didn't *hide* from the fact that they were robbing you. It's also off the beaten track from those droves of news hacks forever hanging around for whatever sensational snippets of gossip they can prise from the tight-lipped apres-opera crowd drifting out from the Ring Road and along their way. We can discuss what's next, in there, over a cool beer or two. First one's on me.'.

'In that case, make mine a bourbon.' Frank had no sooner spoken, when he saw something to change his mind. He tapped Myers on the arm. 'Hold on a sec. You go on ahead and wait for me there. I'll be along to join you shortly.'

'I hope that's just your bookie come to collect, and not something else we can well do without.' Myers words trailed out with a growing serious tone, as his eyes searched in the direction that Falzoni was screwing a tense look. 'Well, *is* it?'

Falzoni didn't answer the query.

Myers nodded in understanding. 'Right. But be sure to make the words short and snappy. Long ones will take the cool from my Stiegl.'

Sure enough, just coming into view in the shrouding shadows of an oblique-angled alley down the street, was a saloon, blending into the surrounding darkness with its own black body. The dark shape came alive with a shudder with the Renault's six-cylinder engine coughing, to purr away in readiness at Falzoni's approach. Pulling open the back passenger door, he got in. Better to have everything you need to see in front of you. Moulded in with the car interior's obscure outlines, sitting in the driving seat, was the dark figure in astrakhan-collar coat and black Homburg. Vechev Zhaekaly. Former Inspector of Istanbul Police.

A click had the dark interior relinquish some of its secrecy with a faint light coming on, so that eyes looked at eyes in the small rear view mirror. Falzoni gave the briefest of nods to the dimly lit image. What the limited scope of the small rectangle left out was already familiar to Frank. Had the man been contested with the best thoroughbred of racing camels, he would have come off as winner by a long nose. You saw the answer to the whereabouts of half that gold mysteriously gone missing after the war, when he occasionally, *only occasionally*, dropped his guard and chose to proffer his truly hospitable self with a broad smile that could dazzle a blind man with its flash. But the smile was absent at this moment, the lips being held tight in their grip round the ivory cigarette holder. With only the back of the large head facing him, Frank could still see those deep crevices cutting into that gnarled leathery face with its devious charms that waylaid many an unsuspecting dupe in faulty dealings. All this while still protecting the people as an upright officer of the city police force. His was a labyrinth of a mind, not unlike those many back alleys carrying the city's bilge of felony through from its Byzantine and Ottoman eras.

When his questionable behaviour eventually came to light, and he was suspended with trial pending, face was saved for all round by his conveniently vanishing from the scene, his 'venial sins' buried in dusty record logs, to be forgotten forevermore. A much ruffled post-war European/Asian situation presented a multitude of unprecedented paths to be crossed – as did Falzoni's and Zhaekaly's.

Frank could vividly recall seeing for the first time that swarthy Turkish face, its great nasal protuberance putting Cyrano de Bergerac in the shade, standing out from that crowd of wandering vagrants wretchedly displaced by the war with nowhere to go. That had been not long after ending his duties as deputy military advice attorney at the Nuremberg Trials, to take up full time official posting in the active field of military intelligence—*espionage*.

The wealth of information on contacts and 'things' that Zhaekaly had to offer had proved to be too valuable to be ignored by Frank in his new role. In return, he had done favours for the Turk that set him up as legitimate freelance entrepreneur.

With the Turk's natural acumen for administration protocol on merchandise, permits, visas, for back road border routes and customs posts along the Russian/Turkish frontier, Frank reckoned it to be useful for him to tap in on some of that 'commercial' knowledge.

'The opera was to the Major's satisfaction, yes?' Brightly polished gold and dentine 'piano keys' flashed in the mirror.

'Great, just great. At least it would have been if I'd been able to give a little more than half an ear to it. Like I said, great, just great.'

'The dedicated pilgrim finds those stepping stones across the river of life, not with his weary blistered feet, but with the destined steps of his mind.'

'I'd prefer PAN AM myself, but yeah, I'm with you there. Lots on the mind.'

'Then this we shall discuss while bathing your taste buds in the heavenly delights of my country's finest seafood dish of arpa sehriye soaked in oyster sauce, along with a bottle of rich red Papazkarasi. It is the restaurant of my cousin, who is not my cousin, but who likes to be known as my cousin because he is not my cousin as he would like to be known as.'

The gears went through similar double utterings to let the car move away.

'No, no, Vechev, time is short. In the car will do fine. We can just do a short spin, and then you can drop me off in Stephansplatz, or near there. I can find my way back to where I need to be from there. Okay?'

'As the Major so wishes.'

10

With an aerial view, from 35,000 ft, of sharp pointed spires taken over by rounded mosque domes, and 'hearing' the inner soft peel of church bells being replaced by lilting melodic Islamic prayers shed down from on high upon Allah's faithful from slim 'condiment-shaker' minarets, you knew not to look for pork on the menu. This was confirmed with Sultan Ahmid's blue dome mosque sliding past smoothly below, at the plane nearing Istanbul's Yesilkoy Airport.

Stepping out of the cool shelter of the plane's interior, Falzoni felt the heat hit him like a broadside blast from an open furnace. It didn't matter how often you came, and he had been before, you never could get so used to the sudden change as to not feel the first few stifling seconds effect of the warm air on your throat and lungs. He put his hand over his mouth and nostrils and breathed slowly for a few seconds to adjust.

Having survived the boring shifting and waiting routine of getting through Passport Control protocol procedures, Frank was at last able to throw his bag onto the passenger seat of the car he had found for himself and climb in. A battered, sun-bleached Volkswagen, it suited his purpose of keeping a low profile and losing himself among the noisy rabble along seemingly endless alleys filled with market stalls and open street traders, where bartering was done with tongues at Gatling-gun speed, while eyes searched elsewhere to snatch the secrets of those passing by.

Turning the engine on, Frank leaned forward to peer up into the sky at the roaring sound of a military aircraft overhead outbidding that of squawking voices. An Apache AH-64D helicopter heavily armed with AGM-114 Hellfire missiles, Hydra rocket pods and M230 chain-gun. Likely as not from the Cigli Air Base, over in Izmir Province.

Letting in the clutch, he drove off.

He tried to drive without incident along the roads that were primed with a natural potential for mischievous 'incident'. Given the emotionally bubbling nature of the town populace, anything could happen at any time. Anything. Violent outbursts of angry crowd disturbances were liable to break out, any time, any second, as a naturally occurring feature of the day, where instability simmered constantly beneath the surface.

He tensed inside for a second, when he saw the roadblock in the distance, with the policeman frantically waving down an angry crowd with his baton. His tension dropped as he drew nearer. It was a market dispute over fruit fallen from a broken-down lorry that looked to be in a worse state than the rotting fruit. Slowing down in approach to the crowd, he carefully negotiated his way through a sea of melons scattered across the road.

Worrying for long enough if the engine would fall out before he got there, the car won the bet and he arrived. After a tug on the bell rope and a brief wait, the wooden gate, with its brass arabic inlay, swung open. The sight greeting the eyes as the gate fell back slowly was quite surprising. In stark contrast with the dry sun-drenched dust-choked terrain outside the walls, that within the walls was a visual explosion of lush green life. The trees and plants, fed on water pumped from God knows where, filled the courtyard up to the peripheral cloister that was pillared by slender Moorish columns of marble mosaic in gold and blue. Perhaps this colour was meant to match the blue peacock, too proud in its strutting to acknowledge Frank's presence. Only the white parakeet in the tree greeted him with its soft muffled prattle. What tree was Omar Khayyam hiding behind?

Frank had been here before. A private guest house nestling quietly on the city outskirts, it was a good place to lie low. Whilst not officially registered as a 'safe house' by the Consulate's CIA station room, it was still reckoned to be reasonably 'clear'.

What sure as hell did nothing to alleviate Falzoni's brooding agitation, was the normally azure sky deciding to draw dark clouds across itself to let loose a heavy downpour of two inch hailstones. Waiting between progress reports from Army Intelligence HQ or Langley, either one would do, he was gripped by a mind-grinding impatience. It was his practised technique to see every action performed written up and set up as the springboard for the next phase of an operation. So he was always anxious when news took a long time coming in. With Sheldon Myers being none too receptive to his enquiries when he called in, and Vechev Zhaekaly nowhere to be found, matters were not made any easier for Frank's anxiety. To be expected at this phase in an operation, and something you got used to, not getting used to.

It was a long overdue relief when Vechev Zhaekaly eventually *did* turn up to 'collect' him and take him on a reconnaissance exercise. 'Scraping', Zaekaly had called it.

'*Scraping?*' As he put the question, Frank's mind already held a dark picture of them inflicting facial injuries.

'As in scraping the ground to see what's disturbed underfoot, Major.'

'I get you.'

The faint tone of disappointment did not escape the Turk's notice. He had become accustomed to the Major's moods shifting in seconds, so as to watch and position them carefully. Like that cutlery properly placed on the formal dinner table; knives, forks, spoons – each serving its specified purpose -- leave nothing out – especially the knives.

'So where the hell is this mystery tour taking us? I hope it's not going to be a waste of time. Mind you, I can do with a break after that thick black stuff they served as coffee. I wasn't sure if I was to drink it or chew it.'

'With a little endeavour, hopefully, Allah be praised, the night should prove to be fruitful.'

'Yeah, well let's hope Allah's listening.' Falzoni followed him into the night.

Being more used to working on his own, with a rough layout of the ground he intended to cover on a mission like this, Frank had not only the darkness making him careful of where he was stepping on what could only be called a blind run. Being led by the nose by the Turk, so to speak, he was not sure if he was annoyed by this; but he was sure of one thing. He was warming to the stirring undercurrent of things getting on the move again, after his long boring hours of waiting around.

The places they visited were no different from the sort that Frank was apt to frequent in a typical covert run of searching for information. Dark doors, with forbidding airs, opened only to coded knocks, or after long scrutiny – from somewhere, you couldn't see where – but somehow you could hear and feel, a little uneasily. Doors were opened by wardens from 'Hades', giving access to dark dens of even darker iniquitous dealings. But no handful of lire for 'French lessons' hosted by harlots got you through these doors.

Frank let Zhaekaly do the talking. It made sense to do so, with him not having an inkling of what all that multi-syllabic tongue-warbling chatter was about, or where it was leading them specifically. But the concept of a prize calf being measured for fatness prior to sale didn't escape him. In this game you never gave up the idea that you could be that 'calf' in a surprise turn-about deal sprung on you. Letting the others do the talking, Frank watched and listened, while looking around everywhere familiarising himself with the best means for rapid exit, if needs be, from a dangerously dire theatre of activities. No faces registered, being as rough and uninteresting as the surrounding walls. They seemed to be prisoners more of their own inner wretchedness, than of those grim walls pressing in on them. It would appear to be that so far, he was still under the opposition's radar.

Piercing words brought Frank's attention back to his side. '---- damn Englander with you, then?' Zhaekaly didn't suppress his grin quick enough to escape Frank's eye, with its aroused look. Frank's surprised expression gave way to a faint one of tickled humour.

'*American*, pal; all *American*, head to foot, excusing prosthetic alloy accoutrements.'

The man speaking to Zhaekaly, introduced to Frank as Franz Hauter, an 'occasional business acquaintance', rose from his chair and motioned them to follow him into a black recess of a backroom that Frank had not noticed in the gloom. They were allowed the amenity of a candle. From what he could make out in what the poor light allowed him, Frank reckoned that the guy would have served Goebbels' purpose ideally in a propaganda poster, as the gloriously epitomised superior Aryan male. Not a single scratch or blemish on that undoubtedly handsome firmly moulded bronze-tanned face, topped by its thick thatch of lank blond hair. Sharply pressed flannels and short-sleeved summer shirt, and catching a glint even this poor light to boast its price, that Breitling Swiss chronograph clasping the broad hairy wrist tightly with its huge strap of stainless steel links. All said successfully enterprising businessman, just as the Turk had indicated. Only the faded rectangular patch on the breast betrayed memory of the past, where the small palm tree motif of the Afrika Korps insignia had once been proudly displayed.

'Did you really think it was clever meeting me here, and bringing someone along with you? I consider it downright stupid, in fact!' A stainless steel folding knife materialised magically in the strong had, the blade rasping the terrazzo table top beside them in the man's expression of anger. 'I told you to leave me alone!' Knife fury lessened to a quieter scratching on the stone, as Zhaekaly calmed the man down. 'Who is he anyway, this --- *American* --- that I should know I can trust him?' Zhaekaly leaned in closer, to give a soft placating tap to the hand holding the knife. 'It's okay, Franz, it's okay. He's an old friend from way back; I owe him a favour – or two. And if I owe him one, so do you, indirectly, for the times he's turned a blind eye to my dealings. He needs your skill with the camera and photographic equipment.' He turned his head round to throw Frank an enquiring look. 'And possibly some other items, whatever they should be, that he may be requiring.'

Frank could barely hear the other two speak, as they stood tete-a-tete, the knife, with its blade now folded away, lying passively on the table between them. With uncertainty lingering on Hauter's face, he took a long stare at the American, before looking back at Zhaekaly, to give a slow nod of consent.

Talking at an end, they shifted apart.

Frank suddenly realised that the flow of words coming to ear was in full-bodied English – that the man was addressing *him*! He looked round to see what Zhaekaly had to say. Zhaekaly wasn't there. Frank turned round, looking everywhere that he could in the unrelenting darkness, but could not see what he wanted to see. Zhaekaly had gone completely. Having done his part, the Turk had gone off, letting Frank get on with his lot. That was how he operated mostly, as the 'uninvolved in between man'. It suited Frank. Good one on you, Zhaekaly.

Taking his time to take out two cigarettes, and giving one to the German, Frank lit both of them with his gold Manhatten-Bendix lighter. Standing inhaling and exhaling their smoke, they looked each other over, measuring each other, only their affected smiles bridging the silence between them. The one waited, listening. The other waited, thinking over which pawn to move first.

'Your English is very good, Herr Hauter.'

'That is correct, Herr Major.'

'I'm guessing that you spent some time in England or the States, to learn it, right?' That's what they all said when that question was put to them.

'That is not correct. I had an English governess to teach me. She was very good.'

'And I'll bet that it wasn't just *English* lessons she gave you.'

A moment's twitch of a widening smile and no more, was the German's answer to that innuendo.

Taking out his cigarette to stub it out underfoot on the rough stone-flagged floor, Frank then took out a large buff envelope from inside his corduroy jacket. From this, he slid out another two smaller buff envelopes. Taking up the larger empty envelope, he folded it up and put it away in his pocket. Pushing the two envelopes apart on the table, he placed a thick wedge of US dollars on the table between them. The agreed sum, as bartered between Zhaekaly and Hauter.

Hauter examined the contents of the envelopes, slowly, carefully. One was for passport and ID details for frontier and Custom inspection posts along the Russian/Turkey route. The name: **Vladimir Ivan Seigianov**. The photograph: that of 'former' Georgievich (COMPASS). Should things fall through on that frontier route, at least the forgeries wouldn't be traced back to CIA. The second envelope was only for passport and new ID details. The name: **Michael James Parker**.

Hauter's eyebrows drew together as he made a closer inspection of the photograph, before looking up at Frank for confirmation. Frank gave a positive nod. 'Yeah, I know, my mugshots are always lousy.'

This second lot was Falzoni's lever for prising himself out of a tight corner, should it ever become necessary. It was not outside Falzoni's logic to reason how he would cope, with his 'back to the wall', in an 'unexpected contingency', if ever at some time in the future, he should be deliberately dropped in at the deep end, be it the holding up of a public scapegoat for political reasons, or worse, a frame-up by a double agent. Frank had already had more than enough of a wrongful rap across the knuckles from CIA's 'modern' method of trial and punishment rolled into one. And yes, that can happen in this game. *Anything* can happen in this game!

His false ID papers and passport would be duly put to 'sleep' in discreet little hideaway safety boxes in widespread locations; in large cities, in quiet out of the way little towns, to be used only at that time you hoped would never come. The time you needed to vanish from the scene – to become non-existent.

Hauter slid the papers aside across the table, to pick up the money and start counting it carefully. Happy with his thick handful of dollars, Hauter beamed a wide smile of thanks to Frank. 'Danke, Herr Major.'

'Likewise, Herr Hauter. Danke.'

Both parties satisfied, the German returned to his Schnaps and chicken schnitzel, while the Major emerged back out into the night, to rediscover the phenomenon of fresh air.

In spite of the night mist swarming up from the Bosphorus River and over the embankment's rusting iron balustrade, Falzoni could still discern a 'camel' sitting beside a palm tree. But the palm tree was of black cast iron adorning the iron seat end, while the camel seated on it was adorned with its familiar astrakhan-collar coat and Homburg. Vechev Zhaekaly beamed his smile of a million blessings of Allah in golden ingots, and the cigarette glow brightened for a second on the end of its ivory holder, just ahead of the large hirsute nostrils flaring out their smoke.

Frank sat down on the cold iron seat beside the Turk.

Neither of them was in the mood for a plate of eel soup, sickly green like the mist, and so turned away the disgruntled vendor, who trundled his barrow along the uneven walk-way, calling down a million oaths of Allah's displeasure between each bump of the wheels. Zhaekaly spared some of his preoccupation between exhaling smoke and waving away the mist, to give some attention to the American. 'Your friend sends his apologies, being otherwise detained.'

'I see.' Falzoni had hesitation in his words that suggested the very opposite. 'Go on, I'm listening.'

Zhaekaly, in perceiving this very point, allowed himself a deep guttural laugh, without loosening the golden grip on the ivory stalk. 'Ah, but truly another exquisite example of the Western solidity of statement, with its face-saving curtness. You continually say what you do not mean, rather than concede to the defeat of a moment's confusion. One can see how, with a ready salvo of such concise replies to meet the diplomatic fire on every front, your country has no fear of lowering its flag. Whilst others hold steadfast over their transgressions by the measure of guns, the Americans remain so by sleight of tongue.' He waved a hand at the fog, looking down at where the river water was behind it. 'But for the banks on which they stand divided, our two nations are so very much unalike. This fog, for instance --- so cold and secretive, yet reliable in its consistency of occurrence. Just like your evasive words.'

'I'd say better the mist that clears with the dawn, than that which forever dwells in the mind to cloud its judgement.' *And what of that in his own mind?* What Falzoni found to be more anomalous than anything so far mentioned was the Turk's suffering the weather, here on the river embankment, when it was so obvious that he much preferred the comfort of Istanbul's luxurious Grand Bazaar Hotel, where he was staying. Zhaekaly's dedication to duty was to be measured with care. But for the fact that Frank and he were both 'policemen' of sorts, they were otherwise just like their respective countries, so very much dissimilar in character.

In a hand's flash of gem power rivalling New York's Tiffany's, Zhaekaly took out a sealskin wallet to remove from it a fold of paper. He passed the note to Falzoni. It was a note confirming that Myers was unable to keep his rendezvous, being detained elsewhere on special duties, so appointing the Turk as impromptu courier in his place. The words and signature were of the same hand, but that meant nothing, since Falzoni had never seen a specimen of Myers' handwriting. He could only assume that all was well under the circumstances, as stated, and play each card as it was called.

Falzoni read Myers' report following their last meeting in Vienna. Omitting varios parts where necessary, he passed the rest of the information on to the Turk.

Zhaekaly listened attentively with an inclined head, seemingly weighing up each word by the syllable as if it was gold dust. Not fully understanding the flexibility of English idiom, he frowned at the American's classification of Reds as their 'friends', when it was clear that they were their enemy. Frank noted the look, but filed it away in his mind as the key to a possibly different interpretation. Zhaekaly leaned in closer, while fussing with the cigarette in its holder. 'And the plans? There has been no specific detailing of your friend's intended plan of action, for instance?'

'Specifically, no. However, there is the generalised proposal for a series of trial runs.'

'*Runs? Please?*'

'Sorry, exploratory trial exercises spread over deliberately random locations, so as to defy systematic prediction, with the purpose of avoiding criticism of surveillance efforts in their incompetent mishandling of the situation, that would call for a tightening of security measures.'

Zhaekaly paused for an extra-long draw on the slender stalk. 'All this he expects from just a number of trial *runs*? I'm wondering if, like a typical American, he is being a little over ambitious in expecting too much from too little effort.'

'One must have caution to bear in mind that these are merely the trial efforts.'

'Ah, yes, of course. One infers, therefore, that from these trials there shall develop larger events – perhaps the one largest *ultimate event*.'

'My reasoning, precisely.'

There was little more information that Falzoni could relay in exact detail, as they conversed for several minutes more, so that Zhaekaly eventually touched on his personal business subject as expected. 'And you are sure that there has been no clear rendering of how these activities are to be financed? Where the money comes from, and how it is circulated? No mention of names and contacts along the lines, for instance? No mention of whether or not gold currency is being used?' For a moment the Turk's eyes almost glowed brighter than his cigarette.

All Frank could give in answer to the digging look was a negative nod.

They rose at last, to amble back slowly in the direction of Zhaekaly's horse-drawn Broughham and restless hoof-shifting sorrel mare, waiting to gracefully spirit him off to a more improved mode of evening leisure. The Turk turned to Falzoni. 'Perhaps the Major would care to share my carriage?'

'Thought you'd never ask. Thanks.'

Suddenly looming up out of the mist in front of them was an ominous great ogre of a hump-shaped figure. It materialised to block their way before they could enter the carriage. You wondered how that great mass of carpets slung over the puny bundle of scrawny bones beneath the loosely flapping striped kaftan robe that made up the old Arab vendor failed to crush him to the ground. Determination driven by desperation. The pathetically wailing sales talk was in keeping with the forlorn expression, so that Zhaekaly gestured with an angry raised arm for the old man to move on.

They climbed aboard.

While Zhaekaly busied himself with the fitting of a new cigarette in his holder, Frank voiced a nagging thought. 'Presumably the Captain was summoned away elsewhere in great urgency, only at the last moment?'

Zhaekaly applied the flame and inhaled strongly, to establish a new red glow. 'Correct, as far as I am given to understand. But perhaps *eagerly*, more aptly than ungently, would best describe his swift manner of departure.' There was a faint token twitch of the eye in what Frank took to be a wink. 'Strictly between the two of us, I rather suspect that the good Captain makes fast his gallop to take up pace with some fine mare that is a beautiful woman. Truly, minds can be universally agreed on this one subject at least, regardless of ideological conflict.' His cigarette appeared to taste all the more satisfying as he dwelt on the thought. Before they had moved off, a little beggar girl, virtually covered in dirt, but for the bright red silk bandana round her forehead, had come up to linger outside the window on Falzoni's side, holding up and rattling her tin cup.

Zhaekaly could only flick his cigarette ash with contempt in the direction of the beggar, at the same time telling the driver to move on. But Falzoni told him to wait, concealing his amusement as he leaned out the open window to clink a 50 lire note into the proffered cup. Zhaekaly looked round in amazement at this act of charity, snorting his own personal disdain aloud. 'Rewards have to be earned by measure of sweat and blood. Personally, I'd have her whipped until the bones come out to shine in the sun.'

'Oh, we did do something like that over in my country at one time; it did cause just a teeny bit bother, though, when the North disagreed with the South.'

'*North, South*? I'm sorry; once again I do not understand your curious idiom.'

But Frank smiled, waving the matter aside.

Watching the carriage moving further away until it finally disappeared, the little girl turned round to walk towards the dark outline of a figure standing at the side of the road. Sheldon Myers stepped out of the shadows, approaching the girl to take the note, along with the coded message wrapped inside it, from the tin cup and put it in his pocket. He replaced it with a crackling fresh 200 lire note. 'See and don't go spending it all on mascara and eye-shadow, kid. Get yourself a big Mac burger and french-fries. You can keep that silk thing. My using it a second time as a signal would be conspicuous.'

As he turned to walk away, the little girl started to follow him. 'Buzz off!' he said over his shoulder at the sound of her tiny bare feet slapping the hard stone surface behind him. But after stopping for a hesitant moment, she started trailing after him again at a longer distance.

11

Walking across the car park, away from West Berlin's Tegel Airport terminal, Falzoni held up a hand to shade his eyes from the afternoon sun, scanning the vehicles for Marley Goodblood's car. His other hand held the slim leather-covered steel document case with a steel chain leading from the handle and up his sleeve, to be secured around his shoulder. But the car beside the figure waving to him was white and tiny compared to the palatial black Rolls Royce Phantom that Marley drove with 'regal' ego. The 4.4 litre Morgan Aero 8 two-door roadster caught the sun beautifully, with the gracefully curved gleaming white body giving off a holding allure of the *femme fatale*. Marley consulted his watch with a rueful frown as if blaming Frank, and not the plane, for being fifty minutes behind schedule. He looked up with a smile that 'exonerated' Frank, whilst patting his new car. Shed of the formality of the Rolls and usual three-piece tweed, Marley was now suitably clad in blue open-necked shirt, white cotton flannels, suede loafers and blazing bright red skip cap, to match his racy sports car.

'Your new toy, Colonel?'

'I'm just trying it out for a few days.'

'Oh, well, after those few days, maybe you can pass it on to me.'

Marley gave a mocking chuckle at this futile, if only joking, remark. 'You couldn't afford it on your pay, Frank. It's a birthday present for the kid, my son, Marcus. Or maybe I should say a *bribe*. Because that's what it amounts to. I pour out the dollars by the truck-load, virtually kiss college governors' asses to get the kid through Berkeley College and Harvard, to get him those academic bits of paper to get him in the right shape for climbing aboard the family flagship of the Goodblood Global Consortium for Commerce and Industry --- and what does he do? He goes and throws it all away, dropping out, to say he wants to take up 'guitar-twanging' for a lifetime career!'

'And you really think a glitter piece will be enough to get him to change his mind, considering what he's so resolutely decided to cast aside?' It was Frank's turn to pat the car to highlight his point, the open expression of doubt on his face not very pleasing to the spurned father.

'Whose side are you on?

'Oh, on *yours definitely*, Colonel, definitely always on *yours*!'

Getting into the car, Marley slammed the door with understandably inner annoyance. 'Jump in.'

Frank 'obediently' got in. He didn't bother to hide his wide grin at the flashing display of colours beside him. 'We're going to go into the office with you in that loud gear?'

'Wrong guess, funny man.'

'So where?'

Goodblood put a cautioning forefinger to his lips to hush Frank. 'A wise camel waits to get to the waterhole to quench its thirst.'

'Can we leave the coded jargon to what we have in here.' Frank tapped the case in his lap, still secured by steel to his safe-keeping. 'So where are ---?'

'We'll wait and see, shall we?'

Marley let in the clutch, allowing a gurgling guttural growl from the exhaust, before they shot forward with a powerful loud roar, heading off for the autobahn. 'Glad you got here,' he said.

'In that case, do I get 'trick or treat'?'

'Patience, Frank, patience.' Marley said slowly, stalling not only over Frank's question, but also over what was scratching another corner of his mind. 'Wires have been humming between here in the Station and Langley all the while you've been away, so that I've not had the opportunity to discuss the mission with you and Myers.'

Frank nodded, glancing aside to see the other's cheek muscles jerking slightly from inner reflex; he could see that Marley was having difficulty marshalling his thoughts, trying to get them into order along their proper lines. 'I didn't bother packing personal gear, only *this*,' he thrummed the steel case, 'when your message instructed me to take a *'short train'*

'You did right, Frank. Don't worry, I'm not aborting the mission.' He paused. 'Were you thinking that?'

'The idea had its moments. Spoiled my enjoying a bourbon on the flight.'

'And *now*?'

'Now I'm waiting for you to pour out the good stuff – or the bad stuff -- whichever it's to be.'

'Let's wait and see.' Giving Frank a wry smile, Goodblood turned his full concentration back to his driving, his mind apparently cleared of its juggling antics. For the moment, anyway.

With conversation limp – more accurately – discouraged, as they coasted along, Frank looked outside, taking stock of the surroundings. He noted that the density of buildings around them was not thickening – rather, it was thinning, ergo they were not heading into the city. Structures around them continued to slide past, faster and faster, as the car accelerated on its way out of the city. Steadily losing its grip on the Morgan, the city continued to break up until it at last it disintegrated into a random scattering of outskirt dwellings. Wheels turned faster, so that what had been a great metropolis now decreased to a roadside colony that held on as long as it could, before being snatched away as they broke clear of it into the open countryside.

With a sudden dropping of gears, the car slowed down to turn off sharply into a narrow side-road. Marley waved to the old man tending to flowers at the roadside's wooden shrine of the Virgin Mary. The man waved back. Frank made his private sign of the cross.

After a quarter mile distance, loose stones and turf took over, taking them on to be swallowed up in a long leafy arbour of double trees, to eventually pass through the archway in the ancient stone wall. The tall

17th century baroque baronial castle, Marley's place, was familiar to Frank. He'd been here a couple of times before. As they rumbled over the wooden drawbridge spanning the small private moat, and onto the castle's own private island, Frank was puzzled when the car didn't pull up in front of the massive stone portico, but kept on going. They were going round the back, it seemed. That made a change, as he'd never seen the place from that angle before.

As always, Edwina Goodblood needed no persuasion in ardently following the Goodblood family tradition of doing things in grandiose mode, so that you were not surprised that the massive steel structure, that was the barbeque cooker, looked as if it possibly had been designed and 'built' to cater for the hungry masses on board an ocean liner. And she was managing well with the smoothness that was her natural aplomb as hostess, circulating among her hundred or more guests. But she did look damn comical in Frank's eyes, with her tall chef's hat and wide, flappy-legged, yellow dungarees, in contrast to her usual elegant image in diamond tiara and tight-fitting evening gown studded with 'priceless' sequins that she wore for her normal gathering of the city's elite at her formal soirees. That explained Marley's breaking out in the national flag's colours, even if he did miss out the stars.

'Afternoon, Edwina.' Frank enjoyed irking Edwina with his cheeky first name greeting, instead of the stiff 'Mrs Goodblood' that she expected of him in their infrequent meetings. Marley gave him an odd look that wasn't quite clear in its message.

Frank returned it with an innocent grin and raised eyebrows that feigned ignorance of any misdeed.

'Major Falzoni.' Her curt reply was all that she was permitting herself to give the Major, vexed as she was at his turning up, uninvited, to her 'little' afternoon gathering for 'friends'. She flashed a cutting venomous look at Marley, transferring his attention by his following her eyes as she looked pointedly across in the direction of her 'friends'.

He got the message. Yeah, he accepted the difference. They were a sharp lot, all of them in their silk cravats, stiff shirt cuffs, with their sparkling links --- and Frank's dishevelled presentation in tired suit, wrinkled and rumpled from travel. Funny thing was, a leper attending with dripping bare ass, was welcome at one of Edwina's 'small' functions, so long as he had received her imperious summons of an invitation. That was Edwina's strict personal protocol.

Marley felt that Frank needed 'rescuing'. It's all right, Edwina, we're going inside. The Major's brought important stuff that we need to go over. He's had a long day travelling. He's tired and, I'm sure, could do with something to eat.'

That last part had a look of horror jumping up on Edwina's face.

'No, no, relax, Edwina, *I'll* grab something from the table while Frank goes inside.' He looked round at Frank. 'You go on ahead, Frank, while I grab something for us from the table. You know where my hideaway-hole is, don't you?'

'Roughly. Don't worry, I'll find it --- I think I can manage the mileage of stairs and corridors.'

Just as he recalled, the establishment on the whole was an ancient one that favoured the military over the scholastic. In a former era you were likely to have encountered scarce females in the austerity of dark wooden-panelled chambers, where only an old warhorse was as much at home on his charger steed. Polished steel flashed not only on the huge banqueting-hall table, but also on the walls, where swords, bayonets, halberds and armour guarded smoke-blackened portraits of grim-faced generals. Along the seemingly endless corridors, more morose faces looked down from the walls, their stares forever suspended, along with smaller polished blades, that were still a little too large to be called cutlery, mounted between them.

Confronted by so many identical wooden doors, a stranger would have virtually dithered over using a compass or diviner's stick for guidance through the place's maze-style warren of passages. But Frank had been here before, so just missed needing either. The endless climbing of stairs, trekking along passages and turning round corners, was having its toll on Frank's already tired legs.

But he found Marley's den.

The sight directly confronting him on his pushing open the door would have been truly astonishing had he not seen it before. A blazing log fire greeted him with its flames and smoke twisting up to disappear immediately *beneath a clear closed window above it!* So where the heck were the flames and smoke going, your brain's logic would wonder. He knew, but still walked over to the fire in natural reflex.

The conundrum dissolved when the brain plucked up the wisdom to realise that the smoke escaped for dispersal to the outside via flues cunningly located each side of the fireplace. Closer inspection of the vents suggested that this ingenious brainchild of a design was not so much a three hundred year old 'vintage', but a more recent one.

'Clever, eh?'

Frank looked round to see Goodblood, laden with two large trays piled with an odd assortment of victuals looted from under the noses of that lot partying on the lawn down below, standing in the doorway watching him. He saw Marley's smile open wide like the good boy scout expecting a pat on the head, if not a badge of merit, for positive endeavour.

'Yeah, terrific. Your idea, was it?'

'The window gives a great panoramic view and I didn't want to spoil it; but it can get quite cold up here in the winter, so I had them install it. It can be difficult trying to write with your fingers frozen together with frostbite like hogs' hooves.'

'Sure.'

Marley put the trays down on the Italian walnut desk. 'Pull up a chair and get your mouth round that roast beef steak. One of Yanouf's specials from the kitchen. Edwina was just short of screaming when she saw me grab it.'

Marley sank heavily into his chair behind the desk. Picking up a tiny morsel of cheese from one of the plates, he settled back in his chair, nibbling slowly, while watching Frank feed his hungry face. Both got on with their busy lot of masticating their mouthfuls, while waiting for the other to make the opening salvo – good news or bad news. That was the essence of the game, as anyone and everyone eventually came to know.

'So let's have it, what have you brought me? This cheese is melting before I can chew it, it's more nervous than me waiting.'

'I could ask you at the same time, why you called me in so urgently from the field.'

'I'll let you know when we collectively analyse what comes up after throwing both reports into the melting pot and stirring well.'

'I thought you had it all in hand, monitoring me in the field, and everything else, from back here in the Station?'

'One wrong turn in a mission can, if your luck's down, sometimes extrapolate into a whole handful of choices with no certainty over which one is the right one to take.'

Frank chuckled. 'That's variety spicing a boring game up a bit.'

Goodblood shot Frank a sharp look. 'Yeah, and crude jokes should be confined to spicy Chinese cookie crackers --- *Major.*'

Frank held up his knuckles as if chastised with a red hot iron. 'Right, I'm all ears, go on --- *Colonel.*'

'The Red Fleet has suddenly switched their ICMF (Inter Communications Manoeuvres Frequency). Attempting to monitor this, to get cross-bearings on which way their cruise routes are likely to go, without revealing our submarine positions, is giving rise to unforeseen problems. Our lines at sea are stretched, as it is. These damn peekaboo search beams springing up to constitute a pain in our asses are so far numbering more than thirty – with every indication of increasing. And we still don't have any clear knowledge of where or what they're generating from. Cruisers? Subs? Trawlers? We just don't know.'

'How about unmanned double-functioning sonar/detection units; submerged just below the surface to be undetected by us?'

'Yeah, that fits in with the idea of their escalating manner, like a kid's soap bubbles. Good thinking, Frank.' Goodblood shifted in his chair as if a new thought coming to him was as uncomfortable as his buttocks were. 'But like those goddamned soap bubbles, they manage to skip out of the reach of our limited facilities. As far as we can see, a ruddy great whale wouldn't be any the wiser identifying one if it swallowed one and had it nestling comfy in its belly.'

'Can't we call in Strategic Air Command Surveillance, for additional 'eyes and ears'?'

It was Marley's turn to laugh with a mocking note. 'Now that *is* a good joke that belongs in a Chinese cracker, pal.'

'Yeah?'

Marley shook his head at Frank's naivety of administration matters. 'Your suggestion to bring in the Air Force would give rise to further problems, as if we don't have enough already, as it is.'

'*Trouble?*'

'*Money* --- with a capital M.'

'Surely our Expenses Exec could give those Treasury people in Washington a nudge?'

'You clearly haven't occasioned the unique smell of those mean little money gnomes on Capitol Hill, with their fists forever clenched tight and never leaving their deep pockets. Reams and reams of expense reports, officially endorsed with Exec's signature and stamped with his own ass print, would not shift that damn bunch of Treasury bastards an inch, once they've made up their minds to turn their backs on us and play deaf.'

Frank had had his fill of sinking ship tales. Pushing his plate away, he sat back upright in his chair to look Marley in the eye. 'So let's get this straight. Let me guess: you've called me in from my current assignment in order to provide you with my help by paddling, alone in my canoe, into a 'little Navy problem' in the North Atlantic – square it up, smoother than Captain America could --- and we all live happily ever after. *Right?*'

'First part partly right; last part definitely wrong. I can definitely tell you that, Frank.'

Waving a hand, Goodblood pointed at Frank's abandoned plate. 'Don't let me interrupt you, Frank, carry on eating. There's plenty there. Here, I'll help you.' So saying, he took up a fork to spear a generous length of Bavarian smoked sausage and set about attacking it with savage lion's teeth.

Frank shook his head. 'Nah, I've had enough, thanks. And thanks to Edwina, especially. But I'll have some of what's in that bottle. What is it? I can't see the label.'

'It's Yanouf, in the kitchen, you've got to thank. All Edwina does is hand him lists of what she wants for her next big 'little' do.' And it's one of Barbaresco's delightful wines -- Gaja, in fact , from sunny Italy's Nebbiolo grape.' He emptied what was left in the bottle into the glasses. 'Drink up.'

They each took up their glasses, holding them high with a salutary: 'Salute!' before sipping the wine slowly, feeling the refreshing effect on their mouths and throats, dry, after all their talking.

After a long silence and a final swallowing of the wine, Marley placed his empty glass down on the desk with a marked firmness that announced the end of their little interval, and pointed at Frank. 'Drink up. If what you have in that case merits the strength of its chain, then I'll just have Edwina's, and *only* Edwina's, whining complaints bombarding my ears, and not those of the Intelligence Operations Strategy Board lot.' A pause and a deep breath to take in the touchiness of the issue. 'But only a careful computer analysis will decide that. A large percentage by machine, and after that feeble man is finally allowed to get a word in.'

'I'm forecasting feeble man smiles all round.'

'It's hardly yours to suggest, you know that. But I think it might do, if what you've given me so far is anything to go by.' If Goodblood was expecting Frank to beam with gratitude for that complimentary attitude remark, he was disappointed. He carried on. 'If what you're saying is anywhere near correct, then asses will jump from their seats to get things moving in the Operations Control Centre.'

'Well, from what you're saying, that'll be for 'Money-Bags', the Finance Controller, to wave his little green flag.'

'What we want is a *big* green flag, if anything's to be worthwhile.'

'Marley's face lit up bright, like the end of the fresh cigar he'd just put to his lips. 'Grand Comrade Admiral Barovi will shit himself if we put into full operational execution the resultant compilation of their fleet exercises, that we're picking up from our observations.'

'You reckon so, do you?'

'Yeah, Frank, I fucking do.'

'How?

'Jeez! I'll tell you how. If the Red Fleet's Commander-in-Chief is worth the 'scrambled egg' (gold braid) on his cap, he'll have to appreciate that our combined NATO movements mirror their very own movements. He'll have no option but to conclude that our subs are not out there looking for baby octopi for Luigi's Bistro. With this scathing news passed to him, Barovi will stamp on the First Soviet War Deputy, after which lights will burn brightly overnight in the Kremlin.'

'Do you think he'd get away with it --- all the trouble he'd be stirring up, I mean? The buck is bound to stop with him, surely?'

The Red Admiral butterfly may not be able to survive the grim conditions of Siberia, but this Red Admiral will. He's a tough old bird, as well as having strong 'connections' in the Politburo.' He'll survive.'

'If I'm catching you correctly, Colonel, with their knowing that our subs are deep down, scratching their ships asses passing overhead, what about their reciprocal tactics?'

'Do you mean are they secretly listening in on what brand of maple-syrup chef's putting on the toast for breakfast?' Marley took a long pause, drawing in the cigar's smoke and letting the twin blue streams out into the air, above their heads. 'You're not that naïve, Frank, and neither are they. Those guys are already lying comfortably settled in our waters, savouring not only chef's special dishes, but your mom's original pumpkin pie recipe, as well.'

'I don't really care if those guys are tuning in to follow the swing of the match odds of the Grand Hollywood Bowl ball game. Up until now things have been kept hush-hush on both sides. But openly using NATO exercise monitoring of real Russian Fleet tactics is tantamount to rubbing the Red Fleet's nose in its own red flag, as far as I see it. And if I'm correct, that can cause one heck of a lot more than a nose bleed.'

'And you'd prefer we kept things nice and quiet, Frank?'

'Isn't that what I'm paid to do in the field --- namely, tread cautiously at a discreet distance to avoid alerting the prey by stepping on his toes?'

''Agreed, Frank, agreed. But just as Judgement is God's providence, let's leave the tough screw-ball thinking to those guys in DC with bigger tin badges on their caps than ours.'

'I suppose so.'

'At least we both hate red tape, but follow it like good dogs wagging their tails.'

'Yeah, don't we just.'

Marley leaned forward to forage among what had now become an untidy tumble assortment of food for an odd bite. Taking up a succulent flank slice of roast boar with garlic on black bread, he bit into it, looking over at Frank with a smile that was overshadowed by a long searching look behind it. Chewing until only a small corner piece of toast was left, he threw it to bounce off the steel case lying at Frank's feet.

'So what have you got to show me that won't make what I've eaten go sour?' he asked Frank, while giving all his attention to pushing the trays aside to clear a space on the desk. He tapped the cleared space, signalling Frank to put the case down on it.

Removing the chain from the handle, Frank inserted the small key in the case's lock, but didn't open the case. Taking the key out again, he threw it across to Goodblood.

'You're sure you fixed things safely with this Turk guy, Zhaekaly?'

'He knows people who know people.'

'As do you.'

'As do I.'

'And he's straight?'

'As an Irish shillelagh.'

'That's what I hear from Myers.'

'Don't worry; I've got his nose on a hook.'

'As I've said, that's what I hear.' He gave Frank another fixed stare. 'I've convinced Operations Finance that we need to let out enough rope to allow for an unusual angle in planning to mature, and keeping our heads above water at the same time. At the same time ----' The repeating of these last words, uttered slowly as Goodblood pressed the inner corners of his eyes with finger and thumb, and passed his hand down his face, conveyed his stressful hesitance to Frank.

Frank waited, Goodblood's inner uneasiness spreading to him.

'--- there's something of a seesaw of wavering opinions developing upstairs, over the reliability of our prize catch, Georgievich. Is what he's giving us worth its onions, or are we being duped?' That's the burning question.' Marley thrummed the desk hard, his eyes boring into Frank's for his answer. 'Well?'

'That's *always* the question, Colonel. We let it burn on, but on a fuse long enough for us to cut it when we deem it necessary.'

'And how do we judge that, exactly?'

'The anwer's in your hand.'

Goodblood looked at the steel key in his palm, twisting his face, where uncertainty still lingered. He tapped the case. 'And you think that answer's in here?'

'Not at this early stage, no, but it should give us an idea of the length of the fuse. It should help, or partly help, them to settle their differences of opinion upstairs.' He hoped that would calm Marley's inner simmering doubts.

Goodblood gave a cynical laugh. 'Listen, pal, the difference between what satisfies us two, actively running the game, and what satisfies those think-tank guys sitting on their idle hands upstairs can sometimes be enough to rock the universe an inch or two.'

'Just as it did when you were first running the game alone in the past?'

'So you've had your nose in archive records. What else have you dug up, that you shouldn't see?' Seeing that Frank wasn't going to give out anything more beyond a cheeky smile, Goodblood went on. 'Yeah, well, I was young enough, or maybe that should be dupe enough, then to challenge their moves on an interdepartmental chessboard, and so vain to not realise that the pawn very seldom reaches that last line and be promoted to higher station with a bigger punch.' Goodblood sat back in his chair and gave a little sigh. 'It dowses your enthusiasm. So that's why I'm now sitting in this chair, and you're sitting in that chair. Capisce?'

'Sure,' Frank nodded in soft affirmation of the other's good sense.

The heavy silence that came over the room enabled them to suddenly become aware of the very faint strain of laughter from those below on the lawn, coming via the fireplace's flue vents. At least some people had good cheer in their minds.

Marley opened the case. While he sifted through the technical details dangerously purloined by Geogrievich from Red Army top secret safes, Frank looked round the walls of what was unquestionably a male den. He followed countless rows of firearms fanning out diagonally along the walls on both sides of the fireplace. Matchlocks, wheel-locks, flintlocks, and snaphaunces, all rallying to the command of a wigged general on either side, in silent skirmishes depicted in dark oil paintings. Leaning over, to swivel a naval muskatoon's heavy brass cannon aside, he looked at the line of dull photographs lower down. Air reconnaissance shots carried the message clearer than oils or written reports could. The group sets were nostalgic of the camaraderie formed by the action of those days. Foch and DeGall were allowed to stand out for recognition among the faded smudge of uniforms. Patton was unmistakable, in that familiar proud stance, speaking with a dust-faced commander leaning out the top of his battle-scarred Sherman tank, with its sharp American star still showing through despite the burns on the metal plate. A larger, clearer picture caught Frank's eye. Two soldiers standing in conversation beside the burned-out wreck of a 7.4 ton M8 armoured car, nicknamed 'Greyhound' because of its rapid speed as reconnaissance car for what had been Frank's very own old lot, the 2nd Armoured Division in the Ardennes theatre of conflict in WW11. One of them was Goodblood. The other, somewhat diminutive figure in sheepskin jerkin and cockily side-slanted beret, was General Dwight Eisenhower's all too often adversary in planning room decisions for Operation Overlord, General Montgomery. Rumour was that the pair didn't get on too well as buddies, in spite of the broad smiles they gave together for the press cameras.

Frank snapped his mind out of the aura that was floating in the military past. That was then; this was now. He looked at his watch, shifting his feet restlessly as he waited for comment from Goodblood pouring intently over the stolen papers.

Without breaking his concentrated examination of the papers in his hand, Goodblood spoke at last. 'We don't want to give them the excuse to play their hard cards for departmental dominance to say that our operation has not proven to be reliable, but is also costing too much of tax-payers' money.' Marley wafted the page in his hand up into the air so that they could watch it floating in its lightness back down onto the desk. *Was* it too 'light'--- of no valuable 'weight'? '*Is* this a waste of our time and money?'

Frank didn't fall prey to showing weakness that would have come if he'd given the least sign of faltering in his conviction. He held firm. 'Georgievich isn't going to risk his valued position – and his neck— pursuing in something he believes isn't worth continuing.'

'Unless that's what he's *officially* been instructed to do.' Marley's quick reply was cutting in its implication.

'Yeah, there is that. Let's face it – you're the skipper at the helm of this boat heading into white-water rapids leading to the deep dive of a waterfall beyond.'

'I think the message is clear enough, without having to bring in the 'Hemingway' stuff.'

'Understanding is one thing – navigation's another thing entirely.'

'The weight's on your shoulder, Colonel. How we proceed from here, and what we tell that lot upstairs, is for you to decide.'

'Strategic Planning is a trust, Major. Under its terms, how it happens to tilt the national budget is part of its purpose. So it's imperative that we have to show a profit at the end of the year.' Goodblood stood up as if in sudden resolve, passing a hand across his face in nervous distraction from that lying behind it, tickling his brain. 'I'm going to find out what it's costing. We can't go on otherwise without potentially putting our heads on the block waiting for the axe to drop at the discretion of the Secretary of the Treasury.'

'The Turk is a good bet, Colonel; he's proven his worth many times before. If we cancel this operation now, it could radiate out a bad effect on a whole range of indirectly associated plans.'

'In your opinion?'

'In my opinion.'

'Well, I'll bear that in mind when I see what it's costing. Now how about that chicken leg? Are you going to have it?'

'No.'

'In that case, I will.'

Chicken leg jammed in his mouth, Goodblood stood staring at Frank, thinking over his words for a moment, before biting a lump out of the thing and pulling the rest away to speak. 'I'd better level with you, buddy,' he said through a mouthful of chicken, 'your report's screening by the Committee for this mission is so far not showing much favour, but if needs be, I'll block it if there's what looks a sure sign of a motion for closing down the plan. The trustees for Operational Funding have virtually relinquished control of the great load of dollars we need to pour into things, but they will still be in on the letterhead, *somewhere*, of the Strategy Mandate journal to be mentioned in the annual budget accounts. Let's hope that helps. Otherwise, control has been dumped on my shoulders by the Committee for Naval Warfare that runs the U.S.N. Naval Analysis Group for combined US/NATO Operations and European and Group-North NATO Undersea Warfare Staff in Bremerhaven.'

'I see.'

'You'd better be sure to put Myers and Georgievich in the picture regarding close down danger. That is, of course, without letting the Russian in on too many details. Make sure he switches his searches to recent naval equipment developments. We need to know more about these 'floating/submerged bug things' you've come up with. You got me?"

'I'll see to it, Colonel.'

'You're damn right you will, Major.' Goodblood. Looked at his watch. 'Right, that's it, I should think.' Still chewing his chicken, Goodblood managed to beam a broad smile, without choking, to brush aside the heaviness of what had just been said. He read tiredness in the Major's face. 'I guess you'll be wanting to get back to you own place, Frank.' He walked over to the desk in order to get at the phone. 'I'll phone for Bexer to drive you back.'

'Right.' Having removed the chain from around his shoulder and down his sleeve, Frank placed it on the desk, beside the metal case. 'Here, you can have this as well—see and not get yourself tied up in too many knots with everything.' He smiled over at Marley. 'Joke.'

As Frank walked out the door, Marley called out after him before he disappeared along the corridor: 'Oh, and Frank, see and go out by the front door. We don't want Edwina getting upset again about you disturbing her crazy guests.'

The only response to Marley's 'request', was heavy footfalls receding along the long corridor.

12

On leaving Goodblood's 'tiny country abode', Major Falzoni re-directed Bexer to drive him, not to his own place, as instructed by his boss, but on a diversionary route into the city centre, just off from the wrecked tower remains of the Kaiser-Wilhelm Gedachtniskkirche, and along the bustling Kurfurstendamm thoroughfare, where he got out. Turning right, down JoachimsthalerStrasse, he headed casually for the small Azimut Café. Still walking at a deliberately slow pace to let out enough 'gum-paper' to catch any 'flies' buzzing around. It was a fair measure of the 'opposition' to see how quickly the 'buzzing' built up on his arrival back, after his little sojourn out of town. He reached the café to push open the door and step into the dimly-lit seating area that vied with a postage stamp for space. He took his usual position in a seat by the window. It was a good spot that accommodated for both ends of the spy-game two-way 'peep-scope', where you watched your watcher watching you watching him back in return. Fair's fair. Who said Queensbury Rules went out with the dinosaurs?

Sure enough, the last table, just visible at the very end of the row of pavement iron tables outside the window, eventually grew two fresh shadows, the sunlight pushing them further across its top, as the couple approached to take the seats. They sat down, man and woman, hands clasping hands tightly across the table in the affected typical guise of the romantic couple interested in no-one else but each other. But their thoughts were on the American who had turned his head towards the waiter that had approached his table.

Frank ordered his usual white kaffee and apfel strudel. When the waiter returned with the American's order, the American held up his cup in what seemed to them to be a greetings gesture. But not being trained in lip-reading, they had to decide, going by the American's wry expression, if the latent message conveyed by his lips might or might not be classified as outright rude.

Frank's curt 'Guten Tag,' to the couple as he passed them, went unanswered, too totally engrossed in a kissing embrace as they were, to be aware of the American passing by. No kidding! His grabbing a cab and having it drop him off two streets away from his apartment gave no difference to what he expected. Walking thoughtfully back to his apartment, the monotonous drizzle of rain that had suddenly come on was not enough to distract him from noticing the dark limousine, a Merc, that was tailing him, moving along slowly beside the kerb some yards behind him. Mercs were plentiful enough these days; there were half a dozen or so in their own pool. But this was one of theirs. Either they did a good job of tailing the cab without being spotted, or the cabbie was in cahoots with them, passing them the message of where he'd dropped his load.

Well, let them tail their damned asses off, if they wanted to. If they wanted to talk, let them come up to his apartment for some stiff Kentucky mouthwash. He could do with one himself. Otherwise whatever they wanted, they could go to hell. Even once in the shelter of his rooms, he couldn't escape from the dullness of mood that was seizing his inside. Unable to apply his mental resources to any gainful task of the work strewn forlornly on his writing bureau, urgently needing some attention, he stood at the window, staring out solemnly.

But it wasn't the greyness of the weather that was bringing on his grey mood. It was something Goodblood had said, or *hadn't* said. Or was it the *way* he had said it? Even with a second glass of bourbon, on top of what he'd drank earlier at Marley's, inside him, he wasn't too far gone to think that it was just the Department's expenses sheet that was giving the chief an extra ulcer to worry about. No, it wasn't that. And it wasn't a chink in the US Naval/NATO strategy, worrying as that was to the Top Brass. No, it was that unease from uncertainty that was causing imbalance and the midnight oils to burn long in Langley Intelligence War Game Rooms; and like a viral infection, was reaching out to affect Frank.

Did they have a Red fish in their net, or were they going to find that *they* were being cunningly enticed into a Red net by the *fish*?

His mind was solidly united in certainty with one thing --- the rain; united in its unfailing determination to bombard all that lay before it with its cruel coldness. Showing no mercy; no damn mercy to anything or anyone. Rivulets ran down the panes, twisting all the while, changing their routes, changing their destiny. Just like their fish, Georgievich, – or *was* it? Was he *really* changing?

The street, as he looked down on it, seemed to answer his curiosity with a silver spectral glow reflected off the wet stone. No-one was about; everyone swept indoors, off the street by hostile sheets slanting down from the sky. Correction, a dark form skulked about the railings two doors down, across the road. The prowling figure looked up in Falzoni's direction, their eyes meeting somewhere along an invisible line in the darkness. They were of two minds alike in their furtive stealth. The figure stepped back to disappear into the depth of the basement stairs.

Depression was glowering down on the city now with icy pellets of rain granting no quarter. Street lamps having come on, flickered feebly through the watery mesh, in futile effort to lessen the drabness. Or was that his mind? That other great deluge of biblical times may have sufficed in purging mankind's wrong-doings, but this great splash-down would not be enough for that; not in this city, anyway, with its great chessboard of spooks, 'red' against 'white'.

Frank felt drained of energy. He turned round, and with tiredness in his limbs that surprised him, crossed over to throw himself down on the sofa beside the fireplace. Sitting in silence, he stared into the gaunt recess with its cold ashes, their energy, like his, also exhausted. They were grey now, but had started out black. And in reverse? From light to dark? Was it as simple as that to change? That brought them back to that surreal chessboard wargame, where a wrong move could result in the contrasting colours of the squares being bleached to nothing by a nuclear flash.

With this theme of contrast bugging his mind, his thoughts oscillated to and fro in search of answers. The mist outside may have lifted in the streets outside, but in his mind it persisted still, swirling around and around in his rational attempt to claw at it for clearance and explanation.

The shrieking phone jerked him out of his heavy ponderings, to have him up promptly on his feet. Picking up the screaming piece before it could take its threatened jump off the cradle, he listened for a moment. 'Tomorrow, at noon? Yeah, right; I'll be there. So long as I can get a good night's sleep and a solid breakfast inside me.' He listened for a few moments more. Anger flushed up in his tired face. 'Is there something wrong with this line, or am I not speaking clear enough? Didn't you hear me? I said I'll be there. Count on it. I'll be there. Okay?' Having had barely four hours sleep over roughly forty-eight hours, alcohol and fatigue were now joining forces to put him down.

Going into the bedroom, bothering only to take off his shoes, jacket and trousers, he pulled the duvet away and lay down on the cold bed to let tiredness get on with its job of letting him fall into deep slumber.

<h1 align="center">13</h1>

Major Falzoni checked his watch with the hunting-lodge style tavern's ebony baroque carved pendulum wall clock, the grimly hewn cuttings reflecting the dark mood of the surrounding old oaken walls and pillars. Whilst maybe lying about its true age, the sombre atmosphere of the place was enough to make you take it for real.

Sheldon was damn late. Damn! And he was the one who'd told *him* to be here at noon sharp. The fact that he was fussing over the time made Falzoni admit to his edginess. Maybe it was nearer the time for his scheduled medical check-up than he'd realised. He made a mental note to have his secretary, Rosalyn, make an appointment for him with the department's counsellor. Soft name for 'shrink'. Probably he needed some iron tonic pills to combat the effect of mountains of paperwork, endless interim committee meetings, and not forgetting those marathon miles of his legging across Europe, sniffing out its dark spots. He was certainly due for some furlough, but that would have to wait. Goodblood, going by his latest whining, would definitely have insisted that Frank waited.

In normal circumstances involving a possible security leak, their office would have set the machinery in motion. But this was being viewed as 'cagey'. The damage, whilst not certain, could still be hovering there, waiting to drop on them. Five months solid Langley had been waiting, and still said waiting was safest. But at the same time urged Berlin's CIA

Station produce substantial material, either way, beyond hollow conjecture. You couldn't help wondering if, across or down in the crossword, there was a word balancing that contradiction.

Twenty minutes on and the door still hadn't swung open with Myers' celery-stick frame half-filling the doorway space. Hopefully those lost minutes were not going to contribute any crucial difference in stopping their boat from floundering on the rocks. More realistically, Goodblood, now lumbered with additional official office of Committee Director for Naval Warfare, would be putting in his wrangled view on behalf of the US Naval Analysis Group, with the Group-North NATO Undersea Warfare top brass in the Pentagon. Fingers crossed, the session would reach the Secretary of Defence, R.S. McNamara, no less, helping him tidy up and sweep 'awkward things' under the carpet in preparing President Johnson for the monthly Committee for Internal Security. He was certainly the man to do that, having virtually pushed Johnson's elbow up in salute of more young G.I.s marching into Vietnam, in a broad scale escalation of America's involvement in that conflict. One hell of a big hoovering job was going to be needed there if things went awry.

But this wasn't the only reason for holding back. If you jump forward with a report like this now, the general enquiries that ensue are going to demand more selective investigations, and that is tantamount to putting the cat among the pigeons. No, to catch the pigeon, rather than frighten it away, you need a certain degree of stealth. You need to make 'discreet' enquiries through round- about channels, rather than through the direct central channel. That was why he was waiting, and fuming inside with impatience.

'It's two minutes fast,' said a voice behind him, cutting through the hubbub of lunchtime chatter like a knife.

Frank looked round at Sheldon Myers standing there, magically materialised out of nowhere, like the genie released from his lamp. 'For someone who's supposed to be leading *me* in the field, you have one hell of a funny habit of forever being behind me.' Frank looked round at the doorway and then all around, finding no other means of entering the place. 'Where the hell did you come from, anyway? How the hell did you get in here?'

Myers gave a shake of the head that simulated the master disappointed with his pupil. 'You've obviously gone lapsed in our basic training of 'plugging all holes', Frank.' A short pause to smile and sigh. 'Yeah, I suppose we all become so smooth in our actions along the way through time that we can forget the small, but *still important*, points. *Someone* forgot to check the kitchen back-door. Okay?'

Frank was beginning to become irritated with Myers' with precision-correct remarks. 'You forgot to finish with: Quod erat demonstrandum.'

'Yeah, very droll, Frank, very droll.'

Frank took another sip from his glass of bourbon and became more serious. Like they both should have been a few moments ago, instead of all their silly talk. Reassurance on the validity of their mission going the right way was what he was worrying over – what *both* of them should be worrying over. But a little softener first. 'I suppose after that, yours will be a double brandy?'

'You couldn't have put it more precisely, Frank. That will do for starters.'

Frank pulled his annoyance back and forced out a neutral expression. 'So how do we proceed responsibly from here?'

'To be precise, no. Probably the whole lot of us, the whole damn human race, if we care to look at it that way. No, not yet; it's quite difficult to hold a one man vote on who gets the noose at this early stage.'

'Right, that's made everything clear – clear as a broad's piss.' With the barman looking his way, Frank bobbed his head up and down in deep thought while signalling the barman to bring over the pre-ordered brandy. He went back to his own drink. When the barman brought it over mistakenly to him, Frank took it and handed the chunky glass of triple brandy to Myers. His eyes met Myers'. 'Put that away, buddy.' The gesture, with its brevity of words, allowed Frank a few seconds to put up his guard against Myers' astute senses. Office gossip saw perpetual rivalry between Myers and Goodblood. From straight out of Marine boot camp, and progressing up through the Army ranks, Myers had come into the spy game, on the heels of Marley Goodblood, his boss. Goodblood had field experience but not as many good years of active service as Myers had behind him. But with his natural aplomb for post-war military/legal administrative duties for back-up, Marley had landed in the position of being Myers' boss. But for his lack of Socrates and Sophocles, Myers could have been sitting behind Goodblood's desk, and in all fair probability would have made a better job of it. Frank, seeing this, accepted it, knowing that Myers probably thought along those lines, and was forever on guard against his periodic snatches of biting humour.

Frank eyed Myers for a moment over his glass before lowering it. With Myers looking away across the room, his broad profile gave off a strikingly different image to that of the narrow face-front image. Like two different persons; just like the mythical Janus, looking two opposite ways at once. Or was he thinking of Georgievich being double-faced? 'You sounded anxious on the phone.' Frank's face held the question loaded in one raised eyebrow as he searched Myers' eyes, as he turned back, for what they were holding back.

'As did you.'

'You could tell that, could you?' Frank said cautiously, wondering if, indeed, his voice had betrayed how anxious he had felt last night.

'Usually that, and a lot more.' Myers' iron-grey eyes twinkled with cunning anticipation as he sensed that he was on to something, as well as touching a raw nerve in Falzoni's otherwise controlled composure. His chin went up slightly to verify this point on Falzoni.

'Let's go over there,' said Falzoni, and they got up to get away from tables too close-bye, to go over to a quieter spot round the corner of the bar's end. They both looked around themselves for any eavesdroppers. But this was not really necessary. Nobody could hear what anyone else outside their own conversation was saying, as well as the general clamour of voices and clinking and banging of glasses down on the bar making bugging an impossibility. In public places like these, if you were going to suspect anyone and everyone of talking shop over their Perrier and garlic baguette, you were going to have to put in a colossal amount of bugging time that would have your expenses sheet running out of space, leaving no room for including paper clips.

'Truth of the matter is, Frank, they're not happy upstairs about us possibly having a 'hole in our net'. Myers went on to relay, in somewhat pedagogic monotone, what upstairs had relayed onto Goodblood, what he had in turn relayed onto Myers. All the time he watched Falzoni's face for reaction. Frank conceded no expression beyond the occasional jump of an eyebrow, looking down all the while into his liquor, swirling it round in its glass. Myers finished and waited.

After the lull, Frank looked up. 'So you want me to change my shoes for roller-skates, to move faster, smoother, down the line; upset the dust in places labelled strictly taboo, to get your shining report in faster? What about our possibly minnow-come-shark, Georgievich? Is he going to obligingly hop, skip, and jump to your new whim? I wonder?' Frank half-closed his eyes in mock forethought. 'As far as I can see that's going to call for a lot of unauthorised door opening between the departments. Unofficial and all that. Stepping on people's toes, and causing interdepartmental friction. Some people are not going to like that. Somebody can get his fingers caught in the door in something like that.' He shook his head slowly and blew a silent whistle.

'Then you just damn well make sure it's not *your* fucking fingers that get caught in the door. That's what you're paid for, Frank.' Myers shifted uneasily as he recognised Falzoni's game of playing awkward. 'Not *unofficial*; just off the Index and without a file, for the time being.'

Frank saw the chance to be dogmatic to the points in the book and jumped in sternly for shear devilry. 'If it's not unofficial, it's official, and how can it be official if it's not entered in the Index?'

'Don't be bloody awkward! There's no time for it – for me – or for you! You know damn well what I'm implying!' Myers was openly vexed now, and Frank was enjoying it.

But enjoyment could only be had in small spoonsful. 'I know what you mean, and I know only too well what can turn out to be difficult.'

The mischievous twinkle in Frank's eye spread out into a cheeky smile. 'You make it sound as if you don't want to be the bearer of bad tidings to our masters upstairs – or to Goodblood, for one, anyway. Am I *Right?*'

Myers all but felt Falzoni's smile burn into his own face. He gave him a fiery stab with his eyes, before gulping down his drink and looking away. Of course he was bloody right! He knew that Falzoni was bang on target with that point as well the earlier one. Bearers of bad tidings, as he had put it, were almost inevitably lumbered with the task of salvaging the sunken ship. If they failed, their heads generally rolled. He may have been Frank's case officer and handler in the field on a piece of paper, on a mission, but off the field he couldn't make the man wag his tail an inch.

Frank enjoyed that thought as much as he was enjoying his bourbon.

Myers scratched his face to hide the fact that he was momentarily lost for an immediate answer.

The small victory was enough for Frank so he stepped down his attack. 'So where to from here?'

'Whatever way, it's not making itself clear enough from here.' Myers was surprised at Falzoni withdrawing his wedge so soon. He usually liked to push it in as far as he could to inflict what little discomfort he could for his own stupid amusement. 'No, with all the technicalities he's encountering with his being recruited for GRU work --- of all things! --- we have to get Georgievich extending his search into extra-Ancillary Register territory. Do you follow? Do you *agree?*'

As if on cue, where some answers were needed, Goodblood's face became one of the many in the crowd bustling around inside the doorway. Frank saw the face and watched him scanning the place for them, systematically checking everyone along the counter, before coming through into the public bar. Their eyes met, and Goodblood elbowed his way through to them.

Sheldon made a show of rummaging in his pocket for money, but Goodblood held up his thick wad of dollars to stop him. Which Sheldon did promptly.

'Got to look after my boys -- since it's still working hours and not leisure time.'

Myers broke the sharpness of their boss's message with a smiling: 'I'll have a brandy and his is a — --- what *is* that you're drinking, Frank?'

'Bourbon.'

'And he's having --- '

'I caught it,' cut in Goodblood, clearly not wanting to waste more time with repetitions. Ordering two brandies and a Kentucky bourbon, he pointed and nodded for the barmen to have one for himself, and keep the change from the large two hundred dollar bill beating the polished bar for 'shine'.

'Danke schon.'

Marley turned back to his 'boys'. 'So, have we reached something agreeable --- something that's *workable*?' He read their faces. 'It doesn't look like you have. I didn't think you would.'

'It's a bugger of a position to move forward from, if we have only one half of the stalemate panel upstairs on our side.' Frank looked at the others for agreement. He only got one – from Myers.

'But nevertheless, move we *must*.' Goodblood was adamant on that. He looked round at Myers. 'So what have you got lined up – or *half* lined up – for Frank, that we can agree on as workable?'

'More or less what you went over with me last night.'

'I don't want less – I want *more*. So go on, I'm listening – refresh my memory.'

Like the stern master waiting for errors in the Latin verbs being conjugated before him by the pupil, Goodblood listened on intently to Myers repeating the details they'd discussed the night before. Well, at least from what he was hearing, it did reassure him that he'd made the right choice of putting Myers in as Falzoni's case officer for this assignment. He ventured a question to Frank. 'So far you've managed to get Geogievich to pass on to us plans of mechanical components. What about the electronic programmes for these? It's imperative that we have these from him. Without them, our counteraction against their Atlantic onslaught is virtually rudderless.' A short pause told Frank that what was coming was what he didn't want to hear. 'But more than that, I'm sorry to say, if you're thinking the workload is already too heavy.'

'Let's have it then.'

The slowness in Goodblood's words betrayed the fugged-up state of hesitation he was experiencing. He looked round at Myers. Myers held the look for a moment before rocking back on his elbow on the bar, shaking his head in mock amusement and turning to Frank and back to Goodblood. 'Yeah, go on; cheer us up, Marley, with more good news. Then we can all die laughing.' The words rang too close to ominous, for Frank's liking.

'Our very own Chiefs of Staff can sometimes be our worst enemy when they're unanimous in sending us out along diverging avenues of paramount importance. The East-West confrontation has been avoided in Vietnam, but is acute in the sphere of development of nuclear weapons' delivery systems and the counter measures to defend against them. McNamara has just nudged Johnson for a formidable US spending of $5,000 million to create an antiballistic missile defence system. Russia is already setting up a like system. Nor is that Moscow's only tactic that gives the United States the impetus for further nuclear build-up. We've also got incoming reports of a new super nuclear bomb they've hatched, that can attack us by a low-orbiting space rocket --- and of our ability to shoot that bomb early in its orbit.

Pentagon statistics assure us that we have 1,710 intercontinental ballistic missiles, 656 of these carried in our submarines. All of these directly pinpointing targets inside the Soviet Union. Pentagon reckons that even if the Russians were to launch an attack without warning, nine-tenths of our land-based missiles would survive to strike back. There's also reports of us developing a space craft that can carry nuclear bombs, no less. By re-entering orbit, we see it being able to direct its bombs to targets anywhere in the entire expanse of Russia; even those our Polaris missiles can't reach.'

Myers couldn't resist thumping the bar in jubilation 'So shouldn't we be shouting hallelujah! If our big chiefs upstairs know their stuff, and all you're saying is strictly kosher, we're giving the Reds a mighty damn boot up the ass.'

'But just how likely are they to leave it at that, Sheldon?' Goodblood looked at the two empty expressions, knowing that they were playing dumb to see how the magican would play out his next card trick. He continued. 'For every point where they see us leading, they're bound to strive to equal that point and then go beyond with their improvement giving *them* the lead. To do that, they're going to want to see how our little ballistic popguns work, and how they can pluck the corks clean out of them. While we, in turn, need to know just how they go about this.'

'Double snooping on both sides, then. That'll call for a lot of digging.'

'Yes, exactly, Frank; that *will* call for a lot of digging,' said Goodblood. 'And Georgievich is the one who came to us saying that he had the spade to do it.'

'So we'll have to set him up along a lot of new lines, in addition to what I've already got him doing.'

'And Marley and I'll need to be freshening you on a few new points, as well, Frank.' Exhaling with relief at what seemed to be the sum-up of their 'pow-wow', Myers turned to the bar for more 'fire-water'.

At this, Goodblood raised his voice to regain Myers' attention. 'And we're still not finished yet, are we?'

'As if we didn't have enough, as it is.' Myers' groaning remark earned glance of rebuke from Goodblood.

Cleared of interruption, Goodblood continued. 'There's still the Ho Chi Minh problem in the Vietnan theatre. He's so far rejecting the President's offer to stop our bombing of North Vietnam on the condition that the North ceases infiltrating troops and supplies into South Vietnam. In spite of our concentrated bombing power grids in the North, portable diesel generators, as far as we know, are surviving our aerial bombardment by being hidden in tunnels. We need to be able to locate these tunnels in order to eliminate them. Another point is where starvation was critically looming in the North, Chinese and Soviet food supplies are effectively warding this off. So all in all, that little nuisance of a faraway corner of trouble also needs our concentrated attention no less.'

'So you want me to get Georgievich to get access to the appropriate master-plans and sub-unit subsidiary plans, make copies and finally submit them to us in the West? That's one hell of a lot of snap-shots to be taking, from what you've just said, without the fingers being snapped in a trap.' It wasn't the sort of thing you felt confident about, and Frank wasn't confident saying it. This was very much apparent to Goodblood and Myers.

'You have to *try*, Frank. We've supplied him with all the specialised equipment he'll need for the job. You've got to *try*. You can see that, can't you?' It wasn't usual for Goodblood to put his words forth in a pleading mode, but he was doing that now. He looked at both of them, quietly pleased at their calmly relieving him of the shoulder-load landed on him from Top Brass on high. The conversation was over; like a cough lozenge having given up its last bitter suck. They all three tried to digest what they could of it in a moment's silence. It was a long heavy silence.

The hubbub of conversation around them, now magnified to catch their attention, broke their spell.

Goodblood stepped back, about to take his leave. 'I'll leave you two to get down to working out some plans. Anyway, I've got to go.'

Myers pointed to Marley's glass of brandy on the bar. 'You haven't finished your drink.'

Goodblood waved this aside. 'Things to do.' With no more ado, he turned and pushing his way back through the babbling crowd, disappeared out the door.

With Goodblood gone and Falzoni steeped in thought, Myers went to the phone at the end of the bar. He deftly jabbed in the cover number of their Embassy's CIA extension safe house number. With their number of agents the system they worked was like picking your contact for the job off a supermarket shelf. That was good old American commerce for you. Myers gave his pre-arranged cover name and that of his contact and waited. His attention came away from the general noise in the lounge as the tiny metallic voice pricked like an insect in his ear. He listened as the monotone voice of the duty officer gave the rendezvous and time and then clicked off. He put the phone down with mixed feelings stirring inside him; relieved that things were starting to move, but a little uneasy over *where* they were moving to.

As they waited for their cab to pull into the kerb, Myers turned to Frank. 'That was sure one hell of a mouthful Marley gave us back there. Now I'm going to have to repeat it, or some of it anyway, to a pal. He's a finicky sort of guy who likes things put to him with a straight logician's tongue. You can do that better than me, Frank, with your first-hand experience.'

'Who exactly is it we're going to see?'

'No one you know, or would waste a second glancing at in public. He can be quite prickly when he's in a nasty mood.' Settling back in the cab seats, Myers abruptly put a hand on Frank's arm. 'So I don't want you pouring out horror stories of what we've just heard from Marley. We want answers. We need answers. To get that, we simply use merely suggestions at this stage. *Right?*'

Frank wasn't quite sure how to answer that *at this stage*.

14

Nervous and restless from waiting for the American, Colonel Georgievich's spirits rose at seeing the small black dot of a car coming along the road beside the curving stretch of stagnant canal that was only one of Haarlem-en-Leyden's many. Tinged a bleak yellow, from a weak morning sun scratching its way through heavy cloud, the canal's poor light reflected how it had dimmed from being once part of a shining network of waterways 'bulging' with barges serving the city's commercial needs. Having served its days, it was now truly a backwater – long forgotten.

The Colonel's spirits dropped, as the car drew nearer, when he saw that it was a large black V-8 Volga sedan. Not quite what he had expected the American to be driving. And *definitely* not so, with that hammer and sickle emblem flapping on the small triangular consular pennant mounted on car's bonnet.

The black door swung open, to let out a similarly dull black suit. The man beckoned. 'Get in.' No diplomatic politeness there. But KGB officers were not expected to be politely mannered.

Geogievich got in. Two doors slammed shut and the engine started up sharply with its heavy purr, efficient like its driver. As they moved off, the man gave what was not a friendly look at Georgievich. 'What the hell are you doing here? Why aren't you where you should be, in s-Gravenhage (The Hague), with your Trade Delegation crowd. We've been frantically searching for you everywhere. We've even had to call on the help of these local stupid police, saying we needed to get you back to see your dying mother.'

'My mother passed away many years ago.'

'You know that, but *they* don't! Idiot! Like I said, what are you doing here, of all places?'

'I just relished the opportunity of treading the same terrain as Van Goch, who, I've reason to believe, sought inspiration for his creations in this very area.'

'If he looked for inspiration in this deader than dead back-of-nowhere dump, I can well understand why he went mad, running around cutting off people's ears.'

The fact that it *was* a quiet out of the way region made it a suitable place for Georgievich to meet the American, as they had agreed. It was the standard security procedure that both of them waited for a maximum of thirty minutes, for a maximum of three consecutive days, for the other to turn up. If the other failed to turn up, the meeting was aborted. This was the third day – the only day that the Colonel had managed to get away from his Trades Delegation colleagues and get here. All for nothing, alas, it seemed.

Georgievich was puzzled by the route they were taking, away from The Hague. 'Why are we going in this direction? This is not the way back.'

'Haven't you grasped it yet? We're heading for the airport.'

Located at 13ft below sea level, between the city itself and Haarlem-en-Leyden, Schiphol Airport served as Amsterdam's buzzing international flight centre. Amsterdam, with its ninety-six islands linked by three hundred quaint bridges in a glittering lacework of canals and glass boats, was a sparkling diamond indeed, to the tourist's eye; but for the KGB officer driving a government scientist to the airport on a deadline mission, the city was a nightmare, even if it was daytime. No matter where they turned, there was an octopus of a white-helmeted traffic policeman waving them down to let some wretched pedestrians cross in an endless tide while they waited forever. If this wasn't the case, then it was the tourist bus being too long to turn out of the narrow bridge in one go, or it was the students protesting with their placards, between the vehicles, across the squares. Whatever it was, it made the seconds tick by as the KGB man tapped impatiently on the steering wheel. He had said in his last phone call that he would get the Colonel to the airport by two o'clock, but that didn't seem possible now. Still, it was something to be grateful for that, with all agents put into the field within the last twelve hours, they had eventually managed to track down Comrade Georgievich.

Georgievich looked at the man beside him who was not inclined to give out too much information. But apparently the Dutch police had been conducting a frantic search for him, and when they had finally located him in the backwater vicinity, had politely insisted that he remained there until one of his own people came for him. He had been implored not to wander off, but to stay put until he was collected. After that, the KGB man had arrived. But the more Geogievich thought of it, the less he was able to fathom the reason for all the fuss.

But in spite of his lips being clamped tighter than a sprung bear-trap, the KGB officer had let it slip that he had received the message from their Consulate informing him that Comrade Georgievich was required to return on the gravest national urgency. The exact nature of this had not been clearly stated, since no one at the Consulate knew what it was either. And that face beside him, shut as tightly as the hands gripping the steering wheel, said it had no knowledge further to that behind it.

Georgievich was used to being whipped off, as a top electronics engineer, to government to Soviet installations in Russia and satellite Warsaw Pact territories. So he didn't mind being interrupted in this hectic manner. His work, on the whole, was rewarding, inspecting and improving on Soviet Defence's technical countermeasures to the West's NADGE (NATO Air Defence Ground Environment) newly updated FLS-88 radar units and the improvised relays of the new Marconi 5227 height-finder radar systems. His satisfaction with the equipment made up for his annoyance in not having time to see it all. NADGE involved NATO's European members in the West's defensive umbrella stretching from Western shores through Norway, Denmark, Germany, Holland, Belgium, France, Italy and Greece, to the eastern frontier of Turkey, and comprised eighty-four sites, with thirty-four data processing complexes that interfaced with Britain's air defence network.

The complexes were among the most important of Georgievich's work, with their multiple general purpose computers for analysis and distribution of target information from site sensors, and the correlation of data from other stations, received by data links and conventional communication channels. In all, NADGE was designed for air defence against aircraft flying at heights up to 100,000ftby the control of interceptor aircraft and surface-to-air missiles. The system didn't provide for the detection and countering of missiles, or low level sub-radar threats. But that had so far not been on of Georgievich's concerns.

Now here he was, in the custody, there was no doubt about that, of this quietly grim thing by his side. He stole a quick glance at the man. He wasn't really that old for a KGB officer.

The man looked back at Georgievich for a second. To stop any further questions, he tried buttering the Colonel up with some reassurance. 'Not to worry, Comrade Colonel, by official order, the plane will not take off before we get there. Or should I say: until *you* get there?'

'Won't you be accompanying me on the flight? Or is it your sole duty to deliver the 'goods' without handling them?' Georgievich's playful remark was to hide his emotions as his inside flared up in fear of what he imagined was coming, his heart-beat accelerating at thoughts of a warm reception in Lubyanka's ever welcoming rooms with their speciality service provided for guests made to feel readily forthcoming with their confidential information.

The KGB man examined Georgievich again. Probably about the same age as his own old man. He decided to engage the Colonel in harmless conversation as a means of diverting his mind and stop him bombarding him with questions. He, himself, didn't know what all this was about. Only that all his Department's foreign assignments were temporarily suspended, and that this operation was top priority, under the direction of the GRU's Comrade Colonel Zilianov. He couldn't understand *that* bit especially – GRU going over the head of KGB. But his was not to reason why and all that blah blah.

'Sure, I'll be coming all the way to deliver you up the gangway, and safely on board, Comrade Colonel. So long as you're on board, the flight is complete. But I'm sure that you're already familiar with all this sort of VIP procedure lavished on you by Moscow, aren't you?' He looked at the Colonel for his reaction.

'Yes, that's true, I am. But I'm presuming that you're not exactly without your own experiences. I can't believe that you mean nobody cares if you come along or not. I wouldn't have it otherwise on a boring flight in an empty plane to Moscow. And people usually take my judgement as fairly reliable.' With that, he settled back in his seat, hoping that he'd played out the part convincingly enough. But with confidence dipping in a moment, he had to blurt out: 'So why am I being so suddenly summoned back to Moscow? What is it all about? Or have they not said, as is their usual mode?'

'We're not going to Moscow.' Again, he didn't enlighten the Colonel any further.

Seeing no purpose in pursuing the issue, Georgievich left it at that.

As they patiently waited on the policeman trying his best to untie the traffic knots, they became aware of a man coming up from behind their car and looking in for a moment, before walking on. He went up to the policeman and spoke for several seconds. The policeman started instructing the cars in front to move up onto the pavements. Reflexes tensed as the policeman came back to their car, first knocking on the driver's window, then opening the door.

'I.D. papers, please,' he said in said in a quiet, but controlled, voice that wasn't without its trace of authority. The plainclothes man, having come up to join the uniformed policeman, held up his warrant card: **Interpol**. He put the warrant card away.

The KGB man's tension dropped. Both his and the Colonel's papers were passed out to the Interpol officer. Making a long careful scrutiny of the diplomatic documents, the man finally looked up to nod to the policeman. He passed them to the policeman, who handed them back through the car window, motioning the driver to move on.

Thirty minutes later they arrived at the airport. The white and blue Russian YAK-40, with its AL-25 turbofan engines running, was ready for take-off. But the KGB man had to first go on board alone to make a security check. Finding no-one on board but the pilot and co-pilot, he went out to bring Colonel Georgievich on board.

Seat belts fastened, they waited for the tower's clearance signal. With it finally coming through, the plane slowly taxied round in a wide 'pirouette', to head for and straighten out, on reaching the take-off runway.

Seeing the gleaming plane gather speed along the runway, to gracefully lift off from the long black streak, like a great steel goose, the Interpol man, watching this from the Visitors' Gallery, decided it was time to make that phone call. He shut himself in the soft quiet of the glass and steel booth and picked up the phone. Watching the other travellers ghost silently past, he waited for the operator to get through for him, on the Embassy code and then a special nine digit code. Only a select few in Embassy official circles and an even smaller minority outside the city, knew the number. He was part of the smallest minority out outside of Langley to know that number. Telephone codes circuits raced the call through miles of wire banks that were shrouded in the shadowed security of concrete government basements of CIA Overseas Communications and Signals Division. It got through at last, scrambled, to an office in Foreign Intelligence. There was no pipping sound in the receiver. Only a sharp click and a calm female voice saying: 'Code?'

'Short Weekend, Rotterdam,' he replied, following security screening procedure.

'Transfer; one moment please.' Another click, and another voice, male this time, spoke: '*Yes?*'

'Hello, *ALBATROSS?*

'Yes.'

'This is ZULU Amsterdam. MAGPIE in flight.'

A sharp click of the phone at the other end.

Having delivered the message, and the small clip of microfilm he'd taken from Colonel Georgievich's ID document now safely stowed in his pocket, Major Falzoni put the phone down and walked out the booth.

15

04.21hrs (GMT), Somewhere over South Korean territory, heading for Seoul.

The whole world could be shaking, for all you could feel all around you. But it wasn't. It was the hulking great frame of the Lockheed C-130E Hercules USAF transport plane juddering from the might of its four 4050hp Allison T56-A-7 turbo-prop engines, with their four-bladed Hamilton Standard propellers tearing their way through the violent air turbulence of East Asian sky. Wind shrieked and engines screamed, hauling the 14ton body load onwards towards the South Korean capital. Its cavernous hold with a volume of 4300cu ft, was carrying 240mm M1 howitzers, three 2.5 ton M35 trucks, one Lockheed AH-56 Cheyenne helicopter, along with 114 troops. And Major Frank Falzoni.

Frank looked along the row of young raw G.I. faces sitting across from him, their loose helmet chin-straps swinging in unison side to side. Like pendulums marking their time. He wondered whose would be the first to stop – and after that – and after that? Decked in camouflage fatigues and strapped with auxiliary equipment of morphine needles, rations, first aid kit, canteen, two smoke grenades, gas mask, trench knife, and fragmentation grenades; a small number also managed to carry in addition, two cans of machine-gun ammunition holding a total six hundred and seventy rounds of .303 mm calibre and .45 calibre. They also shared a common faraway stare of nervous waiting, hugging the 7.5lb 20-round

5.56mm M16 assault rifles that they had faith in to get them through it all and safely back to their moms, dads, and sweethearts. As for faith, well, he hoped that the Big Guy upstairs would deal him some good cards.

In contrast, Frank was in a civilian diplomatic outfit of light safari jacket and trousers and white Panama hat. Yeah, well, last week he'd been masquerading as an Interpol inspector, so now his role was as diplomatic liaison between US Army Intelligence and local Korean civilian authorities. More precisely, he'd initially be having a polite coffee and cookies chat with the C-in-C of the United States Indo-Pacific Command, himself, no less. A very busy guy, he would expect Major Falzoni to excuse himself promptly upon swallowing the last drop of coffee.

Frank could then see to his real task of having a parley with anyone who could give him information. The kind that never rose above a whispered 'rumour' and was never written down. The kind he'd have to ferret out from devious characters that didn't exist and could only be encountered in dark corners and alleys where it isn't easy to differentiate between the dying and the dead fouling up the gutter garbage. His only piece of 'hardware' for protection was his .45 ACP calibre Colt automatic, in a shoulder holster beneath the jacket.

04.32hrs(GMT), Landing at USAF Kimpo Air Base K-14. west of Seoul.

The whirlwind of dust died down with the plane's four propellers coming to a halt. Moments later, the tail-end door came down, revealing the gaping mouth of the transporter's cargo hold. The helicopter rolled down the ramp first. Next came the three trucks with their M1 howitzer loads, followed seconds later by the double line of newly recruited, fresh from training camp, hoping *not* to die for their country, soldiers. Frank waited for the last of them to reach the ground, before walking down the broad steel slope himself.

Having stepped out of the hold's dark shelter, into blindingly blazing sunlight, he took out and put on his sunglasses with their silver-mirrored lenses. Good for scanning people around you without any betrayal of your eye movements. Noticing the mangled, burned-out, wreck of what had been a Douglas C-45 transport plane shot down by Korean People's Army Air MiG fighters, across on the far side of the landing strip, he started to walk over for a closer look at it.

'Excuse me, sir. It's this way. Can I help?' It was a young officer who'd come away from the crowd of newly arrived troops to help the civilian whose walking off action he'd mistaken as one of being lost – not quite clear of things --- *like he was himself.* 'I don't know what your mission here is, so I won't ask.' He looked around the vast expanse, pocked with mortar-bomb craters, searching. 'A jeep, or something, perhaps?' he muttered, more to himself than to the man beside him, whatever he was.

'It's all right, Captain, I believe I have someone coming to meet me.' Frank was saying these words on catching the movement, in the corner of his vision, of a figure, distinctly female, by that unique movement of the hips, coming closer in his direction. Just before turning to face the approaching figure, he pointed across the way, for the sake of the Captain's attention. 'Perhaps your help is required more over there, Captain.'

'*Sorry?*' The young officer looked round to see a soldier hammering away angrily at a BGM-71 TOW anti-tank missile launcher being mounted on top of a 3 ton M8 'Greyhound' armoured car.

Saying that with a laugh, Frank walked off to meet what he presumed was his reception party.

'Major Falzoni?'

'Correct. And you *are?*'

'Lieutenant Hoddin. Sir!' The salute was sharp and stiff.

The Major returned it. He reached out to lift up the ID tag hanging from the leather strap around her neck. '*M, L?*'

'Mary Lee, sir. PR Division of Second Battalion of Twenty-fourth Indo-Pacific Marines. I've been assigned to provide you with any assistance you may require during your stay on Base K-14'

Frank wondered how many times the young thing had recited those instructions, in their red-lettering, at the top of her duty roster, to get the elocution perfectly flowing. He smiled. '*Any* assistance?'

'Yes, sir. I'll show you to your quarters, in the residential block, on the far side of the base, facing the town.'

'By all means. Lead the way, Lieutenant.' Frank reckoned she could lead many a man on, the way those lovely rounded buttocks moved as she walked on a little ahead of him.

16

Mostly shrouded by cloud as it was, the moon gave off enough light to catch the gleaming sheen of the wet dirt track receding in a graceful curve into the distant trees. It was also enough light to catch the polished radiator grill of the Citroen car that was nosing cautiously out of the bushes in response to a moment's blink of torchlight from out of the darkness. The car returned the signal with a sharp flash of its headlights. Suddenly it was not just the trees that stirred softly in the breeze. Materialising out of nowhere, a host of figures ghosted up out of the night to form a double line alongside the track. Frank reckoned their number to be about over a dozen, as far as he could see, as he got out of the two-door cabriolet.

Three of them that approached him preferred to keep a tight grip on their .45 calibre M3 sub-machineguns, rather than offering smiling handshakes for greeting.

One of them, what appeared to be the leader, fancied himself as a modern 'Gingachchook', sporting the Mohican-style headband and twin feathers with trailing pony-tails in place of the Army regulation M1 helmet. Plainly a needle-shot of the good old coke gave the guy enough reassurance that feathers were a better bet than steel against his brain being blasted to a pink mash by a 7.62x54mmR bullet from a Chinese T67-2 machine gun. Best of luck, pal, you're going to need it – plenty of it.

Frank looked at the figures closing in around him –enigmatic dark shapes that revealed nothing but for the moonlight giving glints of steel in their hands. Weapons and sabotage equipment supplied by chopper droppings that the poor pigeon couldn't manage – sub-machine guns, grenades, plastic explosives with their pencil detonators – and for silent, smooth, lightning-strikes from cover in the undergrowth, ugly but efficient Welrod silencer pistols. As if this was never enough, Chinese Mauser 98 rifles and MP 40 sub-machine guns could also be useful whenever they could be seized. But he could also see the fretful expressions in those young but haggard faces, smeared with streaks of black 'war-paint' for camouflage; so far away from the safety of their cosy hometowns, that they had to be forever wary not only of enemy bayonets and bullets, but the jungle itself all around them that teemed with death from creatures they saw previously only in their nightmares.

For sure enough, the troops, young kids most of them, faced terrifying things in the Vietnam jungles. There's more to worry about in the field than just the enemy. While the North Vietnamese are the primary enemy, the jungle presented entirely unexpected challenges of its own. Plants held the power here, with thousands of species per square mile battling with each other for control. Even trees were strangled by matted creeper that in turn was devoured by fungi.

While troops were earning Purple Hearts and Congressional Medals of Honor, fully engaged in fighting off the *visible* military enemy, they were also fighting off an invisible creeping, crawling, enemy that made your skin crawl. Vipers, cobra, krait, giant scorpions, snakes so large that even if they were not venomous, constricted you to kill you in your sleep. Another pest of a menace was the Weaver ant, nicknamed the 'communist ant', because of its red colour and seemingly not attacking enemy troops. Apparently it was immune to the bug spray issued to our guys. That left you the choice of using either your Colt automatic or your trench shovel to kill them. If you were in a tank with them, then you either jumped out of the tank fast, buddy, or drove the tank in your damn birthday suit!

Yeah, Lieutenant Mary Lee Hoddin had given it to him full blast, no holding back, reading out from the officially issued warning pamphlet, in deathly droning monotone, all the quick ways of going to meet your Maker, courtesy of Nature. An incredible one was her description of 'innocent' plants, yellow like daffodils, that hung low from tress, and were known to lift, yes, *lift*, troops up out of their personnel carriers, grabbing you by the arms or neck as soon as touched. All beautiful trees and pretty flowers, no kidding --- Heartbreak Grass, Flame lilies, Twisted Cord Flowers, Bark Cloth Trees; yeah, all very pretty – all they did was kill you if you touched them, or blind you if you fancied a change from your iron rations, and ate them instead. Not forgetting danger from leopards, tigers, bears, elephants, water buffaloes and even giant cows that could end your days for you in a mad murderous rampage that your trusty M-16 isn't likely to stop.

He'd taken the pamphlet from her and taken it with him like she'd strongly suggested. Now, standing here with it freshly on his mind, he felt instinctive reflex make him glance around at the blackened foliage.

'Gingachgook' stepped forward. 'Sergeant Bronowski, Thirty-First Rangers.' He eyed the man, so out of place with the military setting in his safari suit, up and down slowly. 'So who might you be, pal? Only Army vehicles bother to take picnic runs down along this way. Lost your way taking the wrong turning, driving your civvy jalopy across town, I'll bet'

But perhaps that was the very reason why Frank was wearing the 'dupe suit'; namely to present a non-threatening neutral image to any trigger-happy Vietcong militia he should be unlucky enough to cross paths with. He showed Sergeant Bronowski his diplomatic pass.

'You still haven't said what the fuck your business is right here in this fuck of a place.'

And Frank still didn't. He just stared at the man who was staring back at him with equal resolve. Some boots around them shifted restlessly. Better to defuse the tension. Frank took out the piece of paper, holding it out the soldier. 'I want to get to that place.'

Bronowski shone his torch on the paper. After a second's inspection, he looked around searching for a face among his men. 'Hey, Hoogie, wherever you are, bring me that goddamn map on the double. We can't afford to keep this guy waiting, can we guys? Hell, no, not when he's wearing a diplomatic white hat. And see and clean your hands, Hoogie. We don't want your dirty marks on government paper.'

Snatching the Panama from the 'diplomat's head, 'Gingachgook' held it up to his own head. With the feathers getting in the way, he decided it was no go, tossing the hat to his men who passed it around, after trying it for size on their own heads.

Playing it safe, Frank joined in the general laughter all around. There's no telling what crazy antics a bunch of battle-worn, stoned out of their minds, kids will turn to for a little innocent fun to relieve their stress.

The hat eventually got back to Sergeant Bronowski, along with the map. Fun now abandoned, he concentrated his serious attention on the small circle of torch light as it moved about, searching, on the muck-smeared 'government paper'. 'You're going to be touching on the western border of the Hau Nghia Province, just near the Go Dau Ha river port. Not an area you'd want to take your grandma to on Sunday picnic. No, definitely not, pal. But that's your business --- *White House* business, I'm supposing, not mine.' He paused to think for a moment. 'True, we have strong fortification with heavily bordered military zones in that specific area; but as that smart English guy, Newton, said, "To every force there's an equal and opposite reaction." That means we're under constant threat down there. Rumour has it we're barely hanging on by our teeth. I kid you not, pal.'

When Falzoni nodded slowly with inner agreement from his own information source, Bronowski smiled. 'Ah, so you're not a dumb cookie after all; you already know what you're letting yourself in for, heading down that way.' He looked around at his tired dirt-faced crowd, once upon a time pink-faced kids, now trained and fully fledged in vicious killing. Looking back at the diplomat standing there in his relatively spotless hat and outfit, he shook his head. He even felt a tiny touch sorry for the guy. 'We'd like to help you, but we're all needed here, each and every one of us, until we're either recalled, or until we fall. You're going to have to make it on your own, pal. Sorry.'

Frank took back his little piece of paper and put in in his pocket. 'That's okay, Sergeant. You've been of great help with your map directions. So I'll be on my way. Maybe next time I'll have time to join in a booze-up round the camp fire.' He turned to get back into the car.

'Hey, and hear this, buddy, if you're stopping along the way to get out and water the plants with a piss – make sure that it's your dick that you're holding, and not that bloody giant three foot – yeah, no kidding -- almost three bloody feet of bloody Chinese centipede! If its poison doesn't finish you off, you can be damn well sure that its bite will hurt like hell.'

Yeah, Mary Lee had mentioned something of that, Frank recalled. What was it exactly she had called it? – *Scopal* – no, correction – *Scolopendra subspinipes*. Nicknamed the Chinese 'redhead'. Extremely aggressive and highly venomous. 'Your advice is duly noted, Sergeant. Thanks again.'

The road, stretching south seemed to be the only one in that region, with just narrow tracks and streams popping up occasionally around it, where only the widest of them was visible wriggling out from under cover of the dense jungle foliage by aerial reconnaissance planes. Frank had seen jungles before, and knew first-hand the value of trees sparing you being spotted like an ant on the ground from the sky.

Stealing an occasional glance up at the dark sky, willing dawn to appear, as he drove along, Frank felt a shiver coming over him. Let's hope all those jabs that Doc had given him before flying out were doing their job and staving off tropical infection. He felt cold. He certainly could do with warming, just like Mary Lee had warmed his bed with her body three nights ago. But the jungle floor's magical phosphorescent glow from decomposing vegetation began to fade. Peeking through swaying treetop branches, a purple sky lightened gradually to pink.

As ever, as he drove along in the mysterious half-light he heard noises that were not entirely of the engine; distant sporadic bursts gunfire and explosions -- and from the undergrowth on either side --- sounds of --- what?

When the sun did manage to scrape through from behind the clouds, it struggled to find its way through the forest roof. Reaching down with golden fingers, it probed around on the ground's carpet of rotting vegetation to give an image of itself shifting to and fro.

Daylight brought on a strange silence, where concentration was now on the road ahead, and not on trying to identify sounds from the darkness that had shrouded both sides during the night. The river, a puny tiddler width to locals of half a mile across, pushed its winding way into the scene. Of a dark brown colour, it looked stagnant until you saw the surface broken by a mutilated human body floating past with its grim message.

The air was now humid and hot with relatively no motion, so virtually anchoring low clouds, like great fluffy zeppelins, to the spot. That was something to be thankful for; such weather didn't encourage enemy planes to fly low over the mountains. So, with relatively no danger of aerial attack removing the need to dive for cover under the jungle canopy, Frank's progress on the ground was steady, if monotonous.

Here at the river, the forest gave way to a gap, allowing the sun to come out and warm the air. A twisting serpent of molten gold flashing in the sunlight replaced the flowing mercury shine the moonlight had given the water the previous night. With daylight signalling relative safety to animals, Frank could hear the sounds of them scrambling down to drink at the river's edge. 'Safety', alas, was all too often rent by screams and frenzied splashing as patiently waiting predators moved in to take their prey. A hearty breakfast for some, not so for others.

With the ground gradually drying out and becoming firmer, the old Citroen seemed happy to surge forward at a better pace to make good time. But Frank's progress was halted twice in the following three hours. The first time to wait for room to negotiate his way carefully round an ox-drawn cart, the poor animal so emaciated that you could virtually play the old xylophone number on its ribs. The second time was to get out for a piss. Standing out in the open, with only the soft purring of the car engine in the background to distract his hearing, Frank listened intently. The faint hum of a distant plane. Growing louder, closer. If he knew his sounds right, it didn't sound like one of theirs. With the car on the road, there was no point in hiding in the trees. He waited, looking up. It was a Beriev Be-6 maritime patrol seaplane, Soviet manufactured for deployment by the Vietnamese People's Liberation Army. Maybe you can see me, pal, but we can also look in on your lot.

Thanks to USAF Black Shield reconnaissance flights by Lockheed A-12 jets, like 'great black darts', flying out from the Kodena Air Base at Okinawa, refuelling over Haiphong, Hanoi and Dien Bien Phu, to refuel again over Thailand's demilitarised zones, we now had clearer pictures of 70 of the so far 190 known North Vietnam surface-to air missile launching sites.

But that was another matter entirely. High altitude aerial reconnaissance would not solve the difficulties Frank would be encountering in this assignment. It was going to be a tricky business unearthing and establishing the locational co-ordinates for bombing those tunnels housing diesel-powered generators supplying much needed electricity for Vietcong survival.

17

As the last yards of miles and miles of jungle rushed past, the thick foliage suddenly cast itself aside and the Citroen burst out into open space in all its unrestricted freedom of panoramic vista. Happy to escape from the jungle's grip, the car seemed eager to surge forward at a faster, smoother pace along the road that was now relatively drier and firmer. Frank saw the shapes looming up ahead, closer and closer.

It was a veritable eyesore of social impoverishment at its worst – an absolute scrap-heap of a dilapidated refugee campsite of shabby dwellings scattered around each other in no particular order like a fortuitous roll of the dice. Shoddy thatched wooden huts and crumbling arrangements of stone and hardboard, supposedly houses, with strips of tin and canvass for roofs. Roasted relentlessly by sunrays beating down on their moisture-laden surfaces, the roofs gave off a softly twisting mist with mirage-like effect. Through it, Frank could see a quivering outline of Go Dau Hu near to the river port of Go Dau Hai. That was where he hoped to track down his quarry.

The high-pitched sound of children's voices came to ear as they played and scrounged about for anything remotely edible among vermin-infested garbage strewn wantonly where there was space on the ground, as well as around infection-ridden open sewers. All in all, a right Purgatorial stop-over, for sure, where the only chance of things getting better meant going to meet your Maker.

So mortality in these parts was not entirely due to B-52 mass bombing after all, then?

A tall crane of ancient teak and rusting iron supports beamed down from aloft to herald Frank's entering the scene driving along Go Dau Hai's riverfront. Just as rust-coated was the old freighter securely roped, long abandoned and forgotten, to the half collapsed wooden jetty.

Greeting him from ground level was a long curve of jumbled oddly-shaped buildings dominated by an imposing customs house complete with its own tapering spiked tower and barbed pinnacles. At least that's what his intelligence dossier was saying it was. Further along the quay were stone warehouse structures of once brightly coloured facades of varying hues, their peeling paint flakes now rendering them to drab shades no better than naked brick.

Frank's eye quickly picked out the long low wooden structure with its high pole and limply hanging flag. Local militia quarters. That same sun's bleaching effect had turned the building's glorious Communist Red colours to a mocking weak pink. Can't those Commie guys ever have the sense to see the 'writing on the wall'?

Now all he had to do was root out McGavin's place, wherever it was, in this muck-up of a town.

Laurence Gary McGavin; former captain in the USACE (United States Army Corps of Engineers) until he was booted out in 'dishonourable discharge' for his devious dealings, in early '46. Not that he was alone in that kind of shaming dismissal, there being quite a few guys, emotionally lost and discontent now that the fighting had stopped, who turned to breaking a few of those martial rules to make up for their disillusionment. He was just one of an outflowing wave. You could say that it was like putting your soldiers back in their proper boxes, discarding those that were too damaged or broken to be kept. So he had been made to go off on his own separate maverick way. According to Records, he had later applied for posting with a then very 'young' CIA. But Recruitment, after careful consideration, had turned its back on him.

Now a new war was favouring him, it seemed, with the critical need for supplies and trading in the Asian theatre of conflict enabling him to run his own successful enterprise.

With his dossier giving no specific address whatsoever for McGavin's supposed place, Frank's patience waned and his eyes tired with long searching through street after street of the town.

Then he saw it.

LGM ENGINEERING: Repairs & Supplies

You had to appreciate McGavin's ingenuity of design shining out at you as it did from the deep brass chunk lettering standing out from the wooden background board, the bright yellow metal defying the sun's merciless attempt to bleach it colourless as it had done with painted surfaces everywhere else. So maybe the guy was getting it his way at last. Frank sure hoped so; otherwise his coming all the way out here was a waste of time to no-one's benefit whatsoever.

Inasmuch as McGavin's business brought in handsome profit, it was also of great assistance to the Vietcong war effort. It was now McGavin's turn to help the United States war effort. It was Sheldon Myers who had put Frank in touch with an informer for British MI6's Far-Eastern Desk who'd pointed out McGavin as the best possible bet, as far as he could see, for solving their current problem of locating Vietcong tunnels for their B-52s to bomb. True, McGavin was pulling in a fat packet of dong banknotes for his invaluable servicing of the Vietcong diesel-motors and other underground machinery; but perhaps he would welcome an even thicker wad of dollars, or Swiss francs if preferred, in a most gratuitous gesture from Uncle Sam that would enable him to escape from this junk-hole of a place. Or *would* he?

On and off --- on and off – the rapid bursts of light flashing again and again in the dim interior of the open-fronted building beckoned Frank to go in and throw a few questions around. It was a figure with no face --- only a black plastic panel fronting its leather-hooded welding mask through which it was peering closely at fussily fusing metal plates. You couldn't see who was behind the mask.

But it wasn't McGavin. It couldn't be – not with the way the oil-stained boiler suit was pulled tight round the figure's rear end, with the ass filling out the curve the way only a dame's could, better than any guy's ever could.

Like a great spluttering fountain of light, giant menacing sparks arched out in all directions causing Frank to step back promptly as some came near to him, just missing his face. 'Serves you right if you get hurt, mister,' said a shrill trilling Asian voice that betrayed the soft female form lurking behind the otherwise rough outer appearance. 'If you don't know where to step to keep out the road, then it means you've no business being here. Are you hiding in here to avoid being arrested by the militia? Are you in trouble, mister?'

The sparks suddenly cut out at the same time as the grim mask went up. Much prettier than her grimy overalls, and with a friendly, if cheeky, smile. But belied, alas, of her being younger than the deep wrinkles ringed around around her eyes allowed her to look, as her race's genes decreed. Free now of the mask's protective visor, she saw the stranger in all the relative splendour that the diplomat's outfit afforded him, so dazzlingly pristine white, to outshine her in her dirty greasy garb.

Taking off one of her large leather gloves, she searched in her pocket, to bring out a crumpled cigarette. She reached down for the blowtorch, to light the cigarette from the fierce hissing jet flame. Taking a drag, she then blew out the long train of smoke before speaking. Stopping to peel a tobacco flake from her lip, she went on. 'You do business with *Waurence*, maybe? *Waurence* no here, Mister. He away odder place. Me do work when he away. You no see *Waurence*, Mister.' Her tiny hand gestured to shoo him away. 'You go!'

Frank tried a diverting tactic to get round her stubbornness. He bent in closer to inspect the metal plates she was working on. 'That's a really swell job you're doing there. Yeah, really good job.' But he hadn't an inkling of what it was she was actually doing. He gave a little cough and smiled to compliment the comical silliness of his remarks. 'All right, so what the hell *is* it you're doing?' That brought out the laughter it deserved from both of them.

'Better question is: what the hell are *you* doing here? And you've come a hell of a long way for whatever it is. It's a long time since I've heard an American voice, so I'm not quite sure if that pleases me or not.' McGavin's frame didn't quite fill the space in the doorway that had opened in the back wall of the workshop. In fact quite the opposite, with him 'towering' over the girl by barely an inch. And she hadn't reached Frank's shoulder. Not exactly what you expected an engineer to look like. But what does an engineer, or anyone else, outside of the presumed stereotype image, look like?

McGavin was a short-framed figure with a bustling energy that seemed to want to burst out of his constricting shortness. The head seemed out of place – stuck on the wrong body – honed to a sharp hatchet-like front that sliced the broad Zapata moustache in two. He certainly couldn't have had that during Army days. His hands and arms moved about everywhere needlessly without any spoken words accompanying them. What a shrink would see as a neurotic syndrome. Probably one of the reasons CIA had turned down his application. Perhaps also partly due to his agitation in being tied down to a humdrum job, when what he had wanted when enlisting was a shot of the action with a paratrooper regiment.

But McGavin reckoned that his squat stature had always worked to his disadvantage. Especially with the coming of war. The Army Selection Board had not placed him with a fighting unit, as he'd wanted. Instead, because of his technical background, they'd placed him with the Engineering Corps. Prior to the war, he'd worked with the Pittsburgh heavy engineering company, Huntly & Brenns Engineering. Back then, the company had specialised in its manufacture of large bore commercial steel tubing and drilling components for the oil-rig industry. When war was finally upon them, they changed to making 0.5"- 6" armour plating, and wheel-track plating for the British 42 ton Churchill tank; sub-contract work had them also producing the tubular sections for the tank's Grundach rotary 360 degrees prism periscope.

Frank walked about slowly, looking at, and stopping to finger, weird-shaped metal pieces scattered all around him, without knowing one damn piece from another. 'Great stuff,' he said. 'Great stuff.'

It didn't escape McGavin's notice that the stranger wasn't really interested in technical things themselves, in spite of the technical questions he threw out over various pieces of machinery. He plainly wasn't a 'technical things' person. No, McGavin saw a shrewd mind making rapidly sharp assessment of him, as he no doubt did with other individuals, predicting their reactions to his descending upon them with his interfering barrage of personal questions.

Frank couldn't make out in the poor light if it was a gun the man was carrying in his hand as he walked up slowly. It was a hefty monkey wrench. In spite of the guy's small stature, his expression said that he was more than happy to have a go at cracking a skull swinging that bloody great thing.

'*Easy*, pal, *easy*. I'm here to talk business, McGavin. *Money* business.'

'What's *your* name, bye the way? You know mine. What do I call *you*?'

'*Mister* should do for the time being.'

'Ah, so it's *that* sort of game we're playing.'

'Got it in one, right on the nail. You catch on quick. I like it when people catch on quick; makes for less time wasted pushing them aside when they become obstacles blocking my way when they refuse to follow my reasoning.'

McGavin didn't like the subtle menacing under-tone of the stranger's words. His grip tightened on the heavy steel tool. Frank noticed this and continued to stare at McGavin without batting an eyelid.

'And you're thinking you can persuade me to follow your reasoning, do you – *Mister*?

'I'm thinking it's a safe bet that I can. If you'll just bear with me and hear me out.' Frank half-turned round in the girl's direction, jerking his head and making a slight hand motion to signal having her leave them so they could talk alone.

'It's okay, she won't understand us.'

'But she speaks English – so she *understands* English, however rudimentary or *broken – take your pick* -- it is. That's substantial reason enough, I should think, for not having her ears pick up on possibly what could be upsetting for her. Get rid of her.' The other, more serious, consideration was that she could quite possibly leak the information, however inadvertently, to a dangerous source.

McGavin was feeling a growing disliking for the stranger, not sure if he was happy with the way the guy was issuing demands, even if he did appreciate at the same time that it signified they would be talking 'serious' business. He gave out a strange babble of words that Frank certainly didn't understand to the girl.

She replied in the same lilting foreign tongue, shaking her head violently as she did.

'She doesn't want to leave her work unfinished; says she has still a lot to do to finish the order. She's a good worker. I wouldn't want to lose her.'

Frank shifted with impatience that was loaded with annoyance. 'Like I said, McGavin, I can't spare the time for to and fro ping-ponging with words. If you'll just hear me out on the serious proposal I want to put to you.'

'And if I don't? If I simply refuse to listen, am I to expect you to call in your 'heavies' to work me over?'

'Hell, no, I can't stand the sight of blood; makes me feel squeamish.'

'Yeah, sure, and my name's George Washington.'

'Now that you mention Washington, there's another president in that town who's ready to hold out his hand with a handsome reward for a great favour you could put his way.' Frank rubbed a thumb and forefinger together in an enticing sign of big money. '*Plenty* of it.'

'Oh, *yeah*?' I find that hard to swallow, with me being strictly *persona non grata* over there, in that great land of so-called liberty and freedom. That's a laugh.'

'Yeah, really, and no fooling around; with a deal all officially approved and signed by presidential seal, no less.' Frank stopped to look round at the girl and then back at McGavin. 'But first, can we go somewhere quiet where we can have a cosy little parley.' He pointed at the monkey wrench. 'And I think we can do without that now, don't you?'

Lingering with indecision for a moment, McGavin plumped the heavy tool down with a loud clank on the large drum of diesel fuel. He turned round sharply to head for the back door. 'This way.'

A door on a small storeroom building across a short yard behind the workshop opened into a long room of metal pieces that spoke of mechanical aptitude if not genius. Machines and tools abounded with seemingly miles of rubber tubing and metal contrivances of all shapes and sizes, to fill all the benches and shelves with a clinical trimness that made for precision engineering.

'Like I said before – "liberty and freedom" over there -- that's a laugh; what about the liberty of others?'

'You're meaning, of course, *these* people?'

'That's right, buddy, that's exactly who I mean.'

'You do a good job for them, I gather?'

'Yeah, keeps things flowing smoothly; what of it?'

'We want you to plug a finger in the hole, so to speak, and stop the flow.'

'What the fucking hell does that mean?'

'You do a lot of work on their electrical supply, don't you?'

'Yeah, so again, what of it? Heck, where's all this leading?'

'We want you to implement a short circuit, so to speak, if you follow me.'

'You bet I fucking follow you! You mean for me to bloody sabotage not just one system, but the whole bloody network, don't you?'

'Not quite that exactly. *We'll* do the damage. You can safely leave that to us. We'll take care of that end of it. We just need you to give us the precise locations. But otherwise, you took the words right out of my mouth.'

'Yeah, I'll bet! You've had those words ready on your tongue long before you came in here.'

'So what do you say?'

'You've got to be joking, pal!'

'Couldn't be more serious than God naming today as Judgement Day.'

'Well it would be tantamount to Judgement Day for me if I went along with your lunatic plan. I run a really hot number of a business here supplying their needs. And that fulfils my needs in turn, giving me money for food to keep my head above water.'

Yeah, you could see that. Where McGavin lacked inches in height, he was compensated in girth, where a proud belly said it liked its bowls filled to overflowing with their rice, beans and noodles.

'I build their machinery, service it where necessary, and replace it with new parts – imported from across the water, by the way, – from China? Did you hear me – I said *China*! So how do you think President Johnson would like me if he knew that, trading with the enemy, eh?'

'He already does – down to the last bolt, screw and rivet, believe me.'

'Yeah, *that* I *can* believe. It's just like you CIA guys, with all your secret security checks, to know the safe threads to tread on the spider's web, better than the bloody spider itself.'

So McGavin was still embittered by the CIA, as well as his country, more or less, turning him down. Hence his "trading with the enemy"
'Is that a no?'

Giving a hardened smile, McGavin nodded his silent defiant answer.

Frank toyed with a strange-shaped piece of threaded piping lying on one of the benches. He looked up after a moment of thought. 'Am I to believe that you really intend to spend your entire life here, ending your days viewing the idyllic panoramic view around you, from your old rocking chair on your verandah? Don't you ever dream of escaping – yeah, I say *escaping* – from this shit-hole of a place? The two million dollars you would definitely be paid by the United States Treasury would enable you to do that smoothly with no hitches whatsoever.' A long pause 'What do you say?'

But McGavin's eyes were staring right past Frank, their attention focused on something behind him.

Frank turned round slowly. He noted that the man was not armed, but his firm stance and bearing said that his importance carried some weight in the local militia contingency. Frank nodded with a quiet smile. The man returned the gesture with a polite bow of the head. Businessman to business man courtesy.

There was still the unanswered question hanging in the air between Frank and McGavin. Frank looked at McGavin, raising his eyebrows as he did so to prompt an answer from him.

Nervous indecision was the only fleeting answer passing across McGavin's face as his mind wrestled with the issue. After very long moments, he blurted out: 'Give me twenty-four hours to think it over.' He glanced nervously at the militia man, fearing he was reading the thoughts in his mind.

'You have it.' Turning to go, Frank paused as McGavin called out.

'Where are you staying in the town?'

Frank looked back at McGavin with a conniving smile that said he was giving that information out to nobody. Absolutely nobody. 'I'll be in touch.' Flashing a glance from the militia man to McGavin, he muttered in low voice a strengthening point for his offer: 'It'll be better than anything your sweat would ever earn for you here.'

Once again, businessman to businessman, Frank smiled politely, a curt bow of the head returning the gesture. But behind the Asian face's placid expression, there was steely hardness and inquiry in the dark eyes that bored into the back of the American walking away and disappearing out through the doorway.

18

Washington's goddamn peak hour traffic, had slowed his official limousine down, in spite of its 'presidential' glisten, the vehicles crawling along inch by inch, bumper to bumper, to slow Marley Goodblood's progress through the capital's flowing rivers of metal, so that he was late for the Pentagon War Room Committee meeting. Entering through the tall doors of the committee room, he followed the solemn blank-faced naval adjutant leading him to his place down the long room. The chair, looking so condemned in its isolation, was placed just inside the open end of the horseshoe arrangement of tables with its threatening pincer closing in positioning. Just like those Roman army generals strategically positioned their soldiers to trap the enemy. Clever guys, those Romans. Taught us a trick or two about battlefield manoeuvres.

For those butt-brains crazy enough to believe it, the horseshoe is a bringer of glad tidings and good luck, if not that pot of gold itself. Well, this one certainly didn't look like it would; not when it was made up of those sharp uniforms bristling with their refulgent arrays of brass buttons and 'gongs', along with fruit cocktails of campaign ribbons and glaring gold braid that spells out the military 'modestly' broadcasting their trade like only they can. Prim straight backs and firmly set expressions fitted the straight high-backed chairs with the usual rigidity you expected from Top Brass, their inverted reflections on opposite sides of the long polished table-tops doubling the splendour of their uniforms.

In all, an urgently summoned assembly of contacts from Naval Intelligence, Air Intelligence, Army Intelligence and Joint Services Counter Intelligence. One hell of a swell military parade. Normally only the hush-hush guys sat down to these time-wasting meetings, watching the flies on the wall watching them in turn counting the seconds ticking by on the clock. So someone's gut-rumblings had deemed the situation urgent enough to call in this jamboree crowd of Top Brass. With Goodblood feeling nakedly alone in his civvies, in contrast to that around him, he felt like the plucked turkey on Thanksgiving Day before it went into the oven for its roasting.

No, correction, he wasn't alone. Sitting there at the far end, on the horseshoe's arch, in a pin-striped three-piece of charcoal grey, was Barrington Gilberts, Committee Chairman, and political guru Chief Advisor to the US Secretary of Defence, McNamara.

The guy was still rambling on, with no hoped-for sign of his speech coming to an end. The droning self-satisfied voice going on and on. At last it came. 'In all, we have in its build-up, the first waves of a bad storm coming our way, in its material way, politically and economically, for want of better words.'

Goodblood was tempted to clap his hands to compliment the long-winded grandiose words; Shakespeare was lucky to have lived in a different century, as he would otherwise have been put out of a job by Gilberts' rhetoric.

Taking his hands away from the table's edge and resting them on his buff folder, Gilberts sat back upright in apparent judgement of his 'subjects' seated before him down the length of the room. Peering owl-like over his silver half-eye reading spectacles for a second, he took them off for a better look down the long double row of tables. Marley couldn't see Gilberts' eyes exactly at that distance, but he could imagine their intensity staring at him. The old bastard hadn't been too pleased with his 'modified' report. The foreboding crisis held in Gilberts' scathing words to everyone centred on the Vietnamese Leader, Ho Chi Minh's threat to launch nuclear projectiles at the United States from that tiny

Communist country. What you might have considered to be something of an impudence, considering the colossal difference in size of the two opposing sides; perhaps they should remember the 'headache' that a relatively diminutive David caused Goliath to suffer. Ho Chi Minh offered to withdraw his threat if President Johnson issued an immediate halting of the US bombing of North Vietnam. Neither side withdrew its threat, so that, needless to say, the war continued on its not so merry way.

With no immediate sign of a solution to our armed forces' lamentably poor faring in the Vietnam conflict, eyelids all round blinked and fingers twisted a file's dogged corners as minds went over Gilberts' last twenty odd minutes of searing oratory.

Somewhat like a gaping Gothic gargoyle, Gilberts leaned forward searching for – *anxious* for – a gleam of inspiration to come into the face of at least one of the sea of empty expressions before him. Something, *anything*, that wasn't just a tired service memo. His eyes found Colonel Goodblood easily, standing out against the colourful uniforms, as he did, in his civilian attire of quietly chequered country leisure jacket, American styled whilst cut to give a subtle North European tone.

But Colonel Goodblood seemed to be giving more attention to his watch than his committee agenda notes and appeared to be far away in his mind from the meeting. Whilst others in their boredom fidgeted with pieces of paper and written reports in front of them, Goodblood's preoccupation appeared to be elsewhere. Restless mood swings had him shifting from elbow to elbow. When his mind came back into the room and he caught Gilberts' eye, Goodblood's face failed to release an expression or identifiable signal that went beyond a defiant stare. He simply fingered his chin, holding back what he was thinking, before looking down at his notes.

Gilberts returned his attention to his duties as Committee Chairman.

Seeing that the Chairman's attention was back with them, and not distracted as it had been moments before, Brigadier General Grovesby spoke: 'What came to my attention like a horror story was the report of our CH-46A Sea Knight choppers being brought down like swatted flies!

How the hell are those midget 'Cong managing to pull off that kind of undetected strike action? '

'Look to Moscow for that answer,' said another voice.

'No, no, no, you've got it all wrong. They were definitely not shot down by the enemy,' said Goodblood, anxious to put a pin in the bubble of gross misunderstanding. 'Sure, I can see how you're thinking that – we thought that ourselves when it first happened in --- ' a quick sifting of pages in the folder to find what he sought ' --- in August thirty-first, one of our Sea Knights on medical evacuation mission to USS *Minnesota* disintegrated in mid-air killing all occupants.'

'Damnit, Colonel, I already know only too damn well about that blasted crash; for God's sake get on with it, man!'

Goodblood waved a hand to quell Grovesby's angry outburst. 'Bear with me, Brigadier; just bear with me. Thanks.' He went on: 'Next day another CH-46A experienced a similar incident at Marble Mountain Air Facility, making all of that type of chopper to be grounded, except for emergency cases. And that cut our Marine Airlift capacity in half. With repeated occurrences of crashes registering virtually identical technical details of damage – yes, we also concluded that they had been shot down. But with technical analysis of the damage details rendering virtually identical results, our minds shifted.' Goodblood paused to take a deep breath in his keenness to clear up this mess of misunderstanding. He went on: 'In fact, it appears to be a shortcoming of our own. Investigations conducted by a Joint Naval Air Systems Command/ Boeing VTOL accident investigation team revealed that the structural failures were occurring in the area of the rear pylon, resulting in the rear motor tearing off in flight and may have been the cause of several earlier losses.'

'You're saying *we're* at fault! How the hell can you reach that preposterous conclusion, Colonel? How the hell can you say that when we have our dollars stacked on Boeing's VTOL choppers as the best machine possible? Tell me that, Colonel.'

'In that case, Boeing VTOL have a lot to answer for.' Goodblood's cutting reply had everyone waiting for explanation. He obliged them by continuing: 'The technical team recommended structural and electrical systems modifications to reinforce the rear motor mounting as well as the installation of an indicator to detect excessive strain on critical parts of the aircraft.' Goodblood paused to take a deep breath before finalising. 'And that, for all I'm personally able to fully comprehend of all the technicalities, is what I'm given to understand is how the situation stands.' He looked around to see how all this had affected everyone. Sullen and needing cheering up. 'As far as I'm given to understand, the CH-46A should be returning to service hopefully by December.'

'The only way I can make sense of that, Colonel, is that you're implying that we have a Commie sympathiser working with Boeing VTOL; that we have to root out a saboteur in the company's construction people. Is that what you're saying?'

'Like I said before, look to Moscow for that answer,' said that voice again, this time with a jocular note.

As if to clear the air by shifting to a different issue of concern, Army Intelligence's General Towdrey felt the need to voice his worrying point. 'What I want to know is this. 'At the beginning of '67 the United States was engaged in a steadily expanding air and ground war in Southeast Asia. Since its inception in '65, Operation Black Thunder the bombing campaign against North Vietnam has escalated in the number and significance of its targets, inflicting major damage on transportation networks industry, and petroleum refining and storage facilities. Yet the campaign shows no signs of achieving either of its stated objectives. Our air attacks haven't broken the Hanoi government's will to continue the war, and they're not halting or appreciably hindering the flow of PAVN (People's Army of Vietnam) troops and supplies into South Vietnam. North Vietnam has been able to repair damage and develop substitutes for destroyed facilities rapidly enough to counter incremental escalation of our air campaign. With Soviet and Chinese assistance, the North Vietnamese have built a large and sophisticated air defence system. Its guns and missiles extracting a toll in pilots and aircraft for every one of our raids. On the ground in South Vietnam, our US force build-up is approaching completion. More than 380,000 US troops are in the country, alongside over 730,000 Army of the Republic of Vietnam (ARVN) soldiers and some 52,000 soldiers from other allied nations. After a year of base building and intensifying combat, I believed that our forces were ready for major offences that would seize the battlefield initiative from The PAVN and Viet Cong (VC). But now, with the PAVN/VC conducting their own build-up, including the infiltration into South Vietnam of regular PAVN divisions, it's not so clear what to believe.' He stopped, to look around to see what his words so far were making the others believe. He continued: 'It's clear that these units, along with VC guerrillas and light infantry formations, are countering our challenge. Within South Vietnam, the PAVN and VC are seeking opportunities to inflict casualties on our forces in large and small engagements. They're also concentrating troops at various points on South Vietnam's borders to create a strategic threat to our allies and compel the Military Assistance Command, Vietnam (MACV) to disperse its reserves. In Operation Bison – a major operation in southern half of the demilitarized zone north east of Con Thien, the PAVN 90TH Regiment ambushed the 1rst Battalion of 9th Marines; we suffered eighty three killed, one hundred and seventy wounded and nine missing.' Grovesby shook his head, at the same time bringing a clenched fist down hard on his table. 'That made it the damn worst one-day loss by our marines in the whole Vietnam conflict. In all, as far as intermediate estimate tells us, out of our total of four hundred and eighty-five thousand US troops, we've incurred eleven thousand and one hundred and fifty-three dead and one hundred and forty thousand injured.'

The General sat back in his chair. After that long mouthful of negative download, you could see he needed a breather. 'Can anyone answer that?' He looked around to see if anyone could.

Gilberts closed his folder on Operation Bison and looked at the others, then with particular scrutiny at Goodblood. Even at that distance, Goodblood could sense the man's mood had worsened on account of the crisis, so that brooding fire burned through the bloodshot eyes, where 'fish nets' of dilated blood vessels pulsed over yellowing white sclera.

Pushing the folder away in quiet distaste, Gilberts put on a more amiable air. He put on a benign smile that he thought would please everyone. 'A moment perhaps, everyone, for wetting dry mouths.' Smiles and relief broke out all around at this move to change the subject. Hopefully one that would prove to be lighter.

Gilberts pulled his folder back to sift through the sheets, thin as they were, but heavy with distressing data. 'So what do we have so far on that, Colonel Goodblood?' He looked up at Goodblood. 'If you would care to enlighten us, please don't let us hold you back.' His fingers tapping to demonstrate that degree of official impatience that a governing chairman was allowed to have.   Like a synchronised system of puppets, a double row of heads swivelled round atop their uniforms to fix their attention on the Colonel.

With all the room's attention focussed on him, Goodblood pondered for a moment between what he knew, and what was best for the committee to know of the situation. *His* situation. 'One can well appreciate your annoyance, for want of a better word, General, at the seeming result of all our forces' combined action showing little, if no, effect on the enemy. Yes, that does grate the mind, I grant you. But it basically boils down to the fact that their large network of underground tunnels housing electricity generators and other essential machinery, along with other vital supplies provided by China and Russia enables them to seemingly defy our B-52s' massive aerial bombardment.' Goodblood paused to look around before giving a final point, stinging as it was. 'And – they are a resilient people. But perhaps it's not so much a case of what the source of the problem is, but more a case of what has to be done to resolve it.'

'And *are* we, Colonel --- doing something *"to resolve it"*?' Gilberts putting his stick in again. 'Perhaps you would care to fill us all in with another revealing explanation, if you have one. *Do* you have one? One that can put our minds to rest with something that is not too difficult to accept?'

How to reveal without revealing? That was the little puzzler tickling Goodblood's mind. 'We have an ongoing covert operation down there to contact and negotiate with a source with plans for exact pin-pointing of the Viet Cong tunnel locations and so enable our B-52 bombers to destroy them outright, once and for all.'

'For God's sake, Goodblood, we're not bloody pigeons! We want something more than a lousy scattering of crumbs to satisfy us.' General Towdrey was plainly angry with impatience. 'Have you, or have you not contacted this source?'

'Yeah, we have.'

'*Well?* Is the damn so-called source in full swing agreement for implementing our plan or not?'

'We're waiting for confirmation on that.'

'Waiting! Waiting! That's all we seem to do. Goddamn it, can't you speed things up a bit, Colonel?'

'Alas, we're experiencing a spot of bother there.'

'What the hell does that mean?'

'Yes, I don't follow you, either, Colonel,' cut in Gilberts. 'Aren't field reports coming in?'

'We've only had silence, in place of signalled transmission at regular scheduled timing. It seems our man has gone to ground; that is, if he hasn't been taken into custody by militia and handed over to Chinese or Russian interrogators for their 'friendly' grilling. We can't afford to send in 'feelers' and jeopardize the whole thing by attracting unnecessary attention, if he's simply keeping a low profile. We *have* to wait a little longer.'

'Good God!' Gilberts was greatly dismayed. 'I don't doubt that that you operatives in the field can do the job better than pen-pushers like me. Yes, that's right, I'm a pen-pusher. That's what I get paid to do, and I do the job satisfactorily, even if I say so myself. Are you doing *your* job to its satisfaction, Colonel Goodblood? Forgive me if I'm inclined to see question there.'

But Gilberts sensed that Goodblood was not going to give out anything beyond that. He saw that the Colonel was not in a position to make solid standing statements over weak ground. He was right.

Goodblood confirmed what Gilberts was thinking by looking up at him with an expression of restless impatience. He then looked down pointedly at his watch to push the message home. Inasmuch as Gilberts, as Chairman, didn't like *his* meeting being hurried on to its end by another person's prompting, he appreciated the Colonel's need to get back into the field. Rising up, he announced the meeting's closure, giving the date of the next month's meeting. If you detected any icy intonation in Gilberts' words, it was for the benefit of Colonel Goodblood's ears.

A notable rustle of papers being thrust away briskly into briefcases said that Goodblood was not alone in his urge to vacate the room. As everyone began to leave, drifting in a crowd of small-talk towards the door, the spider on the chandelier got the message that yawning-from-boredom time was over, and abseiled down the side of the glittering crystal glass in its decision to come down to earth.

19

Falzoni shared his room in the abandoned factory-cum - 'happy house'-brothel perched on the river bank with a colony of ants. A thin winding line of them trekked across the rough wooden floor, humping great loads of leaf and dirt ten times their weight to disappear through a crack in a bent plank that had seen better, more honourable, days serving as part of a foreman's desk. Neither man's intrusive giant boots nor those man-made earth-shattering explosions outside was going to stop them. You couldn't help but admire such determination.

If the same tiny room had been let out to a flea circus, those agile insect performers may well have been induced to ride piggy-back in order to allow for elbow-room. Bearing in mind, alas, that many of the wretched unfortunates of this war-torn land didn't even have elbows. He knew that feeling well enough with his prosthetic left forearm as companion reminder. Spartan, the tiny squashed-in cubicle space of a room may well have been by Western standards, but a veritable luxury to these people, granted by the power of Allah, or whoever it was they saw as their big boss 'upstairs'. Never mind those new Commie masters stamping out centuries-old cultural beliefs with their indoctrination declaring religious thought of any kind strictly taboo. If the peasant mind harboured a sacrosanct thought deep down it was there for keeps, and no shifting it.

Settling down as best he could, Frank lay down on the low-slung bed, its wooden stump legs barely thicker than the coarse straw bag mattress. He only then he noticed his knuckle was bleeding; the result of his scraping against the rough wall coming up the stairs. Alcohol was not without its effect on his already tired senses. He'd downed a whole wooden jug of a weird concoction of 'house wine' at the tiny 'bar' in order to quell any suspicions of why he was here in this dung-pit joint with lots of money to splash out. But it didn't satisfy that obvious question behind those querying stares of why he didn't want to take a female with him up to his room. He thought of the subtle remarks that had come in his direction from all around, cutting through with raucous laughter, honing his alertness for a more seriously toned question being put to him.

Like the bruised knuckle, he was taking his chances in scraping by. But as the room spun wildly around him, his remaining sobriety told him that he perhaps may have just escaped a knife across his throat. And that was just for tonight. What would it be like tomorrow? The fear and thrill of it had him muttering himself quietly to sleep. The nearness of the bed to the floor proved to be useful with his Colt Automatic resting inches from his hand on the floor.

But any sleep that Frank managed to catch that night was greatly unsettled. A river of nightmares swam through his mind. Through the darkness came the putrid odour of excrement and bodies rank with sweat, that reminded you of the endless story of human desolation and wreckage all around outside. Dozing fitfully, he jerked awake between ragged patches of disturbing visions, trying to orientate himself to his squalid surrounding, and escape from scenes that had upset him. Distorted dream visions, ungoverned by daytime's sanity, ran amok through his mind, playing havoc with his emotions. Convoluted mood changes took him from a morose past, to a precarious present that harboured a great fear of the future. Overriding all these melancholy wraiths spiriting through his mind came the scary questions. What were the odds of McGavin's VietCong business contacts tumbling to the reason for this new American turning up on the scene to offer him a different sort of 'contract'? Could he be connected to Goodblood through Myers? Had he overlooked anything in his cover story – any tiny point that could be the difference between life and death? Did he let her down? Had they quarrelled that much that night? Had he pushed Charlie into something that had proved too dangerous for her? With his mind struggling to grasp some inward shelter from discordant jabbering beyond his room's thin walls, sleep at last claimed his mind solidly, clapping his brain tight to its dark abysmal bosom. He rested inwardly undisturbed, until some blasted cockerel announced it was time for morning ablutions, or whatever else it was that a damn bird does at that wretchedly early hour.

But he had to thank the bird for its screeching reveille call. It had him awake and alert just before the heavy hammering sounded on the door. Just enough time to push the Colt and holster inside the mattress through a hole he'd cut in it earlier. From the authoritative tone of that voice on the other side of the door, it would not be a good thing to be found carrying a firearm on his person in a body search.

He made a point of opening the door none too slowly – suspicion shown by slow caution on one side of the door served only to generate suspicion on the other side of the door. The man, or was it boy -- difficult to ascertain age in the sallow thin-faced Asian features – looked up at him. Tiny as he was, the .303 Lee Enfield bolt action rifle he brandished earned him his due respect. Especially with that great naked bayonet sprouting up from the muzzle's end.

Not understanding a single word the guy was shouting at him, Frank still understood, by the forceful tugging of his sleeve, that he was being invited on a 'blind date' of sorts. As he half turned to close the door behind him, Frank was yanked away violently by the man who was blasting him with another volley of more words he didn't understand. At the same time, the guy's colleague got an equally fierce hollering of words in his ear ordering him to stay behind and make a thorough search of the room.

Clumping noisily down the wooden stairs after his armed escort and out through the doorway into the cutting fresh morning air, Frank saw that his presence was important enough to warrant an extended escort of three more armed guards – Chinese, this time, as the small red stars on their helmets indicated. For back-up they had the great 11.1 ton,

6.63 m long, 6-wheeled green beast in welded steel armour plating, embellished with its own large red star. The BTR-152 armoured personnel carrier, manufactured by the Soviet Union and supplied to Vietnam for deployment by Ho Chi Minh's belligerent Communist cronies, and as in this case, the PAVN. Powered by Diesel engine and provided with an improvised new gear box, Frank appreciated how it meant bountiful work for McGavin to build up the coffers.

Pushed brusquely into the rear of the vehicle, and its steel doors slammed shut behind him, Frank was enclosed in darkness but for the slivers of light slicing in through the side observation slots. Like the low-slung predatory alligator it reminded you of, the great thing gave a deep snarl and shudder, readying itself, before moving off.

The engine made most of the noise as they sped along, with only a few quiet words exchanged between the guards. An occasional smile or cheeky wink from him to them received only three stone-faced stares in return. He couldn't tell exactly how long they had been going since they'd confiscated his watch – along with his artificial forearm; yeah, these wary guys were taking no chances. After all, there could have been an atom bomb or too concealed in that short length of hollow alloy tubing. But as far as he could reckon, it seemed to be after about something like thirty minutes or so that the monotonous drone of the engine changed down to a lower tone that signalled a slowing down. At last they stopped.

At a first glance through the opening doors, it seemed to Frank that there was nothing there, and yet everything was moving, as billions of tall grass blades frisked about in a sea of green ripples along the broad expanse of the sloping coastal headland. But stepping out of the carrier into the strong breeze whipping up his hair and collar, he saw, looking to the side, that there was a lot more than nothing there – a *hell* of a lot more. Isolated lower down on the open plain before him, the building looked smaller than it was, squashed into the ground by the overwhelming urge for flatness between sky and plain. Simple shades of whitewash and black tiling gave a maritime air to the structure. Whilst ground floor windows shrank back in precious privacy, protrusive dormer windows stared out to sea in an endless watch for the enemy. What may once have been an idyllic retreat for the reclusive philosopher or artist was now serving as a military observation post. This, Frank deduced, from the bustle of activity, distant as it was, going on around the tower. Like ants under a hypnotic spell of urgency, tiny figures and vehicles criss-crossed in a flurry of unceasing hurried movement. What Frank recognised from old experience as the familiar preparatory build-up prior to active manoeuvres. In true oriental spirit, a twisting serpent line of low-slung supply trolleys somehow managed to weave and twist its way through the general bustle without actually causing collision. Bombs, Frank guessed, from the way the 'serpent' was heading towards the great Russian 'Bear', the Tupolev Tu-95 four-engine turbo prop powered bomber, its Kuznetsov NK-12 contra-rotating propeller tips moving faster than the speed of sound, making it one of the noisiest aircraft around. That is, according to our technical data wizards back in Langley.

Over to one side, three Vietnamese missile crews, having probably undergone six to nine months training in the Soviet Union, were practicing with S-25 Berkut ground-to-air missile launchers. Again, so our Langley lot were telling us. In fact, like it or not, twelve of our aircraft so far had been brought down by some damn ace of a sharpshooter, Lt Vadim Petrovich Mirbakov, all by himself.

At the runway's end, the 'Bear' was turning with the surprising lightness of a ballet dancer to taxi back up. It moved over into what looked like a service bay that was dominated by a large hanger and an orderly double-lined formation of hunchbacked corrugated metal huts. The hanger's gaunt mouth widened to let a long 'beetle' with lots of wheels speed out towards the 'Bear' to tow it inside. The massive bulk of the great grey beast receded slowly, inch by inch, into the hanger to gradually disappear behind the deep shroud of darkness within.

Aloft, directly above Frank, sentinels wearing the tower's black and white livery circled around in long scrutiny of the American approaching the military encampment. The seabirds gave out their hoarse warnings before finally moving away. They'd done their bit, leaving the rest to another to do a better job. And there it was, hovering two hundred feet overhead, a two-ton tadpole swimming against a background sea of azure sky.

Frank looked up at the helicopter twinkling with lights, sucking in all that below through its powerful 300mm telephoto lens and into its Kalimar SR-200 single lens reflex camera.

It was the last he saw before a blindfold was put over his eyes.

20

The metal door flew open with deliberate extra force to give a resounding crash to upset the prisoner. Major Frank Falzoni looked up, without seeing, towards the loud disturbance that had shattered his quiet concentration. He was still blindfolded, his wrist still secured behind his back by chain to iron anklets. What sounded like the same guard was hollering, in his same hoarse voice, words that were wasted on Frank's ears. But the way the guy was pulling him up and out of his hard chair suggested that they were going places. And in a hurry – the way the guy punched his arm and shouted to hurry him on.

Frank reckoned they had arrived at wherever it was they had been heading for when the guard whipped off the blindfold to let light flood into Frank's eyes. They were standing outside the door of what was likely to be the 'boss', with his rank and title in large Chinese letters on the metal surface.

The guard hastened to remove his prisoner's chains and ankle shackling. The noise of this was evidently enough to alert whoever was within the room to have a commanding voice calling out.

The guard opened the door to enter and make a weak bowing gesture before removing himself faster than lightning.

Perhaps not quite the grandiose air of a general's office, the basic spartan furnishings of the room – desk, folding metal bedframe and mattress, two wooden storage chests and one filing cabinet --nevertheless served adequately for a commander in the field to bunk down in and issue his commands from. No photographs of loved ones or colleagues – an aesthetic man married to his stern career. Behind the desk, mounted on the wall, the proud blade of a Saracen scimitar shone out its glory of the past.

For several seconds two minds connected solely in silent staring, the American major studying the Chinese captain, and the Chinese captain studying the American 'civilian'. Taller than you presumptuously expected of a Chinese, the officer was slim and trim in his sharp khaki tunic with brown leather belt, double-tongued brass buckle and Sam Brown diagonal shoulder strap, to meet all requisite points of dress code in the soldier's manual.

'Was it interesting? Did you find what you were looking for?' said Frank, breaking the silence.

The Captain inclined his head to signify not understanding the American's question.

Frank held up his empty left sleeve end and pointed at the desk with his right hand. Looking fresh out of an Edgar Allan Poe tale, the artificial forearm piece, removed of its cosmetic black leather glove, gleamed with the message of a menacing claw.

'Ah!' Understanding now, the Captain picked up the piece, along with its glove, and came round from behind the desk to return the items to their owner. Giving a polite bow, he handed them back to the American. He held out a hand, gesturing towards the chair. 'Please.'

'Thanks.' Frank sat down.

Going back behind his desk and sitting down, the Captain pulled open a folder to study its contents. The only sound breaking the room's heavy silence was his turning pages as he read on, looking up occasionally at his 'guest', but saying nothing. Not a single sound came from outside either, where tumultuous hollering of squad formation commands had rung out earlier. Perhaps with an American present on the base silence was the order of the day. It made for a tense, if not oppressive, atmosphere.

But Frank wasn't that thick. Only a fool would be beguiled by this new polite reception he was now getting. He recalled only too vividly his episode at the Wyoming 'debriefing' compound, courtesy of the CIA psychological interrogation team, where friendly smiling expressions and the *assured* absence of 'thumbscrew' tactics only served to weaken you with disarming confusion over what to *really* expect from your jolly inquisitors.

While he waited, Falzoni re-attached the prosthetic piece once more to his upper arm. He was tired from not having slept well, his having spent the night in a room, totally deprived of heating, that could hardly be compared with a four-star hotel's Emperor Suite. Whilst not as openly brutal a physical mode of extracting confessions as that used by the ancient Spanish Inquisition, modern mind games could prove to be just as effective in the end at achieving their objective.

After some concentrated reading, the officer looked up at his visitor. 'You are Mr Porter? That is correct, yes?' The last syllable in the name was stretched out in high tone, Oriental style, as if a porter was actually being summoned.

'I would have thought that was halfway round the camp by now. Yeah, that's correct. I'm Mr Porter.'

'I am Captain Sakamura.'

'*Sakamura*? That sounds more Japanese than it does Chinese.'

'My father, in his early youth, was compelled to flee the land of his birth, and that of his forefathers, on account of blemished honour, and sought permanent residence across the waters in China.'

Frank threw up a hand to stop the explanation going further. 'I get the picture! I get the picture!' In reality, Frank didn't want to be cajoled into weakening his resistance by the classic interrogator's ploy of using friendly family small-talk to inveigle his way behind the prisoner's defensive barrier.

The Captain sensed this, either by instinct, or as trained interrogator himself, recognising the American's move for what it was. He changed tactic. 'You are a traitor to your country, Mr Porter.'

'I prefer to see myself as a survivalist and keep my head above water.'

'And for this you put your faith solely on money, with your conscience totally devoid of any degree of national spirit?'

'Yeah, well it pays to keep the popcorn piled high.'

The jet-black Japanese eyebrows almost nudged each other in a frown where the American's idiom was confusing.

'Money is like water – it eventually finds its way everywhere, regardless of whatever religious chant or political doctrine attempts to brand it as taboo. It makes no difference if it's Karl Marx or Zurich bankers doing the preaching – doesn't matter if it's national banks or river banks holding the 'water' in; it will still flow between those banks to join the rivers, that join the seas, that join the oceans, across the globe. There's no escaping it.' Frank paused to let his message sink in. 'And let's face it – we're both here to help this country by providing supplies it needs – and to do that we use good old-fashioned money.'

'And *bombs*, Mr Porter, and *bombs*! Your country – your *forfeited* country -- the United States of America, claims to be helping this country, while, in the same process, killing hundreds of thousands of innocent men women and children with its horrifically unceasing barrage of aerial bombing. Is this how it means to *liberate* this country from Communist dictatorship – by securing initial foothold on the land and thereafter trampling the land underfoot by establishing its own dictatorship of economic superiority? Yes, I must concede to you being accurate in that point, Mr Porter – money does come in to it.'

'You got it in one! Great! We all of us make deals. That's why I'm here, as you should well know, if you're reading that file right.'

Sakamura looked down at the folder, sifting through the pages. 'You intend supplementing material of a more newly developed superior design than that already provided by the ---,' he paused to read further down the page, '--- LGM Engineering Company. Is that right?'

'Yeah, that's it. But understand, I'm not cutting McGavin out of the deal. No way! He'll still be the exclusive provider here; I'll get a cut – a *handsome* cut – for transacting arrangements for the deal binging together these better just-of-the-drawing-board designs and a new Chinese engineering works.'

Sakamura looked down again at the file. 'The Ho Lin Wu Light Industrial Plant in Guandong Province?' He paused to think. 'Unless my memory deceives me, it's in the south eastern area of the country, bordering Hong Kong and Macau; the capital, Guangzhou, sits on the industrial Pearl River Delta region.' Another pause, looking up at the arched metal roof overhead, scouring his memory. 'Yes, I know of it; if I recall correctly, the city's architecture is mainly of nineteenth century design.'

'Right on the nail.' But Frank saw where this could possibly be going, and moved in quick with his next response to avoid being caught out with a trap question. 'I can't otherwise corroborate you on the geography; I've never been there in person. I only know the place through business connections.'

'And you are able to procure these technical details, which surely must be of seriously sensitive privacy classification? *How*, may I ask?'

'I know people, who know people, who know people.'

The Captain said nothing to this. He simply sat back for several seconds, nodding his head in deep thought. While he did this, Frank's thoughts were on who the hell had 'shopped' him? Was it the militia guy he'd encountered briefly in McGavin's workshop? Or was McGavin, turning down the offer of a fat bag of loot, finding that he hadn't the backbone to go back to the States, tinted, as he would be, in disgrace?

Sakamura lifted the American's contract documents out of the folder. 'These would appear to be authentic in their content.'

'Right; so with that all cleared up, can we get on with it?'

'They *appear* to be authentic. But to finally decide, we must have proper authentication. Agreed?'

'Do I really have a choice? Sure, go ahead, by all means.'

The Captain gave what looked like a wicked smile and nod, while at the same time, pressing a button on the desk.

Frank prayed in his mind, hoping that those expert forgers at Langley had done their job; if they hadn't, they should be sacked. He didn't like to visualise what his own fate would be in that last instance.

After several minutes of waiting with tension, for different reasons, in their minds, the door finally opened, following a faint deferential knock, and a guard stepped in.

'Bring him in,' ordered Captain Sakamura in Chinese tongue.

Distracted by this new entrance of a Soviet Army officer in his bright regalia of sparkling buttons, broad epaulettes, and red and gold cap and collar tabs, Frank's attention didn't take in the colonel's face until the last moment.

When it did, Frank's inside jumped; he wasn't sure if from surprise or from unease.

Colonel Antonin Yuri Seirganov Georgievich!

21

In writing up a progress report of a mini-operation within an operation, Sheldon Myers entered Colonel Georgievich's codename as LEASH. Because that was the role he'd assigned the Russian to play in pulling in a 'stray dog'; the 'dog', previously known to Georgievich as 'Lewis', now being known as 'Porter'. This devious game of name-switching, in all its subterfuge, was becoming quite familiar to the Colonel, presently enmeshed, as he was, in his own irrevocably perilous game of breaching highly classified Red Army security measures. At the same time placing him in the straits of impasse with a dilemma. Namely, how to fasten the 'leash' to that 'dog'. If he denounced 'Porter' as the spy with potential plans to implement sabotage, he would be scuppering large scale US military operations; alternatively, if he spirited 'Porter' away from the grip of his Chinese captors, he would be virtually suspending over his own head a cloud of serious questions of loyalty, and possibly death by firing squad thereafter.

This gave Myers his own share of headaches. As case officer and handler in the field, his responsibility was to ensure the smooth running of an operation – second, of course, to maintaining the safety of that agent in the field. In pulling one of his charges out of a deep pit, he was causing the other one to balance precariously on the rim of that chasm. And the importance of both these agents was paramount. Losing these two men would be costing a lot more than just two lives. And it hadn't escaped Sheldon's thinking that one of the reasons, if not the *sole* reason, for GRU officer, Major Zilianov, taking on Georgievich as technical watchdog, was for the Colonel, *himself*, to be watched. It hadn't escaped Georgievich's thoughts either. Myers could all but hear the click of a double dice roll against him.

Myers' looked out the window of his hotel room, down into the 'tired' little square. That was the kindest way you could describe the horror of a space that had once been a royal 'square', now rendered, by massive aerial bombardment, totally bereft of the least semblance of its former dignity from noble walls encircling an ancient Daoist temple palace. In its place, the colossal mountain of debris: stone, wood, metal, – *human bodies* - gave off its dying sigh with clouds of smoke and pulverised stone dust swirling up and around, seemingly searching for a way to go, lost in their aftermath confusion. Little flames lingered here and there, licking the overall great wound.

And to think that he could be lying down there among that sorry lot. Less than fifty minutes ago all the circumstantial building-blocks of so-called 'norm' had stood down there in their proper places; they had all now been displaced – all but one – this hotel. It had rocked violently from the outward-directed force of exploding bombs, but still held loyally to its foundations. But only just. The building had still sustained enough damage, to fear that it was possibly ready to collapse – if not immediately, *soon*. That the window had survived without as much as a teeny crack was no assurance that things were okay. Sure, some pieces of furniture, the writing desk and the wicker chair, had taken it upon themselves to walk across the room, in time with the vibrations. The bed had faithfully decided to stay put, but relinquishing two legs, so that the side dipped down on the floor.

He'd just missed being wiped out, *caput-mortuum,* by his own people. But then, that's what soldiers did, didn't they, giving up their lives in their duty of serving their country. That included the ones serving in civilian gear like himself. And he wouldn't even have got a medal or public citation for it. Only a minuscule of commemoration by way of a petit flag on that board in the CIA building.

Like panicking rats, on hearing that the dreaded vermin-exterminator was afoot, everyone was in a hurry to vacate the building. That was good, in that it meant his leaving the hotel ahead of schedule would not be viewed as suspicious, like it usually was when he was forced to make an impromptu emergency exit.

A sudden knock on the door made him jump. It was a servant, going round knocking on doors to alert people of the urgent need to get out fast as they could. Seeing Myers was in the process of literally throwing all he could lay his hands on into his battered leather Gladstone bag, the servant ran into the room to help him, looking around for things to pick up. He saw the gentleman's jacket lying in a crumpled heap on the bed. Just as he stepped over to pick it up, it slid off the sloping bed to land on the floor with loud thump that said something very heavy, like metal, was inside it.

Glancing sharply at the young guy's face to see how he'd registered with that revealing sound, Myers stepped over quickly to pick up the jacket with the 9 mm Beretta in its specially strengthened deep inside pocket. But the guy got in there before him. Trying not to look too worried, Myers put on a friendly smile and seized hold of the jacket, careful not to wrench it away in a flustered movement that would betray his anxiety. But maybe the guy had noticed, since he gave Myers a funny look.

Holding the concealed automatic in a tight grip, Myers felt around for his wallet amongst the bundled folds. But whether he was put off by the gentleman's behaviour, or fearful of the floor, and the whole building, collapsing under his feet, the young guy had turned and was gone out the door before Myers could get the money out to pay him. That was message enough for Myers. It was no hard decision to reckon that it was time to make a hasty retreat from this potential death trap of a hotel.

Checking to make sure that the safety-catch hadn't come off when it had fallen, Myers returned the automatic to his pocket, grabbed his Gladstone and left the room. That young guy had the right idea – make haste, make safe. Outside, in what, less than just an hour ago, had been an orderly setting, disorder was everywhere. People, like ants moving in on a dung feast, were crowding in from everywhere to try salvaging what they could – and what they *couldn't*, alas.

Moving away from the scene, while everyone else was moving in on it, brought a good many curious, if not suspicious, looks in Myers' direction. Maintaining his brisk pace, while holding a casual air, he kept on walking, ignoring those sharp dagger eyes on his back.

Marley Goodblood and Barrington Gilberts, along with the Secretary for Defence, McNamara, sipped their lukewarm coffee as best they could while resting for five minutes from the commotion in the war room next door. With land and water now bristling with 'primed steel', both sides were now bristling with fear of pressing the wrong buttons, and so pressed their respective computer buttons to assess and reassess the situation. If they got their sums wrong, they could end up with more scrap metal than that on the opposition's side. Either way, both sides ended up with a lot of scrap. The military-minded senators on Capitol Hill argued themselves hoarse with their points, while the pentagon experts tut-tutted and shook their heads. In between the messages, the cypher clerks shredded up the code paper like a sideline confetti business. But then you wouldn't dream of throwing confetti at a funeral. Goodblood pondered over the message that had come in from Myers, saying that he was accompanying Georgievich and Leash. The thought of Myers actively joining the active chase would normally have made Marley feel his age; instead, he felt that their different ages meant nothing where time was about to burn out in a dazzling frizzle.

While any report of Major Falzoni fell into silence, to worry an exclusive small number of heads in their operations, some field operations still surged on under their own momentum, like the frantic antics of a headless chicken still trying to put in as good a performance as Fred Astaire. This suited Goodblood, since he had a few things to try out before his last card was played out.

'It's merely a temporary setback, Mr President,' said Marley, trying to sound convincing, while playing down his own dismay. The President hadn't thrown up at this logic, but he had looked very worried. Especially now, with votes dropping like finger-scalding boiling raindrops in his already weak constituencies of Pennsylvania and Arizona. True, what had been the other chance was now the only chance. His always-to-be-heeded political 'wazir', Barrington Gilberts had not required to add any more than his customary nods and grunts to emphasise that they now desperately needed Major Falzoni to acquire that vital information. He was agreed in the wisdom of the President making generous arms concessions to Israelis, in return for their releasing of Palestinian 'nationals' held in Israel – as well as to the rogue traitor McGavin, least-deserving as he was, yet ultimately the key factor to resolving this little headache of a problem.

Goodblood looked at the general pushing the tiny tank across the large table map and reflected how he bore a faint resemblance to his late brother, Harry, who would have been about the same age now, had he not been killed in action in the Ardennes conflict. But that was as ancient as it was morbid, and about as useful as a free duodenal ulcer, with prepaid medical expenses thrown in. He shook the thought from his mind and made an effort to concentrate on what the general was saying to those around the table. In rooms all over the globe men were bent over their tables, studying their maps, pushing their tiny tanks. No need to be reminded that these weren't toy tanks lifted from Junior's Christmas box. While the Kremlin continued to wonder, the Whitehouse continued to worry and the Pentagon continued to whistle through its teeth. Russian troops were building up towards the Western borders in massive land manoeuvres, while Chinese troops shuffled towards the Vietnam border. Bolder air manoeuvres saw the giant swallow bomber cast aside its top secret cloak to fly out from its Moscow military air base on flights 'straying' further and further into Western air territory. Flying with these, in greater number, were giant Topulov TU bombers scraping the sky with their 164ft wings, like clouds of locusts gathering for a colossal gorge.

Back here in the city, swaps were taking place in less dramatic entourage, with diplomats calling on each other with the punctilious regularity of duelling seconds. But professional face meant revealing little. If embassies could admit to vermin scratching away behind the skirting boards, they could admit to the devious presence of secret service people behind the scenes. The Russian Ambassador was as friendly as he was adamant with the American diplomat, haranguing him over Russia's right to maintain vigil over the West's naval movements, at the same time carrying out its own naval exercises to guard against the invasion of Russian territorial waters. Ambassador Green listened, remembering from wise experience that sore points were often reached, not by mentioning them, but by patient noting of what was *not* said between the lines. Behind their practised waxy smiles, neither of them knew what the hell was really going on, except that their security people were scurrying about like nervous beavers plugging their dam against rising waters that signalled imminent flooding. When Green passed through the anteroom on his way out, he recognised the man speaking to the Russian naval attache as the British guy, Broaley. Outside, a man stepped over from a limousine to ask the Ambassador if he would care to wait for Broaley. When Broaley came out, he invited the American into his limousine, and they rode off, tete-a-tete, into the city's crowded lunchtime traffic.

Goodblood put the phone down and marked up yet another appointment in the afternoon in his diary. Handing the sheaf of memo notes to his secretary, Rosalyn, for typing up, he pressed the intercom, to tell the car pool to have his car ready for him in ten minutes. With pulses throbbing on the dire situation, his office was inundated with calls from the State Department. Some observers saw the East's build-up as a threatening aggression policy in Russia's new 'imperialist' expansion plan. Others saw it as pure propaganda by Washington warmongers, to widen the gap in East and West trade relations. Publicity speaking, Uncle Sam's political voice was suffering acute 'laryngitis'. *Sotto voce*, however, there was grave concern for United States allies with their defence 'balls-up'. The Secretary for Defence, urged on by the Vice President, sought out the military people. They gave their dire opinions and humped the urgency of finding their missing 'intelligence link' onto the back of the Intelligence people. Their mess – theirs to mend.

The Central Intelligence Agency was spotlighted and the finger pointed at Goodblood. Meanwhile, the Russian Embassy expressed its strong wish for a spokesman from the US State Department to attend and explain the present policies of the United States Government. Why, for instance, in flagrant violation of the peace treaty, had innocent Russian 'trawlers' been fired upon by American warplanes? Never mind that the 'trawlers' had been purloining, by electronic means from afar, from an American naval vessel stopped with engine trouble at sea. Besides, they were a 'rogue' crew, Bosnian sympathisers, commandeering a Russian vessel; not at all the responsibility of the Russian Government. A complete U-turn, perhaps? The US Embassy made similar appointments for urgent talks with the Russian Embassy. The Russian Foreign Minister was at present in deep discussion with the American Defence Secretary and the National Security Advisor. He had already dispatched a summons for the Russian Ambassador to attend for a separate talk later. Bearing in mind that all this political hotchpotch was of those with the big voices, those with the big power. But what of those who had only little voice, who had no power, except that of Allah? Goodblood hadn't forgotten that the court of enquiry into allegations of brutal treatment of a terrorist by Homeland intelligence officers was convened for tomorrow. As he hurried out the door and down the corridor, he decided to call Barrington Gilberts from a public phone booth.

22

Falzoni struggled against the tide of jungle camouflage battle fatigues pouring out of the train along the platform. Outnumbered in his civilian clothes, he edged his way with one elbow, through the contra-flowing river of soldiers, while holding on tightly to his large case lest it should be wrenched from his grasp in all the bustling. All around the same battle was going on multifold for individuals. Shoulder-born supply bags swinging about narrowly missing other bags and their bearers. Scattered about the mass uniforms, threadbare civilian clothes in their drabness reflected the sullen expressions of their weary wearers. Here and there children looked tiny and lost, as indeed they were, amidst the teeming crowd of grown-ups, their wailing cries drowned in the noise of the station's overall commotion.

A plainly distressed mother, wielding an angry fist at those in her way, anxiously sought after her own precious little one. From out of all that milling green and yellow camouflage, a tiny arm stretched out to grasp the mother's hand. That crisis, only one of many, was resolved. Nervous farewells between fighting men, about to depart for their assigned 'fronts', and their women, kisses, tears welling up everywhere. The public address system, with its unintelligible quacking announcements, would still have been unintelligible even if there had been no noise all around. Overhead, pigeons fluttered and flapped freely from girder to girder, wondering what all the fuss was about down below.

Climbing aboard the old battered coach, Falzoni found himself engaged in a new battle trying to make his way along the narrow passage, searching for a seat in a compartment. A 'million' others, alas, had the same idea, so that compartment after compartment was full as he made his way along slowly, like a contortionist, squeezing, wriggling, past others that had decided to stand, if not sit or lie in the crowded narrow passage.

Doors were slamming closed along the vibrating rattle-can structure that posed as a train. The rusty iron gate was closing, when it suddenly pulled open again in urgency, allowing an old British Ferret armoured scout car of the NPFF (Vietnam National Police Field Force) to come through and race alongside the slowly accelerating long clanking mass that 'leaked' its steam rather than spouting it proudly, as a better 'cousin' would have done. With amazing agility, two bodies came wriggling out, like maggots, from the hatch on the steel-plated hulk's hump. With amazing agility, they jumped off the vehicle to land on their feet and ran after the train, to climb on board through a door flung open for them by the guard. This they managed all in one continuous flowing action whilst still grasping their heavy M1 Garand semi-automatic battle rifles. The sidearm belt holsters moulded in a revolver outline were tiny enough to suggest that they held the standard S&W Bodyguard .38 Special snub-nosed pistols.

The NPFF reminded you of the former German *Wehrmacht's Feldgendarmerie* (military police), highly trained in intelligence gathering and counter-insurgency, counter-terrorism tactics. While the German unit had functioned as an extended ancillary arm of the country's main military force, these National Police Field Force super-cops co-operated closely with the Army of the Republic of Vietnam, (ARVN) and also worked in conjunction with the United States Indo-Pacific Command, along with its discreet regional CIA contingent.

This was giving Falzoni mixed feelings. Even although they were potentially allies, he wasn't sure about the wisdom of letting them rescue him by putting him in immediate touch with the CIA lot. That would only serve to highlight his presence here, where he shouldn't be, on his covert mission, as word eventually leaked out, as it always did. That would also, in its turn, spell big trouble for Georgievich, revealing how he'd played a traitor's double-hand by deviously engineering the American spy's escape. That, along with the whole McGavin sabotage plan blown sky high. Knowing that, zealous loyalist GRU officer Major Zilianov would waste no time in having the firing squad line up, priming their rifles and aim, waiting for his order to fire.

Preoccupied with these thoughts addling his mind, Frank pretended to search through his pockets for the ticket that he didn't have, when he saw the ticket inspector slowly drawing nearer along the passage, stopping every few seconds to make his checks. At last the inspector stood before him, staring him straight in the face as he held out his hand for a ticket. Not wanting to draw undue attention to himself with this little breach of rules causing the verbal commotion it was likely to, Frank put on what he hoped was a disarming smile, while his brain raced for an answer that would get him out of this awkward spot.

'Here, Frank, you've dropped your ticket. Bloody hell, you're always dropping things!' The totally unexpected utterance came from behind him, in its sharp unmistakably English accent.

Turning round to retrieve *his* ticket, Frank's eyebrows jumped a fraction on seeing the new face. MI6 agent, Lieutenant George Broaley. He'd last worked with Broaley in Berlin, ferreting out vital intelligence from the East sector and through to the West sector, under the nose of the Stasi regime rigid security surveillance measures. 'Thanks, George; I owe you one. Drinks are on me'

'That's what you always say, Frank, but it still always ends up that I'm the one who digs deep in the pockets to pay for them.'

'That's the price of a true friend.'

With the ticket inspector satisfied and gone, Falzoni leaned in closer to Broaley to speak in lowered voice: 'What the hell are you doing here, Broaley, popping up like the rabbit out of the magician's hat?

'My *apologies* if you're not happy to see me, Major, but considering the acuteness of circumstances, I'm the best measure of assistance that your associate, Myers, could come up with, given the limited window of opportunity that he had to work with, in limited time, in the area.'

'Oh, I'm happy to see you, sure enough; not so sure, though, about having to listen to your cocky answers, Broaley'

'Another of Myers' tricks whisked out of the magic hat for you.' Lieutenant Broaley handed Major Falzoni his new ID papers.

'Hmm,' murmured Falzoni, looking at the mug-shot hastily conjured up by 'magician' Myers. 'He makes me look older.' He inspected the identity section. 'A new day in the life of *Frank Day*. Well, that should put the hounds off scent for a little while, if there's any still sniffing around.' He put the papers away in his pocket.

'*And* --- of LEASH, Frank? The 'magician' never exactly filled me in any on that.'

' "Only what you need to know", ' quoted Frank.'

'Of course. Understood.'

'Although, to be honest, I'm not much in front of you with knowledge on that little issue. We both agreed it to be the best strategy to travel separately after making our exit from the Red Dragon's country-camp lair.' They were both allowed a discreet little smile at the coded language. Probably unnecessary, where there was little likelihood of anyone around them understanding English – but you never can be too sure. 'Alas, He won't be able to stall for long in his own Red lair when it comes to the surface that he was instrumental in helping an American to push through a devious Capitalist plot highly damaging to Soviet State plans and those of her Chinese Communist allies. Enough time, maybe, to grab whatever classified material he can, before making that necessary final exit.'

'You don't sound as if you think he'll manage to do that.'

'I can't say the odds are greatly in favour of it. If he doesn't, it'll be a great loss.' The Major paused for a moment's long thought. 'But it'll be the lesser of *two* losses, nevertheless, if I can't succeed in getting McGavin to throw himself in with our 'business proposal.'

'I won't ask what that is.'

'Good boy.'

Frank tapped his jacket over the pocket where he'd stowed the papers. 'I'm relying on this lot to get me back to McGavin without turning too many heads in my direction.' He looked down at his still too conspicuous, once-pristine white, safari suit, now marked and rumpled as it was. 'The smell won't be noticed in these parts, but the style would. A change of gear would be an asset.'

'And I won't remind you how your tradecraft training instructs you to remedy that situation.'

'That's right, Lieutenant, you *wont.*'

When the Ha Noi to Dong Dang train stopped halfway along its north easterly route at Kep, those two NPFF officers alighted, somewhat perplexed, onto the platform of barely set rough-cast concrete. They had other things bothering them without having to worry about messing up their regulation issue boots. With no photo or facial description details to help them, they had only the name to go by. Thanks to Myers' deliberately wiry scribbling, the letters y and a of Day could be misread as an i and an o so allowing the English Day to possibly look like the Asian Doi. With the absence of limbs being a common feature in this war-torn country, empty flapping sleeves drew no undue attention — not even *that* one where the peasant's ao dai jacket had a pungent aroma of manure and the man's face was partly obscured by his conical rice farmer's hat; both these items costing Frank almost half of Myers' envelope of Vietnamese dong notes that Broaley had handed him. Never mind those: "Friends, Romans, Countrymen, lending an ear", these two peasant guys had seized the money, only after much haggling, with a voracity that plainly said, plebian as they were, they could still manage to lend a *deaf* ear to Karl Marx.

23

The old wrinkle-faced taxi driver was getting her twenty-four passengers out of her tricycle rickshaw in great haste, in her eagerness to take on the custom of the Western man who was beckoning her; and hopefully for a bountiful overpayment for her service, as typically happened with the naïve Western traveller. Unloading her four wooden crates of clucking chickens down beside the vendor sitting cross-legged beside the brazier, with its spit turning another doomed bird over in the flames, she took payment with one hand from the man, whilst tugging Sheldon Myers' sleeve with her other hand, to usher him into her proud yellow-painted taxi.

A frantic farewell of wildly flapping wings, the wind disturbance flapping the woman's black silken suit trouser legs, and she was up in the tricycle seat, and pedalling the rickshaw off on another cross-town dollar-stacking trip.

The taxi's meter ticked away as they headed eastwards, dodging and swerving around bomb holes and rubble all the while. Myers looked out on both sides as they sped along. Desolation from bombing seemed to increase as they headed further east. Finally, they had to stop where the road was blocked, not so much by bricks strewn across the road, as by houses strewn across the road. They had been blown outwards, the bombing effect being so intense. The driver didn't much fancy having to negotiate a way round the blockage by going down a side street, since the damage seemed to be just as bad there. The best thing for it seemed to be to go further on foot. The local rescue and repair guys were already doing their bit, he could see, with heads bobbing up here and there among the colossal wreckage, going about their rescue work.

The driver turned to Myers. 'It is only another street or so past this one – or what is left of it – if it is still there. I will let you off here and you can go round down that side street there.' She pointed. 'That way there, sir. It is only a small number of minutes away, sir.'

Myers payed the fare.

'My much thank you, sir.'

Myers got out and stood for a moment to watch the rickshaw manoeuvre back with difficulty around piles of rubble, as well as entanglements of hosepipes, and then going round the way it had come. He turned and started to step, and where necessary, climb, over and around the mass of broken stone, metal and bamboo, to make his way to where his intended address was supposed to be. He passed a man standing crying and wailing, who was looking down at two shapes shrouded by dirty blankets at his feet. One of the shapes was barely two feet long. A small straw doll protruded partly from beneath the blanket, still gripped beyond death by an infantile hand. With barely the courage to glance quickly at it and away, Myers thought how easily our Top Brass planners could get away with classifying that as 'collateral damage'.

He at last spotted what he thought looked like the place he was seeking. The loose-hanging rope snaking through a hole in the bamboo door-jamb to what he imagined would be a bell somewhere inside, did not seem to be doing its assigned duty --- not after umpteen tugs and nothing happening. Only after half a dozen heavy knocks, and exasperating waiting in between, did the door open cautiously several inches. The suspicious face looking out seemed as narrow as the space it was peering through. The puzzled expression was there, but the man didn't say anything.

Neither did Myers; he left the talking to George Washington, poking his white-wigged head out of the fat envelope packed tightly with more of those national figureheads.

The man stepped back, opening the door wide enough for Myers to pass through, but not wide enough for unwanted onlookers to see inside the premises. Not that they could much beyond the beaded curtain hanging immediately behind the front door. He looked at the plaster on the Western gentleman's throat. 'Does it hurt?'

'Hmm,' was Myers' nodded answer.

The man, owner of the To Jo guest house, was taller than Myers and very fat, with wire-rim glasses perched on the broad bridge of his nose. Chinese dragons twisted on the wide sleeves of the loose flowing gown that were rolled up to reveal more diminutive dragons tattooed on the yellowish sweating arms, down to the massive wrists.

There wasn't much ardour in polishing furniture, it seemed, with all the brick dust that was forever around after bombing raids. The place wasn't exactly officially classified by CIA as a definite safe house, but as far as intelligence had it, the man's ideologies, mixed as they were, leaned more in our direction than the other way. Especially where money figured in it. So it served as a relatively safe 'stopping off station'.

Myers stood there listening to the man rattling on about house rules and other guests in the house. A perfunctory glance took in the shadowy, peculiarly secretive, private atmosphere of the place, with its bamboo and paper walls, leading off into dark corners and passages. Somewhere, above it seemed, the faint monotone droning of a voice suggested to Myers that someone was by-passing Mao Tse Tung for an even greater god. He understood as he listened on to his host, that he was sharing the place with four other individuals. 'Breakfast served at gong of morning seventh hour. If you go out before that, or come down later than that, you forfeit privilege of consuming warm soup and bread. Only one rationed bowl of water to be used for washing. No fires in honourable house -- uses up too much firewood.'

Myers listened on, all the while holding on to his case. His only sign of impatience was his checking the time on his watch. The man noticed this, and drew himself up for his last piece. 'How long you stay?

'Let's say three days.' Myers paused to think. 'Maybe --- we'll see; depends.'

'You no have sure?'

'Let's just leave it at that – three days – for the time being, anyway,' came Myers' lingering, slightly unsure, reply. Not knowing exactly where Major Falzoni was at the moment, or how he was managing to get to the rendezvous they'd agreed upon earlier, time was not a specific commodity. That meant going back and forward, checking and re-checking to see if Falzoni had turned up at the meeting place. And that had to be done without drawing attention.

'You have business?' The man was about to enquire further, but left the question hanging when he saw the Western gentleman's hand removing a wad of notes from the envelope. It was a very fat wad, and the notes were new and crisp. With all that money, the gentleman was welcome to stay as many days, *weeks*, as he wished. He looked down at Myers' tight grip on that heavy-looking case.

That and all the cash he handled easily enough. The man's got to be a dealer, he surmised. Dealing on the black market. This idea pleased him. With all this official constraint on movement, food and goods on the whole, were hard to come by. So, it would not be a bad thing to have someone in the house who knew how and where to get those 'extras' for a good price. Besides, going by the look in Myers' eyes, and knowing dealers for what they are and how they react when caught in a corner, the man could well have a sharp blade up his sleeve. So, no arguing there. 'As you wish, sir,' he said. 'Three days, as you say.'

The money no sooner had appeared in Myers' hand, than it disappeared beneath the other man's robe. 'I shall show you to your room. It is at the top of the house.'

Next to the sky would have been a more accurate description, with bamboo beams and straw teeming with crawling insects' beady eyes looking down at you serving as ceiling. The room itself was no surprise to Myers, considering what he'd seen of the downstairs layout, quiet, with a spartan plainness. With some holy water, instead of ordinary water, in the ceramic bowl mounted on a metal tripod, it would have done as a monk's cell. He looked around at the sparse furnishing. A low short bed with tired-looking blankets; a stool and a small bedside cabinet that was a former tea-chest with a hinged lid standing on its side. There didn't seem to be a wardrobe or any place to put clothes; not that many of those using the place for their 'short nights' would have much beyond what they had on their backs, to worry about storage space. He pulled on a knob on the wall and the bent hardboard door, warped with dampness, opened out to reveal a shallow recess that was the wardrobe.

'Right,' said Myers, turning round to face the landlord squarely. He gave another significant check of the time on his watch.

The man got the message, moving away towards the door. 'My name is Muchu. And *your* name?' How am I to call you – for communication strictly between us? The eyebrows on the thin face jumped up to carry the question.

'How does Kemosabe grab you? Will *that* do?' Myers always liked to get a cheeky bit in somewhere.

Two dark Eurasian eyes, behind glinting pebble lenses, held their searching scrutiny of the two Caucasian eyes, to allow for a few moments thought. Finally: 'Yes, Kemosabe, I think *that* is satisfactory'

Muchu went to the door and then turned suddenly. 'Ah, yes, one more mention; no pleasure happy ladies allowed in the rooms. Can mean much trouble with curfew police patrol inspection.'

'*Hookers?*' replied Myers, smiling, his first smile of the day. 'Understood.'

With Muchu gone, and the door closed, Myers took off his jacket and threw it on the bed. He sat down on the stool. Getting up again, he went over to the door, listened for a moment, then locked it securely. He then started to pull off the plaster with its underlying thick pad of iodine-stained lint at his throat. It had been irritating him for days. When it finally came off, the iodine stain was still there on his throat. But there was no wound or injury of any kind. Not a single scratch on the skin. Another smart dodge put to him by those clever instructors at Langley.

The purpose of the plaster, implying a wound, was to give people who saw it a false reason for him speaking in a difficult unclear voice. This way no-one would ever detect or believe that his accent was American –

that was absolute taboo in this belligerently anti-American land. It was a hard fact that all too often field agents, well trained in their specialised subjects, were uncovered on account of their accents or misuse of their adopted tongue's idiom. Thus, under his guise of a throat injury, he could speak in short, broken, not necessarily grammatically correct sentences, if needs be, and nobody would suspect a thing.

He went over to his case to open it. Taking out the top layer of clothing, he put it on the bed. What was now showing was a high-powered field transmitter. He looked at his watch. It wasn't time yet.

Messages in code were to be sent only at set times. Still forty-seven minutes to go. But he could get ready in the meantime. Taking out the long coil that was the aerial, he stretched it out towards the window. There was another long coil, the power lead; but he could see no electrical connection point anywhere. If there had been, and if he'd transmitted using that power, there was the chance that the impulses could be detected. Being extra safe meant using the transmitter's built-in field generator by means of the crank- handle lever. Forty-four minutes to go.

With nothing else to do but wait, he sat down on the stool again. Looking at the plaster and lint over on the bed, he shook his head, thankful that no medically-minded do-gooder had not wanted to have a look at his 'wound' with an offer to take him to a doctor. That would have shown the doctor a right laugh of a miracle, no kidding.

Myers checked the time again. After he'd sent his message and taken fresh orders from Langley, he'd try to get some sleep. He wondered if his plan of bringing Falzoni all the way up here, far away from McGavin's place, was a wise move. But it was. It was to get his 'hounds' to lose the scent, by his lying low, and consider him gone. Proper plans could then be considered for Falzoni returning, incognito, to the south, to secure that vital information from McGavin and after that hatch a golden egg of a round-about route for returning to the States. And after that, as if that wasn't enough, there was still Georgievich's predicament to mull over and grill those little old brain cells. With that turning in his mind, and by the look of that rough bed, he wondered if sleep was a bit of a futile hope. He had a faint fear that expecting Falzoni to be at the arranged rendezvous on time would be even more futile.

24

The cold night breeze sent the tin can rattling along in an unsure meandering path rolling in and out of the gutter. Stopping and starting again, its erratic clinking cut the night's silence to carry Falzoni's mind back to a time of his responsibility of a different kind; as when he had helped in his grand-father's farm outhouse workshop, amidst the satisfying sound of tools impinging on shining steel ploughing implements, if not on great horseshoes, gigantic to him as a small kid. Hammered and honed like those blades of the valiant *Cavaliere di Corredo*, (Italian medieval knights). As would his grand-father forever intone to encourage him in his craft as well as the country's glorious folklore. That was long before Jerry, the British and the Americans got huffy enough to start planting 'seeds' of a harsh new 1020lbs exploding kind in the beautiful Italian landscape's fertile soil. Only two sections of the storeroom behind the workshop had survived the bombings. And that number was two more than any of his livestock had survived.

There was no time for dwelling on old memories in this work, especially in his present situation Emotions had to be restrained in their lateral wanderings, to be directed forward as a sharpened point that would pierce the enemy's armour.

Frank couldn't allow personal feelings to come between him and what was needed to see this mission through successfully. And Washington was pulling its hair out in its anxiety for him to send in a report of mission accomplished. Strict discipline decreed that all his mental energy should be channelled into the fulfilment of his mission. His failure to bring home a nice fat 'bone' of completion would perhaps not see him put before a firing squad, but he would certainly be in the 'doghouse', fair and square, which meant not being invited by Marley to any more of Edwina's cultural soirees.

On foot, Frank was doing his travelling at night, in order to keep a low profile, rather than using a taxi, or taking a bus. It didn't matter that public buses offered some cover from their crowded capacity, now that he had been 'rumbled', or would be shortly, he considered using the public transport system, what was left of it, to be too much of a risk.

Moving on from his last safe house to the next one along the line would have been an easy shift for him, except that Sheldon Myers' intelligence operations were falling foul from intervention by local Viet forces failing to snare him by only minutes. With militia and security teams across the city alerted to his situation, he was forced to lie low during daylight hours.

Hour upon hour of hiding among ruins of a partly bombed buildings had been worrying as he listened to the voices of men searching among rubble with its unique smell, like a vile signature print, of grim mortality buried beneath; as if it was at all needed to remind you of the wicked deed. He couldn't tell if they were looking for him. Even if they were looking for casualties who had miraculously survived the bombing, how would they react if they came across him? According to emergency plans, when darkness came he was required to go to an agreed point where he would be picked up on the hour, over three hours, and taken to the next safe house. He hadn't been able to be there on the hour any of the three consecutive times, so his 'collector' hadn't been able to hang around for fear arousing suspicion. Instead, he had resorted to the secondary measure of leaving directions in a previously agreed dead-letter box.

Frank had walked many miles as a boy, delivering and collecting for the family business, and then for his toughening-up training at Summer Camp, and later with the Boy Scouts Rangers Movement. All this walking conveniently kept his body fit for the action that would come after his graduating from college and enlisting in the Army at the unfolding of this new war.

Taxi drivers had ears and eyes for recalling their passengers, and their passengers' dropping-off points. In compromise, Frank had let himself be dropped off a good ten minutes walking distance from where he would set off again in a long deliberately misleading circuitous trek to the intended meeting place. At least, what he hoped would be a meeting place. This way, the taxi driver didn't know the exact address his passenger was seeking and so could not be of any help to the police or intelligence people.

The night was cool after what had been a very warm day; but Frank could barely suppress a cynical smile at the puniness of what the naïve traveller would call warm weather, compared to those sunrays burning his semi-naked body as he dug trenches in the hard-baked earth of African battle-fields.

Turning into what seemed to be the right place, from what he could recall of his briefings' details, he stopped to look around. An empty, motionless place. Nothing special that could really be put together as 'details'. That old Ford lorry over there with its back piled high with what looked like in the dark as over-spilling sacks of vegetables. Nothing else. Nothing. No flashing lights, as you would see in that exciting movie. Hell, no such luck. His hopes began to fall.

As he swivelled round slowing, scanning the place, a movement caught his attention in the corner of his eye. Was he mistaken, or had he picked up a quick movement at the lorry's front? He stared at it. Again, a disappointing stillness.

And then the windscreen wipers jerked left to right, once, twice, and then stopped. A few seconds pause, and then the motion was repeated, once, twice, and then stopped.

Frank ambled slowly over the vehicle. No longer having his Colt automatic, he now held a piece of long sharp-pointed stick down by his side. If he was going to be put down by a cruel bullet, he would damn well try and be quick enough to take someone with him on that final single journey.

A shapeless black smudge behind glass was replaced by a thickly bearded mass that the darkness allowed to be called a face, as the window slid down slowly with a shrill squeak.

'Are you looking for a vehicle?' The words came out carefully from the white patch snatching a momentary place amidst the great black hirsute mass. 'Is this the vehicle you are perhaps looking for?'

It didn't quite sound like an Asian voice to Frank. French, maybe? 'Only if it is the vehicle I am *not* looking for,' replied Frank, nervously completing the coded exchange, with the forever present fear of walking into a cleverly sprung trap.

'All right, 'Genghis Khan', jump in quick, so we can head off. It's a tight squeeze, but it's that, or a cold ride in the back with the soya beans.' Frank recognised the voice coming from deeper inside the cabin as that of Sheldon Myers.

Frank climbed up and got in. Before he'd even closed the door, the dense darkness of the place shifted, as a large section of it slid away on four wheels, leaving the rest of it behind with its shrouded secrets of the night.

Two enormous doors running on iron rails, at the front of McGavin's building, awaited Falzoni's strength. But the effort was not required. Just as he was reaching for it, the right door pulled open with a roar of wheels on rail. 'Watch out!' came the warning a second after it was needed, the great steel bar just missing Frank's face by a hair's breadth. Held in the hand that was pulling the door open from within, it had caught Frank's eye just in time for him to jerk his head back.

There was no sign of the girl, but machinery was humming away somewhere in the workshop. Frank looked around checking for her.

'It's all right, we can get some peace to talk downstairs.' McGavin's remark puzzled Frank, as they were on the ground and he saw no staircase. Until McGavin leaned against and started pushing a massive squat metal unit topped by a glistening steel lathe until it started to slide slowly back along its rails. A dirty greasy black trapdoor fringed at its edges with curly metal shavings.

Coming down into the dimly lit cellar, carefully watching where to put his feet on the narrow wooden stairs, Frank could have done with a second warning which, alas, he didn't get. Too late, he didn't notice the gnarled oak beam until his head gave it a resounding thump. Stepping down onto the stone-flagged floor, he was not spared the inches to allow him to stand upright, having to stand with a stooped back, to avoid banging his head yet again, this time on the low ceiling.

'Yeah, I know, it's a bit cramped,' said McGavin. 'You can't deny they certainly are short of inches in this country. But hold on, maybe we can do something about that.' Putting his arms around a fat steel-ribbed wooden crate stamped with bright red Chinese markings, he lifted it, with grunting effort, off its stout bench, to stagger round under the weight and place it down on the ground. Looking round at Falzoni, he held out a hand, inviting him to sit on the now vacated bench.

Frank sat down. Not a moment too soon. Being bent down like that reminded you only too well of all the crouching he had done in those mud-filled battlefield dugouts way back then in his days with the 2nd Armoured Division. It was also better than ending up pre-empting chronic sciatica problems. Removing the empty oil cans from a smaller wooden box, McGavin stood the box on its end and sat himself down on it. 'There, I think that's a little better.' He looked up at the ceiling. 'Yeah, these people are generally much shorter than us, that goes without saying. Yeah, I reckon this space down here would have been where the 'dung-shovellers' would have lived, with the land owner boss occupying the bigger space upstairs.'

Frank looked around the shadowy subterranean surroundings, taking in the atmosphere. Primitive was the word that came to mind. With uneven very roughly hewn rock walls that had shiny rivulets of dampness trickling down them, this was plain enough. He rubbed his head where it was still sore. And with that ever so low ceiling, with its damned beams pressing down on you, perhaps *furtive* was more fitting.

McGavin watched Falzoni, still known to him as 'Porter', inspecting the cellar, smiling and just managing to hold back his laughter at the other's annoyance at hurting his head. 'I'd much have preferred for us to meet in my office,' he said, 'but with the recent step-up of ID inspections by militia in public places, this is safer. You're lucky to get away with them accepting that your own skin is not counterfeit.' Although with the anti-American situation scourging the country as it did, that was not so much a joke as it sounded. He had not intended sounding racist in the least, seeing the connection only as an afterthought. But he wondered if the CIA guy, or whatever he was, sitting facing him, had read his thoughts from the remark. It was hinted, if not actually said, as much as it went round, that these guys were trained to do this, using body-language techniques. To think that he'd actually tried to join them at one time. The bastards had turned down his application. And now they were begging for his help. In that view he was tempted to tell them to shove it; but two million was a great softener, for sure.

He fidgeted with a splinter on the box end for a moment, to slip under what he imagined was Porter's mental radar homing in on his mind. From the way Porter was acting, McGavin had instantly sensed that the guy's visit would be something more than the basic planning of operations, followed by a casual whisky or two. Far more. And he was right. So he had chosen this place for its secrecy to match the urgency. Porter had not kept him waiting either, arriving as he did, just short of helping him lift the heavy steel plate concealing the cellar entrance.

Searching in his pockets, McGavin brought out his blatantly Communist yellow and red packet of 'Stalin-brand' Xiaangtan Zynong Chinese cigarettes. A steady running supply of them at no cost was one of the perks allotted to McGavin for being the Vietcong lot's 'engine man'. He held them out to Porter.

Frank shook his head at the offer.

Shrugging his shoulders, McGavin put one to his mouth and lit it. He took a long draw to get the first taste that morning, then blowing out slowly, used the time to gather his thoughts while looking the other guy over. Whilst it was true that his work in this, as yet, still foreign land, took in a myriad of weird characters and customs, McGavin nevertheless had been sparked with curiosity when first informed that this American business man wanted to have a meeting with him. Again, incoming snippets of 'rumour', rather than 'solid information', had proved useful here in their interpretation if casual innuendoes were anything to go by. It seemed to be the natural native Asian trait to be tight-lipped and refrain from letting slip anything that could prove to be personally harmful in their small talk. A well-greased tongue seemed to be the mark of the Westerner. Apparently, the guy worked freelance in his dealings, totally irrespective of national boundaries across the globe. That fact, if it was true, had been worth a thought or two to McGavin in his anticipation of the guy turning up.

McGavin blew out more smoke slowly as he turned this aspect over in his mind. For *that* particular point, he didn't care if Porter *was* reading into his thoughts. He noted that for the normal white-collared entrepreneur that Porter had pretended to be on his first arrival, the man carried himself with an active outgoing image, with the stature that spoke of relatively good health and *something more*. Quite the man of contrasting parts.

McGavin had to blow out a tobacco flake before speaking. 'I got the impression from your phone message, that you were anxious to see me.'

'You'll recall that when we last spoke, the subject of confidential concern was one that could be of benefit to both of us and others all round in a big way.'

That of skipping my cosy spot in this country that's so far adopted me without a single bark? Yeah, I remember. The possibility of that has been on my mind a lot since then.'

'Alas, we're now at the point of no return that goes beyond simply sitting back and thinking things over,' said Frank gravely, leaning across with a sheet of paper in his hand for McGavin to take.

'Oh, yeah, how's that?'

'See for yourself.'

McGavin tried not to sound too much like being one step behind in this new development. 'What exactly am I looking at? I recognise these co-ordinates and what looks like operation times; but I'm not recognising these names – no, never heard of them before --- hold on --- this location --- that's where I operated from some years ago, before moving to a better place – *here*, in fact. And what's this cell BEAVER?' McGavin looked up at Falzoni. 'I get the funny feeling that this –' he held the paper up, flapping it in demonstration '-- is somehow meant to involve me – dragging me into something I'm feeling I'm not going to like the sound of.'

Frank tapped the paper, pointing with his forefinger 'See here – these last three bombing missions; specially encrypted material directing the flights specifically along precise routes so as to enable them to reach and bomb the enemy targets. The only one who could have known of those particular secret underground tunnel locations and passed it on to the enemy is holding these details in his hand.'

'Are you saying that I'm spying for the enemy – spying for the United States?'

'You've got it,' said Frank, his searching eyes not breaking their unsettling hold on McGavin.

McGavin let out a nervous cough. 'But, hell, I know nothing of this operational data – I've never seen the fucking stuff before! My name's not here, and yet you're pointing me out as the guilty party. I suppose the same applies to you, Porter, or whatever your name really is; your name's not here either, and yet I'll bet you knew all about these damn bombing missions, for sure!

'Granted. I hold my hand up to plead guilty to that; yeah, I'm a good old paid-for-it spook; but at least I know how many stars are on *my* flag. You've only got one on yours. And how long before that gets rubbed out, I wonder?'

'This is a damn bloody frame-up! I'm being set up by your dirty lot!

'Sure thing, you've got that right, pal. Just look at that signature at the bottom. That's the big Brass Hat, with command over all the other Brass Hats, who decides whose house is going to be blown down, like the Big Bad Wolf he is.'

'Have I got this right – am I to understand this to be the penalty for my running out on dear old Uncle Sam all that time ago? You can't stand the idea of me having done well for myself and settled in comfortably here. You want me to double-cross these people after all they've done for me?

Frank sat back abruptly, shaking his head and slapping his knee. 'Are you really that thick, McGavin? Can you really not see that you're tolerated by these people only in so far as you continue to be useful to them. After that ---' Frank drew a finger across his throat. 'And that may come sooner than you think.'

'What's that supposed to mean?'

'Even if your chop-stick pals here are slow to tumble to the game, how do you think Moscow is going to react to knowing there's a rodent gnawing away at their plans for a glorious expansion programme with their Chinese and Vietnamese comrades?' Again, Frank tapped the paper in McGavin's hand. 'When a copy of this *accidentally* falls into the hands of our Lubyanka 'pals' in Moscow, they'll be quick to dispatch one of their specialist 'rodent exterminators' to remove the pestilent factor.' A different line of thought bit at Frank's mind as he thought of another rodent soon to be hunted – Georgievich. With their informing the Russians that McGavin was a saboteur undermining their plans, they were automatically implicating Georgievich as a traitor by way of his covering up for McGavin with his reassurance of testimony that the business transaction documents were genuine, and not forgeries. That was the other side of this game that Frank had to get back to; he needed to get the Colonel out of the trap closing in on him, before it snapped shut.

McGavin felt Frank's distraction giving him a possible means of eluding the other's scrutiny. He picked away at another stray tobacco flake on his lip as spirits gathered momentum in his bid to find and pick a chink in Frank's argument, if not, personal armour.

Frank caught the other's mounting thought of resistance coming his way. 'Don't fight this. You won't find a way out of this mess, the way things are developing. I'm on your side. Like I said before – I'm here to help you.'

'Who mouthed off that phrase first – you or the parrot? It could mean a lot of things – going in a lot of different directions, good and bad' McGavin wasn't going to give up on the point that easily, now that he felt that the stalling time it was giving him could possibly be useful as a lever. 'I'm only interested in the good ones.'

'That goes for me as well. We're both only interested in the good directions.'

'So tell me where this is going. You haven't come here just to gloat and warn me of the noose that you claim is going to be put round my neck for sins I haven't committed.'

'That's right, I haven't.'

'So bloody well get on with it! Fill me in.'

'What I originally promised you – big money; *big, big,* money. And a way out of all this.'

'Pending on the condition that I give you the location co-ordinates of the tunnel layout. *Right?*'

'Right.'

'I can only come up with details on those that I've serviced so far. And from what I've learned of the system, that's only about a third – no – more like – oh, a little bit less than that. You find that it's usually always the ones that keep on breaking down and needing repairing, that go on breaking down, again and again. And before you comment on that, I can't work miracles on run-down machinery that's one stuttering rev away from the scrap heap. It's a boon when supplies from China get through the US naval embargo. You sure had me there, with your offer of a fresh business deal when you first came on the scene. I was ---'

'All right, all right, leave it there. I've heard all I need to hear on that point.' Frank stood up, breathing out a noisy expression of frustration mingled with relief. At least that matter, however much not what he had wanted to hear, was behind them now, settled once and for all in its cold clear certainty. 'Next move is to get out of here and away with what little we *have* got.' He looked round critically at McGavin. 'Have you got those co-ordinate details ready on hand?'

'Upstairs, in the order book.'

'Not in a safe?'

A broad mocking smile brightened up McGavin's up until now dismal look. 'No need for secrets here. I'll leave that sort of thing to you. I'm not a spook, remember?'

'So let's get on with it.' A jerk of the head, signalling McGavin to get up.

Getting up, McGavin made for the steps, then stopped on hearing sounds from above. A female voice, the girl's, by the sound of it. This was followed by the sharp stentorian bark of a male voice cutting the air with its command. An impromptu inspection by Police or 'Cong' militia.

Frank looked up at what was going on above them, and back at McGavin. He searched the man's face with probing concern for a sign of nervous alarm breaking out. He had been rearmed with a 9mm automatic by Myers, but this was not the right time for violent confrontation and leaving tell-tale dead bodies lying around to betray their presence in the area. Seeing McGavin reaching out for a heavy gear cog wheel for a weapon, Frank tapped the man's arm, and waved his forefinger to stop him.

With only their silence pulsing away between them as they waited, they stared long and hard up at the trapdoor.

25

Cobblestones on their own are awkward to walk on; wet with rain, and they are a bother; but cobblestones wet from rain and on a steep slope, and they constituted an absolute hell. And it had been raining. So Colonel Georgievich cursed quietly to himself as he wobbled and slipped on the unkind surface of this street that wanted to dive, rather than lead, as other decent streets did, down into the hilly district on the outskirts of Moskva (Moscow). Why did all these towns have to be built on slopes, he moaned to himself. All right, so his grandmama's place was also on a hill, but you got up and down the hill by way of a dirt track, not wretched cobblestones. The only bother there was that you had to avoid stepping on dung in the dark.

He would have come down into the town by an easier way, if he'd been able to borrow a car from someone. But it seemed that he was busy with whispers of security surveillance checks. So baring this in mind, he'd risked taking a bus that went along the mountain road, to be dropped off above the quiet outlying district. His irritation was balanced with a faint humour of what old Narena would have made of his new habit of swearing that he'd developed. But then he had learned of late, how to do a lot of other far more nasty things in his involvement with that American who, in manner of the chameleon, forever changed from name to name, the last one, as far as he knew, being 'Porter'. Now he was on an assignment that could see him arrested and shot, if things went wrong. And that was also because of Porter.

What would his dear old *babushka*, Narena, think of her cherished grandson now, if she had been able to see what he was involved in, colluding with America; she would have seen it as betraying his country. Never mind that her country had betrayed *her*. Tradition can be blinding in its bloodline hold through generations. *Dedushka* Ivan would have only stopped short of having him whipped, instead, ordering him to leave in exile from his beloved land, to join his new compatriots far across the great waters. Well, grandad, that's what I'm trying to do now.

As he made his unsteady way down the treacherous incline, something odd caught his attention in a house window. It couldn't be – but it was. What he had mistook to be an ornamental piece had shown itself to be alive with its jerking head movements. A live proud chest-puffing cockerel no less, with jerking bright red comb, standing on the steering-wheel of the black Zhigulis saloon parked half on, half off, the pavement. With food being scarce as it was, hoarding livestock in one's car did not unduly imbibe the eye with surprise. Georgievich went over to the window for a closer look at the bird as it lifted a leg in majestic slow motion.

Hinges moaned out their agony aloud as the official-looking door, badly in need of paint, beside Georgievich opened. A surly face poked out round the door jamb, followed slowly by the rest of a large body in dirty open-collared *Politsiya* tunic with acute button shortage. At least the hip holster, with its Marakov pistol, *was* buckled closed. The hard face lines wrestled themselves into a more amiable expression for greeting and for doing possible business. 'The good Comrade would perhaps be looking for information – for *food*?

Knowing the severity of food shortage and its strain on drastically low wages, Georgievich realised that this was not as outlandish a remark as it sounded. It also meant that in these circumstances, the price of the bird would be steep. The man was only a sergeant, but Georgievich didn't pull rank on him, now dressed in civilian clothes as he was, not wanting to reveal his identity to a policeman if he could help it. 'No, thank you,' said Georgievich brusquely, stepping aside to be on his way.

But the man stepped in front of him, blocking his path. 'Comrade does not think my cockerel is of good quality? He insults me and my cockerel, implying it is not of prize stock?' There was unmistakable hostility rising in the man's voice.

Georgievich wanted only to be cordial and not cause a street scene in a silly argument over a damn bloody cockerel that could possibly lead to something more serious. At all costs, he had to keep a low profile and not become tangled with municipal authorities who would pass him down the line to a locally stationed GRU unit.

The policeman wasn't giving up, changing tactics. 'Perhaps you would wish to hire my car, maybe?' He looked over at the Zhigulis and then back at Georgievich. Giving a wry smile, he held out his hand, rubbing the thumb against the forefinger in sign of payment. '*Yes?*'

True, a car would be very helpful, but a policeman's vehicle would be easy to trace if word went out of it going missing, as it would, if he took it. 'Is that possible? Isn't it a breach of regulations, hiring out an official vehicle to a civilian?'

'As the district's sole representative of the Law, rules are as I see fit. Here, in the suburb, away from the city centre, we have to mend our locks and cut our keys ourselves, and I always like to make sure that I have a spare key in my back pocket.'

'I'm sorry, Comrade Sergeant, but I do not have any money.' Hopefully that would quell the bugger's persistence and let him be on his way.

But the man gave a grunt of disbelief, reaching out to take a hold of Georgievich's jacket sleeve. He rubbed the sleeve slowly with his thumb, feeling its rich fibre. 'For someone who has no money, the Comrade is dressed well.'

Georgievich's wits raced to beat this. '*On me*, I mean,' he replied with a playful smile, tapping his pockets to show what he meant. 'I don't have any money *on me*, Comrade.'

This seemed to bring a lighter gleam into the man's eyes. It also caused the grip on Georgievich's sleeve to tighten. There was no hiding of the animal pleasure showing in the man's unshaven face as he openly inspected Georgievich from head to foot, and then up again, savouring the goods. A good catch. 'Comrade can always pay another way and not worry about money.' The dark eyes came in closer to Georgievich with their horrible leer.

His mind being otherwise frantically engaged, it was only now, at this closeness, that Georgievich noticed the disgusting smell of woman's perfume on the man.

Georgievich ran his mind over the tricks of the trade that Porter had shown him in hurried rough lessons of unarmed combat training to get him out of 'sticky corners' like this one. But he also remembered Porter telling him, not that he needed to be told, not to blow his cover by drawing unnecessary attention to himself. To put down this great lecherous lump of a despicable 'fairy', who was also probably the district's only representative, no matter how odious an example, for Soviet Discipline and Penal Statute, here in the street, would be doing just that.

Looking round abruptly at the car, Georgievich blurted out: 'Quick, it's moving! The brake's slipped!' With the man jerking round to see, Georgievich used the distraction to yank his sleeve free from the man's grip, and stepped away swiftly down the slippery slope, cursing and chuckling acidly as he slipped and stumbled over the wet cobblestones.

With the slope eventually levelling out, he was at last in the main body of the town. He had a marked preference for back passages, away from the very surprisingly heavy volume of babbling crowds, here for what must probably be market day. And away from those heavy roaring engine Red Army trucks passing through on their way to manoeuvres of one sort or another. He needed to keep away from prying eyes, no matter who they belonged to. And yet not even down these narrow dark alleys, with their fair quantum of cow and goats' dung, away from the blinding glare of wider sunlit thoroughfares, could he be sure that he was not being watched – every breath he took being snatched by silent eyes from behind non-moving curtains.

As he made his way along the long winding alleys, he caught glimpses to the side, in the wider streets, of lines of market stalls, open street traders and doorways, where bartering was done with the tongue at Vickers machine-gun speed, while the eyes searched elsewhere to tug away at your secrets as you passed by. With the din of buyers' and sellers' haggling competing with the bleating of sheep and the braying of donkeys, Georgievich gave up trying to decipher different dialects around him bombarding his ears as futile. It was the town's turn this week for holding market day, and people flooded in from many far away districts to trade their wares. A rare lightening of mood for this otherwise normally very grey grim city, constrained so in strict compliance with Party People's Municipal Legislation.

After ducking under clothes line after clothes line stretched across the way, there was suddenly no more need for Georgievich to dodge flapping sheets. The passage had opened out into a tiny square. Two bent scrawny leafless trees enclosed by a knee-high rusty circular railing claimed the square's centre. A wafting of cooking aroma drifted out from a stall, one of many allowed to occupy the square's space for market day, playing with his nostrils, challenging him to identify the particular cuisine. He was tempted by the thought of food, but he had to concentrate on something more important first, before allowing himself to contemplate on the lesser issue of replenishing his all too empty stomach with a generous bowl of thick warm farmer's potato soup.

It was perhaps the best kind of dish you could hope for these dark days. In those days long gone by, a popular flourishing of Georgian restaurants had served their diners with a rich host of dishes, lobio, satsivi, shashlik as well as chicken livers and caviar. Moskva's famous Aragvi Restaurant had topped the list of those dining venues, but today it was virtually the only remaining one providing such delicacies of the palate. Georgievich, himself, had once enjoyed a privileged place at table there as a young man, when just newly promoted lieutenant, served by an army of waiters in dazzling white ankle to chin aprons and 'mutton chop' side-whiskers, dashing to-and-fro like neurotic penguins, eager to serve their particular table's diners.

Alas, today those waiters' loyalty of service was reserved for their security-minded masters, where the Aragvi was now a buzzing nest of spies and KGB officers. Khrushchev's Chief of Security henchman, Yuri Andropov was said to frequently 'occasion' the place.

With that, in association with food, on his mind, and his hungry feeling persisting, Georgievich could easily believe that no matter how experienced you were, no matter how many missions you completed successfully, and put behind you, this nervous feeling never left you completely.

Being jostled from time to time, as he made his way through the crowd, Georgievich suddenly became aware that he now had in his hand a piece of paper that had not been there before. The barely legible scribbling of 'olives' and four little circles with a bent line running through them. It looked remotely like the Plough constellation. If this was supposed to imply a 'night-time' meeting, then his time was wasted being here in the middle of the day.

He looked around for anything resembling that on the paper. Nothing. And then they caught his eye through the spaces between shifting people. Wheelbarrows! Walking along as casually as he could, he inspected the merchandise on the wheelbarrows. At last he came across a small one selling only olives, black and green.

He ordered a bag of the black variety.

'Large or small?'

'Just black.' Short answers. Avoid unnecessary use of words that may invite conversational words of a prying nature in return. Straight out of the spook's manual – or more precisely, straight off Porter's professional instruction tongue.

Picking up a rolled newspaper conical 'bag' of olives, the man handed it to Georgievich. The olives were green.

Georgievich looked at them, shaking his head and looked up, proffering them back to the man.

The man pushed them back to Geogievich.

Puzzled, Georgievich stared at the man. 'These are not black.'

The man just stared back.

Georgievich returned the stare in defiance, mingling with the feeling that something was wrong. One of that other American man Myers' little charades not working out as it was supposed to?

'You need your eyes tested,' said the man.

Still not understanding, Georgievich shook his head again.

'You need your *eyes tested.*' This time the words were stressed hard to press home the message.

'Ah! Of course! The conundrum dissolved. Needless to say, if he'd asked for green olives, the man would have given him black ones for the same end.

Olives were all forgotten with a small card appearing magically from beneath the man's fingers on the barrow-top. **APPOINTMENT: MOSKVA PEOPLE'S MAXIM GORKY INFIRMARY.**

'Bolshoyespasibo,' said Georgievich quietly thanking the man as he took up the card and turned, walking quickly away.

Retracing his steps back through the alleyways, then into the city's central district, Georgievich searched and searched. The more he looked, trying to identify passing landmarks, he more he felt he was getting nowhere pretty quickly. His vague memories of the city were proving to be deceptive. For several minutes he almost regretted stepping into this degree of threatened exposure from all around him. With angry honking military vehicles, stamping dray horses and gigantic agricultural waggons narrowly missing him, rushing in from all directions, as he crossed unfamiliar streets and squares, his passage was slow and dangerous. Animals and engines were united in common onslaught against him it seemed from the noisy river of traffic flowing around him. He had fleeting moments of seeing himself entering the infirmary as an emergency casualty case, rather than as a daytime visitor. Almost granting his wish, the great Mercedes roared past on its 60hp four-cylinder bi-block engine, sparing him only by inches, its polished brass accoutrements flashing warning to other suicidal pedestrians. A grand Soviet Red Army General's uniform on the passenger in the back seat had replaced the German Wehrmacht Field Marshal's uniform of the former war-time back seat passenger. Waving away the exhaust fumes, Georgievich stepped up onto the haven of a pavement.

He should have remembered and recognised the infirmary from its massive bulk. It stood out from the lesser structures; imperious without being palatial, having had all czarist traces chipped away, to leave a morbid façade of grey scarred stone. Where sisters' and nurses' white headpieces should have flapped in the breeze, like a swarm of butterflies 'welcoming' those wretched with wounds and ailments of sorts, it was sullen figures in vague dirty uniforms, understood as somehow military, by the shoulder-slung rifles, who stood about in the forecourt, monitoring those intending to enter the establishment.

Georgievich entered the building.

The corridors were bleak, with dark tiled walls. Their mood was reflected in the was faces of patients sitting about, listless and 'lost', round every corner. The heavy stride Georgievich's military boots rang out resolutely on the stone floor so that minds looked up tired and fuddled, expecting, as much as they dreaded, seeing white-coated figures approaching with their frightening pointed instruments and 'things'. But the tall man walking past wasn't wearing a white coat – wasn't carrying any of the horrible infirmary stuff. Curious minds, relieved, lost their interest in Georgievich and returned to their inner focused gloom.

Geogievich tried stopping a nurse, asking after directions to the Eye Department. Built like a tank, while waddling like a duck, she carried an enamel bed-pan empty and newly washed but with a faint odour of its recent faecal contents still clinging to her uniform. She wasn't much help, hurrying on without stopping, waving a vague direction with a muttered reply revealing nothing clearer than '---- that way' She hastened on her way.

A porter came along pushing a trolley laden with bed linen sodden with excrement and urine. He wasn't much help either. He didn't know. He couldn't help the visitor. He trundled his trolley-load on along the corridor.

Becoming a little more uneasy by each passing minute, Geogievich wondered if the next person he encountered would be holding out manacles to put round his wrists. He felt the chance of that happening increased with every step he took in this bustling bastion of officialdom. As long as he wasn't caught yet, the odds of him being caught increased.

He knocked on the open door of a small room marked: Reception. The receptionist, bent over a desk covered with paperwork, looked up. Removing his silver pince-nez, the man stood up. An official questioning frown squeezed its way into the pale round face, between the jet-black moustache and the sharp goatee beard. Whilst his function was to receive enquirers, it was made plain that he did not like enquirers. 'Can I help you?' The frigid tone was far from helpful to those members of the public intimidated by the infirmary's oppressive atmosphere.

Georgievich passed the card across the desk to the man.

The man stared down at the card for a long moment, then up at Georgievich, then back down again at the card, before picking it up. The pince-nez came up again for official scrutiny.

Georgievich waited with mounting tension.

With an official flurry of wrist and fingers, the man reached out with an officially rigid arm to return the card. 'If you would care to follow me.' He led the way briskly along another morose dark corridor. With his stiff straight back and official status, the man saw himself as every bit as good as the high-minded medical professors.

Finally reaching a door as unrevealing by its being closed as all the other similar doors were, the man stopped. Telling Georgievich to wait outside, the man went inside. After what seemed a very long several minutes, the door opened, and Georgievich was bade to enter by the receptionist who then took his leave.

On opening the door and stepping inside, Georgievich was surprised to find that the room was already in total darkness.

The door was closed behind him and a hand took hold of his arm. Presumably that of the ophthalmologist – *or whosoever was posing as one.* Georgievich let himself be guided through the darkness across the room until something in front touched him. The patient's chair. He sat down.

Reflexes had him tensed to defend himself when he sensed a movement extremely close to his head. A side light came on somewhere making him relax a little. He tensed again as a strange metal appliance came swinging round to his face, just stopping short of hitting it. Bristling with knobs, dials and 'things', it looked as if it could have done well in a medieval torture dungeon.

The man, now seated on a stool beside Georgievich, fitted the phoroptor to Georgievich's face, somewhat like a giant 'iron mask' that no doubt Dumas would have imagined as fitting for the unfortunate royal prisoner in his legendary tale of sibling rivalry in the royal household. The weird contraption provided two lens apertures for Georgievich to look through. After an adjustment from the hand in the darkness, a series of seven-digit numbers popped up for Georgievich to see *inside* the phoroptor.

'These are the reference codes for the files we need you to procure for us in what little time we have.'

'In what little time *I* have. And *you* are?'

'There's no need for you to know who I am, any more than I need to know who you are. But I'm given to understand that you came with good referral. If it makes you feel more relaxed, I'm the temporary locum replacement for the good Doctor Leonovsky, who was suddenly taken ill.'

'Oh, *very* relaxed – I think not. But what about my new passport and visa clearance documents, I'm supposed to be getting? I understood that to be the reason --- the *sole* reason for me breaking my cover, exposing myself in public --- coming here to collect them?'

'You'll get those as soon as you bring us those important files. Be assured of that.'

Oh, so that was Mr Myers' game, Georgievich thought, with a sinking feeling – the original promise made to him by Myers was now being downgraded a degree to an '*assurance*'. 'But if ------'

'Let's get on with it, shall we!' The words were commanding in their hardness. 'Concentrate on the numbers; you've been trained to memorise things in a short period of time, I gather. I'll give you five minutes to do that—no more. We haven't the time. They can't be written down.'

After the five minutes had elapsed, Georgievich felt something being put in his hand. 'What's this?'

'It's made to look like a small bottle, which it isn't, labelled Eserine Eye Drops. You'll notice what looks like a puncture dot on the label in the middle of the letter e in Eserine. That's the lens aperture for the micro camera that the 'bottle' really is. You'll take the shots by turning the false plastic screw-top clockwise and back. The camera takes fifteen shots.'

'Let's go.' A hand took hold of Georgievich's arm again, to help him out of the chair and lead him back to the door.

'How, and to whom, am I to pass these film shots onto, should I manage to get them successfully?

'Leave that to us. We'll handle that.'

'So, we're still playing that game?

'We're still playing that game.'

'It's a game I don't want to lose.'

'None of us do.'

As they reached the door, the hand tightened slightly on Georgievich's arm to stop him. 'Good luck.'

'I think I'm going to need an abundance of that, for sure, if that's the only thing I can rely on being sure.'

<h1 style="text-align:center">26</h1>

An ominous scraping above them, on the outside of the trapdoor, took over from the silence where the voices had stopped. Someone was trying to wedge a lever in to prise the steel plate open.

Frank stepped back as far as possible to lessen whoever it was's view of them, signalling McGavin to do likewise. Taking out his Beretta, Frank lined it up, readying himself for the intruder to poke his damn head in. As much as he didn't want to worsen their situation, desperate as it was, by taking the guy out, there was no other option. There was no knowing how desperate the orders were for their arrest – if they were to be shot on sight, leaving questions last.

A narrow slit appeared first, pausing for a second, before widening slowly. Caution was tense on both sides of the steel plate. The rifle muzzle with its barrel nosed its way in like a probing snake. Then the head with its dark Asian face.

Before Frank could fire – before he could resolve his indecision over firing or not, the guy did a totally weird thing. The crazy 'Nam bugger dropped his head down and kissed the edge of the hatch opening!

Frank's confusion was cleared at the sight of the red tinge creeping into the black Asian hair, down the side of the man's head. Blood.

'Are you guys okay down there?' An American voice. Myers, of course.

'We're okay,' said Frank, mounting the wooden steps, two at a time. 'Is he dead?'

'He'll live; I hit him with a chunk of steel. Mind you, who knows what the poor guy's bosses will do when he reports that he'd had his prisoners, then let them escape. Maybe be better if the guy had sniffed it, right enough. But hell, he's not the only guy sniffing, around here. If those damn wrinkle-faced midgets are not close on our heels by now, my name is Moses. We'd better be out of here pronto. We've a heck of a lot of travelling to do, with a lot of ground to cover. If we don't move fast, we'll be needing prayers more than we need these.' Myers handed documents to Frank. 'Our documents room guys are going to be running short of printer's ink, with all this stuff I'm having to keep giving you, Frank, to save your skin. For God's sake, Frank, make it be the last time and don't fucking muck it up again.'

Frank grasped what were his precious lifeline papers out of here and made them disappear in his pocket with the same swiftness that magician Myers had made them appear, as he always seemed to be doing all along this mad caper of a mission.

'What about me?' said McGavin. 'Don't I get tickets as well?'

'You're coming with me, pal,' said Myers. 'So I can see you don't get into any more mischief treading on more rotten eggs to ruin things.'

'*Me*, ruin things? What the hell --- '

But Myers waved a hand to shut McGavin up. 'We've done enough tongue-waggling. Let's all get out of here. Drinks are on you, Frank, back in Happyville.'

But for the lingering domination of shimmering temples holding it back, you couldn't fail to notice that ancient Krung Thep (Bangkok), in all its antiquity, was pulling on a new modern commercial age image. Fog was just beginning to lower its heavy mantle onto the dark outlined shoulders of the city, choked with brooding rags of a brooding red sunset. A faint westerly breeze was wafting the mist inwards from the mouth of the Menam River twenty miles away. In spite of the thickening fog, serried rows of shipping were still discernible, standing out at the river windings, hatching the mist with a ghostly gossamer forest of masts and cross-beams. Merchant vessels bearing barrels, bales, sacks and hides that swung through the air, crewmen yelling as they received and directed them with swinging arms.

New sounds drifted up to Frank Falzoni and he looked round to see cranes creaking and pulleys rattling; idle sails flapped flatly on small private schooners, whilst ships pulsed and sounded their base horn blasts as they prepared to get underway. All this reaching Frank's ears through the rhythmic plashy background sound of breaking waters.

But it wasn't what he wanted to hear. Where the fucking hell is the damn bugger?

Hopes jumped for a second as he heard a coarse voice carried in the descending gloom. False alarm. It was a river pilot guide commenting to a happily babbling tourist party for their 'education', and rude enjoyment, of the pleasure houses floating past on the river banks.

Frank walked on slowly, turning round every few yards to scan through brooding eyes at the varying combination of shapes and activities around him. Ominous dark forms loomed up like lumbering dinosaurs to give fleeting glimpses of enormous timber warehouses and crazy watermen's stairs snaking down to massive landing stages that swarmed with smudges of human parasites. With tugs spurting their coke fumes in the faces of these dockside workers, the hazy image of the already blackened stevedores was lost completely. Between newly erected bright buildings, darkness slinked back down alleys that allowed for discreet escape from the revealing public glare and juke-box blare of bars poised on their corners.

Stuck here in this rabble of a tourist joint, Frank thought how easily you could be stranded, if not *'trapped'*, if you had no sense of direction after being forced off your original intended course. And things had certainly pushed him that way. You could never allow yourself to be sure of what action to take until that moment for action came. Things can change instantly and require you to go off at a tangent in a new strategy. So that in a way, you had to see where you were heading, without actually knowing where that was.

Frank likened this contradiction to the frolicking figure of a drunk, looming up closer out of the alley's darkness, repeatedly falling down and then standing up again. In his happy inebriated state, the poor bastard probably could see what was ahead, without a sober appreciation of what it was he was seeing.

As the figure came up close, Myers suddenly stepped back in tensed reflex at the sight of the man's arm jerking up at him. But the man's hand held nothing more threatening than his bottle of spirits. He was offering a drink.

'Thanks, pal, but my mom always told me to drink nothing stronger than good old cocoa,' said Frank, declining the offer. He watched the guy waddle off in pursuit of his wandering destiny.

With drink on his mind, Frank headed for the Mosqito Klong Toey Bar discreetly nestling just out of sight round the corner from the city's affluent Asoke Building-Windsor Hotel facing Pattaya Beach.

But what he saw reflected on the glass door concerned him more than what was going on inside the bar. The flashing blue beacon on the roof of the car had caught his eye first. He watched the man walking up from behind him. Something metallic flashed in the man's hand.

Frank turned round.

It stopped short of just poking his eyes out:

ROYAL THAI SECURITY POLICE
<u>Phan Tam Ruad Ek (Chief Superintedent) --- Muyan Ka</u>
<u>Phon Tam Ruad Ek (Commissioner of Police) --- Suwat Chaengsuk</u>
<u>Phon Tam Ruad Tri (Major General) --- Chakthip Jindacha</u>

The bold words on the card, held a few inches from Falzoni' face, stood out to catch his attention, as they were meant to, with their brazen message. Light shining out from the Mosquito joint glinted on the gold metal shield bearing the royal coat of arms with their central red, white and blue vertical stripes. This helped to reinforce the card's authority, with the Superintendent Muyan Ka's name, and his barely legible cat's whisker squiggly signature and photograph below it. Further official endorsement was made more so by the smudged ink ring of authority stamped over the Commissioner' name. At the bottom, holding command over all this was the boss, the Major General. A sharp tick in ballpoint, along with a small star embossed in the plastic, sufficed here in place of a signature.

Affecting a fake surprised reaction at the card's sudden presentation, Frank made a deliberate point of spilling a great drooping end of ash from his cigarette as he jerked his head back from the warrant card. But he had already summed up the 'royal cop' from his covert glance at the guy's reflection on the glass door. He noted how the man, in open gesture, rested his hand for a moment on the polished leather open-style holster which held what looked like to him to be a Spanish version of a Smith & Wesson revolver. From what he remembered of Ordnance Record details, the pistol probably used French Ordnance 8mm cartridges. All in all, not a man to be toyed with.

'Papers,' the officer said brusquely, deliberately leaving out 'sir' that would have made for a policeman's politeness. He obviously wanted to sound as hard as his power allowed him. Holding his head back, he looked steadily at Falzoni, watching him, as he slowly pocketed his warrant card. Falzoni sensed that he actually wanted him to be difficult so that he could demonstrate his official power. And power he had. But he'd long experienced this kind of situation over and over again so that it would be good enough to get him past, answering the Superintendent's probing questions. Whilst doing so, he ran his mind over old basic training lectures on 'body language', and what facial expressions to pose and where to focus the eyes for different situations. He hoped that he was doing it all correctly.

Feeling the man's eyes digging into him, Falzoni wasted no time in handing over his ID documents.

He could see that the man was disappointed in not finding any fault in the papers as he gruffly handed them back – that he would very much have liked to take him in for searching and interrogation. There was a lightened air of relief, not only in Frank, but all round in those in the bar, when he entered. The little 'official' scene outside had put everyone on edge. Pausing inside, Frank turned to look back through the closed glass door for a parting moment's scrutiny of the Superintendent. With his hand still on the door handle, Frank watched as it seemed that the damn policeman was having second thoughts and was going to come back in to pester him further. He held his breath until the Superintendent turned and got into the patrol car, pausing to look back at him through the car window. They both watched each other watching each other for a never-ending few tense seconds, before the vehicle suddenly lurched forward with a powerful snarl, and moved off up the street, to finally disappear round the far corner, heading back across the city, to Police Headquarters at Patham Wan.

An awareness of noisy incoherent conversation rabble around him came back to Frank's ears as he sat down and ordered a Kentucky Crocodile Cocktail with extra blue menthol – no ice. 'Any chance of a pastrami sandwich with that?' But the barman's vacant look was enough for Frank. 'No, I didn't think so.' He handed the money to the barman. 'Have one on yourself and keep the change.'

Ironically, there should have been no 'animosity' between America's Major Falzoni and Thailand's just recently departed official representative, the Superintendent. In its ongoing war with Vietnam, the United States had Thailand as an assured ally. US government's military strategists viewed Thailand as a logical staging area for American forces because of its proximity to North and South Vietnam. Because Thailand was buffered from the conflict zone by Laos and Cambodia, it therefore made it safer for American personnel. With these factors in mind, the two governments had reached a so-called gentlemen's agreement permitting American forces to use Thailand for positioning military bases. The first base for operations was established at Ta-Khli Royal Thai Air Force Base, located approximately 144 miles northwest of Bangkok. Key bases for USAF operations came later at Korat, Ubon, U-Tapao, Don Muang and Udorn. Of all the bases established, 45 were Army installations; 18 for US Navy and Coast Guard installations; 28 for USAF installations;

and other installations for US government civilian personnel, namely, ambassador staff, 'intelligence analysts', contractors and others.

True, there had been a little trouble - still brewing, in fact, - over servicemen's complaints of suffering side-effects from *alleged* contamination from the herbicide operationally known as Agent Orange containing deadly chemical toxic dioxin. Agent Orange was employed to defoliate the thick jungle vegetation around airfields and other US installations in South East Asia. The purpose of this being to expose enemy forces who relied on the trees for cover. It was the usual thing to see a US Army Huey UH-1D chopper in the distance spraying AO over agricultural land on the Mekong Delta and demilitarised zones. So you commonly saw great stacks of 200 litre drums of AO for US armoured personnel carriers to spray over enemy Vietnamese rice fields. Here, in Thailand, bases at Karat, Nakhon, Phanom, Ubon, Udorn and U-Tapao had been subject to sniper attack, perimeter penetration and combat engineer attacks. Back in Washington, the US Department of Defense had legitimate concern about these threats to US personnel and equipment, thus leading to the decision of using herbicides, e.g. Agent Orange, within base perimeters in Thailand.

This was causing a little ripple of discourse among both Thai and American medical and civilian administration staff. Maybe it was on account of this that the good Superintendent had wanted to pick a bone, so to speak, as an excuse to sink his teeth in. Sorry, I can't oblige you there, pal; petty jurisprudence squabbles are just not my thing.

If Frank had not been caught off guard by the policeman, having privately spied his approach, he was, on the other hand, certainly a little surprised by the next entrance into the bar, now returned to its hubbub of cheerful chatter, with 'official trouble' having left them. It wasn't so much because of the somewhat surreptitious 'sliding' in by the back door, but because of the face, with its beaming expression, now confronting him. And when Marley Goodblood beamed like that, it implied a cane was being raised to rap naughty fingers.

No invitation was necessary for Goodblood to sit down beside Frank at the bar.

Ordering two Gautret cognacs, ignoring Frank's protest, Goodblood used a few moments looking round the room, smiling at strange faces, to ready himself for discussing things with the Major. Having worked with each other for some time now, they both knew how the other's mind worked, so readily saw a mental tussle of wits looming.

Goodblood let the barman put the two cognacs on the bar. He pushed one towards Frank. 'On me,' he said, while eyeing and wondering what the blue-coloured concoction was in Frank's glass. 'And another one of whatever it is he's having in that glass for him.' He held up his glass of Gautret. 'Cheers!'

'Yeah, and a Merry Christmas to you, as well.'

You didn't have to be a consultant psychiatrist to know that when Marley greeted you warmly like that, showering you with drinks, the temperature behind those eyes would be ice-cold in contrast. His little trick of catching you unawares. It might have worked a long time ago, but not now.   Following Marley's logic and train of thoughts when he was in that mood would be much more of a convoluted passage, with more than a few sharp corners to turn. Over the long time that he'd known him, you learned that Marley tended to employ his cunning tactic of saying a lot, 'without saying anything', so to speak. A valued technique in intelligence work for sifting out the 'black sheep' from enemy folds and recruiting them as double agents.

Frank waited with a simmering curiosity, feeling that the details of the reason for Goodblood having come all the way out here would not be coming his way just yet, if at all. Not without a little subtle sideways prompting.

'Am I to take it that reception among your pals in the Senate has cooled down somewhat lately, to get you to seek a warmer climate way out here? Is *that* anywhere near the target?' said Frank, keeping his voice down so as not to be heard away from their table. 'Yeah, well, you'll certainly find the temperature is high here, if you catch my drift.'

Goodblood looked down at his cognac for a moment before looking across at the Major. 'As far as I know — as far as any of us are aware of – nothing has been ultimately agreed upon so far. But yes, as far as preliminary planning has progressed, the prospect of us mounting heavier assault forces in is fast becoming a reality by way of majority voting.'

That didn't sound quite right to be what was bugging Marley. 'Is that *it*?' Frank didn't hide the questioning tone in his words.

Taking the hint, Goodblood went on. 'Prior to launching the broadside of American and multiple allied forces into 'Nam, we're sending in Navy Seals on specific reconnaisssance operations – along with small teams of specially briefed Canadian, Australian and French underwater specialists – with the task of bringing together a co-ordinated front in preparation for an invasion. Previously, our attacks have been scattered, lacking the punch a united effort can give. It's taken goat-headed slowness to appreciate the sense of a co-ordinated set-up to demonstrate what strength can be derived from merging isolated small groups into a larger fighting force.'

Goodblood raised his glass again to Falzoni, in salute at this news. 'Now that President Johnson has been made to see sense, we're gathering our separate fighter groups together in one great solid united front, so that we can at last push Ho Chi Minh's bastard lot out of the way for good.'

Frank gave a wry smile at this, nodding his head. 'And you came all the way from the convenience and niceties of Washington to tell me this. Why the hell didn't you save yourself the bother and send the message to me by a bare-footed runner holding the damn note on the cleft-end of a stick!'

Angry hardness shot into Goodblood's expression. 'Cool it now, Major, before I'm forced to put you down for insubordination.' He allowed a softer expression to take over. 'As you say, it's *warm* here, so I suggest you don't let it get to you. *Right*, Major?'

'*Right*, Colonel.'

Goodblood didn't want to darken his own, what he imagined, shining image of being a good guy of a boss who listened to and understood his team by saying that Frank could sometimes be a right pain in the ass with his obstinacy during discussions. Keeping tempers down between them was one thing, but moving on without explanation for a misunderstanding was virtually a guarantee that plans were not likely to advance from square one without Frank bringing out a sore point of sorts.

Frank broke the silence with a measured degree of calmness in his probing, in the form of a question. 'Can we afford to be that confident? This great united broadside onslaught attack? I mean with the enemy so close on our heels, virtually shadowing all our movements, can we realistically hope to sabotage vital transport and communication installations in preparation for the intended assault operation? Only a few minutes before you came in, I was batting off questions thrown at me by the local *Royal* PD -- or so his ID badge said. You get my point?'

A little puzzled, Goodblood looked round at Frank, waiting for him to expand on her remark. But nothing followed. Frank was relying on Goodblood, with his usual close-to-the-chest better in-depth knowledge of whatever the particular situation was, to take it from there.

Realising that Frank was handing over to him, Goodblood took over. 'It's a nasty reality of a thorn that's given us a sore thumb that we could well do without; but it has to be dealt with.'

'Oh, yeah?'

'Public outcry seems to have broken out, following US government investigation into the growing reports of 'Nam veterans suffering *supposedly* from the effects of Agent Orange. Political reactionists are declaring that the US Government's usage of Agent Orange for military purposes is violating the nineteen twenty-five Geneva Convention which regulates the use of chemical and biological weapons.'

'So how are our Big-Wigs on Capitol Hill handling that one?'

'By definition, Agent Orange isn't a weapon as such; it's a herbicide and defoliate employed for the specific purpose of destroying plant crops in order to deprive the enemy's concealment in their act of ambushing us, and not to target human beings. By similar degree of definition, a weapon is any device used to injure, defeat or destroy living beings, structures or systems. Agent Orange doesn't qualify as a weapon under that definition.' Stopping for a breather, Goodblood looked over at the barman, beckoning him for a refilling of their glasses.

'I think we can say you've read up well on the technical points, there, Colonel. But how are the other side taking that? Am I wrong in wondering if is it enough to shut them up?'

Pushing a newly filled glass across to Frank, Goodblood picked his own up to have a sip, before continuing. 'The way I see it in longshot is, even if it was to be conceded that Agent Orange *is* a weapon, then if the US Government is to be charged on that account of using it as such, then Great Britain, along with her Commonwealth Nations, will also have to bear the weight of dishonour in lowering its head in pleading 'guilty as charged', since they made extensive use of it during their Malayan Emergency. In nineteen fifty, that was, if I remember rightly.'

'Yeah, well, the way *I* see it is, if that barrage of science-backed logic isn't enough to quell their bleating, it'll take a lot more than drowning ourselves in *these,* to keep us happy.' In demonstration, Frank threw back his Gautret and Crocodile Cocktail in double gulp, raising a finger to signal the barman for further replenishing of their empty glasses.

Moments of silence while they waited for the barman to do his bit, saw faint traces of dismay, if not sadness, creeping into their faces as the bitter truth got through to their moral consciences, holding them in its inescapable iron grip of judgement.

'It's not just *our* people who believe themselves to be fighting for the right cause,' Goodblood muttered, somewhat abstractly. 'Supposedly *they* must believe that too.'

'Quite.'

Goodblood shifted his glass around in thought. But the widespread usage of Agent Orange on the Vietnamese general population did cause terrible consequences resulting in cancer, birth defects and a multitude of other 'nasty' ailments. With over 11,969 square miles of forest stock defoliated, and arable crop-land eroded, robbing it of valuable food reserve, it brought starvation level to the door of the civilian population --- but for the supplies provided by China and Russia. In all, it wasn't something to be easily ignored. That was war—with its diabolical incentive for resorting to brutal methods of extorting submission and surrender from not only the enemy, but the innocent so-called 'collateral'.

Possibly with a slight feeling of guilt at this late inner admission, Goodblood tapped the table hard and sat back upright. 'C'est la guerre.' The remark, in its sudden outburst, surprised not only Frank, but Goodblood himself.

For want of relief from his morbid thoughts perhaps, Goodblood changed the subject. 'As if wading through that quagmire bog of a mess, I'm landed with more headaches contending with the calamitous antics of Batman and Robin! God only knows why I assigned Myers and you to work together as a field team! I wish God would tell me! Where the hell is the Myers, anyway?'

'He considered it safer to take a separate roundabout route with McGavin.'

'And what do *you* think, Frank? Do you think it's safer?'

'It seems to be working so far.'

'That's a point that needs serious pondering. So far you two have made a right hog-wash hash of things. The mission blown sky high.'

'Unforeseen contingencies that couldn't be avoided.'

'Yeah, that's for sure, Frank, that's for sure.'

Beaming a smile broader than Alice's Cheshire Cat, Goodblood decided to put that issue aside, and step down from his high seat as judge for the time being. That was Marley for you --- he was liable to switch moods in the flick of a second, shifting them about, to disappear and reappear in different places, with the same magical ease of that damn crazy Cat.

Discussion was agreed to be exhausted when the glasses were no longer taking in refills. 'We'll leave separately,' said Goodblood suddenly. Jumping up abruptly from his stool, he dropped the bills, one after the other, like a loser's hand at poker, onto the bar, and turned to go. He paused to look down at Frank. 'I'll go back the way I came, through the backyard outhouse and out through the side gate into the alley – thanks to Pascal.' He gave a glance of appreciation to the haggard old face behind the bar. He looked back at Frank. 'You can wait for five minutes after I leave before you go out the front way. Okay?'

Frank nodded. 'Okay.'

Goodblood looked at Frank, measuring how he was taking all this in. In spite of what he had said, he did consider his coupling of Myers and Falzoni together for a mission was right, where the Case Officer had to act like a shrink with his patient, handling his agent's situation problems with a calm professional control of emotions; at the same time as sectioning off a corner of his mind to resolve operational problems with cold logical decision. What some might classify as cold-blooded choice. Both of them were competent field operatives, painstakingly advised through long briefing sessions what to expect in their coming mission, with the nerve-rackingly *unexpected* situations it would entail; how to establish, with lightning reflex, an air of innocence and convincing pretext if caught being where one shouldn't be; in all, how to survive under constant close surveillance and preliminary interrogation without breaking down.

Yes, he thought that he'd made the right decision, putting the two of them together for this mission. He had to hold firm with that decision to avoid worsening his headache.

When Frank stepped out of the bar and started walking up the street, he was not conscious of two particular eyes following his movements. They were those of the man sitting in his car, idly twiddling with the stamped metal Afrika Korps Ringkragen gorget memento dangling on its chain from the rear mirror. Parked across the street, beside the small grove of tall slender poplars, ex-Lieutnant Franz Hauter was suddenly fired with curiosity by the face he thought he had just seen. As he watched the figure of Frank moving up the street, his mind sifted through his stock of memories. Searching systematically, he suddenly found it. Nodding slowly, he smiled his satisfaction. 'Porter,' he said slowly to himself. '*Major* Porter.'

With the war's end seeing Wehrmacht officers being recruited by Allied Forces on account of their specialised knowledge, Hauter was duly snatched up by the Red Army as being 'possibly useful' for his experience in covert operations with Afrika Korps in close co-operation with the

Feldgendarmerie and *Feldjagerkorps* as well as *Geheime Felpolizei* (Secret Field Police). So his photographer entrepreneurial business was a cover for his work as an undercover operative for Red Army Intelligence. Aside of scheduled official work for his new hammer and sickle bosses, he was allowed to operate freelance, regardless of national 'flags', brokering intelligence deals to the highest bidder.

This job he was on now had nothing whatsoever to do with the American, but now that they'd just crossed paths by chance, perhaps it could prove to be profitable to follow it up.

Alarmed at the human's approach and the menacing metallic click of the closing car door, the little squirrel scurried rapidly up the slim bole to the safety of shelter among the leafy branches above. Standing in the cover of the trees for a few moments, Hauter watched the American receding further up the street, before stepping out slowly to follow him at a discreet distance.

27

It was too dark to see the face of who it was tailing him; but checking with continual glances at adjacent glass surfaces as they were passed, told Frank that the guy's pace, safe as it was at an 'innocent' distance, was too consistent with his own pace to be mere coincidence.

The watch-vendor thought it was all a great farce bellowing out his sales talk at the stream of passers-bye, whilst backing up his banter of bargains with a double-armed glittering array of 'genuine' Swiss watches, remarkably so, manufactured in and imported illegally from Kowloon.

Ex-Lieutnant Hauter didn't share the man's mood and cursed as he continually dodged around people in his way, trying to keep track of his prey. The American was some yards ahead and didn't seem aware, so far, that he was being tailed. He seemed to be walking on without any sign of caution, holding Hauter's steady, yet 'unconcerned', attention. All the while the pair filtered their way through crowds of shoppers standing in their way. To pass through crowds like this was a good thing if you were tailing someone, but it was a pest if you weren't sure if you were being tailed yourself.

Frank needed to check just that, and the billiard-ball scattering of people as you passed through the crowds made this awkward. He decided to employ the old tactics of sharp turns that good old fashioned street corners and abrupt openings of alleys provided. That way, you could tell if two people were going the same way, without being together or without being pals; just like a flypaper with its gum for trapping dirty flies. Hauter was ready for this trick and slowed down, eventually stopping. He had to think. With his limited knowledge of the street layout, his mind was jammed in trying to come up with a roundabout way of getting back on the American's trail.

Frank found the long tunnel-like close constriction of the alley around him coming to an end, opening out onto what appeared to be the loading bay to the rear of a large building. Stepping up onto the long concrete loading platform and pulling open the broad studded iron bar framed wooden door along its iron rail, he entered into the noisy swirling melee commotion of sellers bartering with buyers in a giant indoor fish market emporium.

Was it the wise Confucius, or Marley, after tickling his tonsils with two grand's worth of his royal Louis Remy Martin cognac, who said that a dazzling vision of true wonder striking the eye new will not manifest itself so ever again? Well, to push that corny philosophy home, there was that face again, and it was no different from the first time he'd seen it. He had picked it out, after minutes of scanning his surrounding over and over again, from among the river of faces flowing in their unceasing tumultuous torrent of shoppers around him. It was not the striking European countenance, standing out against the sea of Asian features around it, that had caused Frank's personal alert antennae to prick up – but the fact that he'd caught those eyes, out of all the 'millions' of eyes milling around, looking at *him*. Now here he was again, his trailer having been caught off-guard, turning away too abruptly to avert his eyes and pretentiously study the squirming lobsters on the stall beside him in a futile attempt to make himself inconspicuous. He didn't want to be caught like those lobsters. Too late for that, pal.

But that face? Was this the second time he was seeing it – or was it the *third* time? Frank racked his brain, trying to think back. Not too far back to a small 'business location' discreetly buried in the seclusion of a conveniently dim-lit backstreet sector of Istanbul.

Suddenly bumped to one side by the moving crowd around him, Frank's attention on the trailer guy was interrupted for a second. Looking round again to where he'd seen the face among the shifting mass of many, he swore. The bloody guy's mug had vanished. He'd damn well scarpered. Or maybe he hadn't? Maybe he was still around here somewhere, but making a better job of keeping out of sight this time.

The tail had gone off. If he had stayed on, Frank would have simply played the game and led him on a wild goose chase. But now that he thought that he had shaken off his tail, he could possibly continue on his way to where he was going. He was relieved all right, but not before shaking off his natural suspicions. He looked back more than once, on his winding way before being convinced that he was not being followed and that his fears were imaginary.

Even so, imaginary or not, the reflexes were hard to keep down and he made a check of all those drifting along the street behind him. A business man carrying a brief case; a mother carrying her child, suckling it openly at her bare breast; a woman in a green plastic raincoat; and two hairy youths in decadent jeans that clung to their bodies like leper skins. They would probably stink like lepers if they came closer. But nobody came any closer and everybody was minding their own business. The rest of the crowd had already been on the move ahead of him and so couldn't possibly harbour his tail. His rational mind no sooner said this than his nervous mind made a sweeping check of everyone around him again. Negative. He was reassured once more and gave up checking – for few moments, anyway.

Still following the American along Charoen Krung Road, in what seemed to be the Sathon district, Hauter kept out of sight behind the archway leading off to a small prayer garden with its holy shrine to the four-faced Phra Phron, lord god of the highest heavenly realm of Brahmaloka, in the unique junk-shaped sepulchral monument of dirt faced with stone that was the ancient Buddhdist temple of Wat Yannawa. He was of two minds whether or not to grab the American. If he didn't pounce on him now, there was the possibility that he would lose him.

On the other hand, if he grabbed him and beat the information out of his skull, it could maybe cost him precious time. Better that he followed him, he decided, for what could possibly be only for a few minutes more.

All moved on silently, like sacrificial mutes on their way to a giant alter stone, their mind reciting the sacred scripts of the torn posters and blinking neon screens in a shared ritual that was peculiar to the solemnly plodding urban pedestrian.

Frank jumped slightly with nerves as someone spoke beside him. 'Money?' said the old man in rag-style clothing, shaking his little tin. A destitute vagrant. Frank took a second to absorb the question through his surprise. 'I'm broke,' he said, shooing him away, and the old man ambled off to annoy someone else and worry others at his approaching and pestering them next. The father with the Goodyear tyre face and immaculate white collar pulled his little boy away gently from a half-eaten apple abandoned on the ground. 'Leave it, son, it's rotten,' he said in a soft voice. Possibly what the true to form pragmatist would seize upon in his hair-splitting argument as veritable evidence that not all of the Asian populace was suffering from severe malnutrition inflicted on them by the war. Behind him, the old beggar shuffled up to swoop down on the apple and tested it with his lips. He stowed it away in his sack, pleased with his cunning.

A bus-stop ahead up the road. People swayed and twisted as they waited. The business man looked in his polystyrene briefcase. The mother gently patted her burping child's back. The woman with the green plastic raincoat felt about inside her pocket. There was nothing in, it but only she knew that. It was part of her camouflage for surveillance duties. She felt the American's suspicious look coming her way so she turned away, to look at the poster featuring the porcelain exhibition at the Suan Pakkad Palace Museum.

People stirred and paper flapped from the wind shifting as the giant glow-worm of a double-carriage bus moaned and slid out of the darkness alongside the patient group waiting for it. Frank got on and stood by the empty space by the door. Only the mother and child and the woman with the green plastic raincoat were with him, he noticed. They paid no attention to him. But it was the common characteristic of travellers on public transport that people became potentially anything, locked away as they were, behind the insular privacy of their minds. Anyone became anybody. So it was pick or choose for crook or cop.

Moving off, the bus suddenly jerked to hard-braking halt again, as some crazy straggler jumped onto the rear carriage, just 'scraping' between closing doors.

Well, well! If it wasn't the Kraut, deciding to come out into the open – or determined not to lose track of his quarry.

Frank stepped up nearer to the rear door of the bus's front carriage and watched Hauter through the transparent panels of the adjoining doors. He now had the woman in the green raincoat between himself and Hauter.

Everyone held on as they moved off again. The bus cut its way through the mass of people and vehicles thronging the streets on its circuitous route across the city. Frank moved his head to let a man open his newspaper. Knowing only a few words of this strange Asian language, he was still able to pluck out of the unfamiliar mass of 'twisted' symbols what he thought he recognised as **bombs** and **Vietnam.**

Forgetting himself, Frank bent in closer to see if he could pick out anything else interesting. The paper suddenly ruffled itself and eyes loomed up, annoyed, over its top. Frank straightened up and looked away, feeling guilty at breaking a universal code of social protocol. Never read another person's paper on the public transport. Be it peace or war, there was never any variance with this indefatigable maxim that was the creed of all cloths. The Pacific Ocean could well dry up, and Everest could crumble and tumble, but you never read another man's paper on the bus. Instructors at Langley had neglected to include that in the rigorous training programme.

Frank turned back towards the glass panel and caught the reflection of the woman watching him just before she whipped her eyes away. It could mean nothing, of course, but his hand still went down to his pocket, to feel the outline of the Beretta.

At last, they reached what seemed to Frank to be the route terminal, with doors opening and everyone squeezing out like parasites from the worm's shiny silver side. Hauter stepped off behind the bustling crowd. The woman got off as well. She dithered about seemingly looking for her bearings, or someone. Frank turned to jump back on again just as hydraulic arms were pushing the doors shut again. Hauter had expected this move, staying as he did on the bus, waiting for him. Before Hauter could be out of reach and lost behind the closing doors, Frank's arm shot out to pull him off the bus. 'Hi, there,' said Frank in a mocking game of play that fooled no-one. 'I'm American. I'm from Arizona. I'm a tourist here.'

Hauter fumed inside at the bus speeding away, leaving him behind to be the one 'snared' in their on-and-off little hide and seek game. He was flummoxed by the noisy onset of the American and his mind could only register annoyance after the initial setback surprise. Frank made up for Hauter's silence with another deliberately 'American loud-mouthed tourist' outburst. 'Gee, but isn't this a swell little town we have here, in spite of the pong of all those pongy chop-chop soya bean rice dishes. I'm absolutely gone overboard with it. Real whackoo, overboard. You know what I mean?' He prodded Hauter hard on the shoulder to emphasize his meaning.

Hauter cracked a smile, playing on with the silly verbal 'no-body's fooled' game. 'Sure. I hope you have a good day.'

Frank grabbed him by the arm. 'Say, don't let me hold you back, pal, but isn't there a statue or something around here in memory of their great wise guy, Buddy the fishy conman, or something?'

'I think your confusing Buddha and Confucius.'

'Yeah, you're right, pal. That's who I meant, Buddy and Fushy the conman.'

Hauter stepped back to stand openly smiling and shaking his head at the American in all his likewise open tomfoolery.

Frank grabbed Hauter's arm again and still smiling playfully pushed him hard against the wall, like the cat with its trapped mouse. 'Say, isn't that just swell of you, pal with your modesty. Always pretending you don't know, when you do know, huh?' Walking beside Hauter, Frank then bounced him against the wall like a rubber ball every time he tried to get away, so that the message became clear. Just to reinforce the message, Frank's eyes glinted through the cheery expression for a second. But only for a second. Otherwise, he was absurdly waggish so as to confound the man.

When the Africa Korps field knife materialised in Hauter's hand, Frank suddenly wanted a handshake and 'accidentally' wrenched the man's hand round in a joint-cracking twist. The knife clattered noisily to the ground and Frank 'accidentally' flipped it with a deft toe so that it slid across the pavement and off onto the road. 'Gee, sorry, pal. I really am sorry. Say, but what was that thing, anyhow? Some sort of winkle-picker, or something?'

Letting go of the man's arm, Frank decided to walk along 'peacefully' beside him, now that the guy had realised how serious the game really was. 'Unless I was holding the street map up the wrong way round the last time, I think I know where there's a cute little place along that way where we can go and have ourselves a nice little chat over some nice drinks. Yeah, and maybe some good *real* American coffee. Not the stuff these foreign joints serve you that tastes no better than burnt-out Detroit Motor Oil. Know what I mean?' He looked at Hauter. 'And give some of us a chance to loosen up our tongues, huh? Come on.'

The two of them shuffled off, as much a mixed bag of a duo, as those attending Alice's tea party, with the American one still cheerfully continuing to broadcast his loud-mouthed wisdom to the street. 'Say, and do you know what? If you ask for it nicely, they serve you a good old pastrami sandwich using good old honey on toasted bread. Do you like pastrami? I sure as hell swear by it, yeah.'

They walked on.

Some distance behind them, the woman in the plastic coat was following them, totally unnoticed by them. She was of a mind to continue after them until she saw the man beckoning her with an arm through the open window of the car that had just pulled up at the kerb-side. Going over to the car, she got in and it moved off to slowly follow the two Capitalists.

28

I'm not even going to try and imagine how you managed to pull that one off, Lieutenant Hoddin.' Major Frank Falzoni's remark was supposed to be a serious question whilst there was a playful glint in his eyes in as he looked down at Mary Lee walking by his side, across the great expanse of the U-Tapao US Military Airfield bristling with activity all around them.

'Nothing to it. I simply put in a GH/3 request to escort you on your final flight out.'

'And was it approved? All the way to *Berlin*?'

'I'm sure it will be -- Colonel Sully doesn't come into his office until later this morning.' Mary Lee gave a cheeky smile up at Frank. 'To make sure I was fulfilling my assigned duty of providing you with my assistance, courtesy of PR Division of the Twenty-Fourth Indo-Pacific Marines, whenever you needed it,' she added, with cheeky connivance.

'There's more to you beneath that cute uniform than meets the eye, Lieutenant.'

'Is that you stripping me naked in your mind, like all you men do to us *innocent* girls?'

'I never said that.'

'And I never said I *disapproved*.'

'Like I said – all the way to Berlin, no less!' Frank tilted his head back, throwing his eyes up at the sky, letting out a hearty laugh. 'To think that

I'm being taken for a 'ride' by a cute 'rookie' half my age!' He swallowed his laughter to collect himself as his eye caught the movement of a jeep curving round in a great arc to seem to be coming their way. He looked down at the Lieutenant, raising his eyebrows in loaded question '*Hmm?*'

She bit her lip nervously.

The jeep came up smoothly to circle wide around behind them and then then coming up abreast of them without stopping, to move along slowly keeping pace with them. The corporal flapped up some fingers to his cap in what was a salute. Major Falzoni returned the salute.

'Plane's turning its guts, ready for take-off, Major. If you'd care to jump in.'

'Good timing, Corporal. Thanks, we will.' Frank gestured for Mary Lee to climb into the vehicle first. He pretended to not notice the corporal's surprised expression at this. He climbed in beside him.

'It's the Lockheed C-130E Hercules, sir; over there.'

'Right.'

'Apart from the crew, there's no other passengers riding 'taxi'; you'll have the whole hold to yourself.' He wasn't sure if he should have made that last word plural. 'Special flight, I gather, Major?' He'd noticed with a quick glance the steel chain attached to the Major's slim steel case's handle, and disappearing into sleeve where he guessed it would run up to the shoulders to be anchored securely.

An awkward pause of not answering. Frank broke the spell with some humour. 'And no recliner seats, then?'

'*Sir?*'

Frank stole a glance and secretive smile at Mary Lee in the back seat.

'Have a good flight, Major.' Waiting for them to get out, the corporal reversed the jeep, to turn and speed away back again towards the main building.

Walking up the broad steel ramp and in through the great yawning mouth, they walked into the huge plane's dark cavernous hold, empty but for them, for the next few long hours it was going to take. Boring – unless you had something to do.

Pulling the great mass of loose cargo sacking together as best they could, they arranged something in the shape of what was hoped would give that satisfaction of a mattress of sorts. Kneeling down on it, Mary Lee undid her tie, jacket and shirt buttons, to strip down to her bra. 'If the assistance I provide you with is *commendable*, do you think you could put in a good word for me to Colonel Sully for extended leave – Major *Frank*?' Taking off her white bra, she held it up and dangled it in front of him 'Maybe you could buy me something nice in one of the fancy ooh-la-la boutiques'

He kneeled down beside her. 'Oh, I'm sure I can do that. Who knows, maybe we can get you a *permanent* posting in Berlin.'

Falzoni bounded up the stairs two at a time, to the sound of Glen Miller, not the usual softly haunting sound, but a more jumpy 'Pennsylvania Six Five 0 0 0!' He took over from singing to humming for a few seconds before, with a mischievous smile, making a deliberate point of opening the outer door to the office with a noisy rattle of the handle, so that Glen's number took a sudden dive.

Stepping into the office, Frank had a lovely view of Rosalyn's lovely curved ass as she bent over her desk pretending to be busily preoccupied 'arranging things'. When she turned to face him, he looked at the radio, giving a cheeky wide grin and arching his eyebrows, to push home the point. Which was that if music was on, then Marley was out. Not actually having instructed Rosalyn not to play loud music in the office, he'd nevertheless given a strong hint of disapproval in that direction. So when the cat was out, the mouse was apt to play naughty, imagining that the loud music doubled her typing speed. It did, but it also doubled her typing errors. If Marley couldn't relate the errors to music, then more fool him if he thought it was because she was unable to benefit from his 'guru' wisdom and guidance in his absence.

'So where's he gone off to, then?'

In answer, Rosalyn pointed to the closed door of Goodblood's inner office.

'You mean ---' Frank shook his head with a puzzled frown. '--- he's still here?'

She put her hand, small finger and thumb extended, to the side of her face to signal that her their boss was on the phone.

'Well I'll be –' Frank grinned at her. 'You mean to say that he's too preoccupied with other things, to not notice the radio playing – and to not notice *you*? That's a heart-breaker of a realisation. You have my sympathy, Rosalyn, you really do,' His smile widened to let out his teasing laughter.

She looked at him and gave a long sigh of strained patience. 'You really can be ever so ---'

'Tiresome – yes, I know; so you keep telling me. Mea culpa, mea culpa, mea maxima culpa,' he said striking his breast in a mocking feigned act of contrition. 'But putting that aside, what's new on the plate to give us – *me*, anyway, -- premature ulcers?'

Taking a large pile of folders off the top of the filing cabinet, she handed them to him, smiling, in what was her turn, in open glee as he looked with obvious dismay at the workload. 'Mr Goodblood needs you to go over these before ---'

'Yesterday – yeah, sure, doesn't he always.' Just looking at them without lifting a finger, was already making Frank feel terribly, terribly tired, after that long flight from Thailand – especially considering that he had not spent the entire time sitting idle, but rather, expending a lot of energy in 'physical activity'.

Rosalyn picked up a small piece of paper from her desk-top and planted it on top of the pile he was already laden with in double-armed effort. 'There's this also.'

'What's that?' The woman's handwriting was hardly any easier to read than her shorthand. She was in the wrong department. She should be with the cyphers crew in the bottom floor, just above the basement motor pool.

'It's the appointment time for you to attend for debriefing with the Operations Review Panel. Tomorrow, at precisely fourteen hundred hours. They phoned in just half an hour before you were due to land.'

'No, no, that's not right. The meeting's scheduled for next week – next Tuesday. What's up with them and got under their collar, that they can't wait?'

'Yes, that's still on – the main meeting with the whole panel present. But apparently there's been a modified adjustment need for strategic technical data details, which by their very classification, is restricted by the critical time available.' A pause. 'This is a preliminary preparatory meeting between yourself and our resident medical officer, Doctor Moray. She said you'd understand.'

Boy, but didn't she just manage that mouthful well without choking on her tonsils. She was certainly learning how to talk like those grand wazirs upstairs – all stiff and measured, like those squawk-boxes at the fair that you popped your nickel into just to be told that your future was dark-clouded, where your horse, with all your bucks on it, needs a wheelchair if it's to cross the finishing line before sundown.

'Yeah, sure, I get it. Have a blink with the shrink, time.' Frank nodded, his face gone all serious now as he thought on other things.

Thanks, Rosalyn.' He stared down at the floor for a moment, deep in thought, then looked up at her. 'Be a good girl and get me the CHARLESBURG code numbers for the Interpol Exchange. You'll find them in the safe, filed under SUBLINE and COMPASS.'

'But Mr Goodblood categorically insisted that no-one was to ---'

'Don't you worry about what Marley said, honey, just you leave that to me. If he wants to come and blow a fuse, let him come and have a good old barney with me. Just you run along and get me those numbers.'

'If you say so, Major.'

'I say so.'

Dumping his load of files down on the desk in his own office, Frank turned around and headed for Marley's office. Opening the door, he entered quietly. Even without him intending to speak, he was hushed by Marley's waving hand, while the other hand held the red security Transatlantic line phone glued to his ear. He stood to watch and wait for Marley to finish his talk across the water.

While listening on, Goodblood darted his free-hand assiduously over a file in typically emergency redrafting of a plan that was required to please his military and political superiors in Washington. Only just returned from heavy discussions, over conflicting difficulties on North Atlantic manoeuvres, in Bremerhaven Naval HQ, where he was responsible for the Undersea Warfare Staff's handling of US/NATO and European and Group-North operations, Marley was now, as always, under close scrutiny from the Top Brass, endeavouring to preserve US security by the surest measures that his office, and the means at its disposal could devise, official or *otherwise*. That last, of course, being unutterable by him whenever he had reason to visit Washington's corridors of power.

Frank approached Marley's desk, to sit on its corner, sliding the file around to take out a sheaf of papers and place it on the desk top that was already flooded with paperwork. Marley paused in his long-distance 'tete-a-tete' from America to look up, leaning back to consider that piece of work. Putting a forefinger and thumb to his eyes to relieve their ache, he stooped over the desk to point out where the specific clauses were highlighted in bright yellow.

Frank then helped himself to one of the iron-handled rubber stampers, banging each page with it in turn. Finished with that, he sifted out the one page from the others, lifting it up for closer consideration. 'I'm thinking that this isn't too clever a tactic, Colonel.' This in a voice quiet enough to not distract Marley's ear from that more important voice crackling through to his ear from the White House. 'I'd much rather that we had more time to dig out some better information on it. Makes it a safer bet. Can't we get Admiral Trennil to delay his advance for at least forty-eight hours until we have more reliable intelligence coming through the wires, to give us a clearer picture on it?'

Finished with the call, Goodblood put the phone down.

'I'm guessing that was the um heap Big Chief in the big White Wig-Wam in Big Town DC?'

'Since you put it that way in your schoolboy antics, Frank, yes it was. And I'm telling you, he wasn't exactly handing me the peace-pipe for a friendly smoke. Not after this mess we've landed in. *Your* mess, but *my* responsibility, so it's my neck that's heading for a stretching, damn it. What's more, he's sending his 'Little Big Chief' second in command, Vice President Montrose, accompanied by Defense Secretary McNamara here as a temporary stop-off before going on to the conference at Brussels. That's how concerned they are in Washington; they want to have a preliminary look at the guilty party before stringing him up on the ceremonial scaffold.'

Goodblood reached out to take the document. 'Hell, yeah, our old thorn-in the-foot annexation to the Saigon Treaty that makes the damn Treaty's stipulation stretch like elastic. Yeah, Frank, I agree the possible ceding of the small border territory would appear to be a knife-edge balance, on the wrong side of which President Johnson would not be too anxious to topple. With the miracles of landslide by-elections and our establishing protectorates over South Vietnam fresh in our wake, I don't somehow see Johnson doing handstands and somersaults and bringing out the bubbly champers to celebrate. Not just yet, anyway. Especially with those Ho Chi Minh supporters in our fucking own back yard states doing their best to stir up trouble.' Marley sat back in his chair to rub his face with both hands, as if that would clear away his exasperation.

'No, leave it with me, Frank, I'll see to it in the morning.' As Marley reached out for his watch resting on the desk, his hand strayed reflexively across to touch the mortar-shell piece standing beside it. Its steel had ripped G.I heads and limbs apart indiscriminately at Arno '44. The small scar on the back of his hand gave vivid testimony of where the same metal had spared his life but scraped his soul with the pain of him surviving, while his comrades had fallen.

'Bloody hell, is that the damn time already!' Putting the watch on, Marley got up and stood looking at Frank, while thinking things out for a moment. 'Like I said, leave it with me. Let's hope that we can amend the Treaty to allow us sending a fleet through the Makassar Straits with less problem than we've predicted so far, to facilitate the ships' Marine detachments launching their amphibious assault craft into operation on the Mekong Delta waters. Maybe added to that, if the Gods care to roll the dice our way, we'll be able to post our military consuls in the area, where they can negotiate for the fortifying of the northern frontiers of Turkey.'

'Right.' Frank picked up the other papers and returned them to the folder.

Goodblood turned round to stare, undecided for a moment, at the intercom unit on the desk, before reaching out to it. His finger clicked the switch to bring out the little green eye on the polished Italian walnut surface. 'A cup of coffee would be nice, Rosalyn.' Another click, and the little red eye came on again. Normally, closed office doors never stopped Marley bellowing out loud to Rosalyn for his coffee, but the weighted atmosphere of the last few minutes had apparently brought on a pensive quietness in him.

Ambling over to the window, he looked down at things four floors below, to see what besmirching political slogan was in vogue on today's rallying noisy crowd of protesters' placards. 'So how are we progressing with Georgievich?' He turned away at last from the window to face Frank.

'Coming along, coming along.'

'You sound as if it's not.'

'For this phase of the operation it's not unusual for things to be stiff, somewhat.'

'Have we salvaged anything of the operation do you think.'

'I'd say we've gained a fair footage of ground, considering the short time we had in the field. It's too early to expect Georgievich to make any positive move in his department without it escaping notice and looking too obvious. At least we have him where we can keep an eye on him. 'Frank paused for thought, pursing his lips. 'Y-e-s, I'd say we can work on the guy to save something of a wrecked mission.'

Goodblood's eyebrows crouched closer together as he stroked his cheek slowly, his expression darkening as he examined Frank's expression. 'You sound uncertain – almost as if you're fighting for certainty of soundness of judgement in what you're saying. Are there grounds for uncertainty? Are you seeing a problem? If so, it's better that we know now of them and so plan our way round them, rather than flounder in the field.'

Frank twisted the corner of a folder for a moment and then looked up into the room's high corner, as if it would help to pin-point a difficult thought. 'It's just that he can be distant – *far away* – in his odd moments.'

'*Odd*? In what way? What the hell are you getting at exactly, Frank?' Goodblood's inside tensed, throwing up a spiked barrier, like those make-shift ones they used to erect outside the trenches to ward of surprise assaults.

'Difficult to say, exactly. Like a good horse that you instinctively see as a sure bet of your bucks but have never seen run fully in form so that you don't know exactly what to measure it by. By all accounts he's certainly a solitary guy – cleverly accomplished enough in his technical work. In fact, I'm not sure how he does it, but he appears to continually predict your next stage of planning just as your bringing it on. But apart from that, I would almost say he's an embittered loner of a guy. Although in spite of what normal circumstances would have him classified as such, he, by virtue of his work, does seem to hold back from falling into that character mould. I suppose you could say that he's the direct reversal of that old adage that no man is an island. Like a great damn ivory tower, in fact.'

'You're saying that maybe we need one of those medieval moving assault towers on wheels things to scale his battlements, so to speak, to get to him. Is that what you're saying, Frank? It damn well sounds like it.'

'Yeah, something like that, I suppose.'

'Jeez, Frank, you've got to quit stalling around with empty "something like that" mouthfuls. We need something solid to work with, if we're going to get anywhere with the guy.'

'Yeah, well, whatever it is, the crazy berk had definitely got his guard up about something.'

'Go on, fill me in.'

'He can be a trifle too snappish, if not short, when answering questions, with an undisguised resentment at your digging in under his person armour.'

'Surely something we come to expect in this game?'

'Yeah, I guess so.'

'You should *know* so, Frank.' Goodblood relaxed, lowering his defence against what had been a few – maybe too many – moments of unnerving worry. 'Then from what you've said, we hopefully should have nothing to fear. From the solitary operator character description you're giving me, he should be ideal material to work with. Remember, it doesn't pay to become too personally involved with your catch. Let it shift around like the little hamster in its cage, and make careful observation of all its otherwise innocuous little movements. You know the game well enough, Frank, and it's not Snakes and Ladders, even if it does mirror some of its points.'

'Don't worry, I'm taking it all in like a good boy, Colonel.'

'Make sure you do.

But Frank was still thinking seriously about the possibility of trouble looming up – somewhere – somehow. In his overall assessment of Georgievich, there were naturally patches of personal obscurity that were left to one side. So long as they had the main part of him to do their job, those blank spaces could be left to one side for the time being. It was none of their business so long as they didn't interfere with the important work of the Department. But these 'blank spaces' kept floating back in Frank's mind for re-examination. Whether or not Georgievich realised it, his occasionally muttered small talk to himself was letting out odd messages picked up by Frank's carefully close observation. If it was not suicidal or self-destructive strains that Frank was possibly seeing in the man, what was it? Whereas other men reached out eagerly for success, this guy, whoever he was, whatever he really was, seemed to be juggling with his professional position, ready to throw it away, as if he hated it.

Frank saw something ticking away like a bomb in that man's mind. Something they had missed out in his personal background file. Something that was apparently accepting, if not wholeheartedly welcoming, the precarious role he was taking on with the same mad compulsion that sent other brains screaming after alcohol or opium. Was it a trait for self-punishment for some old skeleton in the cupboard that was crucifying the inner Georgievich? Maybe that skeleton was beginning to take on flesh to haunt him? The man did seem to be inclined to bang his head on the wall about something.

All this had not come to surface, to be noticed, when he had just been a code name buried in far- away Russia. But now that he was entering within the folds of US security, that enigma swelled up like that damned genie, out of its hitherto safe confinement in the bottle, to tower with menacing growth in front of them. Frank didn't care what form the guy's personal qualms took, so long as they didn't upset the Department's scheduled plans. The crazy berk could go jump off the Empire State Building if it made him happy, so long as it didn't get in the way of operations and he carried out his work as ordered. To hell with anything else that could be deemed as unimportant.

Deeply concerned as he was over this issue, Frank made no mention of it to Goodblood.

'Good.' A twinkle came into Marley' eye as his inner trepidations left him, like Elsinor's foreboding battlement spectre departing, haunting Hamlet no more.

'But we've still got to get him out. So how are you managing with that Frank?'

'Zhaekaly's done me well with good details on border routes and frontier security zones.'

'*Who?*'

'The Turk, Vechev Zhaekaly. He's put a few good favours my way in the past.'

'So plans are all clear and straightforward, then? All loose ends tied up like the Christmas goose, plucked and trussed, ready for the oven.'

'Perhaps "clear and straightforward" is a little debatable.'

'Ah, *debate,* trust not debate, when chance it holds back a dark dagger of fate.'

'Shakespeare?'

'No, Frank – *me.* I may not have picked up all the academic letters and laurels that you did at college, but in the mode of every Goodblood family home, my own library has lots of books on its shelves; I have to look clever in front of my wayward wandering minstrel of a guitar-strumming son if I'm to get him to go back to college.'

'Damn clever, Colonel, damn clever. So you think that there's another side to the Russian -- a side that doesn't quite see daylight?'

A chiding arched eyebrow came with Goodblood's response. ''You're not the only one playing your cards close to the chest, Major.'

'Sorry; just thought you had enough on your plate, as it is. I'm glad that's settled.'

'*Nothing* is settled, Frank, until it *is* settled. But taking things as we see them in this perspective, I suppose we can say there's nothing to fret for the time being.' Looking at his watch, Marley stepped forward to reach out for the intercom and switch it on again. 'Never mind that coffee. I have to go out.'

The long walnut box gave out a squeaking mixture of plaintiff protest and apology, but Marley gave no ear to it, simply switching the intercom off. He was in a hurry, time having been delayed enough, already.

'Where to now?'

'I've got to run over to the MI6 station, to put them in the picture, or the part of it we can afford to, anyway. And I've got to make that as brief a session as possible, to allow me time to get to the airport to meet Defense Secretary McNamara, accompanied by what could be the next presidential nominee, if this mess has failing polls toppling Johnson from office.'

A clock ticked away sedately in the shadowy perimeter of Frank's office that was lit only by a desk lamp. Falzoni was bent over his desk in earnest writing and the imitation nineteenth century oil lamp gave off his enlarged furry outline like a great Troll. Outside, a tower clock was lulling out to the soft warm Berlin evening air that all was well; inside, Frank was earnestly endeavouring to render some better assurance to Goodblood, and all of his bosses all the way up the glorified ladder in Washington DC, that there would be no more messing up on the job. Goodblood had left one heck of a workload on Frank's shoulders while he had gone off to 'entertain' his two VIP guests.

Frank had the heavy task of condensing into paper report what President Johnson had done, after several weeks of discussion with his cabinet, Joint Chiefs of Staff, the National Security Council, and a variety of other advisor, which most definitely included Barrington Gilberts. The President's decision on the Saigon situation was finalised. Frank noted the time of Johnson's address to the nation. Following the course of events since meeting with Khrushchev, with the Russian leader's declaring that the Soviet Union would never allow the United States to overrule Vietnam by force, Johnson's resistance to this was firm. A series of steps for increasing military readiness was announced. Initially, Johnson proposed asking Congress for an appropriation of $3.3 billion for the armed forces, over half of which would go to procuring conventional ammunition, weapons, and equipment. Johnson then proposed to augment the total authorised strength of the Army from 864,000 to I million men and increase Naval and Air Force active-duty strength by 32,000 and 65,000, respectively. A doubling and tripling of draft calls in the coming months was called for; included was the activation of some reservists and certain ready-reserve units; tours of duty for soldiers, sailors, and airmen scheduled to leave in the near future would be extended. Finally, programmes to retire or mothball older ships and aircraft and the deactivation of a number of B-47 bomber and refuelling wings would be postponed. The Secretary of Defence, McNamara, announced thereafter a schedule ensuring that 50% of the Strategic Air Command's bombing wings would be placed on 14-minute ground alert and also that training duties for three of the Army's divisions in the United States would be relieved and replaced by readiness for emergency deployment in East European territories to meet any Asian aggression.

In Operation Torchlight, With the tunnel network hoarding vital Vietcong supplies stretching over a distance of 30,000 kilometres in the Cu Chi district, G.I.s were being trained as 'tunnel rats' to spend hours in them, navigating their long winding routes, and detecting along the way, trip wire booby traps that exploded grenades and overturned boxes of scorpions and snakes on unsuspecting US troops. In support, some 32,000

US troops had launched Operation Oak, attacking the Vietcong stronghold of the Binh Duong province north of Saigon, near the Cambodian border. In Operation Torchlight, US and South Vietnam units took advantage of the Marine Corps Fleet's amphibious assault crafts to attack along the South Vietnam coast, successfully wiping out the 1st Vietcong Regiment. Naval Command was now utilizing amphibious forces as floating reserve for transporting reinforcements to any hot spot along the coast. Especially in conflicts concentrated near to the Demilitarised Zone.

Phew! With a sigh, Falzoni sat back to stop writing, and watch more hot news of this ilk come clattering through on the coded teleprinter sheet, leaving barely time for up-roaring applauding by 'Hawks' and dismayed gasps of 'Doves' on Capitol Hill to die down. Shaking his head for a few moments he took all this in, seeing it not as just words on paper, but as the heavy task that he and Marley were laden with of 'sorting things out over there', taking the pulse of events, good or bad, as they unfolded; so far, the odds were on the latter. Especially that bit about Russia taking steps further to stand in their way with almighty great force, and no kidding.

It was definitely welcome news as regards the US build-up of military strength, but just how exactly Khrushchev's martial lot planned to increase and manoeuvre their heavy and light armoured divisions across the military chessboard was, to counter this, a searing thought. How the enemy changed its positions on the chessboard was taking a lot of monitoring, so that Marley and himself had the hellish task of trying their best to be 'flies on the walls' of Moscow's war rooms. The vital intelligence that he and Marley were gathering from Geogievich was tantamount to stopping the lid flying off that dangerously simmering cauldron of what could be that much dreaded conflict of nuclear finality.

With another grim reminder of time waiting for no man, by a tower clock chiming faintly above the murmur of evening traffic outside, Frank dropped his pen and sat back in his chair for a short break. Rummaging around in a lower desk drawer, he found and brought out a packet of pistachio nuts. But the cellophane bag wanted to play tough guy, engaging him in a mini wrestling contest – and it was winning. Swearing, he lifted the confounded thing to his teeth to rip it open.

'You men are all like babies. Here, let me.' Rosalyn had come in to pick up and take away for typing, what the Major had written so far. Handing back the opened bag to Frank and taking up her new load of assessed files, she stood there looking at him gripping the bag in his 'claw', as she saw it, and him pouring the nuts into his other hand. 'It must have been sore when you first had it fitted. *Was* it sore?'

Frank looked up at her with a reproving smile. What a stupid question to ask. 'Haven't you got work to do?' He put his message across looking pointedly at the pile of folders she was holding in her folded arms. 'Goodblood will expect you to have got through the lot when he gets back.'

'Oh, he won't be back until ---' She broke off at the strength of his long mocking stare at her. Turning round, she stomped noisily back to her office.

Crumpling the empty bag in his fist, and with nothing short of his brilliant Bronx Tigers basketball player's skill, lobbed it across the room to land in the metal waste bin that applauded with a soft clonk. He turned to pick up his ballpoint pen and push on with attacking more files, when the phone in Rosalyn's outer office shrieked out for attention.

Rosalyn was promptly at his side again. 'It's Mr Myers. It's about someone called ML.' An interested pause. 'It's a woman.'

You didn't need to be a shrink to recognise the female insatiable craving for details on a potential budding female rival. 'Mary Lee.' The scant piece of info was teasing enough to have her scarlet nails digging into her palm. 'Put Sheldon through to this connection, there's a good girl.' But Rosalyn was still there, rooted to the spot, waiting for casual snippets of information on the 'other woman'. 'Are you still there?' Frank's admonishing growl was enough to shift Rosalyn.

Lifting the phone when the call transferred through, Frank listened on, expecting something that would not be to his liking, as it always was, when it was Myers bringing the news out of the blue. 'Where are you calling from, Myers? -- And you want me to pick you up three blocks away from there? That's pushing it a bit, don't you reckon. Isn't that district a bit too --- Right, right, okay, I won't argue, if that's what you want. Usual procedure: I wait five minutes, then circle the full three blocks; this three times until you appear. If you don't, I'm off and you're on your own.' No more to be said. He put the phone down.

That done, Frank looked at his intercom with its little red eye staring back at him. Reaching out, he moved his finger along the row of switches, to stop at the one for their underground motor pool. He pressed the switch down so that the little green eye took over from the red one.

'Toni?'

'Yeah.'

'Have a car standing by, ready for me in ten – no, make it fifteen minutes. One of our dummy taxi ones. Better make it one with smoked one-way windows.'

'Bullet-proofed?'

'Nah, ordinary glass will do, so long as the glass is strong enough not to shatter from a punk's head when he's too drunk to find the door.'

29

With the week moving on another week, an almost continuous downpour of rain had removed the slush and ice from all but the sorest memories. Hectic dashing about the city in the approaching Christmas rush was made easier by no longer carrying the risk of fractured limbs. Falzoni was very much pressed for time, hurrying between sessions with Goodblood, while still assisting MI6 with liaison talks, and lending a limb to that department of the Army that sought not to ruffle feathers on Capitol Hill by limiting distasteful field activities.

This latter aspect of security may not have been too obvious to the ordinary citizen, where the city seemingly weltered under the onslaught of military activities. No sooner did a disturbance infuriate the public with its vile desecration of some public place, than it was lost amidst the bellowing of protesting demonstrators announcing another coming insurgent uprising in some particular official city building. Little insignificant things, like the murder of a high court judge, did not hold the public's interest for long, fading as quickly as the rain could wash the pencilling of the vendor's pavement newspaper fly-board sheets. In Washington the public's anger seethed a lot longer over the Navy's humiliation of having three more of its Air Sea Transport planes brought down by ground-to-air missiles fired by Russian-trained Vietcong units, killing the entire three crews, much to the taxpayer's pinching of pocket and senators' dismay.

Nor was public unrest helped any by the agitation arising from strikers armed with pick-shafts roaming the city, vandalising and looting from commercial premises. But it had at least simmered down somewhat to a shade of the earlier horror of upheaval from mob rioters bent on taking over the city, but for the swift iron-handed action of City Hall having seen fit to bring out and deploy extra units of National Guard reserves. At least the heads of the two cities seemed to maintain their public composure by still holding its foreign VIP reception soirees. One minor blessing for President Johnson with this wave of civil unrest served to overshadow the Government's embarrassment over its crushing defeat in minor state bye-elections.

Unable to hold his agonised gaze on the crucifying headlines for one second longer, Goodblood crumpled the Washington Post's pages together and let it fall onto his desk, to join the sheets of teleprinter 'horror' reports of the same news littering its top. Luckily it didn't collapse under the weight.

'Small incendiary bombs for distraction in Moscow, and near to the city, you're telling me now, Frank. That makes how many now?

'A total of seven bombings to date, in fact.' Frank's calm expression in rendering the grave situation as mere statistics gave Marley reason to stare at him, wondering if he should compliment or criticise the Major.

'Bloody hell! seven bloody bombings in two days.! You'll forgive me, Major, if I'm sounding somewhat damn contrary to our original plan, when I say that I'm wondering if we may have overshot our mark.' Hooking his thumbs in his trouser pockets, Marley walked over to the window to gaze – to *search* -- for something – *anything* – out there in that unhappy scenario, that would push away his brooding thoughts. As if in mocking denial of his futile wish, a policeman went down under a skull-cracking blow from a furious demonstrator's placard-pole. Trying to decide if this was a bad omen, or just an attack of morbid spirits before his morning coffee, Marley sought inner counsel by stroking his chin in long silence.

He turned his back on the window's discouraging scene. 'As you already know, I've been tracked down and routed in an awkward corner by our two Washington VIP guests, and needless to say, the two of them haven't exactly showered me with congenial greetings. Like hell, they didn't! Whilst our work normally lies outside the general jurisdiction of the police, it has to be conceded that this situation, with its hue and cry, from the public, has developed the furious bubbles of a boiling pot of complaints over our 'mis-handling', as the press sees it, of security matters. Heads are to roll, for sure, I'm promised most solidly, if proper remedial action is not taken soon.'

Marley returned to his desk to reclaim his seat, so that it creaked back directly under his weary weight of office.

Frank was a little unsettled by Marley's apparent relinquishing of his standpoint so easily without his usual measure of fire-dragon resistance. 'Wasn't it part of our strategy to refrain from pulling out the plug prematurely, so to speak, and hold back until we had all the fish in the pond? It can only be working. With this degree of public unrest, Moscow can only think that we're stepping back in imminent abandoning of US policy of aggression.'

'I can't help thinking of the jockey who holds the horse back too long, in overestimation of the nag's ability, so that he's unable to close that gap between himself and the leading rider, and subsequently loses the race and the damn fortune in dollars that you bet on him and his horse. Our great President is apt to derive one hell of a lot more than mere personal displeasure if we damn well chance to lose *this* race. Would your uniform buttons shine so brightly, Major, in the Officers' Club of that God-forsaken speck of an observation station in some remote corner of the map?'

Frank ignored the disquieting thought of such a punitive posting by lifting the newspaper off the desk to tap the front page with a metal forefinger. 'Myers did say that this job was to be the last dummy run. After that ---?' He paused to give a significantly louder tap on the paper. 'The Big Bang?'

'But he has not yet said where this so-called big bang is to occur or what shape it will take.'

'Not yet, but I'm expecting him to follow up on that shortly. He damn well better, or we're all up to our necks in it, for sure.' Frank looked at Goodblood's shrapnel-piece clock to check the time with his own watch. 'In twenty minutes to be precise, or so he promised.'

'*Promised*? I shouldn't think that that word carried much value in this game.'

'He wants me to pick him up again across the town for another quick word in the taxi. He doesn't want to be seen anywhere near the safe house. His contact in Moscow does seem to be a regular cornucopia of information, if we're to believe it.'

'And going along with that, where do we expect our 'rabbit' to bolt from the safety of its warren?'

'As a rough stratagem, one can't fail to notice the irregular pattern of all the bombings in outlying locations. Whilst the individual point names themselves mean nothing, when joined on a map, they form a circle. They're irregular, yes, but not too much so as to strike one as coincidence. In fact, they're positioned deliberately at a distance in order to act as a decoy. And Georgievich definitely needs that distraction if he's to make his escape from the city successful.'

'Having to make a rapid exit from his hiding place, just a hair's breadth from being arrested, in the last two days, is hardly what I call distant, Frank.' Goodblood swivelled his chair side to side for several moment of silence as if that would be enough to dispel his troubled thoughts in a wistful: '*Close* Sesame!' reversal of the magic phrase. Frank drummed his fingers on the desk in thought. 'One thought does niggle me, though.'

'Only one thought? Marley felt his inside play him up with unkind peptic acids. 'But go on, frighten me.'

'Simply that – well, in the same way that the disturbances have followed a definite pattern for the purpose of misleading them from Geogievich's whereabouts, what if they're also misleading us into thinking we're fooling *them*, when they're fooling *us* by catching onto our deception, and looking in the opposite direction of our deliberately set pattern? After all, they've twice been so close to grab him, but didn't. Are they letting him – or *us* – think that he's escaping? There's a point to scratch your brain.'

'Jeez! Frank, you're like a rollercoaster gone berserk, going up and down with your good points and bad points. For God's sake, tell me something I want to hear, that doesn't make we want to grab my pension and quit.' Marley slapped the desk and sat upright. 'How are we progressing with McGavin? *Are* we progressing?' A grey expression that suggested what he was dreading to hear, returned to Marley's face.

'I can't help getting the funny feeling that he think's he's in a position to attempt bartering with us.'

'Hell, Frank, I'm in no mood for mental gymnastics; give it to me straight!'

'Well, the information we want from him seems to be coming out piece by piece, for something in return.'

'What do you think he's after?'

'As a fair guess, I'd say that he wants to be reconsidered for his application for joining CIA.'

Marley's eyebrows jumped up. 'Should we? What do you think?'

'*Me*? I'll leave it to you and your drinking pals at Langley to make, or not to make, a mistake on that decision.'

'Like I've said before, Frank, sometimes you can have me believing that you're not quite the dumb chicken I take you for.' Marley stroked his chin, feeling the stubble coming through. He needed a shave. After he'd had a double malt along with a T-bone steak and some good old French-fries. Looking at the desk clock, he got up from his chair. 'I'd better not keep you from your appointment with our devious colleague Myers. That clock is four minutes slow, as it is.'

'Six and a half, actually.'

'Six and a half!' Surprised at this late discovery, Marley looked round, but Frank had already gone out the door in haste of his urgent meeting with Myers.

The telephone shrieked with piercing urgency, ripping the skin of silence off the hallway, just as Falzoni entered the apartment. He heard her get out of bed and called out: 'It's okay, honey. I'll get it.'

But Mary Lee came out nevertheless, to lean against the door jamb. Her white heavy towelled bath robe hung open, revealing only pale flesh but for where a scarlet triangular affair tried desperately to stop her hips and thighs breaking out. He liked the way the swelling hips balanced her rounded breasts.

As he put the phone to his ear, he noticed the little white spots on her pantie frills. Or maybe that was her skin showing through the minute holes. Or was it spots dancing before his tired eyes? Questions like that, calling for his annual chat with the MO seemed far away to him, with his fatigued brain squealing out for sleep, the energy draining out of him like water from a sponge.

The effort to put his mind across the line and listen to another mind so far away sapped him, and he passed a hand over his weary face. 'Right, Commander; got it. Thanks, and goodnight – or should that be morning?'

The receiver hadn't quite settled in its cradle, when her arms snaked round his neck and she was upon him, kissing him, like the happy Labrador welcoming, licking, its returning master. Perhaps chameleon was more fitting, since her mood had changed, he noted, as her tongue licked his lips with the same seductive cunning of the lizard. Her dark expression reflected his own, coming over her face the moment she caught his indrawn worried look, as he turned round in her arms to face her.

Running his fingers gently up and down her spine, he pressed himself against her for whatever mood she was in, hoping that he could step into it and leave his work behind him – for a little while at least. 'I did phone,' he said carefully, 'to say I would be late, but you didn't answer.'

'I was probably running the water in the bath, and didn't hear you.'

With her kisses going too lavishly down his neck, truth was obviously being evaded. Besides, you could hear that phone scream above the roar of the Niagara Falls. But he let it go. Close as they were to each in their passionate embrace, there was a strained silence building up between them.

'Who was that on the phone?' she said in what seemed an effort to keep a casual tone in the question. 'I heard you say Commander.'

'My great old uncle in Milwaukee; he runs the local Army Veterans branch of the Salvation Army.'

'Sure it was.' Her nails made an extra hard dig into his neck. 'And he's in desperate need of you to go over there and help hand out the molasses scones and cookies. Right?' The annoyance in her voice didn't escape him.

'Right.'

'At his great age, shouldn't he be a general by now, in the Salvation Army?'

'He's modest.'

'Just like his modest great nephew.'

'Yeah, just like his modest great nephew -- you got it right on the dot, kid.'

Sliding his hand down her back to give her bottom a mild rebuking tap, he moved his lips closer to her ear to whisper softly: 'Are you tired of me already – doing the Houdini and avoiding me?'

Not answering, she simply nestled her face beneath his chin, on his chest, and he held her there, silent and secure. But like a mischievous cat purring with energy, she gave off the feeling that she could leap away with open claws. A feeling of restlessness, wanting to escape from a claustrophobic situation. She was young and wanting fun. The kind his work didn't give him time for, especially at his age. Jeeze, slow down, Frank, you're not on those semi-invalid retirement crutches just yet!

The last thing he wanted was for her to leave him for some other young Adonis gigolo. But he wasn't sure, in his troubled mind, if expecting her to live on with him wasn't tantamount to conflict in its situation. It had been awkward enough securing her a transfer to work here, in Berlin, from Colonel Sully in far-away Seoul. He couldn't split himself between her and his work – his *duty* – at this time of urgent crisis. While the former was claiming more and more from him, the latter was getting much less from what energy was left to spare in him.

The initial attraction between them hadn't been anything more complicated than a mutual need for dealing with the boring isolation and almost overwhelming scorching dry air of that sun-baked military base. Her cover tag for hanging around him on his fresh arrival on the base had been to 'assist him in anything he needed, any way she could', as official PR assigned for the duty. He couldn't remember what door, or even corridor, it was, except that when the door had opened and her shirt top opened down two buttons, his seeing her again after their earlier brief encounter on the airfield had truly dazzled him. Not only were her vital statistics good, but her ready supply of statics of data on the immediate area, and on where he would be heading down south, were good. He'd liked everything about her and what she offered. In spite of the base's Grade One security clearance on her, he'd still had Berlin Station screen her, on account of the Red One classification of his assignment. He had no qualms of conscience over this, since that was what protocol's red tape stringency of the work demanded. Nor had he expected any complaints from her for any mistrust she might have of him. That was the understanding they'd agreed on, without saying it, when he'd accepted her plea for a transfer to the 'big city', when he'd consented to handling the fussy Colonel Sully.

Things after that seemed to be running smoothly enough, considering that she'd be ditching her 'above board' PR work to take up her first duties in PR work of a relatively much quieter hush-hush nature that was the CIA. It hadn't escaped him that she had been a might eager, so soon after joining the Department, to swap her PR work for a stint of codes work in the radio section, scanning all the intelligence that was shuttled back and forth. After that, she seemed quick off the mark to be rallying her efforts parallel to the jobs he was running in active field operations. It gave him an uncanny feeling. Or was he being unduly worried, cautious – paranoid -- even? Those shifting, unsure thoughts about Georgievich that he'd half-revealed to Goodblood earlier? Was that uncertainty now affecting his judgement like an infectious rash? Myers would have said it was the proper way to do the job – trusting no-one. What the hell;

everybody was checked, screened, call it what you want, in this game. She'd said that she simply wanted to be near him. Was that all it was?

His session with Franz Hauter in Bangkok was helping to bring out this uneasiness he was having. He was feeling unsure about a lot of things now. He needed to dig out and read up on his station files, as well as wiring through to Interpol's archives, and Army Intelligence's immediate post-war records on the Kraut.

From the way Myers had been putting it across, Hauter was standing at a fork-junction. Either he had been working undercover for the Abwehr (wartime German Military Intelligence) in his early days, trying to infiltrate the Communist element; or he was a double agent, having caught the attention of, and promptly recruited by, a KGB talent scout in the field. This development, with its important implications, if the worst turned out to be true, was helping to gnaw his brain like a hungry woodpecker.

In spite of this, in carefully weighed-consideration, he'd persuaded Hauter to work for them, filtering intelligence from a now unsuspecting Moscow source.

Now here he was, preparing to jump off at the deep end in the last leg final operation to bring out Georgievich from the Russian bear-trap situation, where there was the dangerous chance, if the dice rolled against them, of fatefully stepping on it, along with that ever-promised holiday in Siberian waste-land, expenses paid, courtesy of the Soviet Union, that went with the job, on your falling short of the target.

She looked up at him and caressed his grey face. 'You look so tired.'

'*Do I*?' He'd pulled his head back sharply from her as if to avoid letting her see what it was that was making his mind tired. He instantly regretted his action fearing it was a tell-tale sign of what he was thinking. He hoped he just *looked* tired, and nothing else. He sure as hell *felt* tired.

Collecting himself as best he could, he put his forehead down gently against hers. 'Sorry, kid, I reckon this old stallion has been out of the stable too long today. I need some shut-eye.' He said this with what tenderness he could muster in salvage from the leaded emotions he was expecting from this fresh young restless mare. It seemed to work. It wiped the scrutinizing look from her face like a magic duster. Or was she just better at this game than he thought, possibly courtesy of KGB training? Immediately horrified at what he had just thought, he realised just as quickly that Myers would have put him right, saying that it was a natural part of the job, suspecting everyone and everything. Yeah, and a Merry Christmas and peace be unto all men. Sure!

He made a special effort to put on a Rett Butler face, looking down at her beneath shrouding eyebrows: 'Frankly, my dear, I don't give a damn ---' breaking into a laugh, '---- but I could do with some coffee.' He stepped back. 'I'll go make some.'

Puzzled at the funny mood she detected behind his actions for a moment, she smiled and put out a hand to stop him going off to the kitchen. 'No. I'll do it, Frank. You go on into the bedroom and lie down. You look like you could do with some rest.'

'Rest can come after some shared invigorating exercise.' He reached out to put his hands under the bathrobe and tickle her.

Letting out a squeal, she drew back, giggling, and threw a playful slap at him, almost beating his parrying forearm. The metal one. 'Oh, that's hard.'

'Only if you're not nice to it.' He moved in through her rain of slaps, to tickle more so that she exploded in more squeals. Letting her scuffle off to the kitchen, he watched her buttocks jostling each other beneath the white robe, like they were in earnest dispute.

While she snuggled and contorted her vivacious body, he felt that she was just not getting through to him in his preoccupied state of tension; that he was embracing her warm flesh like a senseless cardboard effigy. While his body wanted to turn its passion on, his mind seemed so remote from that empty physical need. When her fiery rhythmic wriggling finally ceased, after what pleasure he hoped he'd given her, he rolled over on his back, wondering if she'd noticed his lame performance.

Kneeling up over him on the bed, she leaned down and caressed his chest, while he lay there watching the moonlight glisten on her smooth flesh. He saw the question coming as she pouted her lips with that demure look and tilted her head slightly. 'You keep on looking at that clock when you think I don't see you. Is that what the phone call was about?'

'In a word—yes.'

'So where are you off to this time? Let me guess – Milwaukee, to join the Salvation Army?'

'In that case, Mom would be calling Father Mandini to come and have a word with her erring son.'

'You're in that pensive mood, when you go flying off and just leave me, without a word of when you'll be back, or if you'll be coming back.' He felt her hands working harder on his torso, sensing irritation building up inside her.

'I'll be back, don't you worry, kid. Question is: Will *you* be here?'

'What's that supposed to mean?'

Leaning up, and catching her by her wrists, he held them by her hips for a moment to look at her. If he wasn't awed by her simple beauty, he had to be blind. Cupping her face in his hands, he leaned down to kiss her. Rolling over, he lay back down. 'Go to sleep, kid.'

'Stop calling me kid.'

The room settled in motionless silence.

Lying there on his back, he saw many faces, many things. The ceiling seemed to spin so that he saw a massed semblance of human forms and armoured shapes shifting in great slothful motion towards the golden sunset of a nuclear flash.

As he lay there, the thought struck him, as he had put the question to Hauter. Why had the man been so easy to take the offer to come over and join them? If he was working for Moscow, why relinquish what was surely a valuable asset to them, as well as solid roubles to him? When asked what he wanted in return for his change of loyalty, the man had not said anything specific. Frank thought over the implication of that for a moment. Unless what Hauter and his bosses would be profiting from in return, would be the safeguarding of their planted security leak, their real mole of a turncoat. Geogievich?

Hell! Frank slapped his forehead softly. It could mean spinning a whole carousel of suspect faces in the mind. Each face a picture of innocence, whilst possibly harbouring insidious enmity beneath, in the very mode of this so-called Cold War they had got themselves into. Just like their own mole, Lori Brun, in the East Sector, working deep in the Stasi HQ, with access to classified material. All she needed was someone to draw attention away from herself. And that brought it back to Charlie as distracting stooge. And she had paid the mortal price. The pain stung Frank.

With the fatigue spinning his brain round, maybe he needed something stronger than coffee; some good old Kentucky 'mouthwash'. But no; he needed to sleep in order to get back in form for tomorrow.

Mary Lee lay quiet, eyes closed but listening when he got up out of the bed to start sharply putting on his clothes. Checking his pockets and the contents of his light travel bag, he stood looking at her sleeping form for a moment, before deciding not to disturb her with a light kiss. He turned to go out.

'Haven't you forgotten something? The sleeping form moved, raising its head.

'Sorry, kid; didn't want to disturb your golden dreams.' He bent down and kissed her.

'That's not what I meant.' She looked at him, then towards the bedside cabinet drawer.

'No, it's better left there. Where I'm going, carrying a .44 calibre automatic Ruger can ruffle a few official feathers.'

'You're not going back to Seoul, are you?'

'Hell, no. The mosquitos there are jealous of my aftershave and suck it from me. Don't ask me what the leeches do – that would be 'below the belt'. I've told the pool to send someone round in a car to pick you up for work.'

'How will I know when you're coming back?'

'When I walk in through that door.'

30

The bright spot in the distance gradually grew into the headlights flux of the Chrysler speeding along the narrow road winding its way across the deserted landscape. Following the tortuous bend, it momentarily disappeared as it entered a wood, reappearing as flashes between the leafless pines, and out again into the open. Along the boring long road again. Frank accepted the monotony, driving on and on, determined to get there, in time according to schedule.

But how was his passenger taking it, he wondered. He glanced round at Georgievich seated beside him. 'You looked worried – *hesitant* – before you got into the car,' said Frank quietly, without looking round at Georgievich. 'Last minute nerves? A changing of mind, perhaps?'

'I'm okay. Just a little tired, that's all. Barely slept for a minute last night.'

'Right,' said Frank quietly, still keeping his eyes on the road in front, while his inner attention was on that seated beside him. He shifted the subject to divert Georgievich from reading into his thoughts. 'Light me a cigarette, and put it in my mouth. They're here in my top pocket. And don't say you object to smoking in a confined space. Open the damn window, if you feel the need.'

Geogievich looked round sharply at Frank. 'And you're asking *me* if *I'm* having a touch of nerves!'

But Frank was less worried about being caught and thrown into a Lubyanka dungeon, than he was of presenting a double negative report before the Langley Operations Review Panel at the end of the week, as he would be doing, if he made a flop of this final decisive leg of Operation COMPASS as well.

'There isn't time to worry about getting caught – only space for thinking about *not* getting caught.'

'But if we *are* caught?'

'Goes with the job, pal. As others would maybe say, it was what Allah wrote down on the day's menu, so to speak. Total waste of the little grey cells now at this late hour. We're in it now, and we're in it deep to be caught or not to be caught—and you don't need Shakespeare to quote from that last bit.'

'That's one way of looking at it, I suppose,' muttered Georgievich quietly.

'That's the way *we're* looking at it -- *right*?' A pause. 'Hey, remember, pal, you're supposed to be *for* us, not *against* us now, so let's drop the punches and put fighting behind us.'

That was enough to shut Geogievich up. For the moment, anyway.

Nothing else moved outside around them. Yet far out in the soulless wind-scathed wilderness, two 'trees' looked on intently, one with powerful binoculars of the type issued to Soviet Armed Forces.

Their 'bark' was a dark blue-green camouflage topped with an outer layer of netting holding thin leafy branches, letting the soldiers merge in as part of the landscape, but for the deathly black machine-guns draped across their 'trunks'. Their surveillance orders, as part of their general manoeuvres, were to watch everything that moved without interfering and report when it was necessary. And that could mean doing absolutely nothing, between hours and hours of staring at absolutely nothing. A rife soldier's life. The soldier snapped on a switch and the radio pack strapped on his back came into life. He spoke into the microphone fastened about his head under his hood.

Knocking back the hood, he looked up overhead. Between the crackling squeaks from the headpiece, the two ghostly figures waited silently in the shadow of the pines, their eyes fixed skywards. They were the eyes and ears of a general Red Army field intelligence operation, with a stiff training of waiting and flitting about unseen in the forests with lone wolf stealth and cunning.

Neither of them twitched a muscle until the jiggering chop-chop sound of the helicopter reached their ears from above and beyond the trees. The soldier cracked a smile as the earphone squeaked again, just before the helicopter cluttered past overhead, waltzing beneath its fierce circle of swirling blades, correcting itself, to swoop round and follow the long narrow road that headed in the direction of the frontier.

At the same time, parts of the dense mass of forest suddenly broke out in a sweat of growling armoured cars and tanks coming out into the open. They would never get to where the helicopter was going, of course, but that was just a normal part of manoeuvres.

Looking up at the heavily overcast sky with its ominous darker shade creeping in, Frank caught sight of the twinkling lights of the tadpole that was a Russian Kava 4H1. A naval surveillance helicopter. Its usual duties being to patrol the coastal areas for ice blocks, it was now swooping down to watch the progress of the tiny blue Chrysler racing on in its determined south-westwards direction of what could only be Russia's constituent satellite republican state of Georgia's frontier border touching on Turkey.

The rubber-masked face peered momentarily down from the helicopter cockpit, while smoothly switching on the camera. This sucked in the Chrysler's silent motion along the thin line below on 70mm film. Sweeping down in one swift motion, the helicopter was there and gone. It had done its work and relayed a report of this immediately to HQ.

'And Hell and hallelujah to you as well, buddy!' said Frank, watching the helicopter pull away from them and gradually shrinking to a distant spot before disappearing completely from the bleak landscape. He looked round at Georgievich. 'How about that – we're on film! Maybe some Hollywood talent scout will headhunt us for our good looks. Well, mine, anyway. You could always do a stand-in for Frankenstein's prodigy of a creation.' You could well imagine pock-faced Georgievich in his debut performance taking on the role of the infamous monster in that setting, sure enough.

But the Russian mind could not understand this remark's meaning, so Georgievich could only frown. So Frank's face also took on a more serious shade. 'Which reminds me – have you got the film?'

'You have already asked me that question.'

'Yeah, well, I'm asking you again, to keep you on your toes.'

'For the upteen time – yes, I have it.'

'Umpteenth.'

The constant roar of the engine took over to replace conversation. After that, the roar of the rain. A colossus of fury had been cast down from the dark sky above, with great solid sheets of rain pounding and bouncing with great steaming energy up off the road, or what you could barely see of the road, through the windscreen, blurred with its river of water and wipers groaning in their side-to-side struggling effort. With the ground lying somewhere beneath that non-stop deluge, you virtually expected the roadside flood drains to put up their 'no vacancies' notices. Not content with rain god Yu Shi sending down to earth all this water, Zeus had to join in and cast down his javelin streaks of lightning, with the flashes giving solid visible identity to the otherwise invisible roar of the downpour.

It all stopped as suddenly as it had started. The wetness left behind giving everything a sinister spectral silver sheen that belonged in a monochromatic 'B' feature Fritz Lang horror movie. Yeah, you could well imagine pock-faced Georgievich in his debut role as that infamous monster, sure enough.

With, God knows, exactly how many miles of road they still had to cover, Frank's rough estimate was that with no speed limit out here in the wilderness to hold them back, they could maybe cover half that distance with his foot pressed down hard on the pedal. Both sides gave the same monotonous view of flat empty nothing for mile after mile where the landscape had been scraped clean to allow the sentries in their distant lofty boxes to watch without obstruction the 'insects' rushing along past.

Standing distantly tall and aloof away on both sides, the watchtowers being always there profiled against both distant horizons, were seemingly guardians of time. But the watchtowers with their armed sentries were guarding not time but against transgressors on the road lying between them – or anywhere else they should dare to place an unwelcome foot. From time to time, a watchtower would spring up closer to the side of the road, so that you could quite clearly make out the helmeted figure standing beside the machine-gun; just as it clearly made you out in turn, without the need for binoculars, unlike the sentries positioned further back.

More grim reminders of whose land you were trespassing on popped up periodically just off the side of the road in the form of a 5.4ton Sonder Kfz-1 armoured car with its MG-34 machine-gun, which you hoped would not get some crazy excuse to stop you and strafe your tyres with some of its 900 rounds of 7.92 bullets; or if not that, then a 36ton T-55A tank, maybe.

Frank's attention on the rear-view mirror, at the black dot in the distance that periodically persistently showed up when bends in the road straightened out, was stolen when the windscreen started stippling with raindrops. They were in for yet another drenching from the heavens. Not so much a monsoon this time, but lighter so that they could just make out the outline of what they hoped was the Russian border crossing control checkpoint next to the small town of Vale, in the Samtskhe-Javakheti region, facing on the tiny Turkish village of Turkgozu across the border, lying peacefully in its Posof district.

With sheets of rain lashing the ground and everything else in its way, the dark figure in green rain-soaked rubber poncho hugged the poor shelter of the border control point's guards' hut. What could have been Noah's Arch in the shape of an American Chrysler was coming along towards the crossing, though the great deluge of water would not have surprised the soldier, in spite of such folly of religious belief being forbidden by the Soviet Union's doctrinaire teaching. If the rain wasn't sparing them on this side, it certainly wasn't sparing those Capitalist bastards on the other side of the control point, far to the west.

And still it came on and on, the car doggedly cutting its way through the heavy downpour, getting nearer and nearer. The guard swore, knowing that he'd have to leave the shelter of the hut to go out to meet the car. Stooping slightly, as he huddled beneath the poncho, he stepped out into the wretched rain to meet the approaching vehicle. He pointed to a point on the ground where he wanted the car to stop.

'Please stop here,' the guard shouted through the noise of the torrential downpour. With the car's window winding down slowly, he stepped in closer, holding out a free hand for the papers he needed to inspect, while his other hand got ready to unsling his rifle from his shoulder. 'Papers, please,' he said to the driver. Frank held up the passes, just inside the window, out of the way of the rain, for the guard to read. But the guard was not satisfied with that, pulling the papers out of Frank's hand and stepping back to turn abruptly, going back to the hut to examine the documents more closely.

Sitting there nervous, Frank watched one of the soldiers unslinging his PPSH-41 Russian version of the tommy-gun. But it was only to hand it to a mate, so he could take out two cigarettes. Lighting them both and giving one to his mate, the soldier idled up closer to get a better look at the great Yankee beast of dazzling chrome. A little too conspicuous in Frank's opinion, but it was the best the pool could come up with in the haste to get the operation to salvage COMPASS underway.

Somewhat a little to Frank's surprise, a moderate column of vehicles had built up behind them; mostly dirty dusty workers' trucks that had joined the main road from outlying side-tracks. That black car wasn't one of them. But he was sure he could bet on it still being back there, torturing its thrashing cylinders to bring it closer, faster. Frank even noticed that there was a second red and white- striped barrier pole for them to approach, several metres away. Oh, yes, a second one – that one was for a stricter 'security' inspection.

Engines changed gear up and down, the column crawling slowly forward, red brake lights glaring on and off as vehicles stopped and started to allow preliminary document inspection to be carried out along the line, moving as it did, at a snail's pace.

Inching along, closer and closer to their turn, minds all along the line were dreading the search, with its grim hand of authority, much like the virgin on her first night. Frank watched armed guards leap aboard the truck stopped in front. Another guard came up close to peer through the windows on Frank's side. He looked at Frank's expertly forged passport passed to him by the first guard, peering hard at Frank's face.

'Yeah, I agree, it's a horrible mug-shot; it's the best face my old mom could give me.'

The guard ignored the remark. He looked from the photo to the name. 'Ernst Kluschter? You are naturalised American?'

Frank put on his best smile. 'American mother, German father.'

The guard nodded thoughtfully, tapping the passport in his hand, along with Georgievich's. 'Da.' Understood. But he didn't give them back their passports. Something was still troubling the guy. Turning around, clutching them tightly, he disappeared with them into the guardhouse.

Frank and Geogievich sat in silence.

Frank watched the soldiers swarm over the truck in front like parasites on a host, some of them searching the cargo hold, while others pushed mirrors on rods underneath the truck for a belly shot inspection. A sudden eruption of plaintiff yelps, drowned out by harsh commands, saw the cabin door being wrenched open, with the driver being seized and frog-marched into a wooden building adjacent to the guardhouse. A bubble of angry activity blew up, with a grey military truck pulling up out of nowhere and military-booted figures clambered out. Frank's pulse quickened as he recognised the red and black shield-shaped badge with its central double-headed 'imperial' eagle, insignia of the POCCNR Russian Security Police.

Checking the tightness in their stomachs, Frank and Georgievich looked away from the commotion and waited their turn. It was a long wait. Eight minutes, in fact. The guard came back with their passports. But they still had to wait another two gruelling minutes for the truck in front to be hauled to the side off the road. As they moved forward to stop at the second barrier, for the car's body inspection, Frank's tension prickled. This wasn't helped any, with a small group of young guards moving in closer for a curiosity peek at the flashy American car. They had that collective appearance of being newly appointed in their duty, 'wet behind the ear' and brimming with an open confidence of their job's authority – the one at the front armed with a heavy AKM47 rifle and tapping the chrome door handle with one of the heavy wrist-manacles on a chain dangling from his belt. The vehicle itself had nothing to hide, but nevertheless, that is how the mind behaves in a tight security grip like this. Only a crazy berk would say you got over it with experience in the game. You never did.

After a nerve-racking series of hollow-sounding metallic clonks, documents duly returned and a signal given, the shining striped pole rose up. Starting the engine up with a guttural scrunch of gear change, Frank drove forward slowly, under it, past it, all the time careful not to arouse undue attention by making too eager a departure -- and into Turkey.

As they moved off into freedom, Frank caught the sound, and saw through the rear-view mirror, the commotion of a large black Volga V-8 engine sedan forcing a path through the column of honking vehicles, to get to the front and stopping with a screech of brakes. Its door flew open to let a figure jump out, yelling at the guards to stop the American car. His bright GRU uniform stood out in contrast against the duller border guards' uniforms. Alas, it was too late, the vehicle no longer being on Soviet Union soil.

'I'm guessing that's our Major Mikhail Zilianov. Correct?' Frank looked round with a broad winner's smile at Georgievich.

'Indeed, most correct, Mr Kluschter.'

With enough self-control to balance his impatience, Frank pressed on the accelerator for a little more speed, but just enough to go that bit faster without turning heads. A few minutes had them pulling up to stop in the tiny village virtually vying for street space with a Monopoly board, and was cocooned in its own thick sunny afternoon atmosphere of quietness.

After that close shave of so narrowly escaping arrest, Frank and Georgievich felt a naturally induced reflex urge to put some food where previously butterflies had enjoyed a frenzied flutter. With this tiny border village of Turkgozo not having a glittering five-star hotel, or anything like that to boast of, Frank and Georgievich satisfied their craving appetites by 'dining' at the shish-kebab street vendor's stall. At least it had a small wicker-topped table for them to sit at to enjoy the spicy chicken dish with its rich sauce.

'If we are to get back finally by train, it is obviously not from this village. So where do we go to from here?' said Georgievich.

'We don't have to leave the village at all to claim our seats for the journey.'

'No?'

'We're not travelling by train for the last leg; we're joining a coach party of jolly tourists on a jolly mystery road-tour not realising that their final stop-off point will not be the surprise that they expected – let alone being quite a few hundred miles from where they looked forward to having wine and sherries.'

'Am I to understand that we're involved in an illicit plan that condones the kidnapping of innocent people?'

'I'm guessing that Myers, with his peculiar charm, will have cajoled them to collaborate in our little charade; they'll be generously compensated, of course, courtesy of the US Treasury's fat piggy-bank.'

'Why the change of plan?'

'Yeah, well, that's Myers for you. He likes to shuffle the cards and deal them from a fresh pack.'

'Do you think this is a wise move – this new plan?'

'It'd better be; it's the one we're going to be working on.'

Finding the lame questions getting in the way of things more important, Frank tapped his pocket where the microfilm that Georgievich had given him was. 'Are you sure that you've told me everything that I need to know on this thing?'

Geogievich didn't answer. He couldn't answer. Not with the top of his head blown off, as it would be, by the great 'cannon-ball piece' that it was, of a dum-dum bullet. Issued to him, no doubt, by his Bolshevik masters, to ensure a satisfactory completion of his assignment. Classified as illegal by the Geneva Convention – a totally futile declaration, since it never failed to stop those sadistic enough to use it, from using it. As in this case. Quad erat demonstrandum.

Frank's brain registered this in a second before his paper bag on the table exploded twice as he fired the Colt automatic inside it, killing Hauter outright. He'd collected the Colt from a pre-arranged dead-letter drop spot barely half an hour earlier. Otherwise, it would have blown their attempt to escape sky high to have been caught carrying a firearm at the border control. Even a small delay for questioning over this issue would have spelt disaster with the Russian Major Zilianov so close on their tail.

Hauter's pistol with its silencer fell from the dead hand before the lifeless body collapsed on the ground on top of it. His single shot by silencer had not drawn any undue attention, but Frank's heavy Colt had rent the air with enough force to disturb the village's sleepy atmosphere and make heads jerk up in shock, before people came running.

Frank walked over to the body and put a finger to the neck. No pulse. The guy had gone to that farm in the sky. So the deal he'd made with Hauter to recruit him as a double agent to spy on his Moscow bosses had not been as much as they in turn had promised him in return for wiping out the defecting traitor. This as a brutal demonstration that intending defectors could never elude the grim justice of Soviet Russia's iron rule. Never!

Frank shook his head slowly, looking down at the still shape. The crazy Kraut would have probably said something like: "Nothing personal; it's where the job takes you". He looked from the lifeless heap at his feet, then over to the other one with its 'sore head', and back again at Hauter. 'Yeah, you're right, pal, it's where the job takes you.'

With a conclusive icy laugh to this, he turned round, to face the little anxious group that had come to gather near, stopping at a 'safe' few yards away from whatever frightful thing it was that had happened.

'Polizie! Polizie!' was the best Frank could manage in their tongue. No effect. 'Can anybody speak English?'

'I can speak the English,' said someone.

'Can you go get a policeman, or whoever's in charge in this place. There's no hurry, mind you; this guy's not going anywhere.' Frank walked back to the stall to hand money to the man behind the counter who was understandably shaken by what had happened at his very table. 'Here, this is for the food and orange drink; and that's for the mess on your table. Sorry about that, that pal, couldn't be helped. There should be enough there to even buy a new table if you have to, if you can't completely wash off the bloodstains.'

Taking a final look at how COMPASS had ended up after all Langley's expert planning, Frank wondered how much of this 'bloody mess' he'd be able to rub off *himself* after Goodblood brought his departmental wrath down on him. He turned and walked away at a brisk pace.

'You are not waiting for the police, yourself?' This from the crowd's only English speaker.

'Sorry, pal. I've got a bus to catch.'